continued . . .

The Spirit of Thunder

FROM THE
HEART OF
THE STORM

Kurt R. A. Giambastiani

A ROC BOOK

ROC
Published by New American Library, a division of
Penguin Group (USA) Inc., 375 Hudson Street,
New York, New York 10014, U.S.A.
Penguin Books Ltd, 80 Strand,
London WC2R 0RL, England
Penguin Books Australia Ltd, 250 Camberwell Road,
Camberwell, Victoria 3124, Australia
Penguin Books Canada Ltd, 10 Alcorn Avenue,
Toronto, Ontario, Canada M4V 3B2
Penguin Books (N.Z.) Ltd, Cnr Rosedale and Airborne Roads,
Albany, Auckland 1310, New Zealand

Penguin Books Ltd, Registered Offices:
80 Strand, London WC2R 0RL, England

First published by Roc, an imprint of New American Library,
a division of Penguin Group (USA) Inc.

First Printing, January 2004
10 9 8 7 6 5 4 3 2 1

Copyright © Kurt R. A. Giambastiani, 2004
All rights reserved

Cover design by Ray Lundgren
Cover art by David Cook

ROC REGISTERED TRADEMARK—MARCA REGISTRADA

Printed in the United States of America

PUBLISHER'S NOTE
This is a work of fiction. Names, characters, places, and incidents either are
the product of the author's imagination or are used fictitiously, and any resem-
blance to actual persons, living or dead, business establishments, events, or
locales is entirely coincidental.

To the bride of my youth,
who lives with me still

A portion of the author's proceeds from these books is donated to the St. Labre organization, a group of schools on the Tongue River in Ashland, Montana, that provides educational opportunities to the Northern Cheyenne and Crow people.

FOR THE NEW READER

Imagine a world that began much like our own.

Sixty-five million years ago, North America bade farewell to the islands of Europe from across the newly born Atlantic, Australia stretched to separate itself from Antarctica, and the Indian subcontinent was sailing away from Africa, bound for its collision with the heart of Asia. In every place, Life abounded, and dinosaurs—some larger than a house, and others as small as your thumb—ruled the land, the sea, and the air, living out their lives in the forests and swamps that dominated the coastlands along the shallow Cretaceous seas.

Then the world broke open, unleashing a volcanic fury the like of which had not been seen for an aeon. The Deccan Traps gushed molten lava, covering half of India with a million cubic kilometers of basalt. The ranges of Antarctica cracked, spewing iridium-laced ash into darkening skies. For five hundred thousand years, the planet rang with violence. Mountains were born, seas shrank, and Life trembled. Across the globe, resources of food and prey disappeared as the climate shifted from wet to arid. Populations competed, starved, and then collapsed. Over the next million years, half of all species died out, unable to adapt in time as habitats vanished in a geologic heartbeat.*

In North America, the continental plate was com-

*For a more detailed analysis of this nonimpact theory of the end of the Cretaceous Period, see *The Great Dinosaur Extinction Controversy* by Jake Page and Charles B. Officer.

pressed, thrusting the Rocky Mountains miles into the air. The inland seaway that stretched from the Caribbean to the Arctic began to recede, taking with it the moist marshes and fens upon which the last of the world's dinosaurs depended. The waters ebbed, revealing vast sedimentary plains, retreating for a thousand miles before they came to a halt. The sea that remained was a fraction of its former size: a short arm of warm, shallow water that thrust up from the Caribbean to the Sand Hills of Nebraska.

It was on these placid shores that a few species of those great dinosaurs clung to life. Although they were reduced in size and number, the gentle sea gave them the time they needed to adapt and survive. Eventually, some species left the sea's humid forests for the broad expanses to the north, finding ecological niches among the mammals that had begun to dominate the prairie.

Life continued. Continents moved. The glacial ices advanced and retreated like a tide. In Africa's Great Rift Valley, a small ape stood and peered over the savannah grass. Humans emerged, migrated into Asia and Europe, and history was born. Events unfolded mostly unchanged, until the European civilization came to the Great Plains of North America.

In the centuries before the first Spaniard brought the first horse to the New World, the Cheyenne had been riding across the Great Plains on lizardlike beasts of unmatched speed and power. In defense against their new white-skinned foe, the Cheyenne allied with other tribes, and when the tide of European colonialism came to the prairie frontier, it crashed against the Alliance, and was denied. For a hundred years, the Alliance matched the Horse Nations move for move, strength for strength, shifting the course of history.

Then, through advances in technology and industry, the Americans, led by an officer named George Armstrong Custer, began to make headway and the Alliance was pushed back beyond the Mississippi, beyond the Arkansas, all the way to the banks of the Missouri and the Santee. A few years later that same officer—now President Custer—sent his only son on a reconnaissance mission beyond those rivers, only to hear of his capture by the Cheyenne. In the three years since, young George has lived with the Cheyenne, and has sided with them against his own father's forces.

This is the world of the Fallen Cloud saga.

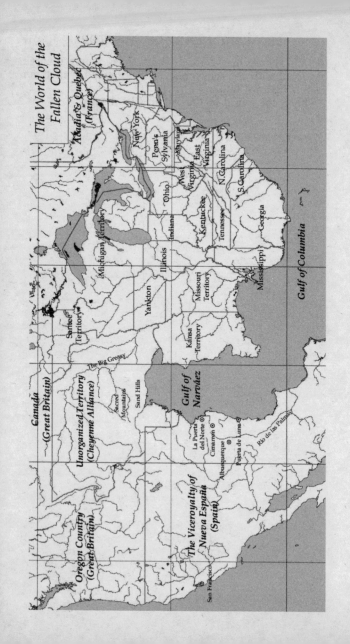

CHAPTER 1

Hoop and Stick Game Moon, Waxing
Fifty-seven Years after the Star Fell
Sand Hills
Alliance Territory

The storm doused the world.

George held the small medicine bag in his hands as the rain pelted down onto his head and streamed through his braided hair. He ran his fingers over the bag's worn quillwork, the leather as old and dark as the skin of the man who had owned it. It had belonged to Three Trees Together, the preeminent chief of the People, a patient leader who had been shot dead pursuing peace for his tribe. George had loved and respected him, perhaps more than he did his own father. He looked up into the rain-dark sky.

"God, damn it all," he said as his vision swam with the sting of tears and cold rain. "Everything, God. Damn me, damn the world. Damn everything."

The storm threw its rain down from the west with a rising, vengeful fury. In the Sand Hills, on the shores of the Big Salty, the temperate waters kept the northern snows at bay, but they could not keep away the rains or the cold winds that blasted down from the great plains of the Alliance.

From a few yards away, George's whistler complained of the bitter chill and sheltered her nose under her tail. For his own part, he greeted the building violence of the storm, shivering in clothes soaked through by the winter's weather. He had ridden for a week to reach this spot, a journey of agony and privation that was an appropriate ending to the devastating trip to Washington

that killed Three Trees Together and nearly killed
George's father as well.

He looked down again at the medicine bag in his
hands. It fit in his palm, a small square pouch sewn shut
to enclose the talismans of its owner's spiritual strength.
From the bottom of the bag hung an uneven, broken
fringe and attached to the top was a long thong of
leather that the old man had worn around his neck.
Made of brain-tanned elkhide, the back of it was bare,
the leather soiled and hardened by decades lying next
to the skin of the old man's chest. The front of it was
sewn with dyed porcupine quills; a geometric pattern
with the right half covered in white quills, the left half in
dark brown. Down the middle were open, wheat-colored
diamonds that represented grasshoppers, and to either
side were blue double-barred crosses: dragonflies. Grasshoppers, he knew, were a symbol of plenty, as they always presaged the buffalo on the open prairie, rising up
in clouds before the herd's advance. He touched the blue
quills of the four dragonflies. He did not know what a
dragonfly meant to the Cheyenne. For the past three
years he had called the People who ruled the great plains
his friends, his family, his own; but still he did not know
all their secret ways.

His vision blurred over, but not with the rain that
coursed over his face.

"Damn it all," he said again, and clutched to his breast
the medicine bag that had belonged to his chief.

Three Trees Together had died on the steps of the
White House, brought down by a bullet meant for the
assassin who had tried to kill George's father, George
Armstrong Custer, Sr., the President of the United
States. He wished now, as he had while staring down at
the bloody stone steps, that the bullet had taken him
instead of the grand old chief. The chief's death had
brought no good, while his own death would have done
no harm.

He looked around at the rain-soaked land. The funeral party, traveling home weeks ahead of George, had
picked a good spot for their leader's spirit bed. Set atop
the limestone cliffs high above the white sand shore of
the inland sea, there would have been plenty of the

leather-winged fliers to come and release the old man's spirit from his flesh. There were remnants of the chief's funeral strewn about: pale bones among the dark sedgegrass and woody thyme, a tattered war bonnet, a dream shield tied to one of the scaffold poles. But for George it was the medicine bag that embodied the chief. How many times had he watched the old man, sitting at the head of a Council meeting, his fingers idly playing with the fringe or rubbing the quills of its geometric design? How many times had the Council waited while Three Trees Together toyed with his medicine bag, his mind seeking the path of wisdom? A man of a hundred summers who, the day before his death, had stood with George on a balcony, catching snowflakes on his tongue. A man whom George loved more than his own father, and who had cared for George in return. Dead. Murdered on the road to peace.

"My fault," George said, his teeth clenched and his breath hard and sharp in his breast. He stood and, medicine bag in one hand, unsheathed his knife with the other. The blade glowed in the dim light, and he felt its bite with his thumb. He looked at the bag.

"I just wanted to help," he said to it, and to the man who had owned it. "I only just wanted to help. But everything I do, everything I've done . . . it always turns out worse than it was before."

He touched the blade to the skin of his arm. It was cold against his wrist.

"What can I do for you now, Grandfather?" He shook his head, the old man's words echoing in his head.

One Who Flies, he had said, calling him by his Cheyenne name. *My heart would be sad if you decided you no longer wished to be one of the People.*

"I know I told you I would go back, but that was when I still hoped. Now . . ." He let the blade score a line across his wrist. Blood rose, mixed with rain, and spread. He drew two more lines across his wrist, and blood flowed down his arm.

There is a family for you with the People, I think, if you want it.

"No, Grandfather. I have no family among the People. Not after the losses I've brought to them. And among the *vé'hó'e* I have been disowned; my own mother told me this. I am alone, Grandfather, caught between two worlds that do not want me. There's only one thing I can do. Only one place to go."

He held out his arm and let the rain wash the blood from his arm down onto the ground. Then, with a quick move of the knife, he reached up and slashed through the braid of his hair. Released, wet hanks fell forward around his face. He dropped the blond braid onto the blooded ground.

"Something of me," George said, "for something of you." He put the leather thong over his head. The medicine bag hung down on his chest.

"Goodbye, Grandfather. May you walk in beauty. For me, there is nowhere to go but to Hell."

He sheathed the knife and tucked the bag under the sodden hide of his tunic. Walking over to his whistler, he mounted. *"Néhoveóó'êstse,"* he said, and the creature rose on its strong hind legs. *"Nóheto,"* he commanded, and they headed off, away from the cliffs. The whistler turned toward the northwest and home, but George countermanded it with a touch of his right toe.

"Not that way," he told it. "Not for me."

Unwillingly, the whistler turned to the northeast and took him onward, into the rain.

CHAPTER 2

Friday, February 7, A.D. 1890
The White House
Washington, District of Columbia

President Custer sat in the wheelchair, able to do little else, as Douglas pushed him down the hall toward the library. One of the chair's wheels squeaked, annoying Custer as only a little thing can annoy a man so swallowed up by larger concerns. There was nothing he could do about the squeaking wheel—the right front wheel, he thought it was, yes, he was sure; definitely the right front wheel, going *heep-heep-heep* as they turned from the cross hall and through the library door—but there was nothing he could do about the larger things, either.

He could not reverse the course of events that had occurred over the last month, could not send back the would-be assassin's bullets, nor save his old friend, Three Trees Together, from the inaccurate but deadly retaliation of his own presidential bodyguard. He could not go back and preemptively remove the ambassador from the discussions that, until that bloody end, had gone so well. He could not clean away the damage done to his body, a body that had been a quiet pride, lean and agile, responding to his every thought, even as advancing age had started to come upon him. And neither could he undo the sadness that he saw in his dear Libbie's eyes, and to him, seeing that sadness was a greater pain than all of his physical torment.

He could change these things not a whit, could not even form the words to express his frustrations. These things were out of his control and beyond his power to affect, just as was the irritating squeak of the unoiled right front wheel on this, his carriage of incapacity.

But unlike those other trials, the wheel was here within his view, and so it constrained his entire focus.

Douglas wheeled him across the library to a place near the hearth.

"How's this, Mr. President?"

Custer, released from the torture of the wheel, sighed deeply. On the rug before the fire, Tuck, the family's old wirehair hound, sighed as well. The fire in the hearth crackled and he could smell the sharpness of bubbling resin as it seeped up out of the burning wood. He looked at Douglas and tried to motion toward the fireplace with his right hand: a twisting, unnaturally difficult movement that was the best he was able to manage.

"Pine wood, sir. Full of pitch, just the way you like it."

Custer closed his eyes and smiled a lopsided half-smile.

"Coffee, sir? Tea? Something to eat, maybe?"

Custer squinched up his left eye and cheek.

"Just as you wish, sir." From outside in the hall came the sound of voices and footsteps. "I'll be right over there, sir. If you find you want anything, you just give me a look."

Douglas was the butler for the house, but for the past month, he had become Custer's personal attendant, perambulating him from room to room, seeing to all his needs and most of his wants, even to dressing him in the mornings.

On the first morning Custer had been scheduled to leave his sickroom, the old Negro had sensed his reluctance at venturing forth wearing only a dressing gown. The man's hands were as strong and black as iron but passed along a gentle reassurance. Douglas had helped President Custer don his undergarments, his trousers, his shoes and socks. He had buttoned Custer's shirt and had tied the crisp knot in his necktie, all without uttering a single word. Custer had never been touched in so familiar a manner by a Negro, and his estimation of this man, butler to seven presidents, was changed by his ability to serve without servility.

By now, though, the regimen had become routine.

Each morning Douglas helped Custer rise, helped him at toilet and bath, cleaned him, shaved him, and dressed him with quiet efficiency. On weekend mornings, he took him to breakfast with the family, while on weekdays he ate alone in his rooms. Douglas laid out the morning paper, turning pages as Custer read the day's news. And three times a week, around noon, Douglas brought him here, to the library, for what Custer considered nothing less than an inspection by the commanding officer.

Douglas took up his post behind Custer as the footsteps neared the library door. The library was Custer's favorite room. On the second floor facing the south, it was a large, square room with one semicircular wall composed of curved French doors that led out onto a balcony. The rippled panes of bowed glass let in the reflected light of day, snow-bright despite the clouds that hid the sun. Reading tables and armchairs stood near the balcony doors, flanked by floor lamps at silent attention. And then, lining the three remaining walls of the room, were the things that had drawn Custer here on the first day of his first term: the tall ranks of bookshelves filled with the imposing collection of history. Journals, atlases, treatises, diatribes. Books on logic, on political theory, on religion. Architectural plans and essays on crop rotation. Dictionaries, novels, plays, and Bibles. Books and folios, skinny and fat, grand and minuscule, bound in leather or cloth as age and style dictated, they all stood shoulder to shoulder, filling the available space with words, knowledge, and wisdom. Custer had loved this room, still loved it, except that now reading was a pleasure stolen from him, as even the simple act of turning a page was beyond his limited muscular control.

In time, he promised the books, scanning their worn and gilt-edged titles. I shall return to you in time.

The footsteps reached the door, and in stepped the oblate Doctor Erasmus Granville, thumbs hooked in the pockets of his waistcoat, his nose raised as if the pleasantest air was somewhere above his head. His balding pate, despite the dark strands of thin hair pasted across it, gleamed in the crisp light, and his eyes looked like sweaty beads behind his round-lensed spectacles. He glanced at Custer and bent in a stiff, slight bow before addressing Douglas.

"And how is the patient this morning, Douglas?"

"He tells me he's fine, Doctor Granville. You can ask him yourself, sir."

"Yes, of course . . . very good, then."

Libbie entered after the doctor, chatting with Jacob Greene, Secretary of War and an old family friend. Upon seeing her husband by the fire, Libbie broke off her conversation and came over to him. She was dressed in a lovely wool wrapper of pale blue merino, trimmed at the lapels, waist, and cuffs in royal blue velvet. A surah of bright yellow silk formed the bodice and front of the skirt, gathered at waist and high collar.

Blue and Gold, Custer remarked to himself. My little dear loves the old cavalry colors.

"Do you like it?" she asked, noticing his attention and plucking at the puffed upper sleeves. She knelt at his side and kissed his cheek, wreathing him in her scent of orange blossoms. "I know, it's a bit brighter than my usual gowns but, Autie"—she leaned in to whisper in his ear—"I'm just so glad that I don't have to wear widow's weeds." She ran her hand across his cheek, and he felt years melt away at her touch. "How do you feel this morning?"

His face writhed as he tried to exert control. His walrus moustache hid most of his lips' contortions, but it did not conceal the struggle entirely. Libbie waited, wanting an answer from him and not from anyone else. His wife's sweet respect drove him to continue through his disablement.

"Mmenh," he said.

"Better?" she interpreted, and he winked in affirmation, the only action he could take with regularity and precision. "That's wonderful, dear. Did you hear that, Dr. Granville? He says he's feeling better."

Granville took a breath large enough to fill an opera house. "I expected nothing less," he informed them all. "The patient will continue to heal from his wounds and build back his former strength. You need not fear, Mrs.

Custer, any relapse into coma; our patient is well beyond that risk. But after thorough examination, it is quite apparent that his abridged faculties of speech, his partial paralysis, and the palsy that afflicts the right side especially, were not caused by the original trauma, but by a stroke brought on, in all probability, by an embolus resulting from the extensive wounds to the neck and chest."

"What is to be done?" Jacob asked from his seat in one of the chairs. "Surely some sort of treatment?"

Granville pursed his lips and shook his jowls slowly. "It is impossible to say, Mr. Secretary, with any hope of accuracy. The nature of each of these cases is so different. Given ample time, some patients recover almost completely while others . . . well . . ." He humphed. "Yes, well, considering the patient's age and the extent of his deficit, it is not impossible to hope for recovery, but it is not a likely outcome."

You dolt! Custer thought to himself. I'm right here! He wanted to shout it to the rafters. Don't talk about me as if I cannot hear you!

"But, Doctor," Libbie said, hand on her husband's shoulder, "is there nothing we can do?"

"I'm afraid it's genuinely up to the patient. Recovery of any kind from a stroke of this severity requires great determination and discipline. It would take many months—perhaps years—before ground could be gained, if at all."

Jacob sat back in his chair, one hand on his plump belly and a faraway look in his eyes. Libbie, standing close by Custer's chair, stared at the doctor. Neither seemed to remember that Custer was even in the room with them.

"Years?" Libbie breathed.

Granville closed his eyes and nodded sagely. "Indeed, madam. Years. Maintaining the patient's morale through such a period is a difficult undertaking, but one that must be ventured. He might otherwise be apt to brood upon—"

Custer stomped on the floor with his good leg. The others turned and stared at him, wide-eyed. Granville's

mouth was frozen in mid-pontification. Custer glanced
at Douglas, then at the doctor, and then at the door.
Douglas came forward and took Granville by the elbow.

"This way, Doctor Granville. I'll take you to your
carriage."

"Yes," Granville said. "Thank you." He bowed to the
others. "Mrs. Custer, Mr. Secretary. And Mr. President,
it's good to see you doing so well so soon. If you need
anything . . ."

Custer glared and Douglas touched the doctor's
elbow.

"Doctor, this way, if you please?"

When the door closed behind the retreating Granville,
Libbie turned to her husband.

"Forgive me, Armstrong," she said, using his middle
name as she often did when distressed. "Please, the doctor simply caught me unawares. I had no idea things
were still so serious."

"Me, too, Autie." Jacob looked like a kicked pup, his
eyes pleading for mercy. "It's a shock. All I could think
is what this means for your administration if you're unable to fulfill your duties for an extended period."

"Jacob!" Libbie said.

"I'm sorry," he said. "I know it seems crass, but we've
got to think about it."

Custer twisted his mouth around a word. "Eereye."

Libbie softened. "Yes," she said. "I know he's right."
She sighed and straightened her shoulders. "Very well,
so it's to be a longer recovery than we'd expected. We'll
just have to work all the harder, and trust a little to the
old Custer luck." She smiled down at him and he felt
better at her resolve.

How much I love you, he said to her silently. How
much you have defined me. Sweet girl. My sweet girl.
I'm sorry things have worked out this way. I'd planned
a different future for us.

She held his hand and looked into his face, tenderness
and love in her expression. He could tell that she was
wondering what he was thinking, and he wished that he
could only tell her.

"Shall I bring in the girls?" she asked. "They would
like to see you."

He jerked his head to the side. "Ayer," he said.

"All right, Autie. Maybe this afternoon?"

He winked and she patted his hand.

The door opened and in scuttled the small frailness of Samuel Prendergast, Custer's former attaché and personal secretary. Samuel was dressed, as was his habit, in a black suit and waistcoat, and a white shirt with high starched collar. Pinned to his lapel was a satin cord that looped up to his pince-nez spectacles. His fringe of feathery gray hair was ruffled, and his slender, ink-stained fingers barely contained the sheets of paper he clutched to his breast. He leaned back against the library door to close it and his gaze darted from one face to the next with nervous anxiety.

"You won't believe it," he said, nearly breathless.

"Good lord, man," Jacob said, standing. "You look like you could use a drink."

To Custer's surprise, Samuel nodded, accepting the offer. Libbie glanced at her husband. If Samuel was given to taking alcohol in midday, something was definitely up.

As Jacob poured a splash of bourbon into a thimble glass, Samuel went to a brocade-upholstered chair and sat on its plush edge. He took the small glass and tossed back its contents like an old hand, and gripped the glass as he grimaced at the taste. Slowly, he released a deep breath.

"It's about the man who shot you, Mr. President. Higgins and Campbell just came in. They questioned a young woman who says she was in the company of the man. She directed them to some leaders of the steel and railroad unions and they . . . I can hardly believe it . . ."

"Speak on," Jacob said.

Samuel pressed forward. "One of these union leaders implicated Señor Silveira, the Ambassador from New Spain."

"You're joking!"

"Oh," Libbie breathed. "But that would mean . . ."

"It is distressing," Samuel said.

"*Distressing?*" Jacob blurted. "The delegate from a foreign power tries to assassinate our President and you call it distressing?"

"Oh, but they said that he didn't intend to kill the President," Samuel said. "It was young George he was after."

"George, Jr.?" Libbie clenched Custer's hand. "But why? The ambassador was the one who brought George here in the first place. After all that, why would he want him dead?"

"I don't know, Mrs. Custer. And neither does anyone else. Higgins and Campbell just made their report to Vice President Morton, and they frankly said that none of the people they questioned can be trusted. Everyone has a motive to lie and point the finger at someone else. We will probably never know what really happened, or why."

"But Levi," Libbie said. "What does Levi intend to do about this information?"

Samuel shrugged and put the thimble glass down on the side table. "Without stronger proof, the Vice President's actions are limited. He is considering now what he will do."

Libbie knelt at Custer's side. Custer looked at her face, her dark hair curling across her wide brow. She stared at nothing, trying to deal with facts and realities from which he'd always tried to shelter her but which now were here, in the room. Long ago, the violence of war had left its first mark on his mind, but now, after twenty-eight years of wedded peace and partnership, not only had it marked his body, it had also succeeded in worming its insidious way through to touch Libbie. All of the battles and all of the campaigns and all of the raids and skirmishes and ambushes in which he'd played a part—he had been able to keep all of them where they had ended, out on the field. The "Custer luck," as she had named it, had always brought him home, sound and hale, until now, when at last, war had walked up and struck him down on his very doorstep.

He looked at the hand that held his own. Libbie had tiny hands, delicate and dimpled, and she stroked his fingers with an absentminded affection, love without conscious thought. As she and Samuel and Jacob discussed the ramifications of Morton's ejection of the New Spanish ambassador, as he heard his wife ask questions in his stead, he saw a gulf open between them. His infirmity had changed her role from wife to caretaker, and he could not keep the tears from welling up in the corners of his eyes.

I do not want a mother, he said to her. I want my wife. I want my partner. I want my love, and my dear sweet girl back.

His right hand did not want to move when he told it to. His left arm was weakened by the wound to his chest. His right leg would not bear his weight. The right side of his face felt like a taper in the sun, slowly melting, drooping.

But the doctor, for all his pomposity, had said that recovery was not impossible. Perhaps the old Custer luck *had* done its work. Else, his wife's bright colors of blue and gold might very well have been the black of a widow's weeds.

With deliberate slowness, he reached his left hand inside his coat. It shook, but he clenched his teeth and made it do what he wanted it to do. Inside, he felt the pocket, and the small square of soft cotton within. He withdrew the handkerchief and, holding it in a trembling hand, dabbed at his eyes and wiped his running nose.

Libbie turned at his movement, concern knitting her brow.

He wanted to say something to her that would express the depth of his emotion and love for her. He wanted to give her hope and smooth the worry from her lovely face. Such words, however, were beyond his ability to speak.

Anything that isn't impossible can be done, he told her in his silence. It'll be as it was when I was on campaign, when we were separated by miles of wilderness. I'll write to you, every day, and work on coming home to you as quickly as I can.

And so, he began his first letter, committing to memory the words he promised himself he would one day recite, when he had bridged the canyon that separated them:

My Dearest Sunbeam. . . .

CHAPTER 3

Thursday, February 13, A.D. 1890
Embassy of New Spain
Washington, District of Columbia

Alejandro stared at the unfinished letter on his desk. The afternoon sunlight glinted off the brass base of an unlit lamp, throwing a warm splash of light across the salutation:

> *To his Lordship, Emilio Serrano-Ruiz, Viceroy of New Spain, San Francisco, Alta California.*

It was the third such letter he had composed in the last month, not including similar letters he had sent to his brother-in-law Roberto, the Governor of Cuba, asking him to speak to the viceroy on his behalf. None had been answered, though he knew that all of them had been received.

He sighed and ran a hand through his silvered hair. His tenure as ambassador from New Spain to the United States had been less than exemplary. It had begun with trouble: with the scandal of his predecessor's death in a New York brothel. From there, it had gone from bad to worse, with his own ship going aground on the coast of Indian-controlled territory, with his rescue and return to New Spain at the hands of the savage inhabitants, and with his ambitious attempt to form an alliance between New Spain and the native tribes in hopes of gaining a foothold in the disputed territory.

Alejandro sighed. Even with all that, he could have

saved the situation; but he had let it go a step too far. He had let his desire for personal vengeance take him beyond the scope of his office, made unwise by his hatred for Custer—once a junior officer, now President, who, during the War for the Tejano Coast, had brought defeat down upon Alejandro's regiment and cost him his position at the viceregal court, a generalship in the military, and his future in Spanish society. Alejandro had let his hatred for that man push him into acts that may have cost him everything, and the silence from San Francisco was ominous.

Still, he reasoned, though a watched pot never boils, neither does an unheated one.

He dipped his pen into the inkwell, tapped away the excess, and returned to his letter's closing paragraph.

> *In conclusion, my Lord Viceroy, and as I have iterated in my prior letters on the subject, it is clear that this proposed alliance between the Spanish crown and the native tribes of the American plains still has much to offer. I say again that we should not, in my estimation, abandon the prospects that we have discovered there, despite the recent difficulties. Please advise me at your earliest convenience. As always, I await your instructions.*

He signed the letter, blotted it, folded it in thirds, and folded the ends into the middle. Then he struck a match. It flared with a hissing smoke that blued in the slanting light of late afternoon and filled the air with the taste of metal. He touched the flame to the wick of a candle, and picked up his stick of red sealing wax. The wax smoothed and grew shiny in the heat, and he twirled it to keep it from dripping. When it was ready, he stubbed the liquefied end onto the seam of the letter, leaving a heavy dollop of bubbling wax behind. Then he pressed the face of his signet ring into the wax, cooling it, and embossing into it the arms of his family crest. When he let go, the wax held the letter closed at all seams and would have to be cracked before the contents could be read. He turned the letter over, addressed it to the Viceroy, and was about to put the letter in an envelope when there was a knock at his office door.

"Enter," he said.

The heavy door opened and Enrique came in, bearing a large stack of letters.

"Excellency, the afternoon post has arrived."

"Bring it here."

During the few months that Alejandro had kept residence in the embassy, Enrique had acted as his assistant. A quiet man without family standing or stature, he was an unimpressive forty-year-old who had long ago reached the peak of his ability in the diplomatic service of his country. Alejandro had elevated him to the post he himself had recently occupied, sure that while Enrique might not excel in the position, he was incapable of bringing any discredit to the office he served. Alejandro smirked inwardly at the thought, knowing that his concern for the dignity of Spain would have been better spent governing his own actions than worrying about the conduct of his mediocre assistant.

Enrique put the letters down in the sunlight that bathed the desktop. At once, Alejandro noticed that most of them were returned letters, written in his own hand. He smoothed his moustache as he pulled a few out of the pile. A note of thanks to the senator from Maine. A letter of condolence to the congressman of Penn's Sylvania. A group of dinner invitations sent to the Secretary of the Interior, the chairman of the Foreign Relations Committee, the archbishop of the New York diocese. All returned, all marked "Refused," or "Return to Sender" in a peremptory hand.

Alejandro felt his blood begin to boil at these snubs. His nostrils flared in a building rage, but he clamped down on it, not wanting to shatter his dignity before his subordinate.

"Thank you, Enrique," he said. "You may go."

"Excellency," his assistant said with trepidation. "This came, as well." In his hand was a leather pouch, the shield of New Spain imprinted in gold on its side, and heavy wax seals binding the twining cords that closed it. A diplomatic pouch from the viceregal throne.

Alejandro stood and took the pouch without a word.

Enrique, aware of his employer's simmering anger, bowed and left. The tall bronze-and-wood door closed with a firm *thunk*.

Through the pouch's leather, he could feel the crisp lines of a letter. A thick one. Since he did not expect a long letter of chatty familiarity from his viceroy, he surmised instead that it was an official decree of some ilk. No, he corrected himself. Not of "some ilk." It was a rebuke, a reprimand, or worse.

He tossed the pouch on his desk and turned his back on it. Unwilling to face the letter, he began to walk slowly around the room, enjoying with conscious study the Old World, pre-Carlist touches of heavy bronze and timbered wood, the chambered moldings of the high ceiling, the sharp click of his heels on the stone flooring. He smiled at the brightness of sun on polished wood, relished the desert scent that rose from the thick, Moroccan carpet, and calmed his nerves with the silken feel of his fingers across the back of a leather-clad chair. On the walls, he could spy, in their frames of ornate, gilded gesso, scenes of his younger years—the beaches of San Diego, the broken lands of the Tejano Coast, and the forested heights of the Sierra. Above the hearth was a painting, hung there only a few months prior, of his family's estate above the vineyards in the Sonoma highlands, and below the mantel hung the sword of his command— his last command—along the Tejano Coast.

These were the luxuries of his office and they measured the height of his rise from the disgrace of defeat at El Bracito to the photograph of himself and the Lord Viceroy, taken just a few months ago in San Francisco. His return to Spanish society had been long and arduous, but he *had* returned, and whatever that pouch contained, it could not be worse than the obstacles he had already overcome.

He walked briskly back to the desk and grabbed the letter knife. Its edge glinted in the sunlight as he used it to cut the satin cords that bound the flat pouch. Grabbing the seal on the other end, he pulled the cords out of their seams, opening the pouch. Within was a letter, folded and sealed much like the one he had just addressed to the viceroy. Without further hesitation, he cracked the seal and unfolded the thick parchment and read.

It was not a rebuke. Nor was it a reprimand. It was a dismissal.

In cold, emotionless terms, the viceroy's edict dismissed him from his post as the Ambassador to the United States, and instructed him to prepare for his replacement, due to arrive in two months' time.

Dismissal! A heavier sentence than he had imagined. But a dismissal based on what? No one *knew* anything; no one could *prove* anything about his involvement in the failed assassination. A summary dismissal based on guess and conjecture? It was an outrage; a slap across the face!

He stared at the document, and then he knew what was really happening. The viceroy did not know—no one in New Spain even guessed—but the failure of his mission to assist the Cheyenne Alliance in negotiating a peace with the United States was the excuse that those Madrileños needed to once again put the ambitious Creole back in his place.

Again he was fighting them! He had been forever fighting them for respect and position. As if it was *his* fault that he was colony-born and not a "true" Spaniard. As if *he* had been the reason that control of New Spain had slipped out of Royalist hands. As if, by fighting with the Federalists against Custer and his Americans, Alejandro had endorsed the idea of a Republic.

"¡Dios mío!" he cursed. "I, who have yearned for the royal favor all my life, to be painted as a rebellious Creole. It is . . . I can not . . ." His rage finally came to a boil, setting his hands to shake and peeling his lips back from his teeth in a sneer of hatred. With a growl that rose from the pit of his belly, he reached over the desk and grabbed the brass base of the unlit oil lamp. The growl became a shout, and he hurled the lamp into the fireplace. Cut crystal shattered against the burning logs, and flaming oil spattered across the hearthtiles, rushing up the flue in a roar that echoed his own.

"Damn you all!"

The door banged open and Enrique and one of the

household guardsmen ran inside. Enrique ran to the spatters of oil that still burned on the tiles, trying to stamp out the flames.

"Get *out*!" Alejandro shouted.

"But Excellency," Enrique said, even more flustered now that the toe of his shoe was covered in burning oil. He tried to put out the flames on the tiles, the flames on his foot, and question Alejandro all at the same time. "Is . . . is there anything . . . *ai-ai-ai* . . . is there anything wrong, Excellency?"

"You everlasting fool, I said get *out*! Now *go*!" And when he still did not move, Alejandro pointed to the guard. "Get him out of here!"

The guard grabbed Enrique by the arm and pulled him quickly from the room. The door closed with a boom that filled the tall room. Alejandro saw his assistant's oily footprints on the stone floor, outlined in guttering flame, and outside the door he heard Enrique's hotfooted complaining echo down the long hall.

He couldn't help it. He began to laugh. The whole of it—Enrique's clownish incompetence, the viceroy's brutal dismissal, and even his own failed vengeance against the man who had started his downfall—it was too much to be borne. Laughing, he staggered to his desk and collapsed into the chair, and when his giggling began to subside, the image of Enrique holding his flaming foot in one hand while stamping at flames with the other sent him upward again into hilarity.

"I have failed," he murmured as his laughter turned toward tears. "More completely than if I had tried." He picked up the viceroy's letter. "With a wink and a blind eye you watched for a decade as my Castilian predecessor whored his way up and down the Eastern Seaboard, but now, on the mere hint of failure, it is I who must retreat in shame." His laughter died and his throat tightened. "And with my wife and child within these walls, here to witness my dishonor."

A firm knock sounded at the door.

"Leave me be!"

The knock was repeated.

"Vete al carajo!"

A guard opened the door. "Your pardon, Excellency, but there is a carriage at the gate. You have been summoned to the White House."

Alejandro exhaled. "Summoned?"

The guard was embarrassed to say it. "Yes, Excellency."

The parchment of the viceroy's note was rough against his fingertips, and the broken wax of the official seal gave literal weight to the import of the words it sealed.

"Not altogether unexpected, I suppose."

The White House was a short ride from the embassy. Alejandro took it as a condemned man takes the walk up the scaffold steps: silent, unopposing. He brought no valise with him, and did not ask Enrique to come along. He wanted no more witnesses to his disgrace than were necessary. The carriage circled around the equestrian statue of Washington and headed down Penn's Sylvania Avenue toward the north entrance. They were waved through the gate and drove up the curved driveway. The northern entrance of the White House, with its forty-foot, Ionic columns, towered above the snow-covered grass. Alejandro descended from the carriage and climbed the white stone steps—steps so similar to those on the south entrance but steps that had not, as the others had only a few weeks before, been stained with blood.

He wondered after young George Custer, Jr., the man the Cheyenne called One Who Flies. Alejandro was glad that, at the very least, he had been able to help free the young man from his imprisonment. He liked One Who Flies, and had come to respect him in the few months they had known each other. He had only wanted his death as a vengeance against his father, President Custer, and as a tool to drive deeper the political wedge between American business interests and the labor unions. With the railroad and steel industries blamed for young Custer's death, the unions would have gained the upper hand. Costs would have shot up, profits shrunk, and tax revenues dwindled. The idea of selling the American Plains back to the Indians would have been more than palatable; it might even have been desirable. And an independent Indian nation bordering on New Spain? Well, that would have opened quite a door.

But the wrong blood had been spilled that day. It had been the President who had fallen and not the son and, as a result, the stakes rose incomparably and the stench of involvement, unlike the blood from the stone steps, became nearly impossible to remove.

Alejandro was ushered inside and up the twisting side staircase to the right of the entry hall. On the second floor, where most of the business of the Executive Branch was carried out, he was taken down the cross hall to a well-lit room on the southeast corner, a few doors down from the office where he and President Custer had been acrimoniously reintroduced.

The walls of Morton's inner office were yellow, and the translucent voile drapes glowed white with the afternoon sunlight, giving Alejandro the immediate impression that he was stepping inside of some giant egg. The men in the room, however, quickly dispelled that image.

There were perhaps a dozen men present, two-thirds of whom were in the dark blue wool of the military, gold braid shining on their shoulders, brass buttons bright on their chests. The few other men were in dark suits. Alejandro recognized William Hawkins, the Secretary of the Treasury, and Harrison Strong, the Chairman of the Senate Foreign Relations Committee. Among these solid men of power aides wove and whispered, carrying papers or coffee, attending to the power that inhabited the room.

And in the far corner, backlit by the tall, bright windows, and flanked by two American flags, was a large desk behind which sat a small, pale man.

Levi P. Morton, Vice President of the United States of America, sat in a large, leather chair. His white hair and squinty eyes gave him the appearance of a mole, but Alejandro knew Morton's reputation was more that of a badger: tough, aggressive, and capable of turning around in his own skin to bite the attacker.

"The Ambassador from New Spain," the usher announced.

The guests rose as he entered, though by their faces he could tell that it was formality and not courtesy that brought them to their feet. Morton remained seated.

"Mr. Vice President," Alejandro said as he walked forward into the room. "You asked to see me?"

Morton did not speak right away, but instead studied Alejandro with a narrow gaze. After a moment, he stood and leaned forward, fingertips resting on the desk blotter. "Yes, Ambassador. I asked to see you. I wanted to tell you this in person."

Morton's desktop was neat, everything in its place. Letters to the right. Pen and inkwell in the center at the edge of the blotter. A tidy stack of bound reports to his left. A bust of Jefferson at one corner, and a small lamp at the other. Only one item was askew: sitting diagonally on the blotter between Morton's tented fingers was a creased piece of parchment. Alejandro recognized at once the heavy paper, the floral script, and the cracked red wax seal of the viceroy's stamp.

He steeled himself, knowing what was to come. "What was it you wanted to tell me, sir?"

"I wanted to tell you, to your conniving face, that we know everything." Morton's voice was small and biting, like the edge of a saw, cutting with sharp, offset teeth. "We know what you were planning, we know with whom you planned it, and we know what foiled it. The magnitude of your treachery astounds me, and apparently"—he held up the parchment—"it apparently astounds your viceroy as well. He has written to tell me that he's recalling your miserable hide back to New Spain. If I had enough evidence, I'd send you back in a box, sir, after hanging you as a spy. As it stands, however, I can only honor the viceroy's request, a request with which I cannot comply quickly enough. I want you out of this country as soon as your replacement arrives."

Alejandro looked slowly at the faces ranged against him, matching them fury for fury. To call him here to disgrace him, to vilify him in this fashion, where he could neither defend nor protect himself, it was just another example of the uncouth and pugnacious American character.

"Mr. Vice President," he said, letting his distaste for

this little man seep into his tone, "you do not tell me anything of which I am not already aware."

"Oh, no?" Morton seemed amused by Alejandro's impudence. "Then shall I tell you that the alliance you were working to forge between us and those savages is as dead as the assassin you and your confederates hired? That is, if you really *were* working to forge an alliance, which I doubt." Morton walked around from behind the desk and into the center of the forest of blue and black wool suits that stood to either side. He walked up to Alejandro and looked at him, hands on hips.

"The interior of this continent, *Mr.* Silveira, is United States territory, and shall remain so. I am instructing General Meriwether to expand his efforts against the Indians, to constrain them within borders of *our* delineation, and to support and protect the expansion of our railroads and our settlements within that territory, by any means necessary." He took a step closer, so close that Alejandro could smell the coffee and cream on his breath. "I wanted you to know," he said in a softer voice, "just how completely you had failed."

He turned and walked back to his desk. "Now get the hell out of my office," he said. "And if you step foot outside your embassy gates, I'll clap you in irons, lack of evidence or no."

Once more Alejandro studied the generals and statesmen in the room. Anger and loathing was plain on their faces, so there was no reason for Alejandro to hide his own disdain.

"The pup barks bravely from within a pack of dogs," he said.

Morton looked up with a shocked stare. One of the generals stepped forward but was held back by another.

Alejandro chuckled. "And dogs that are afraid to bite, at that." He took a step backward and bent in his finest, deepest courtly obeisance. Then he turned his heel on the assemblage and walked out of the room, leaving a tumult of outrage in his wake.

At the embassy, Alejandro went immediately to his office and slammed the door so hard as to make the paintings dance against the walls. The lamp he had thrown that morning had been replaced and all evidence of his earlier temper was gone, and only that silent, invisible efficiency of his staff kept him from repeating his outburst. But still, the effrontery! The complete lack of diplomatic etiquette! He held out his hands in the last of the evening's light. His fingers shook with unspent emotion. As a growl built in his throat, he clenched his hands into fists. He walked out of the light and sat in his chair, deep in the shadows, pressing his fists into his temples, trying to squeeze the rage from his mind.

It is my fault, he told himself as he fought the tears. My fault and no other's. How could I have been so wrong? How could I have brought this down upon us? Upon Victoria?

The door to his office opened and he turned away to hide his face. "I do not wish to be disturbed!"

The sound of stiff fabric whispered through the room and he turned to find his wife standing there, her back to the door.

"Victoria," he said in surprise. "What are you doing here?"

"I came to talk to you," she said, her voice soothing and calm despite the concern—no, the fear—that he saw in her eyes.

"Talk to me?" he said, regaining his composure. "Why certainly, my dear. What is it you wish to talk about?"

Slowly, she came forward into the room. Her dress was of a deep Dupioni silk, almost black except where the sun fired it to maroon. Her belted bodice was stitched tight and her sleeves full. The starched cotton at collar and cuffs was simple and reserved, as were the wrapped braids of her black hair. As she came forward into the light, rubies glinted from her ears, but her eyes were made of onyx, and Alejandro felt that they could see through the sunlight and into the shadows where he sat hiding.

"I want to apologize," she said.

Her admission took him aback. "Apologize? What for?"

"For not being a good wife," she answered him. She stood in the sunlight, hands clasped before her waist, her back stiff and erect, her head high. Alejandro had always considered her beautiful, but never before had he seen her like this: a stately noblewoman, regal in surrender.

"Victoria," he said as he stood and walked around the desk to take her hands in his. "My love, you *have* been a good wife. Always you have been a good wife; better than I have deserved. There is nothing for which you need apologize."

She looked up into his eyes, and he could see the darker pupil amid the darkness of her iris, black with flecks of gold. "I have not done anything for which I need to apologize, yet. But I will. I am about to."

He released her hands. "What are you saying?"

"I am saying that I am about to do something that a good Spanish wife does not do, and I wish to apologize for it beforehand."

"What is it you are about to do?"

"I am about to contradict my husband."

"Victoria. I do not care for this game you are playing. Please, I have much to attend to. Please, leave me alone so I can work."

"No," she said. "I will not leave you alone. Not now. Not anymore." She came forward and grasped his arm. "My lord, my husband, I can see what is happening. I can read the American newspapers. I can hear what the staff are saying. I can read your moods and predict your rages. And I will not stand by while you spin yourself down into the depths."

She had never spoken to him in this manner, had never been so forthright with her opinions. He knew well how she had been able to manipulate him during their decades together—with her softness, and with a gentle, steady pressure like water against a stone, she could maneuver him in a thousand tiny ways. But never had she challenged him so openly, and it completely unbalanced him.

"Victoria, I . . ."

"You are in trouble. *We* are in trouble. Am I right?"

"My darling . . ."

"I am Victoria Isabel Baca de Silveira. I am your wife. I am mother to your only daughter. And I have asked you a question. Am I *right*? Are we in trouble?"

He looked into the face of the woman before him and saw the same high cheekbones, the same dark-winged brow, the same Amor's Bow lips that he had first seen forty years ago. And those eyes, those dark, bottomless eyes, they were the same, too.

So many other men of his rank had taken mistresses, but he had never felt the need or the want. His love and his respect for Victoria, and for her steadfast support of him during his years of servitude to his degenerate predecessor, the former ambassador, demanded that he respect her now. The world settled again beneath his feet. His universe now contained a wife who could speak to him so, who could challenge him as an equal.

"Yes," he told her, "we are in trouble."

"How much trouble?"

"We must leave the country."

She took it like a blow, stepping back with the force of it. "Leave the country? But surely the viceroy—"

Alejandro sneered. From his coat pocket, he produced the viceroy's letter, and held it out to her. "The viceroy has recalled me."

Her cheeks colored as she read. "You should say he has *abandoned* you!" She tossed the letter on the desk and walked away from him, her hands in tiny balls at her sides. "I know what you were trying to do, Alejandro, and he should have been thankful for your daring. An independent Indian nation would have opened a door for the Spanish throne."

"He was just looking for an excuse," Alejandro said.

"Serrano-Ruiz was a fool not to support you completely." She came close to him again, took his hand up in hers, kissed it and held it to her breast. "He has always denied you your proper place at court. But he has missed his chance. You will find another champion."

"Who?" he asked her. "Anyone who took on such a challenge would still have to deal with Serrano-Ruiz."

"Anyone but someone higher than Serrano-Ruiz," she said plainly.

"Higher than . . . higher than the viceroy?"

"Yes," she said with a smile. "You must apply to the queen."

He could not think of a response. The queen? María

Cristina? To hope to engage the queen regent in his plans was . . . it was ludicrous.

"Why would Serrano-Ruiz allow me to take my case to the queen?"

"It is simple, my love. He will allow you to go to María Cristina because he believes you will fail, and by going to her, it marks you as a desperate man."

"And if he is right? If she refuses?"

"Then she refuses, and the viceroy wins. But if she agrees . . ."

Alejandro shook his head, trying to maintain his sense amid the whirl of ideas and events. "Why would María Cristina want to involve herself in this mess?"

Victoria's smile dazzled in the sunlight.

"Act boldly," she said, "and bold things will happen."

CHAPTER 4

Big Hoop and Stick Game Moon, Waning
Fifty-seven Years after the Star Fell
Winter Camp of the Closed Windpipe Band
Alliance Territory

Storm Arriving scowled in frustration and stared at the logs that burned in the hearthpit of One Bear's lodge. He took a measured breath himself and tried to explain it another way.

"If we wait until spring, it will be too late," he said. Of the several men who sat around the fire, there were three whose opinion he hoped to sway. First was One Bear, his father-in-law and a respected peace chief of the Great Council whose stature had only grown with the sudden void left by the passing of Three Trees Together. Then there was Two Roads, the leader of the Kit Fox soldier society and a war chief for nearly twenty years, whose word would convince many others. And last there was Stands Tall in Timber, the holiest man among the People and the Keeper of the Sacred Arrows. The others who completed the circle around the fire—while certainly influential men in their own rights—could not play as pivotal a role as the chiefs. The chiefs were key to not only winning the support of the Closed Windpipe band, but critical to building consensus among the entire People. If he could convince these three, they would convince others.

"To us," he continued, "winter is a waiting time. We wait for the spring. We live off the stores and supplies gathered during the warmer moons. Our whistlers huddle close together and prepare their nests. Our walkers sleep under their leaf mounds until the sun's road climbs higher into the sky. We wait."

He looked at the men. The firelight glowed on their dark faces, glinted from their dark eyes. They were old men with hair as white as the snow outside the doubled lodgeskins, and young men with hair still as black as the night between the stars. They were elders, storytellers, medicine men, and soldiers. They were his friends. They were his people, his clan, and his band, and they were the ones he was trying to save.

"We wait," he said, "but the bluecoats do not. For them, the winter is a building time. It is when they replenish their stores, not when they deplete them. It is when they grow fat, not when they grow thin. If we wait until spring to begin our work, the summer will be gone before we can act. The bluecoats will not wait for us. As it is, they will rise before we do. They will act in the spring. They will rise with the first grass and we will spend this year the same way as last year: running from them instead of chasing after them."

Two Roads furrowed his brow as he considered what Storm Arriving had said. The war chief stared into the fire, his hands on his knees, and took a breath but One Bear broke the silence before Two Roads.

"My son-in-law is a fine soldier," One Bear said. "And I am proud of him. His words, though, are a soldier's words, and consider only the soldier's path. We must also consider the other paths of life, and the actions that are appropriate to those paths." He hesitated as he pondered his next words. "For many years we have walked the path of war against the *vé'hó'e,* and yet it has not helped us. We have taken the *vé'ho'e* weapons from the bluecoats, and we have used those weapons against them. We have taken the spirit of thunder from their iron roads, and we have used it against them. And now, Storm Arriving counsels us to adopt the *vé'ho'e* ways of war, to give up our traditions, to war in the depths of winter, even if it means abandoning our families' needs. I cannot see that this will help us."

He paused long enough for Whistling Elk to stretch good manners and slip into the gap to speak. "Storm

Arriving is not speaking of making war, but of preparing for war," he said in his soft, melodic voice. Whistling Elk was a man-becoming-woman known for his story-telling, his healing talents, and his bravery in battle. With his dual nature of both male and female, he often saw things in a way that eluded others, and thus his word carried special weight among the People. "The bluecoats push into our southlands, and we move away, crowding the Crow People to our north. If we do not act now and parley with the Crow People, we will soon be faced with war on two fronts: north and south. Storm Arriving merely suggests that we act now to prepare for this."

"Preparing for war is the path of war," One Bear said, reasserting his right to be heard with a brief glare sent at Whistling Elk. "Three Trees Together was leading us away from the path of war, and in his memory, I say that we should not run to it now. Using *vé'ho'e* ways has not helped us, and so I say we must return to our old ways. We need to renew our virtues. If we fast and make sacrifice and reconnect with the powers of our world, if we reestablish our bond with Maheo'o and the great spirits that stand at the four corners of the world, we will benefit from their strength. The People will be protected. The *vé'hó'e* will not find our camps. The lands they take from us will not support them. *They* will grow weak while *we* grow strong, and then . . . *then* the time will be ready for us to strike and push them from our lands."

He held his right hand palm down and then turned it palm up, signifying his refusal. "I reject this preparation for war, and in my name and in the name of Three Trees Together, I shall work for peace."

Hands signed and voices murmured as some of the group accepted the reasoning of One Bear as truth. Storm Arriving felt his stomach tighten.

"Not I," came the rumbling gravel voice of Stands Tall in Timber. The Keeper of the Sacred Arrows stared into the flames, his eyes narrowed by hard thoughts. "Three Trees Together was my closest friend. From childhood we grew, living and fighting as brothers against the enemies of the People. I sang his death song on the steps of the great White House where Long Hair lives. I bore the stain of his blood on my hands and in my eyes. I bear that stain still." He looked up from the flames, and his gaze swept the faces of those gathered in the lodge. "I will not work for peace simply because it is not war. The Crow People have been our enemies since before the star fell. We have worked long to weaken them so that they would not threaten our northern border, and yet still they are strong. It is time we tried to use that strength, instead of fighting against it."

"Three Trees Together would never condone this," One Bear said.

"Three Trees Together is *dead*," Stands Tall in Timber said. "You can pray for peace if you wish. I cannot tell you what to do. I shall be praying as well, but I shall be praying for vengeance, and for victory."

One Bear folded his arms over his chest and Stands Tall in Timber leaned forward, elbows on his knees. Both men stared into the fire once more, their choices made, their opinions solidified. Storm Arriving knew that One Bear was lost to him; he would never be able to convince him of the wisdom of his plan, just as One Bear would never be able to convince Stands Tall in Timber that he was wrong. That meant two large factions of the tribe would line up behind the two men. He was glad for the backing of Stands Tall in Timber, for an endeavor such as this done without the benediction of the Sacred Arrows was sure to fail, but it left Two Roads still undecided. As a war chief, he was often the last one to argue for war, but if the opinion of Two Roads could be won, it would break any deadlock, and so Storm Arriving made his appeal directly to the leader of the Kit Fox soldiers.

"Prayer and fasting and sacrifice are good things," he said as he pulled aside the yoke of his tunic, showing the scars of the skin sacrifice he bore on his breast. "One Bear himself guided me through the ritual, and I hung from the pole for an entire day. That was the first time we went to the City of White Stone. But when we went, still we died. And still the bluecoats came. And *still* they kill our families, our wives, and our children." He stood.

"Any man who is not convinced, any man who is not sure if war is the path we should take, come with me. There is someone I wish for you to hear."

Storm Arriving walked away from the central hearth, careful not to interpose himself between any man and the fire's light. Then he made his way around the edge of the lodge, pushed open the doorflap, and stepped outside.

The air grabbed him with chill hands, tightening the skin on his face and causing his loins to rise. The snow was knee-deep, and he plowed his way through it toward the packed snow of the well-trodden path. Once there, he turned and waited to see if anyone would follow him out.

The lodge glowed with the light from the fire, and he could hear someone speaking in a low, calm voice. All around him, fir trees stood like white-shrouded sentinels, and from the gap between them, the crescent moon smiled.

Or is it a frown? he asked himself. I suppose it depends on which way you look at it.

The doorflap opened again, and Storm Arriving felt his heart leap. A figure emerged, and he saw that it was only Whistling Elk.

"That was not very subtle," Whistling Elk said, crunching through the snow to stand next to him.

"No," Storm Arriving agreed. "But I needed to make the point. Without Two Roads, I will never gain enough support." He glanced at the storyteller. Whistling Elk wore a woman's dress and when he sat before a fire he sat as a woman did, with his knees together and feet to one side, instead of cross-legged like a man. But he had the heart of a warrior, full of bravery and passion. "Thank you for speaking up, back there. I was beginning to feel all alone in this."

Whistling Elk ducked his head and smiled at Storm Arriving's expression of gratitude. "I only wish I could have done more," he said. "As you said, we need Two Roads, and I do not know where he stands."

Other men began to come out of the lodge.

"We will see soon enough," he said.

First came Long Braid, a respected soldier of the Red

Shield society. Behind him came Sharp Knife, one of the Little Bowstring soldiers. But when Two Roads emerged, Storm Arriving breathed a sigh. A few other men came out after Two Roads, but it was the leader of the Kit Fox soldiers that he had hoped to see.

Two Roads, the hawk feathers he wore in his braid shining in the moonlight, came up to Storm Arriving.

"Take us to this person you want us to hear," Two Roads said.

In all they were eight men, and Storm Arriving led them off down the path. Their footsteps made the snow creak, but that was the only sound in the night. No one spoke as they walked down the slope, away from the more sheltered areas of the vale in which the Tree People had encamped. He led them past the watering place where the women came every morning to crack the ice and dip their water-skins, but when he turned away from the sledding hill where the children played, they all now knew to whose lodge they were headed. He heard one man *harrumph*.

"Why should we listen to him?" Long Braid asked.

Storm Arriving did not answer.

"He's not to be trusted," Long Braid went on. "None of the Wolf People should be trusted."

"Storm Arriving trusts him," Whistling Elk said.

"Storm Arriving saved his life. He has a soft heart for him," Long Braid said. "It has clouded his reason."

Two Roads stopped and turned to face Long Braid. "If Storm Arriving thinks this man has words I should hear," he said, "then I want to hear them."

They began walking again, and Long Braid did not say anything more. They left the path and crunched their way through the deeper drifts. As Storm Arriving pushed through the smooth, unbroken waves of snow, the moonlight glinted from them in sparkling stars.

Finally, the dark cone of a lonely lodge could be seen against the pale field of snow. Storm Arriving frowned at the lack of firelight. Even after being with the People for over a year, the family within was still struggling to find a peace with their new neighbors.

They stopped a few yards from the lodge.

"Haaahe," he called out in greeting. "Are you there? It is Storm Arriving."

Furtive movement and whispered conversation came from within, and the doorflap opened. Knee Prints by the Bank stepped outside, his grey hair blue in the moonlight.

"Haaahe," he said, greeting them.

"I have brought some friends," Storm Arriving said. "We wish to talk to you."

"About what?"

"About the *vé'hó'e,* and what you told me the other day."

Knee Prints by the Bank looked at the men for a long moment and then, in obvious decision, beckoned them within the lodge.

It was very dark within the lodge without a fire. The wife of Knee Prints by the Bank was blowing on the few coals she had banked against the morning, breathing life back into them and feeding them with small twigs. As the men sat down and as a flame was born in the coals, the conditions of the lodge became clear.

Knee Prints by the Bank and his wife, his two sons, his daughter, his sister-in-law, and his wife's mother all lived in the one lodge. As recently as last fall, the wife's elderly father had also lived with them, until an infection in a wound in his foot began to creep up to his calf, to his thigh, and finally reaching up to sour his heart. But even with the old man's passing, they were still seven people in one lodge, without even a separate lodge for the women during their moon-time.

The lodge itself was in a sad state, made from cast-off skins. They did not even have an inner lining to help insulate against the winter's cold. The light grew, and Storm Arriving saw that the women still wore their *vé'ho'e*-style dresses, and that Knee Prints by the Bank still wore his shirt of thin Trader's cloth, all habits born of their time across the Big Greasy. He did not have to wonder why they were not doing better. Knee Prints by the Bank was not a young man, but his sons were not yet old enough to hunt with great proficiency. And, being members of the Wolf People, it had been difficult for them to make any friends among the People, their old enemies. Their *vé'ho'e* clothes and habits were necessitated by their poverty, not by their desire.

The small fire provided light though no warmth, and Storm Arriving could see his breath as he spoke. "I have brought these men to hear your words about the *vé'hó'e,* and why you came across the Big Greasy. I think it is important for them to hear what you have to say and to hear it in your voice."

The women of the family huddled with the children, keeping one another warm as Knee Prints by the Bank sat cross-legged in the *vá'ôhtáma,* the place of honor at the back of the lodge.

"You all wish to hear this?" he asked.

The men all signed or spoke their agreement.

"As you wish." He straightened his back and folded his arms across his chest. "When my father was a boy, my people hunted the lands up and down along the Big Greasy. By the time I was born, the *vé'hó'e* had pushed us out of some of the best lands to the east and south. We kept moving away from them, wanting only to live our lives. We would give them one area in exchange for peace, and when they broke their promises, we gave them another area, hoping that it would appease them. More and more land we gave them, and the land we reserved for ourselves became smaller and smaller, until at last we were left with a tenth of what we needed, and the smallest part of what we started with."

"Why did you not fight them?" Long Braid asked, his disdain palpable in the words he spoke.

"We did fight them, but the *vé'hó'e* fight in strange ways. They do not stop when they are beaten, and they do not fight to victory. They fight to the death, always to the death. Death means nothing to the *vé'hó'e.* They make war as if they have an inexhaustible supply of soldiers, and perhaps they do."

Storm Arriving remembered finding Knee Prints by the Bank and his family along the shores of the Big Greasy. "Tell them what made you leave your reserved lands," he prompted.

Knee Prints by the Bank shrugged. "We were starving. We were sick. The *vé'ho'e* law said we could not leave our reserved lands to hunt. And then the *vé'hó'e* made another law. This law said that they could take our reserved lands and divide them, giving each man his own piece of the land. The bluecoat agents came to us and said we should make a mark on a piece of paper, and they would give us each a piece of our land. I said I do not need to make a mark. The land is already my land, but the bluecoat agents said that if I did not make a mark, I would not be given a piece of my land. I asked them, how can I live on a piece of land so small? I can shoot an arrow from one side to the other, it is so small. How can I live this way? How can I hunt? How can I feed my family?" Knee Prints by the Bank paused in his tale and laughed; a sad, mournful thing. "The bluecoat agent said that I would plant seeds and grow crops." His eyes glared at the small fire.

"I was a *hunter*. I was a soldier for my people. What did I know about planting seeds?" He sighed, and unfolded his arms. "And so we left the lands of my youth and came across the Big Greasy, hoping to find a life here among our old enemies."

Storm Arriving leaned in to speak. "But now the *vé'hó'e* have come across the Big Greasy. Now they are in *our* lands."

"Yes," Knee Prints by the Bank said. "And they will take your land. Hill by hill and tree by tree." He pointed to Two Roads and the others in turn. "They will take your land, and push you back, farther and farther. And you will give up that land for their promise of peace, and then they will come again, and you will give up more land. You will give up land until you can't anymore, until you *have* to fight them, but by then you will be too tired and too sick, and you will have no more room to move because the *vé'hó'e* will be all around you."

The lodge was silent but for the hissing of green wood in the flames. The men sat, thinking, and Storm Arriving hoped that what they heard had upset them as much as it had him.

"Two Roads," he said. "Honoring the spirits and *Ma'heo'o* is fine. But let us do so while we act."

The leader of the Kit Fox soldiers took a slow breath; his quiet way of asking for the attention of the others. "I think," he said evenly, "that we should move, and move quickly. We must send riders to the other bands now, before the spring comes, and we should speak to our northern neighbors, before the *vé'hó'e* send blue-coats against us."

The others concurred, even Long Braid.

"Good," Two Roads said. He rose, and all stood with him. "My thanks to you, Knee Prints by the Bank, and to your family. I would like to send my daughter to you, if I may. It seems that you have not been shown the best places to gather deadwood for your fires."

Knee Prints by the Bank stood a little bit taller. "We would welcome the instruction."

They left, and headed back across the snows. "Spread the word," Two Roads told them. "Tell your friends and neighbors what you have heard here. We shall pay heed to the word of the Council and the peace chiefs, but we neglect the necessities of war at our peril. We meet again at sunrise."

With that last phrase, Storm Arriving knew that he had been successful, for to meet at sunrise was to meet for action. This winter would not pass before the Kit Foxes were in action.

At the sledding hill, they separated, each heading back toward his family and colleagues. Whistling Elk gave him a quick hug before loping off to spread the word. Storm Arriving headed back alone toward the lodge where One Bear still conferred with his like-minded friends, for it was with One Bear's family that Storm Arriving made his home.

He walked up to the main lodge but hesitated. From within, he saw the light of a low fire. On the lodgeskins, he saw the shadows of those men who had remained behind. He heard their voices, speaking in quiet conversation, still deliberating the fine points of their decision.

There was no point to his reentering that discussion. They had all made their choice; they had all selected the path they would take. For One Bear's faction, they chose the course of prayer and inaction. For Stands Tall in Timber—and now for Two Roads as well—it was the path of movement, of change, and yes, of war. But Storm Arriving was not worried by war. He had walked the path of war since his youth, working to keep the lands

of the People free from incursions, and to weaken the
threats from other tribes and from other races. Crow
People, Wolf People, or *vé'hó'e*, it made no difference.

War was war.

He walked away from the meeting place and headed
toward his own lodge. It glimmered with firelight, and
the designs he had painted on the skins—handprints
over lightning bolts and hailstones—rippled like living
shadows. He pulled open the doorflap and stepped
inside.

Speaks while Leaving sat near the hearth, tending the
fire. Her hair was loose across her shoulders, as she liked
to comb it through before she bedded down for the
night. Close at hand lay their daughter, the infant Blue
Shell Woman, swaddled in skins and furs, with only her
rounded cheeks and brow visible in the firelight.

But Speaks while Leaving did not look up to greet
him as he entered, and Storm Arriving knew that this
was not a good sign.

"What have you done?" she asked him as she poked
at the sleepy coals with new wood. Her hair fell across
her cheek and breast, dark as the breath of night, and
all he could see of her face was the breadth of her brow,
the depth of her eyes, and the strong line of her nose.
She was no longer young—neither of them was—but the
firelight was her disciple, and when it touched her features, she was no more than twenty summers old. Watching her, gazing back into flame-lit time, he remembered
their courtship and the difficulty it had brought, for not
only had Speaks while Leaving been the daughter of a
chief, she had also been touched by the spirits and given
to visions of great power. In courting her, he had risked
the displeasure of both worlds.

But courted her he had, and despite a seven-year argument during which neither of them spoke to the other,
they had eventually reconciled, married and, in time, created a daughter.

A daughter he wanted to keep safe. A daughter he
wanted to see grow and thrive, and, in years to come,
marry and have a child of her own.

"I have convinced Two Roads that we must move before the spring thaws."

She glared at him with angry eyes, an affront he would have accepted from none other than his wife. "You have committed yourself to leaving us again," she said. "To leaving your wife and child behind, while you place yourself in danger." She hugged her knees and rocked gently, back and forth. "How long will you walk the path of war? Why must it always be you who leads them into battle? Why won't you leave fighting to the younger men?"

He knew this was difficult for her; it was difficult for him as well, but he did not think she would believe him if he said so, and so he did not say it. "I lead them," he said instead, taking another route, "because younger men do not know how to fight." She looked up, wondering what he meant, and he continued. "If I left everything to them, they would go out to fight, and they would die. They would die because they do not know how to fight properly." He shrugged, wanting her to understand. "I am needed, for as long as the *vé'hó'e* enter our lands, if for no other reason than to make sure our soldiers fight their best, and stay alive as long as they can."

"But what of us?" she asked him. "What of your daughter? What of me? How shall we live without you here?"

"You have your family," he said. "Your father will be here. He has decided against the path of war."

"But I don't care about them. I want *you* here!"

"Why?" he asked, exasperated, torn between duty and family. He pointed out beyond the skin walls. "Haven't you heard any of the people who have been coming up to me, asking that I go back out to war? They ask for vengeance. They ask me to bring back the hands and ears and scalps of the men who killed their own. They ask me to go out and even the tally for their losses. And it will be an *honor* to do so. Why aren't you like a normal wife, begging me to go out against the bluecoats? Why do you want to keep me here like an old man instead of out fighting for our land and our pride?"

She wept openly, and her words were broken by sobs. "I want you here . . . because I . . . because I am . . . afraid."

"Of what?" he said, pushing on her hurt with his own.

"What are you afraid of? That I might gain favor among your clan? That some might come to esteem me more than your father? Or that they might esteem me more than you?"

"No!" she cried.

"Then what? What are you afraid of?"

"I'm afraid that you might not come home!" she said in one agonized wail. "I want you here. With our daughter. With me. I want you here."

"And I cannot be!" he shouted at her. "The *vé'hó'e* send the bluecoats against us. Last year it was small raids of ten and twenty men, but this year it will be more. I cannot be here because I must go out to meet them, to stop them before they reach you and our daughter."

She looked up, and he saw the gleaming streaks of tears on her cheeks. She stared up through the smoke-hole at the nexus of the lodgepoles. "This is not right," she whispered. "This is not what my vision showed me."

"*Eya!*" he said. "Your vision." When she spoke of her visions, there was no argument that he could bring against it.

"Yes," she said, her sorrow turning to anger. "*My* vision. My vision of the yellow metal that we mined, and of the Iron Shirts. Not a vision of killing bluecoats, or of slaughtering *vé'hó'e* while they sleep."

Her scorn hurt but did not dissuade him. "You have your visions, my wife, and I have mine."

"But your visions are wrong!"

He turned away from her and refused to look back.

"I did not mean that," she said, knowing she had gone too far. "I meant only that . . ."

Still he did not look at her. "I will not risk your life, or our daughter's life, on *any* vision, yours *or* mine."

"Yes," she said. "I understand. But I only ask, do not do anything right away. Wait until One Who Flies returns."

"Why?" he asked. "So he, too, can tell me that I'm wrong?" He stood and walked out of the lodge, not caring even to close the flap after him. He stalked off into the snow and the cold and the darkness, but with every step he felt her questions and her doubts follow him.

Her visions. All her life she had been given them, and all her life she had been proven right, in time. Visions of storms, of raids, of floods and droughts. She had foretold the cloud-that-fell and the coming of One Who Flies, and of his helping the People to overcome the bluecoats.

But where was he now? Where was One Who Flies? It had been over a moon since riders had come in with news of his release from the *vé'ho'e* prison. But though he had returned to Alliance lands, no one from any of the bands had reported seeing him.

Storm Arriving knew that his wife was worried for their friend, worried because of her affection for him, but also because of his tie to the realization of her visions. She had never been wrong, in the more than twenty years since the spirits first came upon her. But now, with One Who Flies long overdue, and another year of war with the bluecoats ahead, her vision that tied him to the Iron Shirts was in doubt. For the first time, she was looking at the failure of one of her visions.

It does not matter, he told himself. I cannot decide what is right based on her visions. I must decide based on what *I* see, and on what *I* know. And I know that the bluecoats are coming, and that we must make our land clean of them.

He turned back toward his lodge. He had to pack his things, if he was to leave with Two Roads in the morning.

CHAPTER 5

Big Hoop and Stick Game Moon, Waning
Fifty-seven Years after the Star Fell
Winter Camp of the Closed Windpipe Band
Alliance Territory

Speaks while Leaving stood in the dawn light, an elk hide draped over her shoulders and over the cradleboard she carried on her back. The hide kept both her and her infant warm, but it was the elk's spirit that kept her calm. The sun's light poked through the dark pines and touched the golden fur, awakening the elk's lingering memories of open fields and green grass, filling Speaks while Leaving with the echo of peace. She sighed, and her breath hung in the air, as still as a cloud in the flat rays of sunrise. Mouse Road, her husband's sister, stood beside her, silent, sullen, and yawning, having been kept up most of the night by the wolf songs sung by the warriors who, with her brother, were now preparing for yet another ride on the path of war.

The men tied bundles across the backs of their whistlers, the large, lizardlike mounts that would carry them on their journey. They packed furs and blankets for warmth, satchels of food and supplies for sustenance, and both traditional and *vé'ho'e* weaponry. They carried knives, lances, hatchets, or clubs, each item a deadly tool beneath the decorations of fur, beads, and feathers. Some men also tied on the horn-and-sinew bows and the full quivers that in the past had been the mainstay of a soldier's power, but which were now falling into disuse, having been supplanted by the weapon that no man was without: the Winchester repeating rifle. The *vé'ho'e* rifles, plundered from a hundred raids and battles against the bluecoats, were crucial to the Alliance's ability to defend itself against the *vé'ho'e* incursions.

As they strapped these tools of war across their whistlers' backs, medicine men walked among them, treating the mounts. These old, patient men would dig two fingers into a deerskin pouch and put a powdered pinch of dried whistler-medicine root in the whistler's mouth. Then the man would put a second pinch in his own mouth, moisten it, spit it into his hand, and rub it along the whistler's muzzle and bony crest. If the whistler shook his head, the treatment had worked, and the mount would prove long-winded and spirited in battle.

But when Stands Tall in Timber arrived with his wife, Shining Hair, who carried the bundle with the Sacred Arrows, everyone fell silent. The Sacred Arrows were gifts from the spirit world brought to the People ages ago by Sweet Medicine. Shining Hair carried them in a quiver of coyote fur, which was wrapped in the hide of a four-year-old buffalo killed with a single arrow, and she held them as she would an infant, cradled in her arms.

Stands Tall in Timber and Shining Hair walked among the soldiers. At each man, they stopped and allowed the soldier to speak to the Sacred Arrows, for any word a man said to the Arrows was heard by the spirits. The soldiers prayed to the Arrows for health, for victory, for glory, and Speaks while Leaving heard their prayers as clearly as if they were speaking directly to her. The clearing smoked with the power of the Arrows, the prayers, and the emotions of parting families.

Whistlers groused and squalled at the cold while the quiet ceremony moved from man to man. Some of the beasts fluted in anticipation, sending their rising tones through the long, bony crests that curved back from their heads. They changed the colors of their skin. The drakes flashed aggressive bars of white and crimson along their snouts, while the hens mottled their flanks with stripes of grey and dark green, camouflage amongst the snowy trees.

As Speaks while Leaving watched the solemnities, she had to admit that the war party was a fine sight. Its soldiers were the prime of the Closed Windpipe band, drawn from men born to the tribe as well as some of the Wolf and Fox People who had come across the Big Greasy. They were adorned with tall feathers, which shivered with every step, and furs of rich colors: chestnut otter, white stoat, grizzled marmot, the contrasting stripes of badger, and the golden richness of elk. Earrings of silver and copper winked in the dawn, and shells and claws rattled from necklaces and pectorals. Fifty men, from eighteen to forty summers old, all strong, lean, and fierce of eye. She felt a tightening of her throat. Though the least among them was a man to be feared, that would not save them all. The shadow of war was with them and it would not let them return unmarked.

Finally, Stands Tall in Timber stood before Storm Arriving. Speaks while Leaving saw her husband stand proudly, as leader of the war party, and then turn to retrieve a small parcel from within the packs on his whistler's back. He opened the deerhide and revealed four eagle tailfeathers, a gift for the Arrows, which he presented to their keeper. Stands Tall in Timber accepted the gift in his left hand, went to one knee, and rubbed his right hand on the ground. He passed his hand over the gift twice, then switched hands and repeated the motion with his left hand. Standing, he gave the gift back to Storm Arriving and told him to tie it to the sacred bundle. He turned to Shining Hair, and tied the feathers to the bundle with a thin strip of leather, speaking to the Arrows as he did.

"Please keep the People safe," he asked them. "And give us the courage to succeed."

Stands Tall in Timber put his hands on Storm Arriving's shoulders and then, smiling, turned and began to sing an old war path Wolf song. The others all joined him.

Take courage, they sang. *Do not be frightened. Follow where you see me riding. My whistler will sing us home.*

The singing faltered, and everyone turned.

"Eya," Mouse Road breathed, and sidled up next to her sister-in-law, hiding.

Speaks while Leaving looked and saw a group of men approaching the soldiers, their feet crunching through

the snow. Leading them was her father, One Bear, his
face dark with suppressed emotion. With him were the
other peace chiefs of the band, faces seamed by old age
and new worries. They walked up to Stands Tall in Timber, who stood with Storm Arriving.

"Do not do this," One Bear said without preamble.

"I cannot send them out without protection," said
Stands Tall in Timber.

"It is not what needs to be done."

"How can you know?" Storm Arriving asked him.
"We are faced with an enemy the likes of which we have
never seen. How can *you* know what needs to be done?
Have the *Ma'heono* come to you and shown you what
needs to be done? Do *you* have visions now like your
daughter?"

Every man was silent, made suddenly aware that
Speaks while Leaving was among them. She said a
prayer to the great spirits who had sent her visions of
the future.

Do not ask me, she prayed.

One Bear turned to his daughter, and she saw on his
face the realization that he had not, in all his deliberations, in all his long discussions, ever thought to ask her
opinion on the subject. Never had he asked her which
of the two paths fit best with the vision the *Ma'heono*
had given her.

Do not ask me, she repeated, looking from her father
to her husband. Please, do not ask me.

"My daughter," One Bear said, his voice unsteady.

Do not ask me. Do not make me choose between you.

They all were looking at her. Even the whistlers had
grown quiet. Stands Tall in Timber stepped forward and
walked over to where she stood. She turned away from
them and stared at the ground.

"Daughter of One Bear," the arrow-keeper said. "We
seem to have forgotten you." His voice was as deep and
rough as a grizzly's call in springtime. He stood before
her, watching her nervous hands, but his words were
pitched to the men who stood in two factions behind
him. "We have forgotten that from girlhood you have
seen beyond our world and beyond our time, telling us
of things that were yet to happen. We have forgotten to

consider your last vision, of gold, guns, and the Iron Shirts."

"That vision is done," Storm Arriving said. "We saw the end of it in the City of White Stone, when Three Trees Together fell."

"We have not," One Bear argued. "There is more to come, but not unless we rededicate ourselves."

Stands Tall in Timber held up his hands. "What does she say?"

Speaks while Leaving wanted to run, to leave this place regardless of the shame or trouble it might cause her, her father, or her husband. The vision that had come to her, two summers past, remained a strong memory. White Buffalo Woman, the spirit provider for the People, had shown her how a piece of gold would lead to weapons and other things the meaning of which was less clear: a ship on the water, a chair of carved wood, and a helmet and shield in the old style of the Iron Shirts, the country the *vé'hó'e* called New Spain.

Some of that vision had already come to pass. The People *had* found gold, and it *had* led to weapons with which they had fought back the encroachments of the bluecoats and the settlers. And the previous summer, they *had* met the ambassador from New Spain, whom they called Speaks for the Iron Shirts. And there *had* been ships, and a seat of power, and a visit to the Iron Shirts themselves.

But it did not *feel* finished. She still felt the power of the vision in her heart, and still felt its yearning to become reality. After the vision had come to her, they had danced—almost the entire tribe had been involved. They had danced and she had felt the power of the vision, and the rightness of it. There had never been argument about the vision's inception, but now, with bluecoat raids bringing death upon the People, with their greatest Grandfather slain, and with failures building as *vé'hó'e* still streamed into their lands, there was disagreement about its culmination.

Was it finished? she asked herself. And if it was, why would the spirits give her a vision that brought no benefit? Did they fail? Or was it still in motion? Was her father right? Her husband? Both? Or neither?

"Speaks while Leaving," the arrow-keeper said. "What do you say? Is the vision complete?"

"I cannot say," she told them.

"Cannot?" her father asked.

"Or will not?" Storm Arriving said.

She could hear the contempt in her husband's voice, and it angered her. "I will not say what cannot be said."

"My daughter," One Bear said. "You will tell us, and we will decide how to fulfill the vision."

She broke her gaze away from the ground and glared at her father. He blinked, surprised at her effrontery, and was about to chastise her when she cut him off.

"You," she said, a pointed finger jabbing toward him. "And you," she said to her husband. "You are both so sure of yourselves. You think you know what the spirits are thinking. You think you know what the *Ma'heono* mean when they speak to me." She glowered at them all. "When they speak to *me!*"

"Daughter! Remember your place!"

"I *do,* my father. I remember my place. I am Speaks while Leaving, daughter of Magpie Woman, who is daughter of the woman called Healing Rock. I am the one to whom the spirit-visions come. I am the one who tells you of my visions, and you are the ones who decide what they mean. You, my father, you know that the spirits intend to help us more, but demand first our suffering and our sacrifice. And you, my husband, you know that my vision is done, and that the spirits have abandoned us to fend for ourselves." Her breath was harsh and frosted the air with puffs of anger. "But you cannot both be right, can you?"

She wheeled on the entire gathering. "Am I the only one? Am I the only one willing to admit that I do not know what the spirits want?"

"Wife!" Storm Arriving said, stepping forward and grabbing her by the arm.

She yanked her arm out of his grasp and pushed him in the chest. "The next words I shall hear from you," she said with a wrathful glower, "will be an apology." Bearing the cradleboard with her swaddled daughter on her back, she turned and fled.

"Speaks while Leaving!" her father called.

"Speaks while Leaving!"

She ran.

The snow was still thick and quickly sapped the strength that her anger had fed. She slowed, and finally stopped, surrounded by the silent trees. She unslung the cradleboard and took it in her arms. Blue Shell Woman, teething on a strap of hide, grinned at seeing her mother's face. Speaks while Leaving sat down heavily in the snow, and stared out at the wall of conifers that hid her from the encampment.

Chickadees hung upside down from snowy branches, picking at pendant cones and arguing with one another like old women. On a higher branch perched a grey dove as pale as the dawn, a ring of black around her neck and her throat filled with mourning. Above the birds, the sky lightened with the growing day. It would be a warming day that promised of spring. Snow would sigh beneath the sun's attention, and boughs would drip as their mantles of white began to melt. It would be a day of cold air and warm light, a day of visiting, and of youngsters sliding down the long, twisting paths they'd slicked down during the dim months of winter.

But for her, with the yodels of whistlers echoing up the valley, with the songs of the soldiers filling the air as they started on their way, it would be a dark day, a day of worry. And a day of regret.

Why *can't* I be like other wives? she asked herself. Why can't I send him out to war, and take pride in his bravery?

She looked down at little Blue Shell Woman, swaddled against the cradleboard. Her infant daughter was fascinated by the birds that peeped overhead, her big black eyes gazing after them as they flitted from branch to branch, dumping dollops of snow on one another. She laughed at their antics, her voice as bubbly as a springtime creek.

Speaks while Leaving loved her daughter, but it was not simply for her sake that she was unable to support this war. Should her husband fall in battle, they would both be cared for. Whether against the bluecoats or against the Crow People, men died in war, and the People had long ago learned to care for the bereft. Her father or an uncle would step in to give them a home. Hunters would donate a portion of their kills to the widow and her child. Other relatives would hand down blankets and clothing, items quite usable after a bit of repair. Life without her husband would be hard, but life often was; though she loved Storm Arriving with all of her heart, she knew she would not die of a broken one.

"Then why?" she asked her daughter's happy face. "Why can't I smile like you and send him on his way? Why can't I be a normal wife to him?"

If she ran, she could find them before they left the camp. If she ran, she could see him, and wish him well. She could ask him to bring her back a trophy from his first kill, or promise him a feast to celebrate the many coups she was sure he would count.

If she ran. And if she believed in what he was doing. But she didn't. And so she did not run to find him.

"Why can't I be a normal wife?"

She stood and dusted the powdery snow from her rump, then covered her daughter's face and shouldered the cradleboard. Walking downhill, she could still hear the soldiers' rhythmic song. They were beyond the mouth of the valley, but the day's stillness lofted their voices as clearly as laughter across a glassy lake.

The chickadees followed in her wake, singing *jee-jee-jee* to her daughter. They were nearly to the wood-gathering path when she heard a man's voice ahead.

"You are not listening to me," the man was saying. "It is important that you listen to me."

She stepped onto the path and saw Mouse Road, her young sister-in-law, with Hungry Bear. A full head taller than the thin-boned Mouse Road and over twenty summers her elder, Hungry Bear towered over her in both stature and confidence.

"I respect your brother," Hungry Bear was saying. "He has fought many battles and brought much honor to the People, but in this, I must side with One Bear and the others. And so should you."

Mouse Road stood sideways to him, her arms holding a blanket tightly around her shoulders, her gaze fixed in a scowl that could melt the snow at her feet.

"After all," he continued, "I will not tolerate a wife

who refutes me. It is a wife's duty, especially in matters of war."

Mouse Road's face suddenly beamed with a wide, overly sweet smile. "Hungry Bear," she said, "did you just ask me to be your wife?"

Speaks while Leaving did not think the tall man could stand any taller, but he did, rising as if pulled by a skyward string. "I . . . well . . . yes. I had not expected this so soon, but you know that I wish you to be my wife. My lodge is empty without a wife, and my children cry for a mother's love and caring. Would you be my wife?"

The smile disappeared. "Now it is your turn to listen to me. My brother may have given you permission to court me, but permission to marry will come from me and from me alone. Do not think that my brother rules my heart, for as you ask me now, and every time that you should ever ask me, my answer will be no. No, I will not be your wife."

She turned and started up the path but halted with a gasp, seeing Speaks while Leaving standing there. Hungry Bear looked up and saw her, too, and Speaks while Leaving saw his dark skin flush darker with embarrassment. As Mouse Road looked back at him, his features changed. Speaks while Leaving knew that look, knew that collection of tightness and lassitude.

He loved her. This broad burl of a man was truly in love with little Mouse Road, and her sharp words had wounded him more than she knew and probably more than she intended. Drained of confidence, he turned away slowly—first his feet, taking a step away, then hips turning as well, then shoulders, and, finally, as he began to walk away down the path, his eyes looked away, but in that gaze Speaks while Leaving saw the last length of his resolve and his hope that all was not yet lost.

When he had gone beyond the first turn in the path, Mouse Road ran to her sister-in-law.

"I was coming to find you, but *he* followed me," she said.

Speaks while Leaving took her in her arms and let her cry.

"I don't *want* to marry him," the young woman said, "but he just won't leave me alone. I don't want to be cruel to him, but he won't leave me alone! And now, Storm Arriving is gone, and One Who Flies is still gone, and Hungry Bear, he—he just—"

"Shh, shh," Speaks while Leaving said, stroking her sister's hair and holding her close.

"He just wants a mother for his children."

"I know," Speaks while Leaving said, knowing that Hungry Bear's desires were more complex than Mouse Road suspected, but choosing not to contradict the young woman.

"And I don't want to be a mother. I mean, I do want to be a mother, but I don't want to be *his* mother. I mean, I don't want to be a mother to his children."

"I know. Quiet now. It will be all right."

"I want One Who Flies," Mouse Road said, looking up into her sister's face. "Why doesn't he come back to us?"

Speaks while Leaving did not know, but that was another fact she left unvoiced. One Who Flies was long overdue. Riders from the Tree People—the band One Who Flies called his own—had not seen him, and he certainly had not come to the Closed Windpipe band.

Finding him, she feared, was crucial to many things; from the realization of her vision, to the happiness of the woman who leaned against her, crying at his absence.

CHAPTER 6

Big Hoop and Stick Game Moon, Waning
Fifty-seven Years after the Star Fell
Winter Camp of the Closed Windpipe Band
Alliance Territory

The evening meal was unpleasant. Mouse Road sat in her usual place nearest the door. To her right was Speaks while Leaving, then old Healing Rock Woman, Magpie Woman, and finally, in the spot farthest from the door, One Bear.

One Bear ate in silence, spooning up stew, his face a frown that had nothing to do with the meal's rich tastes. As a chief of the Council, it was incumbent upon him to maintain equanimity in all things, but in her past months of living with Speaks while Leaving and her family, Mouse Road had learned to read the moods of the family's titular head.

He had barely spoken since the war party left that morning, keeping his words to himself if not his mood. He had spent the balance of the day among the family's flock of whistlers, inspecting the animals, seeing which hens were preparing to nest. He worked at the identifying bands of beaded leather that were tied around each animal's foreleg, repairing or replacing them as needed. These tasks kept him away from others and occupied his hands, leaving his mind free to turn over the problems he faced. Mouse Road had learned that whenever One Bear was among the whistlers, he was not to be disturbed, and when the dark, the cold, and his own hunger had finally driven him inside, his distant gaze and clouded brow told that he was still not in a mood to talk.

Magpie Woman sat beside her husband, filling his bowl

with the thick stew of boiled meat, white-apple roots, and cracked corn her mother had prepared, keeping the fire warm but not hot, and trying to ensure that nothing within her control would aggravate his already unpleasant mood. She occasionally glanced over at Speaks while Leaving, as if fearing another outburst from her daughter like the one everyone had heard of that morning.

But Speaks while Leaving sat, eating with a horn spoon from a wooden bowl, chewing small morsels that she spat out and fed to the infant in her arms. Her thoughts and features were as distant as her father's, but where One Bear was biting back anger—at his son-in-law, at his daughter, at those who had so openly disputed him—Mouse Road could see that Speaks while Leaving was holding back her tears.

Only Healing Rock Woman, the ancient grandmother of the family, seemed unaffected by the emotions that roiled about the lodge. She ate slowly, but not because she had to roll the meat and chunks of root over to where she still had teeth capable of chewing. She ate slowly because she was talking so much.

"And when he returned from *that* raid," she told Mouse Road, "he was driving all those whistlers before him. Everyone was amazed that such a young man, all on his own, could do such a thing." She rolled another spoonful over to her good teeth. "Eighty-eight whistlers," she said past her food, "and he sent them all to my father, as a bride price for me."

Mouse Road saw the others nod in time to the old woman's story, familiar with its cadences from repeated hearing.

"But my father refused him again, saying that now he had sent too many!" Her cackle was the sound of river ice in springtime, but it died when no one joined in her good humor. She glared at the others. "You are all stones today, I see."

Magpie Woman spoke up. "No, my mother. They are simply hungry and cannot laugh without losing a mouthful of your stew. Why don't you tell Mouse Road what Father did next?"

"No," the old woman said, looking around. "You are all stones. No point telling tales to stones."

There was a footstep in the snow outside the lodge, and a voice called out in a not-so-quiet whisper. "Mouse Road," Hungry Bear said. "Are you in there?"

Mouse Road could not help but give a little groan, and Speaks while Leaving reached over to pat her leg.

"I don't like that man," Healing Rock Woman said. "He is too brazen. It is undignified. I don't know why Storm Arriving gave him permission to—"

"I'm sure Storm Arriving had good reasons," Magpie Woman said, warding against any friction.

Speaks while Leaving huffed. "Don't defend him on my account, Mother."

"Hungry Bear is a respectable man."

"You would not know it from the way he follows this young one," the grandmother said.

"You just told of how strongly Grandfather pursued you," Speaks while Leaving said.

"That was different," the old woman said. "He was youthful. This man should know better."

Mouse Road felt the blood rising to her cheeks and her heart race with embarrassment.

"Mouse Road," came the call from outside.

"Go away," Healing Rock Woman said.

"Mother," Magpie Woman said, shocked.

The baby began to cry, as the women passed whispered chastisements around the fire.

"Mouse Road," insisted the suitor out in the snow.

"Eya!" Mouse Road said, disgusted with the entire situation. She put down her bowl and picked up her blanket. "I'm tired. I'm going to bed." She stood and headed out the door, hoping to dismiss Hungry Bear quickly as she walked from the main lodge to the lodge she shared with Speaks while Leaving.

Her suitor stepped back from the doorway as she stepped outside. He wore a striped Trader's blanket cowled over his head in the traditional manner of a courting youth, eager to enwrap the object of his devotions within the privacy of a woolen lodge made for two.

"Mouse Road," he said. "Let me speak with you."

She wanted none of it, and walked past him toward her own lodge.

He reached out and plucked at the sleeve of her robe. "Let me speak with you, Mouse Road. Please."

Torn, she stopped but did not turn. "Speak," she told him, gently. "I am listening."

She heard him come up behind her. Though a large man, he moved with the quiet sureness of a hunter's step. Though he did not touch her, she felt his presence at her back, tall and protective.

"I wanted to apologize to you," he said, his voice a rumble. "I have courted you too strongly, and like a wild whistler, you have grown wary of my clumsy approach. It was for my children that I came to you this way. I wanted a mother for them."

His voice was sincere and straight-talking. She could hear the pain that lay between his words, and she closed her eyes and held her breath, not wanting to hurt him more but neither wanting to encourage him.

"But I have taken care of that problem," he continued. "I have given my children to their other mother, my dead wife's sister. She has agreed to foster them."

Mouse Road turned and looked back over her shoulder. He stood, a tall shadow against the darker night, the blanket limned by the borrowed glow of lodge fires, the cowl hiding his features from her scrutiny.

"Then why are you here?" she asked, "if you no longer need a mother for your children?"

He chuckled once and briefly. "You really don't know?" he asked, and she could hear the sad smile in his voice. "Mouse Road, lovely Mouse Road, I may not need you in my lodge, but I still want you there. Can't you see that you have taken my heart?"

She turned away again, for she could see it. She saw that this man—respected, honored in coups, and wealthy in flocks and possessions—did indeed love her. And, what was more, she knew that she was not as indifferent to him as she professed. He was a caring man not given to anger. He was a good provider for his own children and would be so for her as well. He was from a good family that had produced men of bravery and women of practicality. He might someday become a chief himself, with the right woman at his side.

But love him? She did not, but could she? And did she want to?

"Please, Mouse Road. Please, let me court you slowly, and with the respect that you deserve. Let me come and speak to you. Do not send me away."

His pleas overwhelmed her, and she could barely keep the tears from her eyes. She hurried on her way, running toward her lodge, leaving behind her a man who was nearly as confused as she was.

Within the safety of her own lodge, she finally let her tears come. She wanted so many things that were beyond her grasp. Sitting down near the fire, she wiped tears with the back of one hand while she poked a stick into the banked fire with the other.

She wanted her brother to be the great man she knew he could be, but she wanted him to be happy with Speaks while Leaving, as well. She wanted the People to be safe from the bluecoats, but she did not want to lose anyone else to war. She wanted a future with a man she could trust and who loved her, but she wanted to love him as well. She wanted One Who Flies to return to the People so that she could tell him that she had been wrong when she said that he was not a whole man, and wrong when she had said that she was not glad to see him. She wanted to take away the bitterness of their last parting and tell him that it didn't matter to her that her brother had refused him permission to court her. She wanted him to know that what she really feared was that she was unable to be a match for him. The spirits had touched One Who Flies, and the wife of such a man must be stronger than she hoped she could be.

But without him, she had been as miserable as she had ever been. As she went to her bed and curled up beneath her furs, she realized that she would never be able to push One Who Flies into the shape of a normal man, that it was not fair to try to do so. Her only choice, therefore, was to put herself in the role of an extraordinary woman, in order to be the partner of such a man.

She did not feel extraordinary—felt, in fact, so ordinary as to be nearly invisible. To be as strong and as self-sufficient as she would need to be; it frightened her, but it was necessary, and as she lay there, staring at the aurora of flames that hovered over the coals, she reminded herself that to be independent was not to be isolated, and to be strong was not to be always alone.

The night was filled with songs and the sounds of families laughing. She heard the voices of children and the stories of adults. Flames licked the wood with tongues of orange, blue, and green. A plan began to form in her mind, a plan for taking control of her life once more, and becoming the extraordinary spirit that was required of her heart's desire. It would take several days to prepare, and in order to accomplish her goals she would have to lie to those closest to her. But it could be done.

She snuggled deeper under her furs, listening to the consolation of the dying fire. From the woods at the edge of camp came the virile, elliptical tones of a courting flute as Hungry Bear sent a love song out into the night.

CHAPTER 7

Light Snow Moon, New
Fifty-seven Years after the Star Fell
Winter Camp of the Closed Windpipe Band
Alliance Territory

Speaks while Leaving surveyed the world around her and knew that this was not a vision. After years of succumbing to the power of the spirit worlds, she knew the difference between a vision and a dream, and this was not a vision.

Visions always came upon her with a force. They burned her skin and tightened her flesh. The spirits of the world filled her body, overwhelming her, stealing her control and her sight, blinding her with their message. When a vision infused her, she was left with only the ability to speak, to tell others what she was seeing as she saw it. When in its midst, she could feel the heartbeat of the world, the drum of the universe, thrumming with life, and could feel her own pulse answer, rising with the urgency of life. Visions frightened her, for when in their grasp she was as helpless as a hatchling, but mostly she feared them because they foretold of danger, death, or sorrow. After twenty years of living with them, it was a fear she had never lost.

But this was not a vision. This was a dream. It was a strong dream, to be sure, a powerful dream, but a dream nonetheless.

She sat on the cliffs above the Big Salty. The wind, laced with the smell of crushed juniper and the clean scent of growing sage, tugged at her dress. It was summer, which was nice. She liked summertime, even here in the southern reaches of the People's lands. Summer was a happy time, when the People gathered and the allied tribes came to visit. To be sure, with summer came much work—scraping hides, drying meat, following the herd for the hunt, gathering berries and fruit against the winter months—but summers also brought togetherness, safety, and freedom. Summers brought stories around the fire, grand dances that sent dust up to the clouds, feasts of friendship and honor, and the liquefying excitement of courtship. Yes, she liked summers.

But here on the limestone heights, with the dunes of the Sand Hills at her back and the waves of the Big Salty laid out before her, there were none of those pleasures. Here, there were only the remnants of the past: the pale bones of departed ancestry protruding from the rough ground, and the silvered wood of dilapidated funeral biers lying amid the scrub and sedge. Dragonflies zipped and hovered, flashing their glassy green bodies and the iridescent latticework of their wings, while skippers fluttered by on painted triangles, bouncing from flower to flower. Little-teeth soared over the waters on fans of outstretched leather, rising high on sun-warmed winds. Above them, clouds tumbled like boys at play, and atop it all stood the sun, high in the forenoon sky. She heard the whisper of the wind through the grasses, the *kee-kee* of a killdeer calling its mate, and the distant *shush* of the waves. Despite all this life, though, she felt an emptiness here, a sense of being disconnected and apart. No, this was not a vision.

And so she nearly jumped when she saw the man who sat at her left. He was a handsome man with deep-set eyes and a strong nose, but his skin was the color of charred wood. He wore his hair loose and free in the wind, like a cloud of darkness around his dark features, and he was bare to the waist. On his chest were white spots—the symbol of hail—and on his arm was a jagged yellow line of a lightning bolt. He smiled at her as at an old friend, and she laughed. He was a Thunder Being, a spirit in the guise of a man, and she was well-acquainted with his kind.

She turned to her right, and was not surprised to see another of his kind, for these two never seemed to travel apart from the other. She looked at this man's arm and saw that, instead of a yellow lightning bolt on his arm, there was a jagged scar. Ages ago, it seemed, these two Beings had come to her in a vision and showed her of the coming of One Who Flies on the cloud-that-fell. And ages ago, too, she had ripped from this Being's arm the lightning bolt that had been there, and thrown it down upon the forces attacking the People.

That these two men were here told her that this was, indeed, an unusual dream. They sat there, the three of them, and watched as the sun slowly crept to its height. The Thunder Beings played with the clouds. The one on her right folded a cloud into the shape of a fish, and the one on her left puffed up another cloud to make a bear that ate the fish. Then came a cloud that leapt like a long-legged dog, scaring the bear away, and finally a toothsome walker made of cloud appeared and snapped up the dog for a meal. They laughed, the three of them, playing this way as the sun traveled from left to right, and the clouds rolled from right to left. She wondered if the shapes they made meant anything, but when she turned to ask the one on her left, he was gone. In his place was Mouse Road. Turning to the right, she now saw One Who Flies.

Ah, yes, she reminded herself. This is only a dream. A strong dream, though.

The feeling of emptiness returned, and she realized that her daughter was not with her. She looked around and did not see her. The feeling of a void increased, and a panic built within her. She wanted her daughter, needed to find her. The dream was too strong, and she wanted to wake up.

Wake up.

She was lying on her bed beneath her blankets and furs, her heart pounding in her temples and the sound of her moan still in her ears. Her daughter, nestled up against her breast, mewled in her sleep and Speaks while Leaving relaxed at her babe's warmth, the incredible softness of her skin, and the sweet perfume of her hair. She willed her heart to slow and her breath to quiet down.

Only a dream, she told herself. It was only a dream.

Her eyes soaked up the tiny light from the bedded

coals, and she saw the lodge in hues of orange and blue. From the darkness of the smokehole above, the lodge-poles radiated outward, downward, forming the cone of the lodge. The skins wavered in the uneven light as a draft blew across the central hearthpit. She sought the source of the draft, checking the inner skins that had been tied at shoulder height to the inside of the poles, an extra insulation against the cold nights. All were tied snugly in place, but the doorflap was open.

Looking at the other bed, she saw that it was unoccupied. Mouse Road was not there. She looked back at the open doorflap and wondered if she should leave the warmth of her covers to close it.

No, she told herself. Mouse Road probably just went to make water. She will be back soon enough.

Mouse Road had been quiet in the ten days since her brother had left on the war party, but it had not been her usual sort of quiet. Thwarted in love, ordered by her brother to live with his in-laws instead of with her own clan, and instructed further to succumb to the courtship of a man in whom she had no interest, the young woman was understandably prone to a certain sullen moodiness. Speaks while Leaving certainly felt no need to chasten her sister-in-law for brooding—had their situations been switched, she would have been just as unhappy—but thinking back, Speaks while Leaving saw that Mouse Road's reserve had taken on a different aspect. Yes, she had always been where she was expected to be, and she wordlessly agreed to every request and duty. She never had to be sought, but was never really present. Speaks while Leaving could not remember the young woman saying but the merest word in the past week. Mouse Road had been quiet . . . but artfully so, quiet almost to the point of transparency.

She looked again toward the open doorflap. Was there something to worry about? She reached for a folded blanket and pulled it across her shoulders as she quietly slipped out from under the furs, leaving her infant daughter behind in their warmth. The wicker of her bed-mat creaked as she left it, and outside the lodgeskins, a whistler snuffled.

She stepped through the doorway and saw the crouching bulk of a waiting drake—a large, dark mound in the starlight. A shadow detached itself from his side and clambered atop his back.

Speaks while Leaving ran forward and grabbed the drake's halter rope. The whistler shied at her sudden move. The shadowy figure slipped from atop his back and whoofed as she hit the ground on the far side. Speaks while Leaving saw the bedroll across the whistler's back, the parfleches filled with supplies, the coil of extra rope, and the dark gleam of a rifle barrel. The drake pulled at the halter rope, but Speaks while Leaving soothed him with a quiet crooning and a friendly scratch at the apex of his shoulders.

"What are you doing?" she asked.

Mouse Road stood up, peering over the whistler's curved back. "Isn't it obvious?" she asked in return, all her poutful sullenness returning in an instant.

"Yes, actually, it is obvious. Go back inside the lodge."

Mouse Road took a breath to answer, but Speaks while Leaving tilted her head back and glared at the younger woman.

Mouse Road met the challenge and put her hand on the first rope of the whistler's riding gear. "I am a grown woman," she said. "You cannot tell me what to do."

But Speaks while Leaving knew that she would not have to be any firmer with her sister-in-law. The People dealt with insolence in other ways. They did not reprimand their children, but instead let them know the penalties of bad behavior. Mouse Road might be a woman, but right now, she was acting like a wayward child and should be treated as such.

"As you wish," she said. "But if you mount atop that whistler, I will hold on to it and shout to wake our family and neighbors. I will tell them that you are eloping with Hungry Bear, without your brother's permission."

"But you know that's not *true!*"

"You could always stay here and explain it to them," she said. "Or you could go inside the lodge, and you would only have to explain it to me."

Even in the dark of the moonless night, Speaks while Leaving could see the glare that her young sister leveled.

She let go of a quavering breath and the stars glimmered from her tear-stained cheeks, but she turned and headed inside the lodge.

Speaks while Leaving retied the whistler's halter rope to the stake and followed Mouse Road. Inside, she stirred the coals and placed a few sticks on them for light. Mouse Road lay under her bedcovers, hiding, her back to the fire.

"Where were you going?" Speaks while Leaving asked her.

"Does it matter now?" the young woman asked in response.

Speaks while Leaving considered it. "Yes," she eventually said. "It does."

"I was going to find One Who Flies."

That was what she had thought—the supplies and the rifle spoke of more than a simple trip or whim—but how far ahead had she thought things through? "Where were you going to look for him?"

Mouse Road sighed. "South," she said.

"Why south?"

"I . . . I don't know. It just makes sense that he would still be in the south."

"And once you found him?"

Hesitation, and then again, "I don't know. Bring him home, I suppose."

So, she had thought it through far enough to get her moving, but not far enough that she knew what she ultimately wanted. "Why were you going to look for him?" she asked in a calm, even voice.

Mouse Road rolled over, her head peeking up from under the coverings. She looked puzzled. "What do you mean?"

Speaks while Leaving shrugged. "I mean just what I said. Why were you going to look for him? I thought you had decided that you didn't want to be with him."

"I did," Mouse Road said. "But I changed my mind."

"Why?"

Mouse Road sat up, sensing her sister-in-law's honest desire to understand. She ran her fingers through the thick fur of her elkhide bedcover. "I was angry at One Who Flies, because he never tried to be an ordinary man. But then I realized that he can't be an ordinary man. He is a special person, just as you are. You both have been touched by the spirits." She looked up for the briefest of moments, and Speaks while Leaving encouraged her with a gesture.

"He will never be an ordinary man," Mouse Road said, "because he is destined to live an extraordinary life. And it is just that which attracts me to him, and makes all other men seem . . . ordinary." She sighed. "And if I do not want an ordinary man, then it is up to me to be an extraordinary wife."

Speaks while Leaving smiled, surprised at the wisdom of her husband's young sister, but the smile was bittersweet, for in Mouse Road's words she heard Storm Arriving's own challenge: Why can't you be like a normal wife? And she knew that being a normal wife was beyond her, just as One Who Flies could never be a normal man. The visions, the dreams, the drive to work with the spirits toward a future of hope—she could not turn her back on it all. The visions were their future, and One Who Flies was a part of that future. Finding him was important. But where to look?

The dream from that night flooded back to her, filled with the scent of sage and surf, the sounds of waves and little-teeth in the air. The Sand Hills. The funeral grounds above the Big Salty. South, like Mouse Road had said.

"You cannot go to look for him," she said, thinking aloud.

"I can handle myself," Mouse Road said. "I have killed bluecoats before, just as you have."

"This is true," Speaks while Leaving said, staring into the fire, watching the sticks crack and hiss in the heat. "What I meant, is that you cannot go to look for him by yourself."

Mouse Road gaped. "What do you mean?" she asked. "You? And me?"

Speaks while Leaving frowned. "Yes," she said.

"Together?"

"Yes."

"But will it be safe for us?"

"What? Now you are worried?" Speaks while Leaving

asked with a laugh. "We will be fine. I traveled many, many miles by myself before I married your brother. As a healer, I traveled between the bands, between the tribes, and even to the Trader outposts. I learned much from them."

"From the *vé'hó'e*?"

"Yes, even from the *vé'hó'e*," she said. "I learned from their holy men and from ours. I learned of *vé'ho'e* healing, and of our own sacred medicines. It was from the *vé'hó'e* at the outposts that I learned the Trader's Tongue, for the *vé'hó'e* never learn the language of other peoples. But . . ." She looked over at her bed, and saw the chubby fingers and black-feather hair of her sleeping daughter.

Mouse Road deduced her concern. "You should leave Blue Shell Woman here," she said.

"If I woke my mother to leave her," she said, frowning again, "my father would surely keep us from going." She remembered the panic of her dream when she could not find her daughter. "No, I will not leave her." She took a deep breath and consciously removed the frown from her features. "Besides, we will not be gone for very long. A moon's time, or perhaps a little more. We will tell my grandmother, so that they do not worry, but we will not tell them where we go."

Mouse Road was smiling. "Where *will* we go?"

"Just as you said," Speaks while Leaving told her, feeling her own conviction grow with saying it. "South. We will find him in the south."

CHAPTER 8

Light Snow Moon, Waxing
Fifty-seven Years after the Star Fell
Beyond the Elk River
Land of the Crow People

The whistlers sang quietly to one another as the war party climbed the steep hillside beneath the ancient pines. The riders were anxious and edgy. Storm Arriving sensed the men's nervousness in the way they shushed one another, and in the rough way they handled their mounts.

The air was thick with moisture. Mist rose, lazy wisps rising through the bright sunlight that fell from the canopy in lances that pierced the matted forest floor. Droplets pattered down from a thousand snowy branches, and the steaming flanks of tired whistlers created a spice-scented vapor that hung in their wake like a cloud.

"This doesn't seem as good an idea now as it did last week," Whistling Elk said in a strong voice. "In fact, now I think it might even be a very bad idea." Some of the other riders grumbled their agreement with his assessment of the situation.

Storm Arriving looked over at the man-becoming-woman who rode beside him. Though he wore a dress instead of leggings and kept the braids of his hair coiled up as a woman might, he also carried a club, knife, and rifle, all of which he had used well in years past, and it was not like him to complain about the danger of a war party's mission.

"You have ridden into the lands of the Crow People before," Storm Arriving said.

"Of course I have," he said, glancing at some of the

other members of their group. "We all have ridden into these lands before, but why? We rode here to steal whistlers, to count coup, or to take a few women to bring back as workers or second wives. But never have I ridden north with such a purpose as the one you propose."

Storm Arriving was perturbed by this change in Whistling Elk's attitude. Many of the other soldiers respected Whistling Elk for his knowledge, his bravery, and the spiritual power that came from being a man-becoming-woman. Imbued with the nature of both male and female sides of creation, the men-becoming-women were revered for their wisdom and practicality. For Whistling Elk to speak against their purpose in this way was very unhelpful. He looked around and saw the clumped brows, the eyes that watched the shadows behind the bright shafts of light. The soldiers were nervous enough as it was without such talk to worry them further.

"Well, then now you have a new reason for riding to the Crow People," Storm Arriving said, trying to lift the mood.

"A new reason, indeed!" Whistling Elk said, turning to gather the agreement of his fellows. "But we will get an old reception, I think, and I am not the first one to say it." Other riders muttered their support. "The Crow People will not greet us with open arms, I think. More likely, we will get a club in the head or an arrow in our belly. No, we may come to them in peace, but I doubt the Crow People will receive us that way."

Storm Arriving ground his teeth. "Then perhaps you should have gone with Two Roads to gather soldiers from the other bands."

Whistling Elk grinned. "And miss all the excitement?" He laughed. "No, this may be a bad idea, but it will definitely be interesting. I just hope I live through it so I can tell the story when I get home." He laughed again, and the others all joined in. Storm Arriving realized what the man-becoming-woman had been doing, and saw the lightened spirits of the other members of their group.

"You are too sly for me," he said to Whistling Elk.

"In some things, perhaps," the other said.

Storm Arriving called them to a halt before they

crested the rise. Dismounting, he motioned to Whistling
Elk, Knee Prints by the Bank, and a veteran Little Bowstring soldier named Sharp Knife to come with him.
They went forward, keeping low, moving from tree to
tree, avoiding the patches of stubborn snow. They
reached the crest of the ridge and looked down into the
long, deep valley.

The Crow lived much as the People did, in hide-
covered lodges that could be taken down and moved as
they followed the herds of buffalo and other game that
were their lifeblood, ranging from the Elk River far
north into Grandmother Land. It had been over the
lands between the Elk River and the northern course of
the Big Greasy that the two tribes had often fought.
Storm Arriving knew that the People did not need any
of the Crow lands in order to survive, but knew, too, that
the Crow People were envious of the Alliance control of
the southern plains. The People fought the Crow in
order to keep weakening them, and to keep them on the
northern side of the Elk River.

Looking down through the shadowed greenery of pine
and spruce, the quilt of dark trees and bright snow, he saw
a winter encampment much like one of his own camps.
Cone-shaped homes stood in profusion, lodgepoles bristling up from the smokeholes, feather and fox-tail over-
the-smokes dangling; whistlers rested nearby, halter
ropes tied to stakes, their eyes sleepy as they soaked up
the afternoon sun; women scraped skins or carried wood,
cradleboarded babies strapped to their backs or toddlers
close at hand; men fletched arrows or helped to butcher
a kill, and some sat like the whistlers, taking their ease
in the sunshine. Storm Arriving heard chickens and dogs
and even what he thought might have been a bleating
goat. Youngsters played. Grandfathers told stories. Their
clothing was a bit heavier than what the People wore,
and the men were more fond of fur headdresses than of
feathers, and most women wore dresses of Trader cloth
rather than of deerskin, but other than those things, they
were as were his own; regular people living their lives,
wanting peace rather than war.

At least he hoped so.

"How should we approach them?" asked Knee Prints by the Bank.

Storm Arriving eased a few steps forward. The valley walls were steep and rocky, eliminating any threat from three sides. "Here or at the valley top we would have to enter carefully and on foot. That could easily be seen as a raid." He pointed left toward the valley mouth. "If we enter from there, it will be easier to convince them of our purpose." He looked to the others.

"Agreed," said Whistling Elk.

Knee Prints by the Bank signed with his hand. *Yes.*

Sharp Knife scanned the valley from right to left and then agreed.

They crept backward, away from the brink of the valley wall, and once back among the trees, turned and walked back to the others. It was just as Storm Arriving put his hand on his whistler's riding gear that he heard the shout.

With a high-pitched *yi-yi-yi,* the attackers ran at them from three directions.

Storm Arriving tossed his halter rope to Whistling Elk. "Do not move!" he shouted to the others, and ran forward toward the charging men.

There were eight of them, Crow warriors, and one was coming straight at him. The badger fur of his headdress danced as he ran. In one hand he carried a war-axe and in the other, a thin riding quirt. His eyes were wide in a face painted black and red, and his white teeth shone in a screaming grin. Storm Arriving stood, hands at his sides, facing the oncoming Crow.

"Do not move!" he shouted once more, and as the warrior neared, Storm Arriving saw the puzzlement in his eyes.

The warrior raised his war-axe, the dark blade high above, at the end of the arm-long handle, feathers fluttering. Two steps away.

Storm Arriving stood his ground but did not move.

The Crow twisted as he passed, slapping Storm Arriving across the chest with his riding quirt. Behind, Storm Arriving heard other slaps as the Crow counted coup on them with quirts and open hands, touching but not killing, showing their bravery, but disconcerted by the inactivity of their enemy.

"What is wrong with you?" the first Crow said in his own language. He came back over to Storm Arriving and struck him again in the chest with his quirt. When Storm Arriving did not react, he struck him again, counting a third coup, the most that could be counted on one man during a single battle. "Why do you not fight us?"

Storm Arriving looked over his shoulder. His war party stood as still as the trees around them. Only the whistlers moved, shying from the Crow warriors and flashing battle colors of red and grey and white across their snouts.

He looked back at the warrior that faced him. "I am Storm Arriving," he said in the language of the Inviters. It was a tongue that was very similar to that of the Crow, and one that Storm Arriving spoke easily. "We are not here to fight you or to attack you or to steal any of your belongings."

"Then what is a group of the Cut-Arm People doing on my land?" he asked, using the language of the Inviters, as well.

Storm Arriving took a deep breath and willed his heart to slow, for if he failed now, he would never see his home again.

"We are here to speak with your chiefs. We are here to speak of peace between our two peoples."

The Crow reached back and struck him a blow across the face with his quirt, then lunged and knocked Storm Arriving backward onto the ground. Storm Arriving cried out in surprise, tried to shout an order but a kick to his gut prevented it.

Whistlers bugled and the clearing was filled with the sounds of men striking men with fist and club.

"Stop!" Storm Arriving shouted, holding up a hand to ward off the attack. "Soldiers, you will stop."

The Crow held off his next kick, and with a quick glance, Storm Arriving saw that so had the others. One man moaned, a hand to his head, and heavy breaths came from all. Slowly, Storm Arriving got to one knee and rose. He smarted from the blows of the quirt, tasted blood in his mouth, and felt a creaking in his ribs. With eyes politely averted, he repeated his purpose.

"We are here to speak with your chiefs, if you will allow us. We have come only to talk of peace."

"They are well enough armed," one of the Crow said, pulling a rifle from a whistler's pack.

The first Crow motioned to the other. "What of that, Cut-Arm? You all carry the whiteman's weapon, and we found you creeping around outside our camps. Is that how you speak of peace?"

It did look bad, he realized, but was just the way it had happened. If the Crow killed them all here, it would be months before Two Roads sent another party to find them. There was only one thing he could think to do.

"You protect your people well," he said to the Crow. "All of you. But to kill us here would not be your duty—"

Another blow caught him across the face.

"How do you know what my duty is?" the Crow shouted.

"Because I am a soldier, too," Storm Arriving shouted back. "We all are soldiers, sworn to protect our families and our people from those who threaten them. And *that* is why we are here." He wiped at the new cut on his cheek. The blood streamed across the back of his hand. "We are here to tell your chiefs that we no longer wish to be enemies. If you kill me now, I will not be able to tell this to your chiefs, and you will only have done half of your duty. But, if you wait until morning to kill me, I might have the chance to speak with your chiefs, and then your duty will be complete."

The Crow soldier thought it over, and in glances and signs discussed it with his fellows. Their decision was quick in coming.

"The morning will be soon enough to kill you," the soldier said to Storm Arriving. "Take their weapons."

The whistlers were strung together on a rope line and the captives forced to walk behind them. The snow deepened with the shadows as the Crow escorted them down from the ridgetop toward the valley mouth. Winter held on to the land with a grip as cold as stone. Whistlers pushed and slipped through heavy drifts, and Storm Arriving and his fellow soldiers trudged along in their wake, their calf-high moccasins sinking deeper than the whistlers' wide, three-toed feet. As they neared the valley floor, however, their track crossed an established path, and they turned to take it into the village, hemmed in by walls of snow that at times were taller than any man could reach.

They reached a meadow and the snows leveled out. Ahead, Storm Arriving saw the village and smelled aromas that reminded him of home: happy woodsmoke, the resin of freshly split wood, and the low, gentle scent of whistler dung. He saw that there were actually three valleys here that flowed together in this one place. What he had first thought to be a fair-sized village proved to be a major encampment. Lodges were clustered throughout each of the three arms, densely packed in spots. Some of the paths had been worn through the snow, revealing the muddied ground beneath, and deep in the western arm, he saw the dark-flowing mass of whistler flocks, well protected from weather and predators.

The Crow People did not use walkers, as the northern winter months were too long and too severe for the large beasts. But they did use dogs to a much greater extent than did the People, and their barks echoed along the steep valley walls.

Their guide let out a high-pitched yell that cut through all the sounds of home and industry. Storm Arriving heard the sounds first of curiosity and then of fear as the inhabitants came forward and passed back the news of what their guardsmen were bringing in.

Crowds quickly gathered: shouting men with clubs and knives, youths looking in wonder perhaps for the first time on their tribe's hated enemy, and women standing at the back of the crowd, holding their babies closely, cautious but curious all the same.

Storm Arriving also saw the hatred in their faces, saw the weapons in their hands, and suddenly lost sight of how alike they had seemed from up on the ridgetop. Here, where he could smell the rancid frying of bear fat and beaver tail, where he could see the garish decorations on their clothing and their homes, and where he could hear harsh, guttural words issuing from their long, narrow faces, they were alien. They were the raiders of his flocks. They were the stealers of his children and women. They were killers.

They were the enemy.

A man came forward and struck Storm Arriving on the shoulder. Another came forward but Storm Arriving raised his hand and snarled, unwilling to let any more of these creatures count coup upon his person. They retreated then and gave him room, but increased the fervor of their imprecations. The captives were led forward, and Storm Arriving felt like a wild animal being brought forth to the slaughter. He felt a hand on his shoulder and turned.

Whistling Elk walked beside him, his gaze fixed on the road ahead. "Remember why you brought us here," he said. "Remember what it is we mean to do."

Storm Arriving swallowed his anger.

We need them, he reminded himself. There is a common enemy that threatens us all.

He tried to put the jeers out of his mind, but amid the din of shouts and epithets, one voice broke through to him. It was a woman's voice, and her words were out of place. He looked forward and saw her, reaching toward them, held back by others. Her words were not sharp-edged like the others, but easy and light despite her shouting. She was speaking the language of the People, and though her clothing was thick and gaudy like the others nearby, her features told of a different beginning.

"Save me!" she shouted at them, one hand outstretched. "Take me away from here!" As they neared her, she broke away from those who held her back. She came to them, on her knees. She grabbed onto Storm Arriving's leg. "I beg you, I beg you. Help me! I am Bright Star Woman, of the Flexed Leg band. I am daughter to Black Bull. My mother was Sweetgum Woman, who was also known as Sleeps a Lot. Please!"

The Crow soldiers pushed the woman aside and shoved Storm Arriving ahead. But Bright Star Woman scrambled to her feet and followed.

"I was captured when I was a young girl. I was made

wife to a man who beat me and destroyed my honor. You must take me home. I am of the People. I am Tsétsêhéstâhese."

Storm Arriving clenched his teeth. "I can do nothing," he told her in their own language.

"You must kill these people and bring me home!"

"We are not here to make war against these people."

"Then you are cowards!" she screamed. "Cowards!" And as she took breath to scream it again, a man stepped forward from the crowd and struck her a blow across the side of her head. She crumpled across his arm.

Sharp Knife broke away from the others and lunged for the man but Storm Arriving grabbed him with an arm around his throat.

"Let me go!" Sharp Knife demanded.

"No!" Storm Arriving said, and then turned to the rest of the war party. "Remember why we are here," he shouted at them in their own language. "We are not here for personal honor. We are not here to avenge old wrongs."

"Let me go!" Sharp Knife said again.

"I will not," he said. The crowd had grown silent and the procession through the encampment had halted. All eyes watched in wonderment, eager to see how this would play out.

Sharp Knife struggled but Storm Arriving gripped him even tighter. "You have a cousin," he said, "who has a wife he captured from these people. This is true?"

Sharp Knife quieted, but his hands gripped Storm Arriving's arms like talons. "Yes," the man said. "It is true."

"And how do you think his wife would react, should we bring a party of Crow People into the Great Circle of the People?"

Sharp Knife growled. "I do not know."

"You *do* know," Storm Arriving said. "You know *just* how she would react. And you know what your cousin would do, as well."

Sharp Knife pulled again at the arms that bound him, but Storm Arriving let him go. By the way his soldier moved away instead of forward, he could tell that the point had been made and the crisis was past.

From the edge of the crowd, the Crow man held his

moaning wife and glared at Storm Arriving and his soldiers.

"You leave her alone," he told them, and then dragged her unconscious form back into the crowd.

The crowd itself drew back, surprised and perhaps disappointed by the display of control exhibited by both sides. Storm Arriving spoke again to his men.

"Remember why we are here," he said, and with a quick glance and a forward movement of his hands, signed his thanks to Whistling Elk.

The Crow soldiers who had their charge now regarded them with a different aspect, Storm Arriving noticed. As they headed forward toward the heart of the encampment, they were led not by pushes and shoves, but with beckoning hands, with gestures, and calm words. It was not respect, but it was better than being herded like animals. Storm Arriving felt the tension ease in the men all around him.

They were led to a tall lodge in the middle of the central arm of the camp, the crowd following them in relative quiet. The lodgeskins had been painted with designs in yellow, red, and black. Flowers, birds, whistlers, and other animals were in the designs, as were men, arrows, and rifles, all in a jumble, the meaning of which was unclear. One thing was easily divined, however. Storm Arriving nudged Whistling Elk and pointed upward.

The lodgepoles poked up out of the smokehole at the top of the lodge, reaching up into the sunlight. Hanging from several of the lodgepole tips were over-the-smokes, fashioned of scalps taken in battle. Some had black hair that might have come from the neighboring tribes, but many had hair that shone brown, yellow, or even red as they twisted in the breeze.

Vé'ho'e scalps.

The doorflap to the lodge opened and several men emerged. They were older men with grey in their hair and deep wrinkles in their long faces, but their eyes were still bright, and there was an athletic caution in their every move. These were old warriors, men who bore themselves with a grace and power that had barely begun to fade.

Storm Arriving gave an inward groan. Treating with men such as these would be much more difficult than dealing with peace chiefs. These were men whom he may have met in battle, and who may even have borne scars put there by his own hand.

"Broken Fang," said one of the chiefs to the soldier who had found them. "What do you mean, bringing such refuse into our camp?"

The soldier named Broken Fang straightened at the rebuke. "These men are from the Cut-Arm People," he said, naming the People by their tradition of sacrificing strips of skin from their forearms. "We found them on the eastern ridge, and would have killed them, but they said they came to speak to our chiefs, and to talk of peace."

One of the chiefs laughed out loud. "Peace? With the Cut-Arm People? They have been our most bitter enemy since the time of my grandfather's grandfather. This is just a ruse, to keep their scalps on their heads."

"I am not so sure," said Broken Fang, and the chiefs were surprised by the statement.

"Explain," another chief demanded.

Broken Fang looked uncomfortable at having to defend Storm Arriving and his party. "From the very first," he told the chiefs, "they would not fight us. They did not even defend themselves. We charged them, and struck them all several times, but they refused to move, even when provoked."

"And just now," said another soldier, pointing at Storm Arriving, "that one held back one of the others when Red Wolf's second wife came to them for help."

"You saw this?" asked the first chief of Broken Fang.

"Yes. I saw."

The other chief discounted it. "Just saving their skins," he said.

But Storm Arriving saw the glimmer of a question on the first chief's face. He wanted to speak to the chief, and to tell them all of what they had come to do, but these were savvy men. He could not seem too eager, for eagerness could be misconstrued as fearfulness, and a fearful man would promise anything to save his life.

The sun stood still in the sky and Storm Arriving was

sure his heart had frozen in his breast as the others deferred to the first chief, waiting for his decision on what to do with the interlopers. The chief studied him, studied them all one by one.

Ask me, Storm Arriving silently urged him. Ask me.

"Tell me," the chief said, "why I should listen to a man from the Cut-Arm People."

His heart was beating so fast and hard it felt like a herd of buffalo within his rib cage. He felt the tremor in his muscles and feared that his voice might quaver. He prayed for strength, for in front of these chiefs and before the people who were gathered on the slope behind him, weakness was the last thing he wanted to present.

Then, with signs and words, he spoke to the chief.

"I thank you for hearing me, Grandfather, but it is not just the Cut-Arm People who wish to speak to you." He turned to indicate his men as he introduced them. "Three of us represent the tribe you call the Cut-Arm People, but with us, too, are men from our kin the Sage People and the Cloud People. We also bring men from our friends the Inviters, from the Little Star People, from the Cut-Hair People, and from the Earth Lodge Builders. We even bring men from the Wolf People, and from the Greasy Wood People, both longtime enemies of my tribe. We are all here; we have all stopped warring against one another and joined in a great alliance against a common enemy, and it is this alliance that we come to extend to you and the entire Crow People. We can help each other. We can fight this enemy together."

The chiefs looked at one another, dumbfounded by the pronouncement. Some wanted to take offense and spoke to one another in urgent words that Storm Arriving could not quite understand. Behind him, the crowd, too, grew uneasy, unwilling to trust or even think of trusting this offer of peace. But the first chief, the one Storm Arriving took to be the principal chief, held them off with a raised hand.

"What is the common enemy of which you speak?"

"Grandfather," Storm Arriving said, pointing to the red-haired scalps overhead, "I speak of the *vé'hó'e,* whom the Inviters call *wasitchu.*"

"The whites?" the second chief exclaimed.

"We trade with the whites in the north," said another.

"But we fight them, too," one man offered.

"I would sooner trust a whiteman than these dogs!"

Things had shifted, and not for the better. The principal chief was listening to the crowd, gauging their opinion, and if these chiefs governed in any way similar to the chiefs of the People, Storm Arriving was losing the argument.

"Do something," Sharp Knife said.

"What can I do?" he said, hearing disfavor grow in the crowd.

Whistling Elk leaned close. "They must have a reason to trust us. What would convince you?"

Storm Arriving thought quickly, searching his own mind for what a Crow man could do to earn his trust. Strength would not do it, nor would angry words or heartfelt warnings. Gifts would make him suspicious of the giver, and promises were cheap. A sacrifice of wealth or flesh would mean nothing to him. A Crow would have to sacrifice something from within, something that only he could give.

His honor.

"Shall I tell you why you should trust us?" he asked.

The chiefs grew still, and Storm Arriving turned to speak to the crowd as well.

"Shall I tell you why you should trust us before you trust the whites?" he said, loud enough for his voice to echo through the vale. "Because it is time. Because the whites come at us from the east, just as they come at you from the north. Because neither of us can fight them alone. And because it is time, time for those of us who have lived on these lands forever to say, Enough!"

He turned back to the chiefs but kept his words strong enough to reach the crowd.

"Someone must come forward and be the first. Someone must say I have more in common with you than I do with them. Someone must say, even with all our war and all the blood we have shed, I know you, and you know me. Someone must be the first to forgive the other. And I will be that one."

He turned once more and addressed the throng on the downhill slope.

"I am Storm Arriving, son of Yellow Tail of the Tree People band, and my line has suffered at the hands of the Crow People. My great-grandfather, Black Knife, lost two of his sons to Crow raiders. After my father's birth, my grandmother, named Sky Woman, was carried off during a Crow raid; she was taken to the woods, raped, and then cut open and left for the wolves. My father, a rich and generous man, had his entire flock of whistlers run off and stolen by your soldiers, ruining his fortunes and making him a man who had to live on the charity of others for many years, until I was old enough to help him build them back. All of these things have befallen my family, brought on by you."

The litany tore at his pride, and gripped his heart with shame, but to stop now would be to achieve nothing.

"I said that someone must be the first, and I tell you that I will be that one. I say to you all, here, in your midst, and of my own free will, that I forgive these wrongs against my family. I forgive all wrongs my family has suffered at your hands, and say that now and forever, I will seek neither revenge nor retribution against you."

His words hung in the cold sunshine, buoyed up by the stone cliffs and the stunned silence of those around him. No one spoke. No one moved. No one was sure what was to be done next.

"My name is Whistling Elk," said a clear, strong voice. "My father was Running Bear who died fighting a Crow war party at Little Sheep River, thirty-eight years after the star fell. I will be second. I forgive all wrongs done to me by the Crow People, and promise to never seek revenge or retribution against you."

"My name is Sharp Knife, and I will be third."

The testaments and exculpation proceeded through the entire party and when they were done, Storm Arriving turned to the chiefs of the Crow People.

"That is why you should trust us."

The chiefs conferred among themselves. Storm Arriving looked up at the heavens, at a sky as pale as a year-old robin's egg, strewn with white scarves that billowed in distant winds. Though the air was cold, the sun shone with a gentle warmth and a touch as tender as a lover's hand, and he thought of Speaks while Leaving and their last parting.

They had argued before, the two of them, but this felt different. With her, he could never make himself bend. Though he loved her more than any other person in the world, too often he found himself on the other side of the argument, unwilling to give, unwilling sometimes even to listen. He was always aware of whom he had married—Speaks while Leaving, seeress, visionary, a woman whose life was already legend—a fact he could never forget. His spirit fought hers, struggled for its own place next to hers, but he always felt overshadowed or, more truly, outshone.

But here, in *this* place, it was he who shone. Here he was the one making legends come true and, as the sun rained down on his face, he felt it light him and only him. This was his realm; more than just battles, but surrounded by his soldiers, speaking with chiefs and warriors, determining the fate of peoples. He might not be able to see the future, but he could affect the present by influencing the course of nations. *This* was his destiny. This felt right.

Looking back down toward the Crow chiefs, however, he wondered what this role might cost him.

The chiefs had come to a decision, but the principal chief addressed not him, but the crowd of villagers.

"These men may stay among us for a time, while we think over what it is they have said here, and what they offer us. I, Grey Feather, and the other chiefs who stand here with me, vouch for their safety. Any person who goes against this will meet harsh treatment." And to Storm Arriving and the others he said, "You may camp down by the river. Broken Fang will show you where. We will call for you in the morning." He turned and walked back inside the lodge, the other chiefs accompanying him.

Storm Arriving exchanged glances with his colleagues. Sharp Knife looked worried. Knee Prints by the Bank was surprised. Whistling Elk, though, was smiling, and as they turned to head toward their camping place, he put an arm around Storm Arriving's shoulders.

"You see?" he said enthusiastically. "Hasn't it been

an interesting time? This will make a wonderful story when we get back home."

"If we make it home," Sharp Knife said. "We are still a long way away."

Whistling Elk chuckled. "But closer now than we were a short while ago."

Storm Arriving had to agree, but he was reluctant to hope. The crowd had not dissipated, and Broken Fang had to push his way through as he led them down toward the river. The faces that glared at them were still angry and distrustful, though they no longer threatened.

Near the river was a clearing where pines leaned out over the snow-covered banks, and the sound of trickling snowmelt could be heard from under the river ice. Broken Fang and his fellow soldiers tied the whistlers' halter ropes to nearby branches.

"We will keep your weapons," he said, "but you can have your animals. If you want to ride away in the night, it will be all right with me."

"What if someone attacks us in the night?" Sharp Knife asked.

"No one will," Broken Fang said. "You heard what Grey Feather said. He vouched for your safety."

That wasn't enough for Storm Arriving. "Grey Feather also said that anyone who defied the ruling would be dealt with harshly. I don't want to be left defenseless should someone decide to risk it."

"You call us liars?"

"No," he said quickly. "I say that many of you have good cause to hate us, and though I have vowed never to make war upon you again, the Crow People have not made such a vow."

Broken Fang looked to his fellows, and relented. "We will keep your rifles," he said, and then turned over their knives and other weaponry.

The night passed uneasily, and even though they set watches to guard against possible attack, no man slept but in winks and nods. They huddled close together, encircled by their whistlers' hunched forms, listening to the wails of renewed grief that their appearance had brought, and the sounds of raised voices as people argued old causes over dying fires. Through the night,

Storm Arriving wondered what might happen. Even when his watch was through and he leaned back against his whistler's soft warmth, his gaze was drawn toward the tall lodge up in the central arm of the camp. The lodge glowed with firelight, and the dark designs on its skins seemed to dance with one another, even though the fires in neighboring homes had been doused. His whistler sighed—a huge, heaving motion that settled him closer along her side—and he struggled against sleep, watching to see if the light went out in the chiefs' lodge, hoping that it would not, hoping that the chiefs would talk through the night, for he knew that hard decisions never came quickly, but only in their own time.

He awoke not knowing that he had slept. His side ached where the Crow soldier had kicked him the day before, and as he rolled over, the ache bloomed into a pain that drew his breath short. He lay back, waiting for the pain to ebb, and peered at the world.

The sky draped between the valley walls was heavy with cloud and glimmering with the encroaching dawn. He looked up toward the chiefs' lodge. It was dark in the growing light, and no smoke rose from it. The chiefs had disbanded, but he had no notion of when.

Knee Prints by the Bank was on guard, and he smiled a good morning as Storm Arriving emerged from beneath his blanket.

Did you see them go home? he asked with his hands, pointing up to the lodge.

Yes, Knee Prints by the Bank signaled. *Not long ago.*

Storm Arriving smiled, hopeful for the first time.

When the sun had risen enough to light the western rim of the valley, they were called back to the tall lodge. This time, however, they were ushered within and seated on the right-hand side. A new fire had been laid in the central hearth, and across the fire from them sat Grey Feather and several other chiefs, some of whom they had not met the previous day. In front of them lay the rifles that Storm Arriving and the others had brought with them.

"We cannot accept your offer of peace," Grey Feather said, and Storm Arriving felt his jaw drop open. He was about to speak when Grey Feather held up his hand.

"We must first have some assurances," the chief added.

Storm Arriving felt his heart begin to beat again. Not trusting his voice, he signed with his hands. *Yes. What do you need?*

Grey Feather indicated the chiefs with him. "We all agree that the whites are a danger to us. They make like friends, and they trade for our furs, but they bring us the crazy-water that burns the throat, and they take our lands and our game. They have driven an iron road across the land up north, and they kill our buffalo shamefully, taking only skins and tongues, leaving the rest to rot in the sun. They are a dead people, unconnected to living things, which is why their flesh is so pale. We fight them, but they keep coming."

Storm Arriving motioned, now eager to speak, and Grey Feather gave him permission. "That is why we must join our forces," he told the chief. "You cannot do it alone. Neither can we. But if you help us in the south, we will help you in the north. If we work together, we will be stronger."

Grey Feather frowned and looked down at the rifles that lay before him. "You ask too much," he said, "without offering anything in return. Peace between our tribes would be one thing, and if that was all you asked, we should agree, but we will not agree to help you unless you help us first."

"Grey Feather, I wish we could, but the whites are too strong in the south already. We cannot take soldiers away from our efforts there to help you in the north."

Grey Feather smiled. "You are young," he said. "Do you always trade a thing for a similar thing?" Some of the chiefs chuckled at the teasing.

Storm Arriving kept his temper, seeing his error and hoping the chiefs meant no insult. "How is it we might help you?"

Grey Feather ran a finger along the barrel of one of the rifles. "You all have the same weapons, the rifle that can fire many shots without reloading."

"Yes," Storm Arriving said, feeling a glimmer of excitement.

"We have only old weapons that the northern whites

no longer want. But a weapon like this, it would give one man the power of many."

"I see. And if one man was like many, then it would take fewer men to protect your lands." He leaned forward a little, as if asking a favor of the older man. "What if we could get you some weapons like the ones we have?"

The Crow chief looked back across the faces of his fellows. "If you gave us weapons to strengthen our soldiers here," he said, "we could send others south to you."

"How many?"

Grey Feather made a wavering gesture with his hand. "For each soldier we send, you must send two rifles."

"Yes," Storm Arriving said, "but how many soldiers could you send?"

Grey Feather was surprised at the quick acquiescence to his offer. "As many as you need," he said with a shrug.

Now it was Storm Arriving who was smiling. "And if I send you a thousand rifles?"

The chiefs were grinning openly. "You could send us *two* thousand rifles, and we would still fulfill our part."

They talked for a time longer, discussing details of when and where. Sharp Knife volunteered to stay behind as an ambassador to the Crow People, and as a guide for any southbound troops. The next day, Storm Arriving and the others left for their scheduled rendezvous with Two Roads beyond the Elk River.

Have we done it? he could not help but ask himself. Have we really made peace with the Crow People? With such an alliance, we will be the fiercest army on the Plains. The bluecoats will fall like cornstalks before us!

But the agreement of weapons troubled him, and he wondered if he had been a fool. He had walked away with nothing but promises, and the obligation to arm his oldest enemy. A feeling of dread seeped into his heart, a feeling that did not go away as they crossed the Elk River and he saw the face of Two Roads.

"I have news for you," the Kit Fox chief told him, before he could even tell of the events to the north. "It concerns your wife and sister. They rode off in the night. They have left the People to search for One Who Flies."

CHAPTER 9

Light Snow Moon, Waning
Fifty-seven Years after the Star Fell
North of the Sand Hills
Alliance Territory

Mouse Road crouched in the dawn-brewed mist, hiding behind the leathery leaves of a red-heartberry bush, waiting. She breathed slowly, silently, ignoring the cold, the thorns in her calves, and the cramping muscles in her shoulders.

The persistent drizzle that had dogged them for days had finally relented, but still the sky touched the ground, dampening everything. Her clothes stuck to her skin in limp submission and the braids of her hair hung heavy, beaded with glassy gems. Behind her in the copse of oak trees where they had spent the night, life was awakening with the patter of gathered dew and the querulous chattering of songbirds, but ahead of her, the greater world of scrub and sage remained somnolent and torpid, sleeping still beneath the swaddling clouds.

These tiny events, however, did not concern her. Instead, her attention was contained by the small patch of ground before her. In it, several feather-flower plants raised their first bracts of spring, two large elk-heartberry bushes put forth their early flowers, and sedgegrass gripped tight-footed to the delicate soil. But between the bushes and the tufts of hardy grass there was a length of bare ground, sandy and pale. It was a path—a narrow one, to be sure, but a path nonetheless—and across it was stretched a long loop of sinew-string.

Mouse Road had hidden the bottom of the loop under a dusting of dirt, and the dark green leaves of the bushes on either side held the loop up and open across the track. Extending from the loop was a length of string, white in the early light, the end of which she held in her hand and which she had held since the first glimmer of dawn. She had waited for nearly two hands of time, it seemed, the cold sand beneath her, the cold sky atop her, one hand outstretched, holding the end of the snare's loop.

Her patience, though, was about to bring its benefit.

She heard them coming, had known they would come since she had seen their tracks on the sandy path: prairie chickens, large and plump with feeding on springtime grubs and winter nuts. She heard them clucking and singing *oo-loo* to one another, heard them scratching in the leaves and grass, searching for bugs in the morning chill. Then she saw one, a hen in her cloak of barred brown. Mouse Road felt her mouth begin to water at the sight.

The two women and baby had been on the trail for nearly a moon—much longer than Mouse Road had thought it would take. But the weather had been harsh, and coming down out of the snows of the northlands had been difficult. By the time they had reached the Antelope Pit River, their supplies had begun to dwindle, and they had been forced to either forage or turn back.

Foraging in wintertime was difficult, and slowed them even more, but both she and her sister-in-law had been sure that it was forward they wanted to go, not back. So they continued south, and reached the more temperate climes where spring had started to venture. There, they supplemented the last of their dried meat, dried berries, nuts, and roots with fresh curls of fern fronds, nascent tubers of wasp-plants, and fragrant bulbs of skunk-root and elk-mint.

Even with this addition, however, their stores remained dangerously low. The whistlers were hungry, the baby was fretful, and most of their time was spent searching for food, with little spent on making progress toward their southern goal. They were forced to stay close to the wooded lands where traveling was harder but food was more plentiful. It had quickly become clear to them both that they needed to bring in some game, but Speaks while Leaving had little experience with hunting. Now, as Mouse Road lay beneath the thorny branches, she wished that she had spent more time with One Who Flies as he had set his traps during the winter months. While grateful for the tradable furs, pelts, and hides he had procured with his snares and deadfalls, she had never really appreciated the extra meat it had brought into her lodge. Her stomach gurgled at the memory.

The prairie hen was nearing the noose, and Mouse Road gripped her fingers tighter around the thin cord of sinew. Behind the hen strutted the male, his yellow brows bright in the morning light, his two horn-feathers standing tall above his head like rabbit ears. He was wary, and would be harder to catch in the snare, but his larger size meant a larger meal. They cooed to each other, and Mouse Road tried to decide how to spring the trap. The hen would have to pass through the snare if she was to snare the male, provided, of course, that the hen didn't knock the noose off its leafy hangers. No, it had to be the hen. It was the safest course.

She prepared herself, slowly tensing tired muscles, readying her arm for a quick, smooth snap of the cord.

From deep within the copse of oaks behind her, she heard a voice. Speaks while Leaving was calling for her.

"Mouse Road, look what I've found!"

Spirits, send her away! she prayed.

The chickens halted, the male stretching his neck up to his full height to see what the sound might be.

"Mouse Road?" She was getting closer. "Where are you?"

The chickens both stared in the direction of the voice. The female was only a hand's breadth from the snare. If they ran, Mouse Road knew they might run toward the snare, and kept still.

"I found some yellow shelf-mushrooms," Speaks while Leaving called out. "And the cache of a pine-mouse, filled with nuts and seeds."

Her steps grew closer.

The chickens blinked their wax-white eyelids.

"Mouse Road?"

Wings beat the air with feathered thunder as the chickens leapt up and flew away. Mouse Road sagged, tension draining away from every tautened muscle.

"*Eya!*" she shouted at the earth, and then rolled onto her side. Painfully, she sat up, wincing at the cramps in her back, and saw Speaks while Leaving standing under the trees, her gaze following the chickens, the realization of what she had done all across her face.

"Mouse Road, I am sorry. I was sure you'd have given up by now."

Mouse Road got to her knees and brushed the dirt from her dress.

"But look," Speaks while Leaving said, holding out an armful of mustard-yellow mushrooms. "Won't they be good?" And as she stepped out from under the oak branches, the scrub at her feet erupted.

With a squawking gobble and a huge flurry of wings, a turkey ran out from under a bush and leapt into the air. Its flight was low and right toward Mouse Road, who stood and lunged for it.

The heavy bird tried to turn in flight, but failed and crashed into her face. Mouse Road felt sharp claws against her arms as she grabbed handfuls of feathers. She fell backwards, but took the bird down with her, trying to grab its legs. Her world became a storm of sand, flapping wings, sharp nails, and a stabbing beak. Thorns of the berry bush clawed her. The turkey's wing clonked her hard on the head, but she was able to grab it.

"*Eya!*" she shouted. The turkey pecked at her hands as she held its wing, swiveled, and got to her knees. "Help!" she called, and Speaks while Leaving ran in.

"Get it!"

"I'm trying," but Speaks while Leaving was still holding on to the mushrooms and also still had the cradleboard with Blue Shell Woman strapped to her back. The huge bird flapped and jumped and ran and half-flew, dragging Mouse Road in a widening spiral of panic through the prickly shrubs. It cackled and screamed.

Mouse Road started to laugh. The bird pulled her back down to her knees just as Speaks while Leaving—

having left the mushrooms behind—came in again. The bird flapped and hit and gouged. The baby wailed. The women, each finally getting a hand on the turkey's neck, lost their composure to hilarity, but managed to snap the bird's neck and keep hold of it until it grew still. Then, grinning and huffing, blood dripping from a dozen scratches, they embraced in tearful laughter.

Blue Shell Woman continued to cry.

They stayed in the copse of oaks that night, tending their wounds and cooking the bird. Most of it they cooked slowly over warm but smoky coals to preserve it, but some they cooked quickly on hot rocks for immediate use. For the first time in weeks, Mouse Road felt sated, warm, and very nearly happy. Speaks while Leaving sat beside her, cradling Blue Shell Woman in her arms, giving the babe her breast.

Watching the baby suckle, Mouse Road wondered how her sister-in-law's life had changed. "Do you like being a mother?" she asked.

Speaks while Leaving glanced over with a raised eyebrow, as if the question surprised her. "Yes," she said. "I like being a mother."

The baby, her eyes closed, her fluffy black hair askew, grasped her mother's breast with plump fingers and sucked on the engorged nipple with a single-minded intensity.

Hypnotized by the scene, by the warmth, and by the good food in her stomach, Mouse Road asked the obvious next question.

"Why?"

Speaks while Leaving sighed in a way that bespoke of contentment. "Being a mother," she said, "it answers all my questions. I don't wonder why, anymore. I don't have to ask the reason for this or that." She glanced at Mouse Road and then back at her daughter at her breast. "This is the reason why."

"But," Mouse Road began, "don't you worry? I mean, I would. I wouldn't know what to do."

Speaks while Leaving laughed gently. "It is strange," she said, "and I used to worry, but the fact that there is a person who depends on me for everything has somehow made me more *in*dependent. I am stronger for having her need me." She chuckled again, a deep and happy sound. "I know it makes no sense, but it is true."

But Mouse Road had already begun to wonder about what came before motherhood. "And being a wife?" she asked. "How do you like that?"

Speaks while Leaving gave her a sly look. "Do you mean how do I like being married to your brother, or how do I like having a husband?"

Mouse Road blushed, and Speaks while Leaving laughed.

"I see," she said. "Such discussions are usually left to one's mother or other mother."

Mouse Road grew sullen. "My mother never had any sisters, and now she is dead."

"I know. That is why I thought I might tell you what it is like to have a husband, in their stead. If that is all right with you?"

Mouse Road suddenly felt very small and very inexperienced, sitting next to this woman whom she respected and loved so deeply. Speaks while Leaving seemed to know everything, while Mouse Road felt as if she knew nothing. But she wanted to know, and she wanted to be a wife, and a mother, if that was possible. She snuggled up against her sister-in-law.

"It would be all right with me," she said, "but let's talk of it later."

"Is something bothering you?"

She shrugged, unwilling to commit to words the fear that was still only the black edge of a shadow.

"You are worried about him, aren't you?"

Mouse Road shrugged again. "Yes," she said.

Speaks while Leaving put an arm around her sister's shoulder. "We will find him," she said. "The Sand Hills are just ahead, and then the shores of the Big Salty. I had a very strong dream about that place. We will find him there."

The shores of the Big Salty, Mouse Road thought. The funeral grounds.

Late the next afternoon, after a long day's ride through the rough and undulant country of the Sand

Hills, they reached the cliffs over the forested shore of the Big Salty. Surrounding them were the remnants of funeral biers and scaffolding, some recent, some ancient, all dilapidated or sundered by time, weather, or the leather-winged flyers that soared above the seaside cliffs and helped release a person's soul from the body.

Mouse Road reined in her whistler. She saw only a lifeless collection of mounds and sticks and bones that stretched on for miles. The sage and juniper bobbed in the wind, and the little-teeth hung in the skies, balancing on invisible pillars of rising air.

"He is not here," she said, struck by the foolishness of their journey.

"What do you mean?" Speaks while Leaving asked her. "We haven't even started to look for him."

"He is not here. Even if he was here once, he would not be here now. Why did we think that we would find him here?"

Speaks while Leaving stared at the scene. "No," she said simply, confidently. "He is here. We will find him here."

"Why?" Mouse Road asked, feeling the grip of panic in her breast. "There is nothing here but the dead," she said. "One Who Flies has been missing for nearly three moons. You and I could barely last a single moon without extra food. How could he have been here all that time? Unless . . ." She kicked her whistler into motion, but Speaks while Leaving maneuvered in front of her.

"No," Speaks while Leaving told her. "It is not what you think. He is here. My dream was a strong one, and I was here with you, and with him. With *both* of you."

"Alive? Both of us?"

She jerked her whistler's head around and set it running. Speaks while Leaving cried out after her and followed.

The dread that had begun at the campfire the night before now surged into a conflagration of emotions. Was he here? Was he lying here, somewhere among the scrub and the deep ravines? Had he been wounded, or perhaps even fallen from the cliffs? She rode from hill to knoll, no longer scanning the horizon but searching each brush and tussock of saw-grass, fearful of finding what she sought.

The cliffs had been the funeral grounds for the People and their relatives, the Sage People and the Cloud People, for a hundred generations and more. Everywhere she looked, there were bones. Everywhere she looked was a grandfather, a great-grandmother, a cousin, or perhaps One Who Flies.

The longer she looked, the surer she was, and the idea that he had lain here, untended, unmourned, tore at her heart. Weeping, she rode until she saw a single pole, tilting but still upright, and hanging on it, a shield. Even from this distance, she knew the design—the red-winged blackbird and dragonfly design of Three Trees Together.

Crying shamelessly, she stared at the pole and the shield and felt all her courage flee. Speaks while Leaving rode up beside her.

"He loved him as a father," Mouse Road said. "If he was anywhere in this place, he would be here."

Slowly, Speaks while Leaving rode forward. Near the pole, she bade her whistler crouch, and dismounted. Mouse Road watched as her sister searched the ground, and then knelt to pick something up. Standing, she stared at the thing she held. Mouse Road, overcoming her fear, rode ahead to see.

Speaks while Leaving held it out as she came near. Though dirty and darkened with mud, the golden color of the braid of hair still shone.

"He *was* here," Mouse Road said, excited.

"Yes," said Speaks while Leaving, solemnly.

"What is wrong? Isn't this good news? He was here, but has left."

Speaks while Leaving frowned. "But where has he gone?" she said. "Without this, where has he gone?"

Mouse Road realized what her sister-in-law was saying. The braid was a symbol, a connection. Long ago, One Who Flies had thrown away his blue wool Army coat, severing his connection to the bluecoats and the *vé'hó'e*. Now, he had thrown away this, a foot-long braid with a black hawk feather tied to it. For anyone else, it would merely have been an act of grieving, but for One Who Flies, whose connection to the People had always been a fragile thing, she sensed that it meant more.

"He has left the People," Mouse Road said.

"And gone back to the *vé'hó'e*," Speaks while Leaving murmured.

Mouse Road's dread returned, stronger now, reinforced by the braid of pale hair in her sister's hand. Her beloved had cut away a part of himself and left it behind, heading not to his home but into the heart of his enemy's territory. The last words she had said to him were cruel ones.

When will you be a whole man? she had asked him, wanting him only to be as other men, to stay with the People, to hunt buffalo, to raise whistlers, and to love her. But he had not stayed; he had gone away again, to the City of White Stone to meet with his father, Long Hair, in the hopes of building an alliance that would save the People and their lands.

And now, driven away by those words, he had gone back to those who had tried to kill him.

"What have I done to you?" she asked his spirit.

"Mouse Road?"

She turned to her sister, her course decided. "I must go and bring him back. You will have to go home alone. We can hunt for a few days and then you can head north. The Cloud People will be—"

"No," Speaks while Leaving said.

"Yes! My sister, I am going to the *vé'ho'e* place. You will go north without me."

"No, I will go with you."

Mouse Road stared. "Don't be a fool," she said. "You have your daughter to think of."

"And I *am* thinking of her. I cannot take her all the way home, not by myself."

Mouse Road was in agony. "But I *can't* leave him there. I won't just abandon him to them."

Speaks while Leaving held up a hand to calm her. "I am not asking you to do that. I am saying that together, we can do it. Together we can find him. I will not let you abandon him any more than I will abandon you. Together, we are stronger."

Mouse Road did not know whether to cry in grief or shout with gratitude. And though the dread still growled at her from the depths of her mind, her heart was strong. She was going to find him, and she was going to bring him home.

CHAPTER 10

Friday, April 11, A.D. 1890
New Republic
Unorganized Territory

George took the last swallow of liquor from the bottle, feeling its warmth creep down his throat like a lizard of fire. He tasted nothing of it—probably a good thing considering its raucous quality—but it did help to subdue the sour foulness of his mouth.

He leaned back against the building's rough-sawn siding and tossed the empty bottle under its floorboards, where it clanked against those that had come and gone before it. His mind swam a little, but that might have been the sun that had emerged from behind the clouds this afternoon.

The sun. He grinned up into it, even peering at its insolent face, so bright that it left little streaks of blue and red across his vision. But he was glad it was there. After so much rain—days, it seemed, maybe even weeks—he was thankful for its attention. It warmed the skin of his face, the backs of his hands, his knees, even his throat and chest when he leaned back. Warm. Drawing his skin tight around his bones. Warm. But his rear was still cold. His feet, too. He looked down.

He was sitting in mud. Leaning against the building—what building, he wasn't yet sure—he was sitting in mud. Dark mud and green-cast manure and swirls of other stuff he recoiled from identifying. His feet were submerged to the ankles, and his leggings were caked with it. He lifted one foot, wondering if he wore shoes. Scraping one foot with the other, he found that he wore calf-high moccasins. Wiggling his toes, the mud squished and gurgled inside the mocs. His big toe found its way through a hole and George laughed at it.

"What's so funny," someone said.

Wobble-headed, George looked and discovered a man sitting next to him. It was Red Arrow, a man of the— George tried to remember—yes, of the Cut-Hair People, though he had allowed his hair to grow long and his *vé'ho'e* clothes were in just as poor a shape as George's. His deep-set eyes were red-rimmed and his face was as puffy and unwholesome looking as boiled meat. They had been working together for a while now; the two of them and another man. Where was he?

George turned his head—too fast—and the world slewed in a sickening manner. A gurgle of liquid bubbled up his gullet and added its acid taste to the curdled mash in his mouth. He swallowed against it and took a breath to clear his head. When his vision leveled off, he found the last member of their trio sitting at his other side, a *vé'ho'e* they both knew only as Ploppy.

Ploppy was snoring, his long mouth hanging open, his last few teeth jutting out crazily from ulcerated gums. His skin was a field of dark pores that gave him a grey appearance, and his nose was a fiery carbuncle veined with blue spiderwebs. His clothing, too, was stained, torn, and layered in mud, muck, and worse.

George turned slowly back to Red Arrow. "Are we drunk?" he asked, surprised to find the English words difficult to pronounce.

"I cannot say for you," Red Arrow replied, "but I am not drunk." He closed his eyes and let the sun beat down on his swollen face. "I am dead."

"He's lyin'," Ploppy said. "We're drunk. All three of us."

George reached under his breechclout and scratched himself. "How do you know?" he asked, blinking and testing the muscles in his face. "I've been like this so long, I can't tell anymore."

"Naw," Ploppy said. "We're drunk." He reached down and scooped up a handful of filth. "There's no other earthly reason for the three of us to be sitting here in this, 'cepting that we're just too drunk to care." He flung the mud to the ground where it made a sound much like his name. "And I could do with another drink, too. Either of you have any money?"

"No," Red Arrow said.

George absently patted at nonexistent pockets. "No," he said, knowing he had none. He tried to remember how he knew that, but his head was filled with a haze that made remembering as treacherous as slogging through thigh-deep snow in a blizzard. Images rose from the drifts and were swept away by the wind. Dark shapes, bright shapes. He reached for them but they were fluid, amoebic, slithering out of his grasp.

He remembered having money, remembered walking into town with his hair in his eyes and murder in his heart, but murder not toward any man. No, his fury was not directed toward any living thing, unless a man's dreams were alive; for it was the dreams and hopes that lived in him that he came to kill.

In a small shop, he met a large man with a long beard who bought and sold, loaned and collected. The man regarded George as he would a mad dog; an insult that George forgave, considering his appearance. That day, he sold his rifle, his whistler, and just about everything else he owned in order to build a war-chest for the battle he had chosen to fight. The money had turned the trick, too, keeping him well whiskeyed and able to batter down the memories and dreams that tormented him. Whenever they regrouped and charged him again, another silver coin bought another bottle of brown liquor to defend the ramparts of his mind. With every drink, he saluted a memory. He drank to Mouse Road, who had given him love before banishing him from her heart. He drank to Storm Arriving, who had given him friendship before turning away from him in envy. He drank to the unwavering Three Trees Together, who had given him respect, hope, and the dream of a family. And he drank to his father, whose distant, rigid, commanding, abstemious regard had filled George with a loneliness that he had never been able to shake. But most especially, he drank to himself, pouring the liquor on the fire within.

The battle waged, back and forth, between man and

phantom, using up every dollar and peso he could scrounge. For weeks at a time, he would have the upper hand, remembering nothing, but when the money ran out, when he was left with his knife, his rotting clothes, and the small medicine bag that hung around his neck, he began to lose ground. Without drink, the memories returned, the dreams advanced, and hope—damnable hope—turned him on its spit.

Red Arrow and Ploppy had found him then and, recognizing him as a fellow brother-in-arms, inducted him into their tiny troop. In their company, George begged for coin, spending the last of his dignity for a swallow of backwashed swill. They took work where it was offered—shoveling dirt, shoveling coal, shoveling shit—and kept themselves in a miasma of drink, each to fight his own foes.

Ploppy drank against tragedy born of a dead wife and children, all taken down by yellow fever like wheat before the scythe. Normally, this would have been a deep sadness, but to Ploppy, it was the work of God, a punishment for having treated his wife so ill, and for having dragged her to the Frontier on a long and arduous journey that ruined her health and destroyed the last shreds of love she ever felt for him. He drank against a God whose retribution was overwhelming, and whose cruelty at having thrown Ploppy's children into the hazard had utterly broken him.

As for Red Arrow, neither of them knew what he drank against, though George thought it might have something to do with the dollar-sized patch on his scalp where the hair would not grow. George had heard of men having been scalped while alive, and could imagine the shame that surviving it might bring. But Red Arrow gave them no other clues.

"Do we have to find some work, today?" George asked, hoping they would not. He looked up toward the end of town.

New Republic was one of the sloppy gathering places that had sprung up like toadstools after an autumn rain. It was little more than a mudded track toward which faced several buildings of various size, shape, and quality. There was a stablery and smithy with barns and corrals for the upkeep of animals, and a wainwright and a carpentry shop where settlers came for all their building needs. There was the moneylender's shed, which listed to leeward when the wind was up, and there was the dry goods emporium, standing two stories tall and boasting a loft and glazed windows on both floors. There was a telegraph office—neat and tidy and manned by an officious man with a head like a bean—and then there was Haffner's—the drinking place against which they must be leaning—an odd establishment that, due to its unbridled success, had grown from a small saloon into a rambling inn. Already in its short life, it had been added onto so many times that it appeared more like a collection of tossed boxes and crates than a building. Along the street, both townsfolk and settler strolled, stood, or leaned against roofposts to chat. A wagon trudged past, pulled by two mules lashed by a shouting driver, while at the stable's hitching rails horses stood, their fetlocks heavy with caked mud. George even saw a whistler at the far end of town, ridden in by one of the settlers who must have realized that if the Indians could ride them, there was no reason he couldn't do it, too. It was a busy day in New Republic, and there was the chance that someone needed some stalls mucked out or some of the prairie sod busted to make way for a lettuce patch or a small crop of rutabagas.

George didn't want to work, though, not when the sun was out, but as he stretched in its warmth, he felt the small bag that he wore around his neck move against his chest, and that awoke a strong memory filled with the scent of smoldering sage, the ruddy light of a hearthfire, and the image of an old man, his bony fingers toying with the bag as he considered the fate of his People. He shrank from the memory, and reconsidered what ammunition a day's work of mindless toil followed by a few coins' worth of whiskey might provide.

Before he decided, though, the front door to Haffner's creaked open and heavy heels descended the steps toward the planks that gave respectable folk a cleaner passage across the mud puddles between buildings. George looked up as he heard two men step down onto the boards, but from his vantage, he could only see one of them.

The man was tall—or appeared so from George's ground-based seat—and had dirty boots as did every man in New Republic. Above his boots, however, he was dressed in the plain, dark suit of a man accustomed to conveyances and not to horseback. As George looked farther up, squinting against the sun, which glared behind his head like a saint's halo, he could only make out the man's white collar, dark moustache, and wide-brimmed hat. The man spoke over his shoulder to his companion.

"Watch this," he said. He reached into his vest pocket and retrieved a bright, five-dollar half-eagle, its golden rim glinting in the sunlight. George, Red Arrow, and Ploppy gaped as the man flipped the coin high up into the air, its edges flashing as it spun in a tall, narrow arc, bright against the sky, and came down edge first to bury itself in a clump of manure.

The three of them stared at the shitpile, then scrabbled and leapt on it with outstretched hands, each pulling the other back, shoving the other off, laying full length in the muck. Ploppy got the coin first, but it was slippery and spat from his grip like a watermelon seed, landing even farther away. Crawling forward, they tried for it again. George felt his hand touch it, then lose it when Red Arrow slammed against him, then found it again at the edge of his fingers.

"Leave off!" Ploppy yelled, pulling at George's hair.

George jabbed back with an elbow that connected, probably costing Ploppy one of his few remaining teeth, and then pushed forward and grabbed the coin.

"I got it," he cried, and pulled his hand close so that Red Arrow could not pry the coin from his fingers. "Ha! I got it," he said again as he sat up. Red Arrow glared through tired eyes, laboring to breathe. Ploppy held a hand to his mouth, sulking with failure and pain. But George was triumphant. He took the coin and wiped it on his sleeve, which only served to thin the mud that coated it, but it didn't matter. It was his, and it meant a good, long drink; long enough to share with his sullen fellows.

He smiled at the coin, and then up at the man who had tossed it to them.

"I thank you, sir," he said. "That was most generous of you."

But the man, whose enjoyment had lasted only as long as the fight had continued, looked down on George with a revulsion that bordered on the cruel.

"Trash," he said, and spat a thick glob into the mud. "Let's go." He turned and headed toward the dry goods store, walking past the other man, whose face George now saw for the first time.

Memories descended upon him, a screaming horde of memories. Memories of spring-leaved glades, summer meadows, and hard winter paths. Memories of digging in the pungent earth, of soil, rock, and bright gold. The gentle scent of slow-match and the acrid smoke of fast fuses. The ground lifting up, rising, unable to contain the force they had exploded beneath it. More gold, a long vein of it, shiny beneath the prairie sun. Pounds of it. He remembered the weight of it in his hands, the heft of the full bags, the stretching of his muscles as he and the other Indians of their mining team lifted a chest heavy with raw gold into the back of a wagon.

He looked up into that face, saw the old man's eyes, the grizzled chin, and the crooked smile, and he remembered the only other time he had gotten drunk. That time, it had been to celebrate months of hard toil and the purchase of weapons for the People. That time, George—who had followed his father's example and eschewed drink all of his life—relented amid a convivial mood and in the knowledge that this transaction was of mutual benefit. But that one bout of drinking, that one moment of weakness, had cost him a cracked head, a betrayed trust, and a fortune in gold.

And now the man who had exacted that price stared down at him with a look of bemusement. Vincent D'Avignon put his hands on his hips and shook his head.

"*Tabarnaque*," he said. "If it isn't young Custer. Why, the last time I saw you—"

George pulled his knife and surged up from the muck, but his inebriation stole his balance and he went down on one knee, nearly skewering himself in the leg. His heart was a moth in a bottle, battering itself within his chest. He swallowed against the sourness that rose in his throat, focused on his target, and slowly got to his feet.

"You filthy, lying—"

"Now, hold on there," Vincent said with a backward step.

"—cheating, foul—"

"Let's talk this over." Vincent held out his hands to protect himself.

"—festering, maggot-ridden asshole." George felt the antler-grip of his knife rough in his hand, felt the mud smooth beneath his feet, and saw Vincent's tea-colored eyes white-rimmed with fear. "I'm going to spill your guts, Vincent D'Avignon. I'm going to slosh your shit in the mud and piss on your gizzard."

"You've expanded your vocabulary since our last meeting," Vincent said with a nervous laugh.

"I'm going to use your ball-sack as a coin purse. I'm going to use your prick as a chess-piece."

Vincent looked past George. "Hey, you leave that coin alone."

He turned and saw Red Arrow and Ploppy fighting over the coin he had left behind in the mud. Then his knife went flying and stars exploded on the right side of his head. He fell backward into the mud, and Vincent came forward. With a booted toe, he kicked George in the ribs, then in the gut as George rolled into the pain. His breath left him and stayed gone as with a few menacing steps Vincent sent Red Arrow and Ploppy running for cover.

George lay there, back down in the mud, struggling to breathe as Vincent picked up the antler-hilted knife and walked back toward him. As breath began to flow in and out of his lungs once more, his gorge reacted to Vincent's kick. He contorted and regurgitated its contents in a spurt of thin, sour puke.

"*Sacré Mère*," Vincent said as he looked down on George. "What a sorry sight you have become, *mon ami*. I wouldn't have known you but that you have uncommon good manners for a drunk. Psh. What have you done to yourself?"

It was too much. George lay there in his own vomit,

his head reeling from liquor and violence, unable to do any more.

"Vincent," he said as he looked up at the embodiment of his failure. "Do me one small kindness, if you would, and kill me now. It would be fitting, don't you think?"

Vincent's chuckle was a mixture of cruelty and sympathy. "Hardly," he said as he reached down and offered George a hand. "I'm not such a fool that I'd kill the goose that lays the golden egg." He pulled George up by his arm and steadied him on his feet.

"What do you mean?"

Vincent revealed crooked teeth in a lopsided grin. "Why don't you let me buy you a drink?"

With an emptiness in his stomach and knees that shook with anger unspent, the idea of a drink sounded good, regardless the source.

"A drink," he said, glaring at Vincent with an unsteady eye. "Why do *you* want to buy *me* a drink?"

"Why, because this is your lucky day," he said as he took George by the elbow and escorted him around the corner of the tavern. Red Arrow stood near the rain barrel, and George saw sadness in the Indian's eyes.

"Walk free," he said to George, and raised his hand in farewell.

George chuckled. "He's just going to buy me a drink. I'll see you later and bring you some. You'll see."

Red Arrow only closed his eyes. "No," he said. "I see you no more. You go to another place."

"Crazy Injun," Vincent said as they walked toward the tavern's rear. "Drink affects 'em more than it does us white folks."

But to George, Red Arrow's words of parting sounded like a judge's sentence. He stared at the man from the Cut-Hair People. Though his clothing was soiled and his face swollen, the expression on his face was peaceful, and the large hand that he held up was flexed as if he was pressing it against another, unseen hand. George shivered and had the urge to leave Vincent, to refuse this man entirely.

And why shouldn't I? he asked himself. This man who has done me so wrong? Why should I follow him so, as if the past year and a half had not happened?

He stopped, and Vincent, still leading George by the arm, turned. He looked at George, and then at Red Arrow, who stood as still as stone at the corner of the building.

"What? You don't hold with what he says, do you?" He tugged on George's arm. "He's just a crazy Injun, eh? *Mais oui,* crazy and drunk."

George pulled his arm out of Vincent's hold. "Some would say the same of me," he said, "and yet for me, you'll buy a drink."

"Now, listen, George—"

"I should kill you."

"Are we back at that?" Vincent asked, showing the knife he'd taken from George. "Do I have to trounce you again, y'foolish bastard? Because I will." He raised one fist. "I'll thrash you, I will, if you won't come to your senses."

"You *stole* from us!" he shouted. He remembered the battles the People had fought to get the weapons they'd tried to purchase. "Men died because of you!"

Vincent shook his head and looked at him with narrowed eyes. "Ah, *non, mon ami,* not because of me. No one died on account of me. If I stole, I stole from healthy men. I killed no one." He waggled a finger in his direction. "If anyone killed them, it was the man who led them."

The insult was too great, the challenge too open. George lunged at him, one hand grabbing for the knife, the other reaching for Vincent's narrow neck, but the wily man stepped to the side and thrust upward with his fist into George's gut, crumpling him like a paper bag. He fell heavily to one knee, but Vincent kept him from falling farther by grabbing onto his arm once more.

"Settle down, now," Vincent said, solicitous and patronizing. "Come on, and I'll buy you that drink. *Vraiment,* I think you need it."

The desire to harm, to inflict pain, fired in George's heart. He wanted to do something to atone for his sins, to make up for his weaknesses, and most especially to hurt this man who had been author of so much of it. His mouth hungered for the offered drink, but his soul cursed, demanding *some* sort of payment. Vincent was

an old man but he had bested George twice in the length
of time it told to tell the tale. As he knelt on the sodden
ground, with Vincent standing over him like some be-
nevolent Samaritan, he knew he had to do something,
even if it only be a token. He looked and saw Vincent's
muddy boots and the soiled hems of his trouser legs.

He grabbed one trouser leg in each hand and stood.
Vincent was upended like an unbalanced wheelbarrow,
falling down hard into a puddle of muddy rainwater that
had the consistency of cream. With one step forward,
George had his foot on Vincent's throat, a hand in his
hair, and had taken the knife from his stunned grip.

George grimaced through the dizziness his sudden action had brought on. He glared down at Vincent, whose
eyes were white-rimmed and whose ears were puddling
with rainwater. He rotated the knife on its axis and let
its honed edge catch the sharp light of the sun, drawing
bright lines across the face of the man who had cost
him so much. Vincent's mouth trembled and he panted
through a gaping mouth with breath as rapid as a bird's.
The man's fear was absolute.

"So tell me," he said to Vincent. "Tell me why *this*
crazy Injun shouldn't just take your scalp and leave you
for the little-teeth."

Vincent stared up into George's eyes. George twined
his fingers in Vincent's greasy hair and brought the knife
to his forehead, ready to make the hard, thrusting cuts
that would peel back a strip of scalp from the skull.
Vincent's lips worked, trying to form words without the
benefit of breath or voice. He babbled like a pot of
boiling water.

"B-b-but . . ."

"But what?" George asked with a smile.

"B-but the law!"

Doubt stayed George's hand, and Vincent recognized
his opportunity.

"*Mais oui,* the law."

"What law?" George asked.

"Any law. My law, your law. *Oui, oui,* you cannot kill
me. Even your beloved Cheyenne would not kill a man
for theft."

Fury enfolded George's heart. "The People's law is

only for the People!" he shouted. He stepped hard on Vincent's throat, refusing him air. "It does not pertain to you!"

Vincent struggled against the pressure, pushing against George's leg. "It does, it does," he squeaked. "It pertains to people of the same tribe. And you and I are of the same tribe!"

"No!"

George stood up and fell against the tavern wall.

It was the quandary that had dogged him, tortured him for years, through battle and courtship, through life among the People and deliberations with the Spanish and Americans. Was he white, or red? *Vé'ho'e,* or Tsétsêhéstâhese? And now here that question came at him again, cast up at him from the Devil himself; the one question out of a million questions that could stay his hand.

Stay my hand, George thought, looking at the knife he held. Stay my hand from killing *him,* perhaps. There are other ways to end this.

He felt his breast to find the space between his ribs where he might slide the blade in and puncture his own heart. He pulled open the yoke of his tunic and moved aside the medicine bag he wore beneath it. He found the spot—there, just there—beside the sternum, a place where the flesh was softer. The blade of the knife winked at him as he turned it around and placed the tip against the exposed paleness of his skin.

O happy dagger, he thought, and winked back at it. I am spent, with thy help.

For the second time that day, his knife spun from his hand as Vincent slammed into him.

"Tabarnaque," Vincent swore as he held George up against the wall. He slapped George across the face once, then again, and George saw in his eyes a puzzled concern. "What do you mean to do?" he asked.

George blinked. "Isn't it plain?" he asked in response. "I am done here. I am finished." He held his arms open, displaying himself. "I can fall no further. There is nothing more for me to do."

"But there is!" Vincent claimed. He led George—now unresisting—around the back of the tavern, up the rickety steps that led to the stoop, and plunked him down on the splintery wood. "There is plenty that you can do," he said.

"What?" George asked. "What can I do? I have failed everyone I have tried to help."

Vincent cuffed him on the shoulder. "Except the one person who needs your help the most," he said, and leaned down to look him in the eye. "You."

George recoiled from the idea.

"No," Vincent pressed. "I mean it." He stood back and motioned to the world. "I read the papers. I've read about what you've been doing. You've been trying to help everyone, trying to make peace where none can be had. And don't forget, I lived with you among those Cheyenne you love so much. I've seen how hard you worked for them. Trying to build them up, trying to show them the proper way. *Mon Dieu,* what *haven't* you tried to do for them?"

He climbed the steps and sat next to George on the stoop. "But that's no reason to give up, *mon ami. Au contraire,* it is time to start up again, only this time, you need to think of yourself." Leaning back, he pounded on the tavern door. It came ajar with a creak, and Cora, the thin, pale woman who ran Haffner's kitchens, peered out.

"Ah, Cora," Vincent said, smiling up at the woman. He reached into a pocket and passed her a silver coin. "As you can see, my partner and I are in need of a scrubdown. Would you please get some water ready? Oh, and bring a bottle of rye, too, if you please, while the water heats?" Cora retreated without a word.

"Partner?" George asked.

Vincent patted him on the back. "Yes, young man. Partner."

George could only close his eyes against the memory, too tired to fight any longer. "I was your partner once before. That didn't work out too well."

The door creaked open again and Cora slammed down a squared-off bottle of copper-colored liquor before retreating on heavy shoes. Vincent smiled and reached back for the bottle.

"Cora doesn't like me, but she won't refuse my coin,"

Vincent said. George watched as he squeaked the cork out and took a large swallow. Vincent saw the hunger in George's eyes, and handed him the bottle.

George took it with trembling hands, his mouth watering and his heart a-thunder with the closeness of the liquor. He lifted the bottle, smelled the whiskey's bite before it touched his lips, felt his throat tighten and his stomach twist in preparation. Just having the bottle in hand, his mind had begun to calm, the stampede of thoughts and emotions slowing. He held the bottle in both hands, encased the opening with his lips, and tilted back in a series of gulping swallows. He tasted its sourness, its mineral edge, and its heat. It coursed down his throat, burning its way to his stomach where it flared into a bloom of warmth that passed through to his lungs, his heart, his soul.

He sighed, eyes closed, and felt his entire body relax. The presence of Vincent beside him no longer offended. The memories of failure and pain no longer ached. The bottle in his hands was all he cared about.

"Better?" Vincent asked.

"Mmm," George said, taking another drink. He took a third drink and then opened his eyelids a crack to peer at the man next to him.

Vincent D'Avignon had put his fifty-odd years to good use, and the mileage showed. His wavy hair was thin and streaked with silver, and the stubble on his chin was pale, not dark. Lines creased his brow like a farmer's furrows, and drew tributary wrinkles at the corners of his pale brown eyes. His cheeks had been hollowed by long familiarity with hunger, and his nose bore the marks of lost tempers and lost fights. His clothing, too, showed wear, from the worn hems of his coat to the dingy ridge of his button-on collar. Yet, despite his hangdog collection of features, his disposition was as wry, as sharp, and as lively as ever George had known it.

"What are you doing here, Vincent D'Avignon? Why aren't you up north, living a sumptuous life on my stolen gold?"

Vincent sighed. "Alas, the world does have its way of getting back at a man."

"What? Did you spend it all?"

Vincent smirked and glared at him. "Hardly spent," he said. "Lost."

"To whom?"

"To Angus, my purported co-conspirator and the man, it should be said, who jacked you over the head."

George gaped at the older man who sat with eyebrows raised in wistful recollection of the loss of a fortune in gold.

"Oui," Vincent went on. "Just as I betrayed you, so was I betrayed in turn. While Angus and I reveled in our newfound wealth at your expense, he was having the chests of gold loaded onto a coast-bound train. He left in the night, and by the time I rolled my aching head out of bed the next morning, he was headed for the lonesome dales of his bonny Scotland." He reached over for the bottle, took a long draught that dribbled down his mud-spattered chin, and passed the bottle back. "When I heard that the ship had gone down in the shoals off of Greenland, I could only think it was a fitting end and the Devil had been paid in full. And me? I've been down here among this refuse ever since, selling them the things they need, just as I traded with your Indian people. I tell you, the whites are easier to cheat than your friends were."

He turned to George and looked him earnestly in the eye, a gaze that George did not care to meet.

"But that," Vincent said, "is why you and I should be partners again. It's a sign, my meeting you here. It is fate, *peut-être,* we should both come to this place after so long. It's a second chance, and we'll do it right, this time." He grabbed George's sleeve to emphasize his words.

"I need you, young Custer, and you need me. I remember all the spots we prospected, and you know the Cheyenne. Together, we can go up in the Territory and make ourselves a respectable fortune. They'd let you, surely they would, after all you've done for 'em, no? We won't ask for much, you see. Just enough for ourselves. Just enough for two simple men. Enough for us to live out our lives in quiet comfort. They'll grant you that much, don't you think?"

George's head was awhirl with the freedom of the

alcohol and the influx of notions that Vincent was spouting, and he had to concentrate to bring the ideas into focus.

Go back? he thought. I'll never go back.

"I won't go back to the People," he managed to say.

"No, and I'm not asking you to," Vincent said. "Just take us to the Territory. I'll do the prospecting, and you'll be there to make sure I don't get a Cheyenne arrow in my back. We'll stay 'til winter comes. No longer." He leaned closer. "We'll make enough for you to buy yourself a house and settle back and watch the grass grow for the rest of your life. What do you say, George? Partners?" He held out his hand to seal the deal.

George looked at the hand—the hand he had shook once before—and then looked at the bottle, which he held tightly with both hands. He knew that he didn't have the courage to kill himself, though he had been trying to drink himself there. But neither did he have the courage to live.

Do I deserve to live? he asked himself. Do I deserve a future? Or am I afraid to be just an ordinary man?

He thought of all the men and women of the world, and how they were content—even blissful—to live their unremarkable lives. The concept of ease escaped him. That there should be a state wherein he could rest, where all that needed to be done *had* been done, was foreign to his nature. Always, for as long as he could remember, there was always something else waiting to be achieved, some next accomplishment that lay before him. As a boy, it was the expectations of a general's son, and as a youth, it was the demands of teachers and headmasters. Later, it was the challenges of high society, and the scrutiny of the world as it watched the son of a beloved legend follow in his father's path. He had walked the road of challenge for so long that he couldn't see the upward slope of his life. From youth, to man, to officer, to leader, to challenger, to hero, to . . . ? Where would it end? *Would* it end?

Vincent offered again his hand and the pact of mutual benefit, of quiet security and perhaps, George allowed himself to dream, of obscurity. Hesitantly, George released the bottle of forgetfulness he held, and clasped Vincent's hand.

"If you betray me again," he said to the older man, "I *will* kill you."

Vincent nodded. "*Tristement,* I would deserve it," he said with a smile. Then he stood, pulling George to his feet as he did so. "Let's get you cleaned up, for without a doubt, *mon ami,* you stink!"

CHAPTER 11

Light Snow Moon, Waning
Fifty-seven Years after the Star Fell
Southern Reaches
Alliance Territory

Speaks while Leaving glanced over at Mouse Road as they approached the vague limits of the *vé'ho'e* town. The younger woman's knotted brow and tight grip on her whistler's halter rope told of her nervousness in this, her first meeting with *vé'hó'e*.

"They won't kill us, will they?" Mouse Road asked.

Speaks while Leaving chuckled. "I doubt it," she said, but the humor she put into her voice was false. During her travels as a healer, she had met several *vé'ho'e* up along the fringes of Alliance lands, but those *vé'hó'e* had been unusual. Loners in a forbidding land, they appreciated the occasional visit from anyone willing to trade gossip or skills or goods; man or woman, pale-skinned or dark, the opportunities were welcomed.

Here ahead of them, though, were *vé'hó'e* of a different breed. These people kept close to one another, were barely trusting of their neighbors, and were fearful of riders coming in from beyond their borders.

She could only pray that any fear the *vé'hó'e* felt would not cost her and Mouse Road their lives.

Set on the banks of a thin, northward-trending creek, the small town had been settled in the *vé'ho'e* way. Where the People generally set up their camps in circles or in accordance to the lay of the land, the *vé'hó'e* organized their towns in straight lines—lines often in complete defiance of the ground on which they lay. And so, the town was built on either side of a line that stretched upslope, away from the creek, so that only those on the downhill side had easy access to its banks and others had to hike all the way through town to fetch their own water.

Speaks while Leaving sighed. The obstinate minds of the *vé'hó'e* never ceased to amaze her. How much easier would it be if the road had run *with* the river, instead of against it? The desires of nature were easy to see. Even when she closed her eyes and listened to the world, the swells of land and the rush of water were apparent to her, but the *vé'hó'e*, with eyes opened wide, seemed to fight the wants of nature on principle.

They continued onward, riding slowly toward the town, their weapons stowed away, and their hands in plain sight. The smells of manure from the horses soon gave way to the smells of human effluent, which the recent rains and the fresh sunshine combined to ripen.

"It stinks," Mouse Road complained.

"Yes," Speaks while Leaving agreed. "The *vé'hó'e* are not as concerned about such things."

Mouse Road snuffled. "Even a day-old sparrow knows not to foul its own nest."

Speaks while Leaving bid her be quiet with a gesture. "They are a young people," she said.

As they neared the first rough buildings, people stuck their pale faces out of doors and windows. They gaped but did not run. Men and women both stepped out toward the town's main road to stare at the newcomers. Speaks while Leaving kept her gaze lowered, only glancing up occasionally to gauge the mood of the townsfolk.

One man came forward and shouted at them. Speaks while Leaving did not understand his English words, but his tone was clear. She kept her head low and did not challenge him with her eyes, but on the cradleboard on her back, Blue Shell Woman began to fret. The man curbed his tongue, chagrined perhaps at having made a baby cry, and stepped back toward his home.

Up ahead, at one of the larger buildings in town, was a gathering of men, some of whom, by their clothing, might have been of the northern tribes. Hoping to find someone with whom she could converse in a civilized tongue, she headed toward it.

There were indeed men of the tribes at that place; more than she had thought. Of the twenty or so men who loitered near the doors of the building, only half of them were *vé'hó'e*. Of the other, ordinary persons, some were dressed in poorly kept clothes of traditional cut, but most wore trousers and shirts of Trader's cloth, and some even wore cast-off clothing of bluecoat soldiers.

To a man, however, red and white alike, she could see that they were deep in the well of drink. The acrid scent of it rose from them as they braised themselves in the drifting sun of the afternoon. She reined in before them, her heart filled with a fury she could not explain. For the *vé'hó'e* who sat among them she felt nothing, but toward the men of the prairie, she felt a great deal.

While drink was not unknown among the People, it had been proscribed since before the star fell. Sweet Medicine, the most blessed of men to have walked the earth, warned the People of both the *vé'hó'e* and of the foul drink they brought with them. Young men, being curious, sometimes traded for it, sometimes even stole it, and of those who tasted it, some were lost. But the law was clear about its evil, and the evil it often caused. A man in camp found to be within its grip was beaten with quirts, and a man who was lost to it was sent away, removed from the body of the People.

There were youth among them, and mature age as well, but all of it—strength and wisdom—had been cast aside in favor of the *vé'ho'e* water-that-burns, and so it was with disgust and a sense of betrayal that Speaks while Leaving looked down from atop her whistler's back. That she and Mouse Road needed them was regrettable, for these men had turned their backs on their families, on their tribes, and on the gifts of their birth. It was regrettable that she needed these men, but it was so.

The men all looked up at them as if looking at something new in the world. Droop-lipped and blank-stared, there was hardly a thought among them, and she could not tell from either clothing or habit what tribes they might have once called their own.

She reached within the pouch at her belt and retrieved the braid of blond hair she had found at the funeral grounds. "I am looking for the man who belongs to this," she said, trying first the language of the People. "Do any of you know of him?"

The men exchanged glances of slow surprise, and she asked her question again, in the language of the Inviters, and in the Trader's Tongue. Remarkably, it was one of the *vé'hó'e* who responded to her query.

"I seen such a man as might belong to that," he said with halting words. "He was on a beast like yours, and dressed like a red man."

"What does he say?" Mouse Road whispered.

"He thinks he has seen him," she replied, and then turned back to the man. "Do you know where he is?" she asked, holding the braid. The hawk feather at its end shone in the sunlight.

The man shook his head. "Gone," he said. He waved a hand toward the east, toward the creek and the lands beyond it. "Days ago."

Speaks while Leaving bowed her head. "I thank you," she said, and put the braid back in her belt pouch. Then she gently toed her whistler into motion. The men stared as the women started downhill toward the creek.

"He's even worse than us!" the *vé'ho'e* shouted after them, and followed it with a laugh thick with deprecation.

"What did he say?" Mouse Road asked. "Tell me."

But Speaks while Leaving did not know how to tell her that though they might find One Who Flies somewhere ahead, the man they searched for might not be worth the finding.

"Tell me!" Mouse Road insisted, riding up alongside her. "Is he alive?"

Speaks while Leaving sighed. "Yes," she said, and then decided that her young companion was adult enough to deserve the truth. "He is alive, but is like those men back there."

Mouse Road was silent for a long while as they left the tiny town behind. They checked the ties on their belongings and urged their whistlers into the muddy flow of the rain-swollen creek. The beasts pushed against the water's force, singing to each other the words that only whistlers understood, finding the shallowest fording.

"What will we do?" Mouse Road asked as they reached the far bank. "About One Who Flies? What will we do?"

Speaks while Leaving looked at her sister and saw the conflict of fear and wanting in her eyes.

"We will find him," she told her, and then rode her whistler up out of the creekbed. "And then we will decide what to do next."

A wheel-worn path curvetted across the greening hills, drawing a drunken but generally consistent line eastward. Without constant use, the path would disappear beneath the insistent growth of the warming season, but for now, it was plain enough to lead them toward the next town.

And to the next one as well, Speaks while Leaving thought. If it must.

The whistlers' pace ate up the ground, following alongside the path but not on it. The animals preferred the open ground and the prairie grass to the mudded tracks. To either side, homesteads sprouted: dark, squat, sod-roofed mounds or tall, sharp-angled structures that dotted the sun-bathed hills. Around each one, trees had been cleared and the land had been tilled, its fertility broken open in straight lines, ready for the seed. Within a short year's time the region had been settled by the *vé'hó'e* and, as Speaks while Leaving regarded the new habitations that bruised the land all the way to the horizon, she knew that the People had lost this territory forever.

As she and Mouse Road rode past the *vé'ho'e* homes, tired horses lifted their heads in sudden interest, circling their corrals, ears pricked and noses testing the air as if even at this distance they could scent the whistlers; and Speaks while Leaving thought that perhaps they could. The Alliance had learned to count on the *vé'ho'e* horses' fear of the larger, faster whistler. The whistler's spice-scented, chameleon skin was a tool that the People had learned to use, creating panic among the horses from the upwind side, and enabling a camouflaged approach from downwind.

But the main thing that whistlers did so much better

than horses was run, and their long-legged gait brought the two women to the next *vé'ho'e* town just as the sun began to set.

This place was even smaller than the last, with fewer than a dozen of the square wooden lodges the *vé'hó'e* favored. The springtime air had grown chilly with evening's approach, and the path through the tiny town was nearly empty. There were no horses tied to any of the posts or rails, though set back from the path she could see a corral and stable where several horses stood, all nodding their heads and whickering to one another as if gossiping about the town's newest arrivals. Warm lamplight shone through gaps in shutters and from behind draped windows, but along the short way through town, the women spotted only two men. They sat on the steps in front of one of the larger buildings, leaning back-to-back against a porch post. Just as in the last town, these men, too, were thick with drink. Stuporous, they clutched their empty bottles with nerveless hands and slept open-mouthed to the gathering night. She looked down on them from atop her whistler. One of them was *vé'ho'e,* but the other was not. By his features, he seemed to be of the Cut-Hair People, and it was to him that she spoke, using the language of the Inviters.

"Wake up! I want to talk to you."

The two men opened their eyes and the *vé'ho'e* screamed, startling the whistlers. They whined in alarm and darkened their skin, which only frightened the *vé'ho'e* all the more. The other man, however, kept his wits, drunken though he was. With a steady hand he grasped his companion's shoulder and calmed him. The *vé'ho'e* ceased his shouts, but his eyes told Speaks while Leaving that he had never been so close to a whistler.

"I want to talk to you," she said again to the ordinary man.

He nodded—a *vé'ho'e* habit—but before he could speak, the door to the building opened and several *vé'hó'e* came out, some with clubs, a few with rifles. Seeing the whistlers, they cried out in surprise and retreated to the cover of the doorway. Peering out, one of the *vé'ho'e* shouted at them. Though Speaks while Leav-

ing did not understand the words, his tone was filled
with fearful anger.

"What does he want?" she asked the Cut-Hair man
on the steps.

The Cut-Hair man stood up, one hand waving at the
vé'hó'e in the doorway. He said something to them, and
then looked straight at Speaks while Leaving—another
bad *vé'ho'e* habit.

"They want you to go away," he told her, his words
slow and hard in coming, as if the language had slept
within him for a long time. "Go away. They do not want
you here."

She took the braid of hair that One Who Flies had
left and showed it to him. "I want to find this man," she
said. "Have you seen the man who belongs to this?"

The Cut-Hair man stared at the braid, and Speaks
while Leaving saw recognition in his features. He spoke
to the *vé'hó'e*, but they wanted nothing of what he was
saying. They began to come out from the doorway, mo-
tioning at her and Mouse Road, making the whistlers
shy and pale at their sudden movements. The Cut-Hair
man was arguing with the *vé'hó'e* now, but they were
not listening to him. They came toward Speaks while
Leaving, walking closer, shouting still. She glanced over
at Mouse Road and saw the fear in her sister's eyes. The
vé'hó'e waved them away as if they were dogs at a feast
fire. One of them pushed at her leg. They all stood
alongside her, shouting up at her.

She gave her whistler a nudge. It took a smooth, si-
dling step toward the men, shoving them quickly backward, making a few of them fall.

The shouts stopped as the men scrambled away from
the whistler.

"My apologies," she said to the Cut-Hair man. "My
whistler is a little nervous."

A small but knowing smile touched the corners of the
man's mouth, and he passed her words along to the
vé'hó'e.

"Now," she said, holding the braid out again. "Do
you know of the man who left this behind?"

"Please," Mouse Road added. "We must find him."

The Cut-Hair man regarded the two women, and
Speaks while Leaving wished she could know what was
going on in his mind. From his stance, she could see he
still remembered pride and honor, but from the state of
his tattered, filthy clothing and his person, it was obvious
that he had forgotten many other things.

"You know where he is," she said to the Cut-Hair
man.

He nodded. "Why do you want him?"

"I have had a vision," she told him. "I need him to
make it true."

"He is inside," he said, without further hesitation. He
motioned toward the *vé'hó'e* in the doorway. "But they
won't let us in there. And I don't think they will get him
for you."

She made her whistler take a step backward, and she
looked at the building. It was wide, and some segments
had two stories with shuttered windows. If she couldn't
get inside to find One Who Flies, she reasoned, she
would have to call him outside.

"Ho'esta!" she commanded, and her whistler took a
breath and bugled to the sky in a long, honking *haroo*
that set every horse within earshot neighing. The bugling
rose up the scale, became a flute-song, and then a pierc-
ing whistle that hurt the ear. Mouse Road commanded
her mount to do likewise, and together the two beasts
made sounds that brought a face to every window and
doorway in the town. Above, in the upstairs window, a
shadowy figure appeared and then quickly withdrew.

"One Who Flies!" she shouted, adding her own voice
to the din. "One Who Flies!" The street began to fill
with people, and she feared their chance was escaping
them.

"One Who Flies!"

The *vé'hó'e* in the doorway came forward once again,
shouting at the two women. The whistlers danced away,
and with a nudge of her toe, Speaks while Leaving made
her mount turn full circle, its tail keeping the men at
a distance.

And then he was there, standing at the doorway behind the *vé'ho'e* men, recognizable to her only in the
hawklike intensity of his eyes.

"One Who Flies!" The two women grinned at the sight of him.

All the shouting and noise stopped as the men turned to see who it was that pleased them so.

One Who Flies was dressed in *vé'ho'e* clothing: a dark hat, a pale shirt, and close-fitting jacket and trousers. He appeared much as he had on that day when Speaks while Leaving had found him—how long ago was it? Years, now, it was—when the Thunder Beings had brought his airship down to earth in a terrible storm. He was now as he had been then: a reddish moustache above a delicate mouth and sharp chin, a long and aquiline nose, pale eyes of sky-blue set deep beneath a broad brow, his golden hair cut short so that it barely touched the high collar of his shirt. He stood on the porch, looking out at them, eyes snow-moon bright.

Mouse Road was the first to move. Leaping off her mount before it could crouch down, she pushed through the puzzled *vé'hó'e*. He watched her approach and Speaks while Leaving saw him blink and, ever so slightly, recoil. When she reached him, she grabbed his arm, and he looked away, up the road.

"One Who Flies," she said, her words broken by tears. "One Who Flies, I am so happy to see you. I have been looking for you. I was so worried. I thought that perhaps you had died, but then, in the last place, they had heard of you, and pointed us this way. One Who Flies?" She tugged on his arm, but he would not look at her, and it was not just politeness. "One Who Flies?"

At the door was another man. Thinner, older, his neck was as wiry as an old walker's, and his eyes were just as guarded. He hung back near the shadows but Mouse Road spied him. It was Long Teeth, the trader who had come to help the People dig the yellow chief-metal from the earth, and who had stolen it from them.

"No," Mouse Road said to One Who Flies, tugging at his arm as she backed away. "Not him. You must not listen to him. Never again with him."

She pulled at him but he refused to move. With a yank, he pulled his arm out of her grasp, and for the first time looked directly at her.

"Go home," he said, and his words were thick and

indistinct. Speaks while Leaving saw him blink—a slow, methodical closing and opening of his eyes—and knew that he was still steeped with drink. Carefully, she slid down from her whistler and, holding the cradleboard with Blue Shell Woman, walked forward. The *vé'hó'e* parted to let her pass, but she gave them not a glance: Her gaze was set on One Who Flies, filled with him. She saw the slow wavering of his stance, like a poplar in the breeze. She saw the tremor in his right hand. And at the corner of his mouth, she saw a fleck of spittle. She approached him steadily, and saw everything about him.

"The men we passed in the last town were right," she said to him in the language of the People. "You are worse than they are." She stepped up onto the porch planks and stood before him, staring into his eyes. "You are worse than any of them." Then she slapped him across the face.

"Now just a minute!" Long Teeth said, striding forward from the doorway. "You can't just—"

She struck him as well, backhanded and hard, and her knuckles burned with the pain. The *vé'hó'e* around her spoke and stepped closer but Long Teeth held up one hand while he worked his jaw with the other.

"I guess I deserved that," he said to her in the Trader's Tongue.

"That and much more," she said. "And if you were not surrounded by *vé'hó'e,* I should give it to you."

Long Teeth glared at her. "Now look, you, what I did, well, I'm not saying it was right, but I've paid a price for it. *Mais oui,* I've paid a price."

"Men *died!*" she shouted at him. "Hundreds, both of my people and yours. They died without need, over weapons that we could have bought with the gold that you stole. And you say you've paid for that crime?" She spat on his feet. "You've paid for *nothing.*" Then she turned to One Who Flies and reached for his arm. "And you? You need to come away with us. This place has infected you. The People are in trouble, and I need your help."

Again, One Who Flies pulled his arm away. "Leave me," he said. "Go home."

"One Who Flies, we will not leave here without you."

"I will not go with you," he said with a glance over to Long Teeth.

She looked at the two men and wondered what had passed between them that would bind One Who Flies to his betrayer. What had happened to her friend to make him the puppet of such a man? Was it the drink? Or was there more to it?

"Long Teeth, I do not know how it is that you have this hold over One Who Flies, but I implore you: Let him go. Let him come home with us. We have great need of him."

Long Teeth shook his head. "Not a chance, *ma chère*. Your One Who Flies and I, we have a . . . a business arrangement."

And "business," to Long Teeth, meant digging for gold or cheating others out of it. She looked at One Who Flies, but his gaze retained a detachment, as if he watched them from a distance. He was not, she realized, a participant in this discussion. He was only a bystander, either unable or unwilling to take part in his own destiny.

As you wish, she said to herself. Then I will deal with this man in my own way. I will make him *want* to help us.

She turned back to Long Teeth.

"You will let him go," she said, "because I give you no choice."

He laughed at this. "And just how do you intend to do that?"

She indicated herself and Mouse Road. "We will not leave without him. We will not leave you alone with him. We will stay by you both, as close as we can, wherever you go. In every town, we will follow you." She showed him the baby in her cradleboard. "We will tell everyone how you murdered my husband, of how you raped us both, and of how you now have abandoned your own child."

Long Teeth sputtered with laughter. "That's not true," he said, glancing at the gathered *vé'hó'e*, wondering if any of them understood the Trader's Tongue.

"I do not care if it is true or not," she said. "We will say that it is, and if they do not believe us, we will tell

every man of your thieving and your lies, which *is* true.
And when you head north into Alliance lands, we will
alert every tribe of your presence." She laughed at the
growing look of suffering on Long Teeth's face. "You will
not get what you want." She turned and, taking Mouse
Road by the hand, walked back toward the whistlers.

"Tabarnaque," Long Teeth said beneath his breath.
"What in the Devil's name is so all-fired important that
you need this poor boy so badly?"

She reached under her whistler's jaw and scritched its
neck. The whistler half-closed its eyes and breathed a
large sigh.

"We need him to speak with the Iron Shirts again," she
said plainly. "We intend to forge an alliance with Spain."

Long Teeth gaped at her, struck mute by her statement. He looked at the men around him, staring blindly
at first, but soon Speaks while Leaving saw the ideas
begin to bloom in his mind. He looked at her, then at
One Who Flies, then at her again.

"An alliance? Directly with Spain?" he asked.

"Yes," she said. "With the help of the Iron Shirts, we
can pay the Horse Nations to leave us alone. We were
very close to an agreement before, but . . ." She swallowed against the memory of how the talks had broken down.

"I heard," Long Teeth said. "It was in the papers,
even out here. I was sorry to learn of Three Trees
Together."

"My fault," One Who Flies said from deep within his
daze, but the words awakened his mind, and his gaze
came back to the present. His brow contracted in remembered grief and his lips twisted into a sorrowful
curve. "All my fault," he said.

"And if it is?" Speaks while Leaving asked him. "Are
you going to stay here and drink yourself to death?"

"Yes!" he shouted, suddenly animate. He pushed his
way through the gathered onlookers and stood before
her, fuming, his breath surging through flared nostrils.
"If I choose to, I'll stay here. I'm finished with your
visions and your Thunder Beings. I'm through with all
of it. Why can't you leave me alone?"

Speaks while Leaving pointed to Mouse Road who

stood nearby, not understanding the Trader's Tongue that they spoke, but comprehending every look of grief and anger in her beloved's eyes. "Do you want her to leave you alone?"

One Who Flies turned away from Mouse Road. "She's the one who turned me away, not the reverse."

Speaks while Leaving switched to the language of the People so that Mouse Road could understand. "And do you think she would be here if she still felt that way?"

Shyly, almost fearfully, he glanced over at Mouse Road whose broad cheeks were wet with tears that shone in the evening light. She clasped her hands together before her breast, each holding the other back.

"Please," Mouse Road said. "Please come back to us. Come back to me."

Long Teeth cleared his throat and Speaks while Leaving turned her attention to the trader once more. "What about me?" he asked.

Speaks while Leaving sneered. "Why should I care about you?"

"Because you still need me," he said. "Two Injun women and a penniless sot? How do you think you'll be able to contact your Spanish friends without my help?" He waved a hand at the *vé'hó'e* who stood nearby. "Do you expect one of these fellows to help you? No, you need me. You need my wit and you need my coin."

Speaks while Leaving considered it. Some of the *vé'hó'e* had wandered off, no longer interested in the confrontation on the porch steps. The windows and doorways along the road, too, had emptied, now that the excitement seemed to be over. Only a few of the *vé'hó'e* remained, and they were the ones who had first come out the door, ready to attack them. She saw the Cut-Hair man regarding her from his seat on the wooden step.

"What do you think?" she asked him.

The Cut-Hair man nodded. "Take the scrawny white one with you," he said. "You've used up all your luck getting this far. You'll need some of his to get where you're going."

"Why should I trust you, Long Teeth? Why do you want to be involved in this?"

The *vé'ho'e* trader grinned and raised his eyebrows

twice. "Well, *ma chère,* the way I see it, there's a great deal of profit to be made in such an alliance. And if I'm working *with* you, the chances of my waking up with an arrow in my back are just that much smaller."

"Smaller, but not impossible," Speaks while Leaving said, and was rewarded by both a frown from the trader and a smile from One Who Flies. "It is agreed, then. Now, I want to speak with the ambassador from the Iron Shirts. He lives in the City of White Stone. What do you suggest? How shall we get there?"

Long Teeth's smile returned. He bowed to her and with a zealous sweep of his hand, pointed them down the road toward the far edge of the small town. There, she saw a tiny building, low and square, from which rose a tall pole crossed with a bar at the top. It reminded her of the icons the *vé'hó'e* often wore about their necks, symbols of their god who had died and lived again.

Strung from the crosspiece at the top of the pole was a wire, and the wire stretched away to another pole, and thence to yet another pole. Stepping farther into the middle of the road, she saw a long line of poles reaching eastward, the wire hanging between each in graceful arcs that shortened with distance until they disappeared over the curve of the land.

"What is that?" she asked the trader.

"That, *ma chère,* is a telegraph, and with it and a bit of silver, we can send a message from here to your man in Washington."

Speaks while Leaving had heard of this thing. Wire-that-talks was the name some had given it, and she had heard of how Alliance soldiers destroyed them to keep the bluecoats from sending information to the City of White Stone. Never had she thought that she would be using such a thing herself. She turned to One Who Flies.

"This is true?" she asked him. "We can use the wire-that-talks to contact Speaks for the Iron Shirts?"

One Who Flies closed his eyes and sighed. "It is true," he said. "It will take some doing to get a message from here to Alejandro, but it is possible."

"Good," she said, and signed to Mouse Road: *All is well.*

Mouse Road grinned. It was all she needed to know.

They went to the telegraph shack where One Who
Flies translated her words, composing a message for the
Iron Shirt ambassador, Alejandro Silveira. He wrote of
her wish to reopen discussions and of how the People
had not given up hope of an alliance. The sun was setting when the operator put a hand to his key. Speaks
while Leaving watched, fascinated, as the little man
turned a whirring crank and began to tap on his device.
She imagined the words, her lips forming their sounds,
whispering them into the shiny brass lever that tapped
with its odd rhythms; words of magic leapt from her
mouth into the wire, running up to the pole, racing along
the lines that glowed overhead like curved bows made
of red sunfire. She gazed off across the distant hills, her
sight keeping pace with her speeding thoughts, until behind her the sun dipped its fiery head below the earth's
rim, and the telegraph lines disappeared in the growing
night.

They spent the night beyond the edge of town, their
whistlers far away and downwind from the *vé'ho'e*
horses. She had insisted that One Who Flies stay with
them, and not with Long Teeth in the *vé'ho'e* town. They
ate a simple meal of boiled roots and dried meat, and
settled in around the tiny fire. One Who Flies said nothing on his own and answered few questions, retiring soon
after the meal was finished. It wasn't until the moon rose
that he began to shake.

Mouse Road woke and went to him, cradling him in
her arms. "What is wrong with him?" she asked, her
worry growing toward panic.

"Hush," Speaks while Leaving said, rising up on an
elbow. "It will be all right." Beneath the covers, Blue
Shell Woman fussed and Speaks while Leaving lay back
down and pulled her baby close to her breast. She felt
the baby's little mouth seeking the nipple, felt her moist
questing along the curve of her breast, and heard her
whimpers turn to happy grunts as she found her way
home and began to suckle. Warmth spread through her
as her daughter fed, a tingling sensation that relaxed
her entire length. Her baby contented, she turned her
attention back to her sister-in-law.

"This is normal," she told Mouse Road. "I have seen it many times among our own people. He must separate himself from the poison he has been drinking. It is why I insisted he stay with us."

Mouse Road looked down at the man in her arms. He was curled up like a wounded dog, and shook as if he had been brought in off the winter prairie. His entire body shuddered—hands, arms, legs, head, even his chest writhed with shivered breaths—and his eyes flickered from bleariness to blindness. His lips were taut, pulled back from teeth clenched by a jaw locked in spasm, and his skin—pallid as the moon itself—shone with sweat, beads reflecting starlight from above.

He moaned. "Stop him," he said. "Stop him."

Mouse Road looked up.

"He will see things," Speaks while Leaving said to her. "He will rave and he will cry out. But you need not worry. It is the poison he fights, not us, and it is a battle we cannot help him fight."

They watched over him, taking turns, first one napping and then the other. Bats flew through the fire's pale dome of light, darting after nighttime insects, while from far away came a nighthawk's sharp call. Closer, the brush around them was alive with the tiny travelings of mice and rabbits, and once Speaks while Leaving saw the glowing orange eyes of a hunting lizard as it inspected their campsite.

It was when Mouse Road lay in exhausted slumber that One Who Flies began once more to thrash and mutter. His eyes were open now, and he raised his arms across his face to protect himself, though his persecutors were only spirits of his imagination. Concerned that he might bolt in his fear, Speaks while Leaving got some strong buffalo hair rope and hobbled him. The constricting bonds did nothing to ease his distress, but it did much to ease hers.

She retreated to her place by the fire and held her daughter close while she watched One Who Flies shiver and twitch beneath the heavy buffalo skins. When his features were not twisted by tremors, they were sunken and lax, like fruit that had lain too long on the ground. Despite her own advice to Mouse Road, she worried about him. Fighting the effects of the water-that-burns was hard enough, but there was much more that she wanted from him. No matter the causes of his current condition, her needs for the future would be no less demanding, and no less free from peril. Bringing together two such ancient enemies as the People and the Iron Shirts would not be a simple thing. It would require a strength that she only hoped that they possessed.

Is it right, she wondered, for me to demand this of him? I do not even have the blessing of our own Council. Even my own husband and father do not believe in me. Is it right, then, that I should ask this of One Who Flies?

But the memory of her original vision was strong, and the spirit-sense told her that the images of gold and ships and shields and power had not yet been completed. She thought of the Iron Shirts and of the People, and could not imagine them linked without seeing One Who Flies standing between them. He was a man of both worlds, capable of bringing them together. They did not fit otherwise, except as broken dreams of different ideas.

One Who Flies was the key. If she was to make an alliance with the Iron Shirts, One Who Flies was the man who could help her do it, and as he sweated in the cold night air, she prayed that the earth fill him with its strength, and the sky make his breath come easy. She prayed to the guardians of the world, asking for gifts from the four directions, and hoping that when the time came, they would have what they needed.

The sun rose swollen and red, painting the clouds orange and washing the night out toward the west where it lingered in the hilly horizon. Grass grew green in the morning light, and the stars faded into memory. Mouse Road stretched as the dawn touched her face. She rubbed her eyes and blinked into the morning before she suddenly remembered the night's vigil and sat up to see if her charge was still with them.

One Who Flies lay still, sprawled on his back, twisted slightly from when he had briefly tried to remove the rope from around his ankles. His head thrown back and his mouth agape, his skin was an unhealthy pallor except for his eyelids, which were red and raw looking. Had it not been for the thready pulse that drummed at his throat, Speaks while Leaving would have thought him a corpse.

Mouse Road swallowed and looked over to her sister-in-law. "He is well?"

Speaks while Leaving smiled. "He is better," she said, "but not well. It will be a while before he is well."

Their voices roused him. He blinked and winced at the light of day, then uttered one long and pitiful moan before convulsing once, rolling over, and vomiting a mouthful of thin liquid onto the ground.

Speaks while Leaving saw Mouse Road's grimace of disgust and decided not to chide her for it. Much as though they both might care for this man, he was in a repulsive state.

"Go get some water," she said. "I will see to his needs."

Mouse Road bundled up the empty waterskins and went off toward the creek. By the time she returned, One Who Flies had been wiped clean and made to sit up, though he still only squinted out at the world around him.

"What did you do to me?" he asked.

Speaks while Leaving laughed. "Nothing," she said. "And neither did you, for once."

He lifted a trembling hand to his brow. "I feel awful. Do you have anything to drink?"

Mouse Road offered him one of the waterskins but he waved it off.

"To drink!" he said, too loudly for his own head to endure. He moaned again and held his head in his hands.

"No," Speaks while Leaving told him. "We have nothing but water to drink, and water will be good enough. I need you healthy and with your mind sharp."

"Why?"

In answer, she pointed off toward the town. One Who Flies looked that way.

Long Teeth was trotting toward them. He saw them and waved a piece of paper over his head.

"An answer!" the trader shouted as he neared the camp. "We have an answer!"

"Do you remember?" she asked One Who Flies.

"Of course I remember," he said, glaring at her.

Long Teeth slowed as he reached them, his lungs sucking in the crystal air and pushing it out in misted clouds. He stopped next to One Who Flies and, leaning over, rested with his hands on his knees. He waved the piece of paper. "An answer," he said again.

Irritated, One Who Flies snatched the paper from him and read it. "Oh, no," he said. "I don't believe it."

"What does it say?" Speaks while Leaving asked.

"It says," Long Teeth managed between gasps, "that your Spanish friend welcomes your continued interest in an alliance. He will arrange for a meeting in Cuba, where the matter can be discussed at greater length."

Speaks while Leaving felt her heartbeat quicken. "Cuba," she said, thinking of the trip One Who Flies had taken to the City of White Stone. "That is an island, isn't it?"

"Yes," One Who Flies said. "Did you think he was going to come to you?"

Unknowingly, until that very moment, Speaks while Leaving had to admit that she did. She looked down at her daughter, swaddled in her cradleboard. Blue Shell Woman's eyes were large in her infant face, dark, round orbs above shiny round cheeks.

Where am I taking you? she asked silently. But to turn home now, what will we have accomplished?

The baby gazed up at her, searching for her mother's instruction. Speaks while Leaving saw the question in her daughter's eyes. How should I feel, Mother? Tell me how to feel.

Speaks while Leaving smiled at her daughter and waggled a finger closer and closer until she touched the baby's nose. Blue Shell Woman laughed with a burbly sound, and her eyes turned up into crescents of comfortable joy, her every question answered.

CHAPTER 12

Spring Moon, Waxing
Fifty-seven Years after the Star Fell
Between the Big Greasy and Lodgepole
River
Alliance Territory

Storm Arriving lay in the green grass. The sun was a happy warmth from above, heating his hair and shoulders, and the grass around him danced side to side with the rhythm of the western breeze. He smelled the moist earth and the saltiness of his own sweat. They had been a long time on the trail, working their way to the south and east, testing the edges of the bluecoats' strength, seeking its source. There had been no time for amenities, no time for comforts during their small campaign. There had been time only for riding, fighting, and more riding.

But today, yes, he told himself. Today might be different.

Beside him, also lying flat in the wind-blown grass were Sharp Knife, Knee Prints by the Bank, and Whistling Elk. A bowshot behind them down the almost imperceptible grade, were the rest of the soldiers of their raiding party; a total of thirty-two soldiers armed with rifle and bow, lance and knife. They kept the whistlers quiet and low to the ground, for today surprise was their best ally.

Storm Arriving tilted his head to the side and raised it up so that with one eye he could see over the waves of green. Ahead, the grass-clad land sped away and ever-so-slightly downward, leaving him and his three companions on the only thing akin to a high point for several miles. The land here within reach of the Lodgepole River was nearly flat, evened out by a thousand seasons of rain and flood. The bluecoats who traveled toward them across the spongy mat of little bluestem raised no dust, leaving only dark slashes where their wagon wheels cut like knives into the earth.

Five wagons rocked and jostled their way across the land, precarious on their tall, spoked wheels. Each was pulled by a team of mules that were head-down and set in their labor. Two men rode on each of the high buckboards, one with the reins and one with a rifle, eyes sharpened toward the horizon. Atop the wagonbeds were piles of supplies hidden by oilskin tarpaulins, but the outlined shapes told of barrels, kegs, sacks, crates, and boxes that lay under the dark, shiny canvases.

This was their goal; a train of goods bound for the bluecoat encampment some twenty miles distant. Finding it had not been easy, and getting to it would be harder still, for along with the wagons was their escort, bluecoats on horses and more marching alongside.

"I count twenty on mounts," Sharp Knife said, peering through the grass.

"And at least that many on foot," Whistling Elk said.

Storm Arriving counted for himself. Two quartets of bluecoats ranged a quarter mile or more ahead of the wagons, and with each group was a scout on foot dressed in a mix of tribal and *vé'ho'e* clothes. Back behind the wagons rode twelve more riders, and two chief-riders led the train. On the near side of the wagons marched a double-line of bluecoats, five to a line, and since the bluecoats never did anything unevenly, it was safe to assume the same number on the far side. Add to that the men on the wagons, and you had thirty bluecoats on foot, twenty-two on horse. A good bit more than the thirty-two Storm Arriving had in his own party. In recent years, One Who Flies had shown them some new methods of fighting, but Storm Arriving could not apply them to this situation with small numbers and open land.

He looked again at the men with the bluecoats in the fore.

"What tribe are those who scout for them?" he asked.

Knee Prints by the Bank grunted. "I am sorry to say it, but they are of my tribe. It is hard for the Wolf People in *vé'ho'e* lands. Some find it easier to work for the bluecoats than to raise crops."

"We can try to spare them," he said. "Once it starts, call to them if you can." He crawled backward away from the low rise. The others followed.

The rest of the soldiers sat close by their whistlers. As Storm Arriving crept back to them, he saw their eager smiles and ready hands. Unhappy with waiting, they were glad that action was near.

"The bluecoats ride westward," Storm Arriving told them. "The wagons are still a few miles away, but they will pass close to our position. I want four men to stay here with the whistlers. Four others will prepare to ride after stragglers. The rest of us will make a line along that rise of land and lay hidden in the grass. When the bluecoats are close enough, we will fire on them. With luck, we will take them down before they can reach us."

The soldiers looked at one another, brows knitted with puzzlement.

"What do you mean?" asked one of them. "When do we charge against them?"

"We do not," Storm Arriving said. "We fire from the grass."

Sharp Knife chuckled. "He means we fire from the grass before we charge."

"No," Storm Arriving said, emphasizing his words with signs. "We do not charge at all. Not at all. We only fire from the grass."

The soldiers were bewildered. Storm Arriving could see it in the way they looked at one another.

"I will not do it," Stone Wolf said. "What kind of honor is in this? To fire from the grass, like a coward, like a woman. I will not do it."

"Nor I," said Whistling Elk. "What coup can we count from the grass? To kill from a distance is no honor. We must ride to them."

"The bluecoats outnumber us," Storm Arriving said.

Whistling Elk pressed his case. "Storm Arriving, please. It has been a moon since we left the Crow People, and in that time we have fought no great battles and won no glories. Now is our chance." He smiled with an infectious excitement. "This is the sort of day of which songs are made. This is a day for bravery. You have worked hard for us, carefully bringing us here. We all know this, and we all are grateful to you. Now let us repay you with a victory that will make your heart sing! Let us make our marks on the bluecoats, so that we can ride home with tales that will fill our sweethearts with joy."

Storm Arriving could feel the urge. Just at the thought of it, his own blood pounded in his ears, surging, ready, pumping into limbs. To ride in toward danger was to feel the power of life. He had known it, had felt it before. His arms, his chest, they bore the scars of lance and arrow, and his soul had touched the limits of heaven when his existence had run on the silvered edge of a knife's blade. He had known it, and he heard its song now. He saw its promise in Whistling Elk's smile, in the way Red Whistler gripped his knife. They had all known it, and it was all they had known. It was now. It was here.

And that was its danger.

"No," he said to them. "Those days are gone, I tell you. They are over. We fight an enemy that is cunning and dangerous."

"All the more glory to take him down!" Whistling Elk said.

"And the greater cost if you fall!" Storm Arriving said in return. He calmed himself with a quiet breath. "Understand me. The time of a single soldier is gone. The time of *your* honor and *my* honor is gone. Today, we must speak of *our* honor."

The soldiers all spoke at once. Several grabbed their weapons and went to their whistlers, ready to ride.

"This will be a great battle," Stone Wolf said as he mounted.

"I want my share of the glory!" said another, running to join him.

"Hold, hold!" Storm Arriving ordered. "Listen! This fight will last longer than just today. It will last for today and tomorrow and a moon of moons before we are done. It is a *war*. A *war*! It is not a war that you can win or that I can win, but it is a war that we can win together. *Together*. But to do that, I need you whole, I need you now, and I need you until the end." He looked at them all and sent a silent prayer to the spirits of the world.

"When we are done and the bluecoats have all gone home, you can ride to whatever glorious end you want, but right now I need you alive and fighting together!"

They held, listening to his pleas.

"We will share a song," he said. "Brothers, they will sing of us all."

He could see it in their eyes. They were there. They saw it. They saw the greater need and how a battle won together could be an achievement greater than anything they achieved alone. Stone Wolf dismounted. Whistling Elk gripped his rifle.

"We shoot from the grass," Whistling Elk said with a smile. "And together, we leave not a one of them standing."

An easy breath filled Storm Arriving's breast, but the sound of approaching hoofbeats drove it out again. Unthinking, they had let their argument destroy their cover, and the bluecoats now rode up the slope, rifles raised.

"Crouch down!" Storm Arriving yelled as he dove to the grass. "Let the whistlers free!"

Some of the soldiers did as he ordered, but others shouted their denial. With whoops and war cries, they leapt onto their whistlers just as the bluecoats came within easy range. The air was wild with the crack of gunfire, the shouting of men, the bleating of beasts. Dirt flew as whistlers leapt into motion and as horses' hooves churned the earth. The riders rode onto Storm Arriving and the men in the grass. One horse trampled across a soldier, hooves snapping his bones and ribs before it lost its own footing and pitched forward, tossing its bluecoat headlong into the grass. Storm Arriving racked his rifle's lever and fired at the bluecoats as they passed. His shot was wide of the mark. Another rank rode toward them but the horses were fearful of uneven ground, and their riders drove them ahead, toward those on whistlerback.

Storm Arriving made a quick assessment. With him were a dozen or so men plus a handful that had been killed or wounded by trampling.

The bluecoat riders had broken into groups and were pursuing the soldiers on their whistlers. The mounted soldiers, despite their near-conversion to Storm Arriving's ideas, now reverted to old patterns, the hot blood of war driving them to reckless feats. One rider kicked his whistler into a spurt of speed. A bowshot ahead of his pursuers, he heeled in, turned, and yipped at them like a coyote. They fired at him as he charged; they missed the first time, but not the second.

"Our riders will not last long," Storm Arriving said to those near him. He looked back toward the train. The drivers were pulling the wagons into a tight circle at the direction of the two bluecoats on horses. Other bluecoats stood nearby, watching the horsemen chase the riders, rifles ready, feet edging backward. Storm Arriving worked his lever again. "Long Blade, take the rider with the large hat, I will take the other. The rest of you, get the men on foot. We fire our first shot together. Then take the rest as quickly as you can."

He gave them a moment to set their elbows into the earth, take aim, and calm their breath. "Now!"

Their volley sent up a wall of white smoke but through it, he saw men die. One of the bluecoats on horseback tumbled to the ground and others buckled and fell. The surviving commander pointed up at their position and the remaining bluecoats moved quickly in a precision that spoke of long training. They began to form their ranks just as Storm Arriving and his men let loose a second round. More men fell. Horses screamed. The man on the horse bellowed at his bluecoats, but a third round of fire blew him backward and sent his horse bolting for the horizon.

The bluecoats broke ranks and retreated, joining with the drivers behind the wagons. Storm Arriving sucked air through teeth clenched with frustration. The bluecoats could hide in there for hours, fighting them off from every direction.

"Behind us!"

Bluecoat horsemen were bearing down on them, charging with carbines aimed. Storm Arriving fired a quick shot at the man pounding toward him, then rose up and grabbed the rifle by its barrel, ready to swing it like a club. The barrel seared a hot line along his palms and he snarled but kept his grip. The bluecoat's shot buzzed past his head and Storm Arriving swung upward, catching the bluecoat across the shoulder. The man gave a painful shout but kept his seat and rode past. Grimacing at burned hands, Storm Arriving turned his weapon, pulled another round into readiness, aimed, and fired at the bluecoat's back. More riders were heading their way.

"Half forward, half back!" he shouted, and the soldiers split their aim, firing from a nexus of strength toward their attackers. The bluecoats, counting on their charge to scatter their foe, were undone by the quick efficiency of Storm Arriving and his soldiers. The riders went down in two volleys and the soldiers ran in to finish off those whose horses had been the only casualty. Knife met flesh. The scents of blood and gunsmoke lingered in the playful breeze. Clubs and hatchets rose and fell with quiet efficiency. Agony was cut short.

The field was strewn with bodies—soldiers, bluecoats, whistlers, horses—each in its sunken bed of bent grass. A quick count told Storm Arriving of half his men killed, as well as most of the bluecoats. Of his own, death had found all who had ridden off, as well as two of those who had followed his commands—one by trampling and another by gunshot. The survivors lay beside him on the limit of the small rise, frantic fingers pushing new cartridges into magazines emptied in the fight.

The bluecoats, though, had fared far worse: all their riders were down including the two commanders, and half of the infantrymen were down as well. But that left at least ten or fifteen now ensconced within the wagons' circle, and they would be hard to root out.

"Where are the scouts?" Storm Arriving asked.

They looked toward the wagons. Whistling Elk pointed. "They are there," he said. "On the western side."

Storm Arriving saw them, leaning against the wheel of a wagon situated behind the main defensive line. The two men huddled together, their eyes glancing from within to outside the circle, unsure of which side presented the greater threat.

"Call to them," he told Knee Prints by the Bank. "In your own language. Tell them that we will try not to kill them."

Knee Prints by the Bank did so, using the language of

the Wolf People, lying in the grass and shouting through cupped palms.

The two scouts at the wagons looked their way in sudden interest at hearing familiar words. Storm Arriving did not speak their language, but it was similar enough to the Ree of the Earth Lodge Builders that he could keep track of what was being said. Knee Prints by the Bank told them that he fought with the People, and that if they chose, they, too, could work with the People against the *vé'hó'e*. Some of the bluecoats shouted back and fired at them, their bullets buzzing through the grass like angry hornets, but it was the two scouts that Storm Arriving watched. They looked first at the bluecoats and then at the soldiers in the grass, caught between the warring sides.

The bluecoats took up positions near wheels and axles, and pulled down crates behind which to hide. They were well protected, but only from one direction. Sneaking around them was impossible: the land was too open. The bluecoats would spot them and bring them down with ease. Storm Arriving looked again at the two scouts in their hiding place beneath the far wagon. Each man held a rifle.

Will they? he wondered. If I give them the chance, will they help?

"How many do you think we can take down with the first shot?" he asked his soldiers.

"Four," said one.

"Six," said another.

"What are you planning?" Whistling Elk asked.

Storm Arriving pointed to the scouts. "If we can get six before they duck back behind their barricades, maybe those two can get the rest."

Whistling Elk grunted in quiet wonder. "And if they don't?"

Storm Arriving shrugged. "Then we still have six less to deal with."

Whistling Elk grinned. "Take aim," he said to the others. "Fire on the word, and then fire as you will."

The men lay against the earth, barrels trained to their targets, eyes squinting through sights, aiming high to ac-

count for distance and the gentle slope, aiming right to
allow for the breeze that danced from west to east. They
were sixteen, several to a target. Some would succeed.
Some would aim true.

Storm Arriving prayed to the spirits: Let it be enough.
"Now."

A wall of smoke pushed down the grass. Bluecoats
kicked and sprawled as bullets slammed into their positions. The soldiers fired calmly but quickly now, sending
each rifle's ten shots into wheels, boxes, wagon sides.
Wood splintered. Metal sang as lead bounced from iron.
A mule caught a shard in the hind quarter and hawed
and kicked, creating a circle of chaos. Bluecoats scrambled, seeking haven, but no place was worse, no place
was better. They returned fire, but to no effect. The onslaught gave them no quarter.

Storm Arriving watched the two scouts. They lay there
in a bubble of safety.

"Do it," he urged them as he fired at a bluecoat's
foot. "Do it."

The two scouts looked at one another, and then raised
their weapons. They aimed at the backs of the bluecoats
before them. Eight quick shots and all fell quiet. Storm
Arriving and his soldiers had emptied their magazines.
The scouts had nothing else to shoot. One of the scouts
stood and looked their way. He raised his rifle above his
head and gave a cry of victory. The soldiers stood as
well, rising up from the grass, shouting their response.

Sharp Knife grabbed Storm Arriving in a crushing
bear hug. "You did it!" he shouted.

Storm Arriving grinned with the pleasure of victory,
the thrill of survival against the odds. He beamed at the
men who stood around him. They were all giddy, drunk
with their accomplishment.

"*We* did it," Storm Arriving said. "Together."

They saw to their wounded, and went down to the
wagons. Knee Prints by the Bank spoke to the two
scouts, introducing Storm Arriving and the others.

"We are grateful for your help," Storm Arriving said
to them in the language of the Inviters.

The two men smiled and raised their hands in greeting. "It was good to fight against them," one said. "I am

Bear Wing. And this is my cousin, Sand Crane. Is it true? Can we cross the river and live among your people now?"

One of the soldiers inspecting the wagons yipped in delight. Storm Arriving looked as the soldier raised two rifles above his head. "Many boxes," the soldier said. "And cartridges, too."

"Good," Storm Arriving said. "We will replenish our stocks and send the rest north to the Crow People, as we promised."

"And?" pressed Bear Wing. "Can we come across the river? Can we bring our families away from the blue-coat lands?"

Storm Arriving bade Bear Wing and his cousin sit. The two scouts did so, settling down on the trampled grass. They were young men, but judged by their tattered clothes and thin faces, they had seen hard times. Knee Prints by the Bank and Whistling Elk sat down with them. Storm Arriving squatted down on the hams of his legs, one knee slightly lower than the other. He rested an elbow on the higher knee, and reached down with his free hand to caress the bent and broken stalks of grass before him.

"We are grateful for the help you gave us," he said to them. "Our losses would have been greater. You saved lives today."

"But this man," the scout said, pointing at Knee Prints by the Bank. "He said he came across the river. He said our tribes have made peace."

"It is true," Storm Arriving said, "and you are welcome in Alliance lands." The two younger men grinned, gripping each other's forearms in excitement.

"There is something I would ask you, first," Storm Arriving continued. He glanced at them briefly, trying to judge these men who less than a hand of time before had been working for the *vé'hó'e*. The two scouts seemed open and genuinely eager at the prospect of moving into the Alliance lands; they did not seem stupid with the *vé'ho'e* drink; they looked neither devious nor suspicious. He glanced also at Knee Prints by the Bank and at Whistling Elk, trying to gauge their estimation of these young men. His two comrades knew nothing of what he intended, but their easiness and lack of concern about the scouts spoke eloquently of their opinions.

"There are others like you?" he asked the scouts. "Others who are working for the bluecoats?"

The cousins signaled with their hands that there were. "Many others," Bear Wing said. "It is better than trying to grow seeds in the land. And against you"—he blushed and hung his head—"I am sorry, but we did not know that your people had become friends with us."

Storm Arriving pushed the concern away with a wave of his hand. "Our two peoples have greater concerns than our ancient grudges. The bluecoats are our concern, and protecting our territory is our concern. I ask you, rather than coming across the river, would you return to the bluecoats?"

Knee Prints by the Bank was startled nearly to his feet. "What is this? After the help they give you, you send them back to the bluecoats?"

Storm Arriving held up a hand. "They can be of help to us still," he said. "If they return to the bluecoats, they can find others who might also help us. They can send us riders and information. They can tell where the bluecoats are and where they are going. They can be our eyes from inside."

"And what of their families?" Knee Prints by the Bank asked. "Shall they stay in bluecoat lands as well?"

With a flip of his hand, he denied it. "Tell your families to come to us. From what my friend here has told me, your tribe is scattered and lost. Tell your families to come to us. They will be a part of the Alliance. And so will you, whether you return to work among the bluecoats or not. That is all I have to say." He stood. The others stood, too. He turned and walked away. There were dead men to shroud for the trip home.

At evening, as they were packing up the goods for the trip north and as patrols were calling in the last straggling whistlers, Storm Arriving looked over the field.

The sun had fallen toward the place where storms were born and was about to dip below the westernmost clouds. The sky had turned blue and grey and the clouds themselves were solid and heavy. At any moment, he imagined the Thunder Beings might release their hold

on the clouds and let them fall down upon his head, just
as they had brought down the cloud that One Who Flies
had ridden. It would be a fitting end, for he had given
the Thunder Beings and the powers of the world no
respect in recent days, had called upon them only in
times of trial, and had never thanked them for the things
that made his world so precious.

But as he looked upon the cloth-wrapped bodies of
his friends, waiting to be taken home, he did not know
if he *could* give thanks. This battle had seen the death
of fifty bluecoats, and had gained the People two hundred rifles, kegs of ammunition, crates of food, and
boxes of supplies. It was a great victory, and would help
cement their newborn alliance with the Crow People.
That victory, though, had come at a cost. It had cost the
lives of sixteen men—half his strength—and it had cost
them more than soldiers, too.

It had cost them tradition.

The bodies, wrapped in their white *vé'ho'e* cloth,
seemed to burn as the sun dipped its orange head beneath the clouds. The shrouds glowed with the sunset
light, bright and brash against the dark prairie grass. Sixteen men. Men who had died seeking glory, seeking
honor. Too many men.

He could not afford such losses—this he knew
absolutely—but it was possible, as he looked at those
who remained, as they walked about their duties, loaded
goods on whistlerback, tended to the wounded, and
cooked some *vé'ho'e* food over a small fire, he knew it
was possible that these men still left to him had been
changed by the day. These men might have seen what
it was he was trying to accomplish. These men might see
the difference.

If they did not, there was no hope for them at all.

He turned at a sound and saw Bear Wing and Sand
Crane, the two scouts. "We have been talking with some
of the others, and we wanted to tell you," Bear Wing
said. "We will send our families to you, but we will return to the bluecoats. We will help you from within the
bluecoats, just as we did today."

A calm descended upon him, filling him with lightness.
He reached out and put a hand on each scout's shoulder.

The sun, bloated and wavering, flattened itself and rolled off the edge of the world.

"This is good," he said to them. "Come, let us eat."

And when he ate, he made sure to put some to the side of the campfire, in thanks to the spirits that ruled the world.

CHAPTER 13

Thursday, May 1, A.D. 1890
Palacio de Gubernior
La Ciudad de la Habana, Cuba

The eager sun grew bright behind the slate-dark sea and began to push clouds aside with rosy hands. Alejandro leaned against the iron railing that girded the shallow balcony of his rooms at the governor's mansion.

The plaza below, with its central fountain, shimmered with the coming dawn—the whitewashed stones pale, the street-worn cobbles shiny with dew. The tall, unnatural palms rustled their tough fronds and Alejandro smelled the tidal breeze. Salt, he smelled, and seaweed, too, from the rocks that lined the channel a few blocks away and from the encrusted hulls of the itinerant fishing boats that were piled up along the channel walls like driftwood.

Across the channel, the shore rose steep and dark, untouched by the rising sun. The far hillside stood high above the piers and shipping cranes, its flanks clad in palms and shadowed greenery, its head topped by the heavy walls of La Castillo Del Cabaña. The masonry ramparts of La Cabaña commanded the vista above the channel, just as its partner, Castillo Del Morro, commanded the channel's entrance. He looked toward El Morro, just now beginning to glow with the crisp light of the growing day.

The Castillo Del Morro sat atop its promontory peak, its walls like an upward extension of the rocks themselves. From within the walls, the lighthouse stood even higher, so that its beacon light might travel the farther, warning those lost, and guiding those bound for home. But the clean lines of El Morro and La Cabaña both hid their main purpose. For centuries, they had been the strength that stood over the quiet, lazy streets of Old Havana, and emplaced atop their walls were guns and rifles and mortars: batteries that could destroy any vessel that challenged them. El Morro and its partners at La Punta, Santa Clara, Reina, and Cohima all worked together to protect the coast and the approach to the harbor, but it was La Cabaña that chilled Alejandro. At all of the other fortifications their artillery faced outward toward the sea and an encroaching enemy, but the guns at La Castillo Del Cabaña pointed inward, toward the channel and the harbor.

And at him.

He tried not to take it to heart, but it bothered him, such weapons pointed in his direction. His doubts about his past actions brought him enough sleepless, moonlit hours, but now, with full knowledge of the games he was fostering, the people he was endangering, and the risks involved, he found the brooding castle's accusatory fingers increasingly unpleasant.

The windowed door behind him opened and Victoria slipped out to join him in the dawn. Her hand curled around his waist as she stole easily under his arm and into his embrace. The thick satin of her quilted dressing gown sighed and he kissed her hair—as soft as her gown—and took a breath of its luscious scent.

"It is early," she said as she regarded the coming morn. "Something bothers you?"

A small, silent laugh escaped him. "Not really," he said.

She sighed. "What then? Do you plan to wait at the window until they arrive?"

He used to be able to keep things from her but recently—since the day of his dismissal—she had been able to read his every move and with an ease that led him to believe that she had always done so. The difference was that now she no longer bothered to hide it.

"They should be arriving today," he said.

"That's not an answer."

"No," he said. "It isn't."

The sun rose above the hills, shining into their faces, and she snuggled closer to him. Alejandro held her tightly, suddenly grateful for her presence and her constancy in the face of their future. Together, they stood there and listened to the awakening of Havana.

From the street came the rustic disharmony of an ox-cart: hooves tapping arhythmically along, wheels gritting on the cobbled stones, and the driver whistling to himself as he headed toward the wharf. Farther off, a flower vendor's selling song echoed down the whitewashed façades of the old buildings. Women emerged from backstairs doorways, baskets in hand, their sandaled feet scuffing toward the greengrocer's or the dairyman's for onions or eggs. Horses burred in irritation as their days commenced, and men groused at their beasts' attitude. Soon would come the wails of the trains, bringing sugar from the distant mills down to the port. The loading cranes would begin to crank, and the bellowed calls of steamships would sound across the calm waters of the inner harbor as tons of molasses and turbinado left Cuba, bound for the markets of America and New Spain.

The cathedral bell hit its low, dolorous note, calling the faithful to matins, and Victoria crossed herself, murmuring a quiet prayer.

Alejandro wished he felt her faith, her belief in some design greater than the one which men themselves put in motion. In his estimation it was easier for women to believe in such a world where the divine mingled with the mundane; bringers of life, creators in their own right, they were closer to that ideal than were men. Men were closer to humanity's savage past, relics of their own bloody history, and Alejandro could convince himself neither of God's eternal presence nor of Man's essential goodness. He considered the future, and how events of his instigation might embroil those near him, even to this provincial island that stood in the middle of the Columbian Gulf like a stone fence separating the United States and Spain. Like the Great Plains of the north, Cuba also bestrode a less literal gulf between nations. War, were it to come to the prairie, would come here as well.

"Is it worth it?" he asked, and Victoria looked up at him in what was now a rare moment of incomprehension.

"Is what worth it?"

"This," he said, taking in the harbor, the castles, and the whole world with a simple sweep of his hand. "Is what I intend worth risking this?"

She turned under his arm and faced him, still holding him tightly. He looked down into her face as she looked up to study his. Her eyes were so dark, so impossibly deep, and her lips, pursed now in concentration, so enticing. Even the lines that had crept along the corners of her eyes and the creases of her mouth did not detract from her beauty. She was still the woman he had married, but was also so much more.

"Tell me what you risk," she said.

"You," he said. She dismissed the thought with a sound but he persisted. "You and Isabella," he said. "Your future. *Our* future. And Roberto and Olivia, who were good enough to allow us to come here."

"What about them? Olivia is my sister. Of course we could come here."

He did not want to make her peevish and so tried to explain the thoughts that rambled in his head. "My dear, Olivia may be your sister, but Roberto is governor of this province. I have put him in an awkward situation; if he supports my plans, he is at odds with our viceroy."

She huffed and took her arms from around his waist. Hands on hips she looked up at him. "He is my brother-in-law, Alejandro. What kind of world is it becoming when a woman cannot visit with her own sister and brother-in-law?" Slyly, a tiny smile laced the limits of her mouth.

Alejandro nodded and sighed. He put an arm around her shoulder and turned back to the vista of the plaza, the fountain, the whitewashed buildings, the cobbled streets, and the harbor sparkling with newborn light.

"Very well, my dear," he said, resigned. "A visit with your sister. That is a fine enough fiction for now, but what about when the ship arrives? Roberto has been so helpful. I hate to bring him more trouble. He has enough already with the rebels that attack his rails and his mills."

"Roberto will take care of Roberto," she said. "He is clever enough to avoid trouble, and faithful enough to keep secrets. My sister would not have married him otherwise." She patted her husband's belly. "But enough of politics. Let us prepare for breakfast. If the ship is to arrive today, I want you to have something on your stomach first."

They turned and went inside to dress.

From the outside, the governor's palace was a rather low, two-story building of uninspired architecture. Without the fountain and tended gardens of the plaza that graced its entrance, it could easily have passed as a group of apartments, the home of an old family, or perhaps even a brokerage house. Its stucco walls and simple entrance arches were unremarkable in almost every aspect. It had no carriageway, no towers, no courtyard, no corbels, no oriels, no grand doorway, no soaring gables, and no visual interest other than three small triangles of brick and tile along the front façade, the centermost of which was topped by the flagpole and the black, yellow, and red colors of the Kingdom of Spain. A squat square of yellowed whitewash and faded terra-cotta, it was the most unimposing seat of power Alejandro had ever known.

On the inside, however, it was indeed a palace, packed with the accumulated wealth of the Spanish Empire. A long line of lords, mayors, governors, generals, and princes had called this place home and each had brought within its walls their portion of the gold, silver, sugar, rum, fabrics, ores, and timber that passed through the arms of Havana's gentle harbor. As Alejandro descended the staircase, his feet trod on the filigree patterns of Persia, his hand caressed the satiny banister of dark, Philippine teakwood, and above and around him was a vast fortune in gold leaf, carved wood, painted oils, glazed ceramic, sculpted marble, and forged bronze. At his side, Victoria relished their surroundings, unabashed at the opulence. Every station, every nook,

every wall was adorned with an artisan's craft or an art-
ist's work. From the woven carpets to the high ceilings,
it was a jumbled banquet of talents that could not fail
to impress.

They walked into the dining hall and found their hosts
already at table. Victoria went to Olivia's side and kissed
her elder sister's cheek. Alejandro noted again the remarkable similarity of the two women—but for Olivia's
silvered hair, she was nearly identical to her younger
sibling.

"Where is my niece?" Olivia asked.

"Still abed. You know," she said and placed a hand
on her stomach.

"Ah," Olivia said knowingly.

Roberto had risen when Victoria entered, and now he
turned to Alejandro to escape the veiled discussion of
feminine woes. He extended his hand. "Good morning,"
he said in his usual brusque manner. "Slept well?"

Victoria glanced in their direction, a reminder in her
look.

"Yes," Alejandro lied, keeping his restlessness to himself. "Quite well. And how are you today?"

"Well enough. Well enough," Roberto said. He gestured toward the sideboard with its platters and urns.
"Help yourself. There's plenty. Antonia cooks for a
regiment."

Olivia insisted that her household breakfast in the
fashion of the unassisted buffet rather than with a served
meal. She cited as her reason that it was more efficient,
giving the servants more time to see to other morning
duties rather than dishing up for those capable of ladling
their own meal. Looking at the spread of foods before
him, though, Alejandro questioned Olivia's logic. Rolls,
muffins, and corn breads were piled high alongside bowls
of fresh and dried fruit, and platters of cured meats and
steaming sausages. There were eggs in three varieties,
sardines in oil, gruel of both corn and barley, and sweet
rice pudding. With this and more besides, Alejandro
doubted that the staff would have an easier time of it.
But it was Olivia's house, and Olivia's domain, and the
last thing Alejandro intended was to challenge her in
her own home.

"The rebels," Roberto started as he returned to the table. "At it again. Last night. The Chavez sugar mill near Luyano. Killed a guard and set a fire."

Alejandro looked over at his wife, but it was Olivia who spoke first.

"Not at breakfast, Roberto," she said. "You two will have hours to discuss your rebels and your mills and your strategies, but later, please. Later."

Roberto shrugged and subsided, and Alejandro turned back to the sideboard to compile his breakfast meal, but everything before him brought to mind the situation their wives had asked him to ignore. The fish reminded him of the harbor only blocks away, and the orange juice and the poached eggs wrapped in paper-thin slices of country ham reminded him of the valleys of California where the viceroy's estates lay green and fertile. The silvered urn dispensed its black stream of coffee, reminding him of the hillside orchards where the rebels hid, as the sugar with which he sweetened it reminded him of the coastal fields tall with sugarcane and of American businessmen who poured their money into the island's economy, eager to reap Cuba's riches.

As he sat down at table, he spread on his toast the taste of the Spanish sun captured by marmalade served in a crystal dish, and when Olivia asked if the weather was too warm for him, he could think of nothing but the coming ship and the passengers that were so important to his plans.

He stammered his way through the meal, ending his sentences abruptly or remaining awkwardly silent, unable to navigate the banalities without seeing the undercurrents of politics beneath them. Finally, his meal hardly touched and his stomach in an uproar, he stood and threw his napkin down on the table.

"That is enough," he said.

The others stared at him and his rudeness.

"I am sorry, Roberto, Olivia, for the difficulty I have brought upon your house, but I *must* be allowed to speak my mind."

Roberto, stalled in mid-chew, swallowed his mouthful, and motioned with his hand. "Of course. Speak on."

Unsettled, Alejandro took a breath. Several thoughts

presented themselves, but none encapsulated what it was he wanted to say. At last, unable to come to anything else, he sat and said, "Would you please pass the marmalade?"

Roberto blinked, then reached for the glass dish and passed it along to him. "Anything else?" he asked.

Alejandro sniffed, his knife making small scratching sounds on the toasted bread. "Yes," he said, and looked at Olivia. "The eggs wrapped in ham, they are uncommonly good."

Olivia glanced over to her sister. "Thank you, Alejandro. I shall tell Antonia you said so."

Freed from his proscription, Alejandro took to his meal with gusto. "And the coffee! Wonderful. Dark and rich. Is it local?"

The others stared at him as if he were mad, but he didn't care. He ate and drank and spoke every commonplace thought that crossed his mind, uncaring of the political references they conjured. Soon, the atmosphere returned to normal, and all was well until a serving-man entered the room and walked to Alejandro's side.

"Excuse me, sir," he whispered, "but the ship you have been awaiting? It has just been sighted off La Punta."

Within minutes, Alejandro was on his way. The carriage he had made sure was standing ready took him down Mercaderes toward the wharves. The hood had been drawn back, and he rode in the open air. The weather was warm already, but the breeze had shifted to the northwest, bringing with it the water's cooling effect. They passed by the caliginous peasant fleet with its tattered and patched collection of sails. At the sunlit Plaza Vieja a de Cristina they turned right and came around the Bank of San Francisco where Alejandro could see the piers where the larger ships put in to port. The driver reined in alongside the railing and the steps that descended from the street to the docks.

"Wait here," Alejandro told him, and walked quickly down the stairs to the long boardwalk.

He spied the ship making its way inward from the channel. Even at a hundred feet long, the combination sail-and-steam vessel was dwarfed by the large ocean-worthy steamers that slept at anchor and at dock in the inner harbor. From the small ship's bridge, it would have been impossible to see over the deck planks of the taller ships and for a moment Alejandro wondered if it was the right ship at all. But as it nimbly wove a path around a four-masted giant and steered toward the docks, the name *Santa Cecilia* sparkled in white letters along its bow, and he knew it was indeed the gulf-crawler he had sent up to La Puerta Del Norte with orders to retrieve the man who called himself One Who Flies.

The ship danced and jockeyed past anchor lines, dodged lugubrious tugs, and threatened fishing skiffs under sail. It belched black smoke and sounded its horn, issuing twin gouts of steam as it scudded forward through the green water. Men stood at the gunwales, sailors all, and lines uncoiled toward crewmen on the pier. Alejandro squinted, searching the faces on board, but nowhere did he see the man for whom he had sent the ship.

"Hola, Señor Silveira," called out a man from amidships. Short, swarthy, with a dark beard and a head bursting with dark-haired ringlets, he stood near the forward mast.

Alejandro recognized the captain of the vessel, a man of strong temper and skill extolled up and down the coastal waters. "Capitan de Botella. Greetings! Where is your passenger?"

De Botella jerked a thumb over his shoulder to where his crew was setting the gangway ramp from the deck to the pier. Behind them was a clump of people who slowly made their way to the rail.

First to debark were two women, both in Indian garb. Their bleached deerskin dresses had sleeves that were loosely tied, and cinching their waists were wide belts that had been beaded in strong angular designs of blue, red, black, and white. Below the hem of their dresses they wore fringed leggings and moccasins that were also beaded in bright colors. The younger woman carried a leather-wrapped bundle in her arms, while the older bore a burden on her back. Alejandro looked at the older woman again and recognized her as Speaks while Leaving, the wife of one of the warriors who had traveled to Washington the winter before. As she came down the ridged ramp, he realized that it was not a parcel she carried on her back but an elliptical board, against which was wrapped a baby. The child—less than a year old, Alejandro was sure—peered out from beneath protective layers with curious eyes. He walked toward the women but as they stepped onto the dock, they turned, their attention focused back at the top of the ramp, and their hands gripping the railings to steady their rubbery sea legs.

Alejandro looked up the ramp and gasped.

He knew the man who stood on deck, but was shocked at what he saw. It had been only four months since Alejandro had last seen George Armstrong Custer, Junior—the man he knew better as One Who Flies—but the change that had ravaged him was frightening to behold.

The man who only last winter was negotiating with statesmen and presidents, bartering millions of acres for millions in gold, was gone. The creature in his place was a wraith.

Instead of his tunic of sun-bleached deerskin, his red breechclout, and his leggings with their long green fringe that dragged on the ground behind him, a white-man's suit hung limply on his bony shoulders, the thin cloth wrinkled and shiny at the knees and elbows. Instead of a beaded belt and a feather-trimmed knife sheath, a watch chain of dull tin hung between his vest pockets. And where before his shiny blond hair had been pulled back into a single braid tied off with red cloth and adorned with the dark curve of a hawk feather, his locks now hung in unbecoming hanks across his face, having been cut crudely and roughly by an untrained hand.

Most striking, though, was the change in his physical presence. One Who Flies had been lean but possessed of a fitness in both limb and mind; his eyes had owned a falcon's gaze. The man who stood at the top of the stairs was sallow and unhealthily pale except for a ruddiness around his puffy eyes. He had dropped a quarter of his weight and what looked like most of his strength. The skin sagged at his jowls. His gaze was unfocused and unintelligent. His hand shook as he reached for the rail, and his steps spoke of fragility and ill health. With him was another white man, older by many years, who helped One Who Flies descend the ramp.

"*¡Dios mío!*" Alejandro said. Speaks while Leaving turned to him with a quizzical look. He pointed to One Who Flies. "What happened to him?" he asked her in French.

"It was a difficult crossing," the rough-looking man with One Who Flies replied. As they reached the dock, he walked past One Who Flies and stuck out his hand. "Vincent D'Avignon, business partner of young George here, and at your service, sir."

Alejandro looked at the offered hand and again at the man who offered it. Vincent D'Avignon had seen hard days and many of them—days that had obviously taught him a rogue's boldness—but there was a dubiety to his swagger as he tested his way down unfamiliar pathways. Alejandro knew the sort; knew him by the sharp edge to his gaze, by the angle of his hat, and by the eager condescension in his smile. Though the leather of his belt was new, his shoes were worn, and Alejandro would have bet his Sonoma vineyards that the rawhide man before him kept a silver coin inside his shoe, for emergencies.

He looked at the extended hand again and passed it by, walking instead to the man he wanted to see. "One Who Flies," he said, putting his hands on the young man's shoulders. "Do you need to see a doctor?"

One Who Flies blinked and took a deep breath. He looked at Alejandro and seemed to see him for the first time. "Don Alejandro," he said. "How nice to see you."

Immediately, Alejandro smelled the reek of liquor. "A difficult crossing?" he said and glared at D'Avignon. "A difficult crossing? He's drunk!"

"Yes, sir," D'Avignon said. "It helped, you know, with the *mal de mer.*"

Alejandro stepped back from One Who Flies and understood. The thinness, the vacancy, the mixture of florid and pallid skin. The shaking hand, the unsteady step. D'Avignon smiled in an offensively ingratiating manner that betrayed his culpability. Whether he had been an active participant in the debasement of One Who Flies, or whether he had merely stood by, Alejandro did not care.

A hand touched his shoulder. He turned to find Speaks while Leaving at his side.

"He has been ill," she said.

"Ah. Good, you *do* speak French," he said.

She made a sign with her hand. "Yes," she said.

"How long has he been . . . ill?" he asked her.

Another sign. "We do not know," she said. Her French was well formed and, like that of D'Avignon, carried the flat accent of the Quebecois. "He went to the City of White Stone, but never returned to us. We went to find him. We found him among the *vé'hó'e.*"

Alejandro knew that word. He had heard it often during his time among the Cheyenne. One Who Flies had explained it as a word of many meanings, few of them complimentary. *Vé'ho'e.* Trickster. Spider. Enshrouded. Entangled. With a glance at D'Avignon, he had an idea how some of the connotations had arisen.

"My apologies," he said to Speaks while Leaving. "I have been ungallant. I do not believe we have been properly introduced. I am Alejandro Miguel Tomás Silveira-Rioja, and it is my pleasure to welcome you to the island of Cuba." He put a hand to his waist and bowed.

"I am Speaks while Leaving," she said. "And this is my husband's sister, Mouse Road."

The shy young woman behind her realized she was being spoken of. Speaks while Leaving spoke to her sister-in-law in words made of wind. Mouse Road signed with her hands.

"She is proud to meet Speaks for the Iron Shirts."

Alejandro bowed to Mouse Road as well, but chose not to tell Speaks while Leaving that he no longer deserved the title the Cheyenne had given him as Ambassador to the United States from New Spain. The disgrace of his dismissal still galled his pride, but he reasoned that the knowledge of it was irrelevant to his plans with these people. If the Cheyenne women wanted to think of and refer to him as the Ambassador in their quaint vernacular, it would only serve his purposes.

"And who is this?" he asked, indicating the baby on her back.

In a flash, seriousness fled from her face. She smiled and looked at her feet in unfeigned modesty. She slipped the board off her shoulder and brought it into her arms. The leather and wicker creaked as with strong but gentle hands she pulled aside the cloth that hid most of the baby's face.

"This is Blue Shell Woman," she said. "My daughter."

Alejandro leaned in to see the tiny dumpling, brown as a nut, round-cheeked, with eyes that soaked up the world. The baby stared at him, her open mouth shiny with drool. He grinned at the little girl and waggled his fingers, but the cherubic face dissolved into fear and she let loose a long, healthy wail. He chuckled as Speaks while Leaving consoled her daughter.

"She does not like hair on the face," Speaks while Leaving said, pointing to his moustache. "She did not like the captain either."

"Not to worry," he said with good nature. "I will not take it as an insult." He motioned toward his carriage. "Shall we head onward? Your luggage shall be brought after us."

He led them along the dock and then up the stairs to the waiting carriage. Havana was a place of many cultures. Among its elite were businessmen from America, Creoles from New Spain, and aristocrats from Old Spain, while its peasant masses were the descendants of Portuguese pirates, Negro slaves, and Indian natives, many of whom also carried the blood of the ruling class in their veins. But even with such a fusion of peoples on its streets, still the two Cheyenne women drew sidelong looks and open stares. The dockmen were especially rude, making gestures and calling out to them in words Alejandro was thankful the women did not understand. Even the carriage driver was taken aback by the appearance of such unusual creatures, and it took a sharp *ahem* to put him into action.

The women climbed up with trepidation as the carriage rocked on its springs. Alejandro helped One Who Flies up into the box as well, but directed D'Avignon to ride up with the driver. When D'Avignon bristled, Alejandro gave him an honest glare.

In quiet English, he let D'Avignon know how things stood. "I do not know what your role up to now has been," he said, "but it is now changed. If you are lucky, I may find you of use. Either way, do not think you can fool me as to your sort."

D'Avignon raised one eyebrow, but chose not to argue. With a bow, he retreated and walked around to climb up beside the driver.

The streets were alive with morning business. Grocers threw back the covers from their market stalls and presented their wares to the city. Crates bore vegetables of red, green, and yellow. Netted globes of cheese hung like surplus clappers for silent bells. Sacks gaped, showing depths of brown rice and golden corn. Fruits showed off their sensual colors, glistening strings of smoked fish hung from awning posts, and dried chilies brightened every stall with wrinkled wreaths of fiery red and sooty black. Cooks and mamacitas came to buy for their day's needs, inspecting the goods with a critical eye and arguing each price with veteran skill.

The carriage passed through smoke redolent with grilling meat, and through the moister aromas of horse and ox. They passed a woman who carried a squalling baby in one arm, while with her free hand she kept a grip on a brace of equally unhappy chickens. Carts clattered, carriages rolled, horses clopped and cantered. Dockmen called to one another, stray dogs barked at nothing, and seagulls cried like hungry cats, eager for the dropped or discarded morsel.

Alejandro watched his female passengers as the carriage maneuvered through the morning's throng. Mouse Road stared, unabashedly gaping at everything, her gaze sweeping from side to side, from rooftop to streetcurb. She laughed at a group of boys chasing a burro, and was saddened by the broken-down carthorse struggling against its load.

Speaks while Leaving, however, maintained a dignified façade. She sat quietly, holding her swaddled babe in her arms, but Alejandro saw that her eyes were alive with interest, glancing around her, taking in as much as did her younger companion. Her features, though, betrayed neither interest nor boredom, and she maintained a queenly demeanor as they traveled the short distance back to the mansion.

They drove in through the wrought-iron gates, and Victoria was waiting for them along with Roberto and Olivia. Alejandro glanced nervously at One Who Flies and was relieved to see the young man pulling himself together, straightening his ill-fitting clothes and pushing the hair from his eyes. The carriage rattled to a halt and servants came forward to chock the wheels and drop the step.

Alejandro stepped down first and then turned to aid the women. They descended cautiously, their every step another foot farther into an unknown world. One Who Flies alit without revealing his infirmity, though the change in the young man's condition was impossible to conceal.

Victoria came toward One Who Flies, her hands extended and worry on her face. *"Mon chèr,"* she said, almost in tears. She clasped his hand in hers and looked up into his eyes. "Dear boy, are you all right?"

One Who Flies bowed slightly, accepting her concern. "It is good to see you again, Dona Victoria." He turned to his companions. "May I introduce Speaks while Leaving, of the Closed Windpipe band, and Mouse Road, of the Tree People. They are wife and sister to one you may remember: Storm Arriving, who was with me when last we met."

"Of course," Victoria said. "I remember him well. And how is your husband?" she asked Speaks while Leaving. "He is well, I hope?"

Speaks while Leaving shrank a bit at the question. "Forgive me, but I cannot say. He has gone to war against the bluecoats."

"Oh dear," Victoria said, flustered by the Cheyenne woman's candor.

Alejandro stepped into the breach, completing the introductions of Vincent, and of Roberto and Olivia, their hosts. "But I am sure our new arrivals are tired from the long trip."

"Yes," Olivia said. "Let me show you to your rooms, where you can rest and refresh yourselves."

"That would be most welcome," Speaks while Leaving said.

When they had all been escorted upstairs, Alejandro allowed himself to slip quietly away to one of the sitting rooms. The drapes had been pulled back to let in the forenoon light and the arched doorway stood open, allowing the fragrant breeze from the side gardens to wander in. He plopped himself down onto a fainting couch, one heel dragging across the grouting of the large, hexagonal floor tiles. He closed his eyes and put his fingertips to his forehead to massage the welt of pain that throbbed between his eyebrows.

"Wondering what to do now?" asked a voice.

Alejandro sat up and saw D'Avignon, a dark shadow leaning against the garden doorway.

"What do *you* want?" he asked, lying back down on the couch.

D'Avignon entered the room, looked around, and headed toward a cabinet. "Nothing much," he said as he opened the cabinet, peered within, and closed it. He walked to another cabinet. "I just thought we had gotten off on the wrong foot back at the dock." He opened the second cabinet, looked inside, and closed it, too.

Alejandro did not like this bantam rooster of a man, but he had the sense not to say so. On the other hand, he was not about to let this . . . parasite overstep his station.

"I'll ask you again: What do you want?"

D'Avignon walked over to a small bookcase, the lower half of which was closed off with wooden doors. He opened it, and with an "Ahh!" and the clink of crystal, he stood, placing two small glasses on a nearby reading table. Then he pulled out a cut-glass decanter filled three-quarters full with liquor the color of strong tea. The decanter sang a crystal note as the glass stopper was lifted from its long throat. D'Avignon sniffed the contents—a long, appreciative inhalation—and then raised an eyebrow and the bottle in Alejandro's direction.

"A little early, but would you care to join me?"

Impatient, Alejandro gestured. "All right, yes. Thank you."

D'Avignon poured. The decanter gurgled and the

stopper hissed as it slid home. Alejandro accepted one of the glasses and with a perfunctory nod of thanks, sipped. The brandy was mellow and sharp at the same time, ripe with the taste of cream and oak. Alejandro felt the tension seep out of his muscles. D'Avignon seated himself in a large, brass-studded armchair upholstered in dark leather.

"Now," Alejandro said, peering over at his uninvited guest. "If you wouldn't mind answering my question."

"What do I want?" D'Avignon said. "I have it. A drink and a soft, quiet place to rest for a bit was all I wanted."

"No. What do you want *here*? What do you want with One Who Flies?"

"Ah," he said with a wink. "Young Custer." He tossed off the rest of his drink as if it were whisky, rose, and poured himself another. The leather creaked as he sat down again. "I'm concerned for the boy. He's like a son to me—"

"Bah," Alejandro said with a wave and a sneer.

D'Avignon chuckled. "And you, Don Alejandro? Your interest in him is different?"

Alejandro bristled at the insinuation. "Of course," he said, sitting upright. "One Who Flies is a crucial link between Spain and the Cheyenne people."

"So it's only natural that you'd want to have him killed."

The small glass slipped from Alejandro's hand and shattered on the brown tiles. He was on his feet, shards grating underfoot, his pulse pounding in his throat. "Why, you—"

"Did you think I hadn't heard? Even on the Frontier, sir, we get the eastern newspapers. And news of that sort, well, it just takes on a life of its own, doesn't it?" He went to the cabinet and produced another glass, filled it as he refilled his own. "Yes, *Harper's* was especially brutal. 'Ambassador Implicated in Assassination Plot,' it said. Young George and his Indian cause are quite popular in the North, you see, and when it was learned that he was the target and not the President, well, you can imagine." He held out the glass.

Alejandro took the glass and drained it, not thinking

of the brandy's flavor, bouquet, or its astringency on his tongue. He wanted only its bite to shock his mind back into motion and the breath back into his lungs. Staring at D'Avignon, he slowly sat back down on the couch. When he spoke, his voice was raspy.

"What do you want?"

D'Avignon smiled. "I think we both know that Spain won't be any more interested in an alliance with the Cheyenne than she'd be interested in an alliance with the Cuban rebels. Unless, of course, they had something of value. Something worth trading for. Something worth fighting for." He sat down in his chair and sipped his brandy. "Now, young Custer and I, we go back a few years. I lived and worked among those people, and I know that the Cheyenne *do* have something worth fighting for, and it only stands to reason that if you're pushing for an alliance, then you know what it is, too." He leaned forward conspiratorially, elbows resting on his knees.

"Gold."

Alejandro swallowed and felt a sudden sweat bead his brow.

D'Avignon chuckled and leaned back. "Oh, yes. *El diablo dorado.* And they have it, believe me. They have it."

"You still haven't told me what it is you expect to get out of all this."

D'Avignon shrugged and nestled back in the armchair. "I want in," he said simply. "Whatever it is you're planning, I want in. Of course, I'm willing to help."

"What possible help could you be?" Alejandro said, unable to keep the scorn from his voice.

"For one thing, I could keep my mouth shut about your recent misdeeds," D'Avignon said, eyebrow arched. "Of course, I know that a knife in my ribs will do that, too, so I'm willing to be of service in other ways. For instance, let's say you're able to negotiate some mining rights as part of this alliance. Well, when I was with them, I prospected at least a dozen major sites. I could easily lead a small contingent right to the choicest locations." He winked again. "Even a privately funded contingent, if you catch my meaning."

The reins had slipped from Alejandro's hands, and to get them back, he would have to involve himself with this weasel. It was a distasteful choice, but a clear one.

"Very well," he said. "You work for me, now. But one false word and, believe me, you'll get that knife in your ribs. Agreed?"

D'Avignon grinned with crooked teeth. "I am your obedient servant, Don Alejandro."

"Good. Now make your obedient self useful. I want One Who Flies lucid and presentable for dinner this evening. There is much to discuss."

With a bow and a flourish, D'Avignon departed, leaving Alejandro with an unsettled stomach to match the pain in his head.

•

For the rest of the day, the household was whispered chaos. In every hall and through every open doorway, servants could be heard gossiping, trading information in hushed tones, eyes wide with interest or disbelief as they discussed the new houseguests with ill-contained excitement. Throughout the house he found them, in pairs and trios made suddenly quiet by his appearance and then, their confabulation disrupted, they dispersed. He could not fault them for their excitement: two Indian women, a wily frontiersman, and the rebel son of an American president provided fertile ground for wild imaginings. Such speculation was human nature, or so Alejandro told himself until he went upstairs to dress for dinner and found a gaggle of housemaids peering around the partially opened door that led into the room set aside for One Who Flies.

"Ahem," he said. The serving women turned with a collection of gasps and giggles, and Alejandro was appalled to find foremost among them his own daughter, Isabella. The maids departed with curtsies and quick feet, leaving Isabella alone, her hand still on the door's handle. He reached forward and pulled the door gently to.

"It's not what it looks like, Father."

"Oh? And what do you think it looks like?"

Isabella blushed, and Alejandro grew concerned.

Young and destined to be as beautiful as her mother,

Isabella had been brought up in a world of Spanish privilege and Catholic propriety. While he had ensured that she had never known want, her mother had ensured that she never knew sadness. The result was a daughter on the brink of womanhood who was naïve and as impressionable as warm wax.

The previous summer, when One Who Flies had visited them in San Francisco, Alejandro had taken note of his daughter's obvious fascination with the young and charismatic Custer. He had allowed her infatuation to continue because it had served to drive a wedge between One Who Flies and his Indian friends, thus binding One Who Flies closer to Alejandro and his advised plan of action. Of course, at that time, he had not planned that One Who Flies would be around long enough to prove a problem with Isabella.

As he looked at his pink-cheeked daughter, he realized that things had changed.

"I thought you were unwell," he said.

"I am feeling better."

Yes, he thought, knowing the tonic that had roused her.

"Then go and dress for dinner."

"Yes, Father. I will." She hurried away, slippered feet padding silently down the carpeted hallway.

A short while later he descended the stairs and walked quickly to the salon where Roberto, Olivia, and Victoria were waiting. The women sat together in close conversation while Roberto stood near a bookshelf, inspecting the titles on the spines.

"Ah. Good," Roberto said, heading to a sidetable. He poured some sherry sack into a stemmed glass and held it out.

Alejandro took it and sipped. "Any sign of our guests?" he asked.

"None. Been up there all day. Difficult crossing, I heard."

"Yes," Alejandro said, knowing there was more to it than that. There was the sound of hurried footsteps and rustling fabric from the hallway. They turned to find Isabella rushing in, flushed and bright-eyed, the sweeping hem of her dress swaying with her zeal. She caught herself with a hand on the doorjamb and recaptured a parcel of her dignity with a small curtsy to the group of adults.

"Good evening," she said. Smiling, she walked to her uncle and kissed him on the cheek.

"Evening, child," Roberto said, taking in her coiffure of upswept curls, her dress of pale beribboned blue, and her lace-trimmed, off-the-shoulder neckline. "What a sight you are. Lovelier every day."

"Thank you, Uncle. I wanted to look nice for our guests."

Alejandro felt his right eye begin to twitch.

"Ah," Roberto said. "And here they are."

One Who Flies led the group, his head held high but still uneasy in his dark suit, high-collared shirt, and necktie. His clothing neither flattered, fit, nor was stylish enough for the evening's gathering. He had no gloves, his shoes were in need of polish, and the arms of his jacket were too short, revealing an unfashionable width of cuff and sleeve. Alejandro took note of it all and determined that the young man's clothing situation would be rectified before sundown the next day.

D'Avignon walked in behind One Who Flies, looking little better than the younger man but at least wearing clothing that fit. The men's appearance, however, was of little concern to the others, for it was the women who attracted every eye.

Mouse Road was resplendent in her native costume. She had looped her braids up on each side, pinning them with silver disks from which hung long feathers and beaded strings. Her dress of fawn-colored hide was partly open at the left shoulder, and around her neck she wore a choker of tubular shells, a short necklace of silver beads, and a longer drape of beaded leather. She wore a coil of brass around one upper arm, and on each wrist were quill-sewn gauntlets of leather trimmed with fur. Her heart-shaped face was calm and lovely.

Behind her, Speaks while Leaving entered like a grand dame, accompanied by a household maid who had been given charge of her infant. Dressed in a fashion similar to her sister-in-law, her wide, beaded belt accentuated her more mature form to great advantage. While eye contact, as Alejandro had learned, was considered rude among the Cheyenne, it did not keep her from looking about the room, her dark eyes lively as they evaluated what they saw. She took in everything—walls, decorations, draperies, furniture, glassware, lampshades—with detached interest. Far from the fearful, intimidated primitive that Alejandro had expected her to be in such a setting, Speaks while Leaving stood unfazed, aloof, and in control.

"Bon soir," she said to the gathering.

"Good evening," they replied.

"One Who Flies," Isabella said, walking toward him, hand extended. "How *good* it is to see you again."

Alejandro hoped the young man would remain as dumb as he had down at the docks, but was disappointed as One Who Flies took his daughter's hand, bowed, and kissed her fingers.

"A pleasure, señorita. Let me introduce you to my companions."

D'Avignon glanced over with a wink and Alejandro wished the sly old man hadn't been so successful with his first assignment. But as One Who Flies introduced Mouse Road, Alejandro saw something that made him smile. She eyed Isabella surreptitiously, but with a dislike that was so frank and obvious that it dispelled every concern Alejandro had about his daughter's virtues. She would never get anywhere with One Who Flies, as long as Mouse Road was present.

They went in to dinner, Isabella insisting on a seat next to One Who Flies, and Mouse Road maneuvered herself to a seat across from him where she could keep them both in full view.

The meal progressed from a cool melon soup, to salted greens, to braised duck in orange sauce. While Isabella kept up a steady interrogation of her neighbor, Mouse Road worked with quiet determination to manage the unfamiliar utensils while keeping an unfriendly eye on her competition. The conversation, commandeered by his daughter, drifted amiably from subject to subject like a meandering breeze and held about as much consequence. Roberto, Olivia, and Victoria smiled indulgently at the young woman's obvious enthusiasm

for their guest, while for his own part, One Who Flies
responded politely to her queries, with attention to her
anecdotes, but with nothing approaching anything as
strong as interest. He nodded and smiled and made
small *ahs* of comprehension, but Alejandro could see
that his awareness was tied to the deepening frown lines
anchored at the corners of Mouse Road's lips. The depth
of her displeasure governed him, and One Who Flies
made several attempts to bring others into the conversation. Isabella, however, was irrepressible. Finally,
though, it was Speaks while Leaving who sent the idle
talk in a decidedly different direction.

"Ambassador," she began, and Alejandro saw the
looks exchanged among the family members. With a subtle lift of his hand, he quelled their corrections and let
her continue.

"What are our plans?" she asked. "When shall we
speak with your viceroy?"

Roberto cleared his throat and Alejandro sent him a
daggered look. He caught Victoria's glance, and saw her
cautionary advice.

"I apologize," he said to Speaks while Leaving, "but
there seems to be some confusion. We will not be speaking with the viceroy in this matter."

Before he could explain further, Speaks while Leaving
turned to One Who Flies and began to talk to him in
her native tongue. For the first time that evening, One
Who Flies became animated beyond what was mini-
mally necessary.

"Please," Alejandro tried to interrupt.

The two spoke a little more until Mouse Road, who
prior to that moment had remained entirely silent, began
to speak. The Cheyenne words were crisp, alien whispers
that tumbled from her lips. The young woman spoke
at length, marking the progress of her thoughts in the
tablecloth, delineating each one with gestures and signs.
She pointed to Alejandro and then fell silent.

Alejandro looked at his family. They shrugged.

"If we are not to speak to the viceroy," Speaks while
Leaving said, "then how will we work toward an alliance
with your country?"

"Again, my friends, I apologize. This must seem quite

puzzling to you all." He took a sip of his wine and tried to gather his thoughts. "The truth of it is, our viceroy does not feel he is able to make such a decision. Now wait, before you get upset again, let me explain." He sat back and put into his next words as much ardor as he could muster. "The Viceroy Lord Serrano has given me his express permission to take you and our case for an alliance directly to the Queen Regent herself. It is a great honor for us to do this, and I am sure that Queen María Cristina and her advisors—"

Now it was One Who Flies who began to rasp Cheyenne words to the others. The women questioned him, and he responded with growing fervor and visible anger. Back in his eyes was the raptor gaze of the Custer men, and back in his arms and spine was the strength that Alejandro had known him to possess, only now that strength and that sharp eye were directed at him, *against* him.

"It is out of the question," One Who Flies finally said, once again in French. He pointed at Alejandro. "You have us here on a false promise, sir, and I will not allow it."

Alejandro played the innocent. "What falsehood, One Who Flies?"

"Yes," Speaks while Leaving said. "What falsehood? Hasn't he said he will help us work toward an alliance?"

"But with whom?" One Who Flies asked, rising from his chair. "Not with the viceroy. With the Queen Regent. And do you know where the Queen Regent lives? In Spain. Across the ocean."

To Speaks while Leaving this clearly meant nothing.

"Across the *ocean*. Across a water far greater than the Big Salty. It will take us months. The trip that brought us here will seem a morning's stroll to the journey to Spain. And why?" He looked at Alejandro. "Because the viceroy gives his permission? No. Because the viceroy will not back us, you mean. No, I will not have it, sir. I will not allow you to drag us across an ocean on some wild scheme to try to convince your Queen to form an alliance when you could not even convince your own viceroy. No, sir. It will not happen, sir." He stepped back from the table, turned, and left the room.

They all stared after him.

Dios mío, Alejandro thought. Without One Who Flies, without him as intermediary, without his cachet as Custer's son, we haven't a hope.

He turned to Speaks while Leaving. "You must convince him," he said. "We must speak to the Queen Regent or we will fail."

She looked to her sister-in-law, worry creasing her brow. She glanced after One Who Flies, betraying her reluctance.

From the other end of the table, Roberto whispered in Spanish. "They must go. All is at risk. My reputation as well as yours is on the block."

"Press her," Victoria said, also in Spanish.

"I implore you," he said to Speaks while Leaving. "Go to him. Convince him. I fear the very future of your people is at stake here, for without an alliance with Spain, what hope do you have?"

Tears brimmed in her eyes, and a muscle pulsed along her jawline. She made a sign with her hands and the two women stood. The men stood as well, and watched as they left the room, heading upstairs.

Alejandro sat, feeling sweat trickle from his hairline down his temples and the back of his neck. He glanced over at the one guest who had not left.

"If he does not go," he said to D'Avignon, "you will hurt for it."

D'Avignon nodded, and rose. "The meal was delicious, Dona. And if you will excuse me, I must speak to a man about a journey." He bowed to the ladies, and departed.

CHAPTER 14

Spring Moon, Full
Fifty-seven Years after the Star Fell
Lodge of the Governor
Havana, Cuba

Wordlessly, Speaks while Leaving took her daughter from the serving woman and entered the suite of rooms she and Mouse Road had been given. Mouse Road came in after her and swung the heavy door closed on its creaking iron hinges.

"Tell me," the young woman said.

"I do not know what to tell," Speaks while Leaving said.

"By my blood, that is a lie."

Speaks while Leaving looked at her sister-in-law, stunned by her boldness. Mouse Road stood hands on hips, her stance, her glare, even the set of her chin speaking of her resolve. The young woman's conviction pushed at Speaks while Leaving, setting her back on her heels, forcing her to reconsider her words.

A lie? Yes, she realized. A lie.

Shamed, she turned away from such brutal regard and went to the bay window. "You are right," she said as she sat on the padded bench and leaned back against the sill. "I *do* know what to tell. I just do not know how to tell it."

Cradling her daughter, she pushed the window open and let in a night fragrant with the scents of salt sea and night-blooming flowers. Down at the quays, ships creaked with the incoming tide, while in the streets surrounding the governor's massive home people strolled, lamps were lit, and vendors began to close for the night.

The townsfolk filled the air with songs, banter, and arguments. Mothers called to children and husbands. Somewhere a piece of crockery broke. A barking dog was silenced by a curse. A group of young men whistled at a passing pair of women. The vibrations of life echoed from the whitewashed walls, from the red-tiled roofs, and from the cobblestone streets.

"Such a place," she said as she regarded the closely packed city. "So many people and so much industry."

From the upper-story window, she could see over the roofs of the lower buildings, but rather than streets dividing the homes, she saw canyons carved in the solid residential blocks. She imagined the people walking those streets, sandals scuffing the stone, slowly wearing them down, exposing the homes lit by warm lamplight and filled with the scents of cooked corn and grilling fish. She reversed it all, with her dreaming eye, and saw the streets refill. The homes submerged into the earth, and the verdant land was covered over with grasses, vines, trees. Thickets of jungle ran to the rocky limits of the shore, dense and impenetrable, as dark as the waters beyond them. Eyes opening, the jungle fled, the streets cut their paths into the earth, and the city reappeared.

"These *vé'hó'e* are so different from us. They live so close and act so rashly." Northward, toward the horizon, the clouds were piled high. Blue Shell Woman squirmed in her arms and Speaks while Leaving wished she had taken some food from the table to supplement the breast milk that had been the baby's main nourishment since leaving home.

Mouse Road came over and sat down with her on the bench. "Tell me," she said again. "What happened down there? Why did One Who Flies get so angry with the Iron Shirts?"

Speaks while Leaving shrugged, trying to decide where to start. "The chief to whom One Who Flies spoke last year . . . he will not speak to us again of an alliance. But he has given his consent for us to speak with the queen of the Iron Shirts. The journey, however, is long and far."

"And One Who Flies has refused to go?"

"Yes," Speaks while Leaving said. "He does not believe what Don Alejandro tells us. He thinks Don Alejandro does not have the support of his own chief."

Mouse Road picked idly at the pattern woven into the upholstery of the bench cushion. "And you?" she asked, almost nonchalantly. "What do you say?"

A knock at the door put aside any response Speaks while Leaving would have given though, in fact, she did not know what her answer might have been. Mouse Road stood and walked to the door. Opening it, she stepped back, revealing Victoria, Don Alejandro's wife.

"May I come in?" she asked.

Speaks while Leaving signed her permission but caught herself. "Please, Dona Victoria."

Victoria entered, the fabric of her dress rustling like wind through the fronds of the odd, branchless palm trees that stood outside the window. She moved as if across an icebound pond, gliding smoothly, or floating, as if her feet did not touch the ground. She sat beside Speaks while Leaving on the window seat, and took Speaks while Leaving's hand in hers.

"Ma chère," she said, "I wanted to talk to you. These men, their passions become so quickly roused. I just thought that we might speak plainly, woman to woman."

It was hard enough for Speaks while Leaving to consider this alien creature to be a human being, much less a woman like herself, but she did not mention this to Victoria. Instead, she glanced over at Mouse Road who, with a shrug, sat down on the buffalo robe they had laid out in the center of the room, unable to guess at what this *vé'ho'e* woman wanted.

"Of what did you wish to speak?" she asked.

Victoria smiled and patted Speaks while Leaving's hand. Though the woman was pale to the brink of death, Speaks while Leaving could see that she was still very attractive with smooth, dark hair, large eyes, and a generous smile. But her waist was unnaturally narrow, her hips grossly wide beneath the heavy fabric of her dress, and her bearing—though dignified—was so stiff that Speaks while Leaving wondered if the woman was in constant pain from some old injury.

"I understand that you are reluctant to make this jour-

ney, but I wanted to make sure that you saw the whole
of the situation. You mustn't let the passion of the men
override your purpose."

"My purpose?" she asked before she realized it. The
room faded around her, and she sat in a garden, the sun
shining in hard lines of light and shadow. She felt the
influence of the sky, and the cradling hands of the earth.
The air was alive with birdsong and heady with a scent
she did not know. She felt Blue Shell Woman in her
arms, twisting and fussing, and looked down at her little
daughter. "My purpose?" The view faded and she was
once again in the lamplit room with Mouse Road and
Victoria. Victoria was looking at her a little strangely.

"Yes," Victoria said hesitantly. "Your purpose. The
reason you came here."

"Tell me, Dona Victoria. Why do you think I came
here?" Speaks while Leaving tried to keep the room
around her, but it kept wavering. The wind of the prairie
ruffled the fringe of her dress, and she heard thunder in
her mind. The thunder of the sky became the pummeling
sound of the herds on the grasslands of home, the chest-
filling drumbeat of a Sun Dance circle, the hooves of
bluecoat horses pounding their way into battle, the con-
cussion of cannonfire and the explosions that followed.
Through the din of battle, she could hear Victoria's
voice, calm and sincere.

"I think you came here to try to save your people,"
the lady of the Iron Shirts said to her. "One Who Flies
sees only the obstacles that lie in your path. He fears
for your safety—yours, and Mouse Road's—and though
he is a good man, a brave man, his concern for you two
blinds him. My husband, on the other hand, sees only
the possibilities. He does not realize how much of his
own reputation—and therefore his family's future—he is
risking in this. My husband sees the opportunities an
alliance can bring, and likewise, he is blinded."

Speaks while Leaving felt Victoria's hand grip hers
more tightly, felt the soft warmth of this *vé'ho'e* woman's
skin enfolding the roughness of her callused fingers. She
closed her eyes to shut out the visions of war that filled
her sight.

"But you are not blinded by these things," Victoria said. "You see all too well both the threats and the opportunities that lie ahead for your homeland."

"Yes," Speaks while Leaving told her. "I see them."

Again the gentle pressure on her hand. "Then you know that you must look beyond the dangers."

Blue Shell Woman squirmed again in her mother's arms, and the vision broke loose, flying like feathers in the wind, releasing her. Looking down at her daughter, Speaks while Leaving wondered at the possibilities.

What sort of life lies ahead for you? she asked her daughter. What sort of land will you receive when I am gone?

"How long would the trip be?" she asked Victoria.

"A few months, at least," Victoria said. "It is a long way. But I think you would be home by autumn."

Speaks while Leaving looked up at Victoria's face. The woman was intent, eager, waiting to see what she would decide. "But if One Who Flies does not agree to go . . . ?"

Victoria breathed out a quiet chuckle. "If you decide to go, or, more to the point"—she glanced over at Mouse Road—"if *she* decides to go, he will go."

The look in her eye told Speaks while Leaving that this was a wily woman beside her; a woman used to working in the background. Like the wife of strong chiefs among the People, she made things happen quietly, with subtle, steady pressure. Perhaps this was the sort of role that Speaks while Leaving herself would play. Perhaps in this way, she could work to bring about the future she envisioned.

This is my middle road. This is my road of trust.

Blue Shell Woman wriggled again and began to cry.

"*¡O, pobrecito!*" Victoria said. "She must be hungry. Shall I have something sent up for her? Some fruit or some porridge?"

"Yes, Doña Victoria. I would be very grateful."

"Leave it to me," her hostess said as she rose. "I am glad we had a chance to talk," she said, glided across the room, and left.

"So am I," Speaks while Leaving said as she stared at the dark door.

Mouse Road came over. "Are you all right?" she asked.

The breath that Speaks while Leaving took was long and filled with sadness, but when she let it out, she felt lightened. "Yes," she said. "I am fine."

"What did you talk about?"

"About traveling across the sea to see the queen of the Iron Shirts."

"You are going?"

"Yes . . ."

"Then so am I!"

"No," she said. "It will be dangerous. It is a long journey."

"I do not care," Mouse Road said. Her eyes glinted with excitement. "And we've come such a long way already. How much longer can it be?"

"As you wish," she said. "To tell the truth, I would be glad for your company."

"When do we leave?"

"Wait. You remember what One Who Flies said."

"Yes . . ."

"Well, the Iron Shirts will not listen to two women of the People. They will only listen to men. They will listen to One Who Flies, the son of the famous Long Hair, Chief of the Horse Nations. I must find a way to convince him to go with us." Speaks while Leaving peeked over at her sister-in-law's face. "Do you know how I might be able to do that?"

Mouse Road smiled. "I think I might have an idea."

CHAPTER 15

Wednesday, May 21, A.D. 1890
The White House
Washington, District of Columbia

Custer gave Libbie a lopsided smile as he felt the familiar tabletop with his fingers. It was incredibly out of place, this big workhorse of a table, its oak heavy and dark, its taloned legs and its broad surface scarred with ages of service, but it had been Custer's longtime friend, having traveled with him through service both military and political. He had found it in a stable he had purchased up in Michigan Territory, cloaked in canvas, piled high with tools and crates. As old as the nation itself, the table had seen hard use before he had found it, and harder use since. Custer had brought it with him from Michigan to Missouri, through the nightmare of the Kansa Campaign, and back up to Santee Territory before returning home for a brief time to Michigan. From there, he had brought it to Washington, from the Capitol to the White House, and now he had brought it from his offices down the hall to this room, the library, where he spent his days.

But while the table held its own against the hundreds of leather-bound spines that flanked the room, it did less well when compared to the library's finer furnishings such as the plush Queen Anne chairs, the glittering chandelier, or the curved-leg side tables. Next to them, it seemed as clumsy and out of place as he himself felt next to Libbie. Scarred, ungainly, inelegant, it did not grace the oval room; it invaded it.

And Custer was perfectly fine with that. It was precisely what he had wanted, the last phase in the library's transformation. Sitting at his table, leaning against its comfortable strength, he felt like a man again. His damnable wheelchair, the hated symbol of his continued infirmity, stood close at hand should it be needed, but it stood there empty. Custer sat in a chair at his table, a normal man ready for a normal day's work.

Well, he thought as he looked at Libbie, standing beside him—knowing the assistance she was here to provide—perhaps not completely normal. Not yet.

"Are you sure you want to do this?" she asked him.

"Yes," he said, or a close approximation of it, still unable to eradicate the lateral lisp that the stroke had wrapped around his tongue. "Are you?"

She took a wide-eyed breath of air and sighed. "I think so," she said.

"Don' le' him rattle you," Custer said, struggling with the words. "He' jus'a New Yor' banker. No' a Firs' Lady." Though slurred and lisped and filled with elisions, Libbie was so familiar with his speech patterns that she understood him perfectly. Which was, of course, why he had asked her here.

The door to the library opened and Samuel entered, a sheaf of papers under his arm. Custer tried to remember when Samuel had ever entered a room *without* a sheaf of papers under his arm and couldn't recall such a moment. Behind him came Douglas, bearing a tray with cut-crystal tumblers, a seltzer bottle, and a whisky decanter. With a glance, Custer directed Douglas to place the tray on the low table near the chairs that faced his worktable. Samuel came forward and put the papers down on the table.

"You're sure you want this meeting?" Samuel asked as he began organizing the papers.

Custer glanced at Libbie and she answered for him. "He's sure."

Samuel divided the papers into three piles. Each of the piles he further divided into sections, laying out memos and reports in a cascaded order, allowing quick access to any item. He pointed here and there as he turned them around to face Custer.

"Here are the troop numbers we spoke about, and

here, the summary of cables we've received from Yankton."

" 'Amue' . . ." Custer tried.

"These are the transportation numbers, and these—"

" 'Amue'!"

Samuel looked up, startled, his hands trembling over the papers.

"I 'emem'," Custer said. "I' see' 'em."

"He remembers," Libbie translated. "He's seen them."

" 'Ang."

"Thank you."

"Of course," Samuel said. "Of course. You're welcome, Mr. President." He stepped back, chagrined, and began to leave but Custer stopped him and, with a debilitated hand, directed him to stand by him, opposite Libbie.

"I 'ee' you here."

And for the first time in several days, since Libbie had first told him of her husband's plans, Samuel smiled and stood a little straighter.

"My pleasure, sir," he said, and took up his post at his commander's side.

Custer familiarized himself with the position of the papers Samuel had laid out. He knew what was in each one, but he wanted to know precisely where each one was in its respective stack. With his left hand, now nearly as strong as it had been but still not as clever as he wished it to be, he carefully fingered through the pages. Military movements, troop strengths, cables on engagements, and supply requisitions were all in the first pile. In the second were transportation numbers, memos on railway usage, and industrial reports. The third was not a pile, but a simple brown folder. Custer reached over to it and opened it, closed it, and opened it again, practicing his movement. The last thing he wanted during this encounter was to look inept.

As with most things in Custer's life, he had viewed the coming meeting with a military eye. He'd picked his ground, even changed the terrain by bringing in his old worktable and creating an office within the small world of his library. He had arrayed his allies in reserve on either side, and before them had reviewed the reports and memos: his troops. He reached over and opened the folder again.

And you are my cavalry, he told it.

This meeting was the opening of a new campaign. He'd been preparing for it for weeks. Perhaps it would end up no more than a skirmish, perhaps a battle in itself. He did not know for sure, but he felt prepared, and his best advantage was the fact that his opponent didn't know it was coming.

A sharp rap sounded at the library door.

"That will be Morton," Samuel said.

Custer glanced at Douglas, who crossed quickly to the door and opened it.

Levi Morton stood framed in the doorway. Short and pale, he looked like he'd been pinched out of uncooked bread dough, though his expression was pure pickle: sour and wrinkled. He was backed by two taller, more imposing men who followed him as he walked in.

Custer knew Morton's aides by reputation as well as by sight. The shorter—still a head taller than Morton—was a lawyer and former New York prosecutor named Chaucer. Muttonchopped and ostentatiously moustached, he peered over his narrow reading glasses with a constant expression of mild disbelief. Morton's second aide was Yancy, a tall, aged man who still walked with the rigid precision instilled in him by decades of military service. In the past few months, the two of them had assumed increasing roles of power; until now they were treated as Morton's lieutenants, speaking for him in meetings and conferences.

Together, the three men walked toward Custer's table and formed a skirmish line before it, evenly spaced, Morton in the middle, his two aides guarding his flanks. Morton's gaze lingered long and questioningly on Libbie.

"Well?" he said with an imperious impatience. "I'm here. What's so all-fired important?"

From Custer's left, Samuel cleared his throat. "Mister President," he said.

Morton blinked at the unsubtle reminder, his eyes squinting at Samuel as if he'd not seen him there previously. But while he did not rise to the bait, neither did he correct his impertinence.

Custer lifted a hand, inviting his guests to sit in the chairs behind them. Unwillingly, but unable to refuse without rudeness, Morton sat, directing his men to do likewise. Douglas came forward, offering them a drink, which Morton refused. Chaucer gave a wistful look in the direction of the crystal drinkingware, but declined as well.

Morton looked right at Custer. "What was it you wanted to discuss, Mr. President?"

Custer noted the slight change in attitude, and felt he had established his control of the situation enough to continue. Steeling himself, he reached out with his left hand and touched the first row of reports.

"I' bee' kee'i up wi' effor' in Ter'tory," he began.

"I have been keeping up with your efforts in the Territory," Libbie interpreted for him.

Morton's eyes widened. He now understood Libbie's presence, and the idea of having to deal with Custer through an intermediary was not sitting well with him.

"Indeed," he said, trying to cover his surprise.

"Yes," Custer said through Libbie's interpretation. "And I've become quite concerned. You are heading down a dangerous path, Levi."

"You needn't worry yourself, Mr. President."

"Yes, I do," Custer insisted.

Morton sat back in his chair, obviously unsure of the purpose of this meeting. "Mr. President," he said, "things in the Territories have grown very complex in recent months. I'm not sure you appreciate all of the intricacies of the situation."

Custer leaned forward on the elbow of his otherwise useless right arm, inspecting the arrayed reports. "I believe I am completely cognizant of all the details," he slurred and waited for Libbie's words to make his meaning clear. "Though my body has been twisted and bound by the assassin's bullet, I assure you that my mind is clear and my intellect sound." He pulled one report out from the ranks. "But it does not take a genius to see that you have increased troop strengths in the regions between the Mississippi and Missouri rivers, nor a great mind to know the kind of response their presence in that region will elicit from the Alliance."

Morton waved a hand, cutting off Libbie mid-word. "This is preposterous," he said, rising from his seat. "I don't have time to banter policy with—"

"You 'nsuff'ble prick," Custer said, holding up a hand to forestall Libbie's translation. He dabbed at the stroke-weakened side of his mouth where saliva gathered and then, putting every effort into his enunciation, said, "You will trea' th' Firs' Lady wi' proper respect. Now, *siddown*."

Morton wanted to leave. Custer could see it in his eyes. The man may have helped carry New York in the election, but Custer had never liked him, had never cared for his brashness, or his disregard for experience. Since the shooting, Morton's increased duties had given him a taste for power, and his and Custer's mutual dislike had bloomed into something more intense. Now that intensity shone from the Vice President's eyes and he wanted to storm from the library. Only Custer's position as President kept him in the room.

Morton sat, crossing his arms over his chest.

Yancy spoke up to fill the awkward silence. "If I may, Mr. President. We are only continuing in the Territories the strategy of engagement that you yourself initiated."

Custer motioned for Libbie to interpret once more. "But on a greatly expanded front, and in so doing, you leave your southern settlements unprotected."

"But the southern towns are to our rear."

Custer laughed. "I know your service years are well behind you, Yancy, but surely you've paid *some* attention. In fighting the allied tribes, there *is* no rear."

Morton chimed in again. "The savages have left the southern lands alone ever since you began concentrating forces in the north."

"Perhaps, but what sort of engagements have you had?" He looked to Yancy. "Only small force engagements, true?"

"Yes, sir."

"And attacks concentrating on supply shipments?"

"Also true," Yancy said, a reluctance growing in his answers.

"Supplies of weapons?"

"Yes, sir."

Morton leaned forward, hands on knees. "What's your point?"

"The point," Custer said, "is that you have yet to encounter a home camp of these people. Instead of the mounted squadrons I'd deploy, you deploy infantry. You have lost more supplies than you have transported, and you have overextended your troops, sending them farther in than you can protect them."

Morton smiled. "All that is about to change," he said. "I have personal assurances from several industrial chiefs that if I can secure the lands this side of the Missouri River, they will back the expansion and settlement."

"Settlement means taxes," Chaucer said, wading in for the first time. "And taxes mean revenue."

Yancy continued for Morton. "Thanks to the maps made during your negotiations with the Cheyenne, we have learned the extent of certain rivers and have sent troop steamers deep into the Unorganized Territory. Several columns will soon be heading out onto the Plains. They will search for the tribes as they gather for the summer hunts. We'll be heading due west in four columns. When one column finds the Cheyenne, they'll contact the others and all will converge. We should have the situation solved within a matter of months."

Solved. Custer knew what that kind of wording meant, and he found it sickening. It was one thing to fight combatants, to battle against soldiers and warriors for control of territory, but to overtly and consciously work toward extinguishing an entire people . . . Years ago, decades ago, he might have been accepting of that goal. Even in recent years, he'd allowed such an attitude— even encouraged it in subordinates and generals under his command—as long as he could temper it and keep it in hand. But Morton had adopted the idea as policy and was preparing to implement it. Running unchecked, such acts were heinous in the extreme, and without a doubt, Morton was running unchecked. This was not the legacy that Custer wanted to leave behind.

"I cannot condone this course of action," Custer said.

Morton actually sneered. "I thank the President for his concern, but right now, I am the one in charge around here. I shall give your advice all due consideration, sir, but if you will excuse me, other problems require my attention."

"Problems like Cuba?" Custer asked through Libbie's interpretation. Morton stopped mid-stride, foiled in his second attempt to leave the conversation before Custer chose to end it. While the Vice President watched, Custer deftly flipped open the folder and pulled out the thin report contained therein. Ignoring Morton's gaping stare, Custer leafed through the pages of thin foolscap, grey with densely packed typing. "I read here that you have increased our support and shipments to the Cuban rebels. Has Congress been apprised?"

"Where in blazes did you get that?" Morton shouted. "How did you hear it? That's restricted information! Only I . . ."

Custer gave Morton a long look with a calm eye, letting the man's unfinished sentence hang in the room like a bad smell. Then he looked back to the report.

"I heard of it, because I asked to hear of it," Custer said. "Regardless of the fact that you may very well be 'in charge around here,' I am still the President. I have been in this house for four years, and was in the other House for years before that, and 'in charge' or not, I still have a few friends here and there." He put the report back in the folder and closed the cover.

Morton slumped, staring at nothing, trying to understand where he had lost the argument. Custer almost pitied him, but knew that soon, Morton would realize that he'd lost the argument when he'd accepted the meeting, and knew just as well that Yancy and Chaucer would be the ones to bear the brunt of his anger.

"Now tell me, Levi, why have you increased shipments to the Cuban rebels?"

Morton lifted a weak hand. "An independent Cuba," he said, "is the next step in bringing Cuba into the Union."

"I agree," Custer said, and Morton looked up in surprise. "Cuba is on the brink, as near to independence as it's ever been. But why act now, if the rebels are making progress on their own?"

"Our interests there," Morton said. "The Spanish Crown has imposed draconian restrictions on our sugar interests. They're hurting; the shipments barely pay for themselves now, between costs and tariffs—"

"And the damage caused by those same rebels you're supplying."

"Yes, perhaps, but it's a necessary first cost for final victory."

"I see," Custer said, drumming the fingers of his good hand on the table. "I had kept our support of the rebels to a minimum. This increase raises our exposure, and our danger. How do you think Spain will react when they can no longer ignore our supplying an insurrection within their borders? And how will you respond if you have your army wandering around the prairie? 'To protect everything is to protect nothing,' a man once said, but to fight everything is to lose everything."

Through his daze, Morton sensed the rebuff, and shook off his fog. He straightened, smoothed the hem of his vest, and looked Custer in the eye.

"If you will excuse me, Mr. President."

Custer waved a hand, dismissing him. Morton turned and finally, successfully, escaped the room, his aides following him closely. The door closed behind them.

Custer coughed, his throat dry. Talking was difficult and he was out of practice. Douglas came forward, pouring him a glass of iced water.

"I don't know, sir," Douglas said. "That man was either whupped too much, or too little; I can't tell which."

Custer sipped the cool water and felt it slither down his throat and gullet. He wiped his mouth with his kerchief.

"I'm not sure either," Custer said, "but I'm pretty sure he's going to get whupped again, one way or the other."

And if it keeps him from destroying those people, he said silently, *I'll do it myself.*

CHAPTER 16

Moon When the Whistlers Get Fat, New
Fifty-seven Years after the Star Fell
South of the White River
Alliance Territory

Storm Arriving knelt with his soldiers in among the cattails at the edge of the creek. The reedstalks creaked against each other, and the air was thick with the moist scents of warm mud, sweaty men, and broad-leaved foliage. With his every move, the soggy ground smacked its lips like an old man before dinner, and with every breeze, the reeds talked volubly among themselves. The soldiers, though, said little.

He had fewer than a hundred men now, and more walked away with every phase of the moon. Storm Arriving looked up into a blue sky patched by bright clouds and held up by an even brighter sun. Summer was well upon them. The name of the moon said it all: The Moon When the Whistlers Get Fat. Looking back toward the lazy creek, he could divine the outlines of their war whistlers, their flanks a striped green to match the reeds, their eyes closed as they soaked up the humid heat. But their whistlers were not growing fat; he knew from riding his own that their frames were lean and muscled, for that is what the soldiers needed: speed and agility, not summertime complacency.

And out beyond the reeds, out past their hiding place, he heard the approach of the reason for that need.

Vé'ho'e music was strange to his ear. It had too many tones, all crammed in between the handful of notes that his ear could distinguish, all arranged with intricate precision in short phrases that repeated over and over. He found it confusing and boring at the same time, but he was glad for it because before the bluecoats even appeared, their song announced their coming.

The sunken creekbed carved its way through a prairie that barely noticed its presence. The hills, thick and green with summer grasses, lay on either side of it like dogs sleeping in the sun. From beyond one such rise a mile distant came the herald song of flute and drum.

"There," Whistling Elk said, pointing toward the two scouts who ran in advance of the column.

"Good," said Mosquito from his place nearby. "Let's get this fight over with. It's time we went home."

"Me, too," said another soldier.

Storm Arriving frowned. "You cannot leave," he said. "I need every man here. I need *more* than every man here."

"It is summer," Mosquito said. "My family needs me, too, and more than you do."

"Some must stay," he said through bared teeth. "The patrols have pulled back to the lands north of the White River. We are the only ones protecting this land. If we leave, the bluecoats will be able to go wherever they wish."

"And if I stay much longer, my wife and her mother will die of hunger this winter, because I have not provided them with meat to survive it. Besides, the bluecoats grow in their numbers while we only diminish."

"We diminish because soldiers like you leave! And meanwhile, look! Look!" He pointed out toward the column of *vé'hó'e* that had now appeared from behind the gentle hill.

The two scouts were a mile ahead of the bluecoats, their eyes scanning the land along the creekbed. Behind them, the men in dark blue wool marched in easy order through the knee-high grass. Unlike previous encounters, this was no supply train or escort for new recruits. These men walked without fear; their raucous song said as much. There were a hundred or more of them, with pack beasts carrying supplies, and chiefs riding horses near the rear. Each man carried a pack and a rifle.

"This will be a hard fight," Mosquito said.

Silently, Storm Arriving agreed, and then one of the

scouts did something that caught his attention. Like any scout, he trotted for a bit parallel to the creek, then stopped to view the scene, but when he stopped, he also made a motion with his hand.

"What is he doing?" Whistling Elk asked, noticing, too, the odd behavior.

It was not at every stop, but only when he was in front of the other scout, with his back shielding his gesture from the others. Storm Arriving squinted, trying to see what the man was doing.

Running forward, he stopped. His hand in a fist against his chest, he made a motion as if tossing something to the ground and then, hand stiff like a chopping blade, made a forward thrust.

Bad, the first sign said, and Go, said the second.

"He is one of ours," Storm Arriving said. "And something is wrong."

"He is warning us," Whistling Elk said.

"Of what?" Mosquito wondered.

Storm Arriving watched the scout signal again: Bad, Go away. But not away, in the direction opposite the approaching bluecoats. The scout signaled away, down the creekbed, downstream and at an angle. Not the quickest route of retreat. He turned to look across the north side of the streambed.

The land on the far side was as rolling as to the south, and being so, could conceal as much.

"Mount!" he commanded as the bluecoat cavalry rode around a rise, rifles raised and ready. "Let's go!"

Cavalry carbines popped and spat, and the reeds hissed as bullets shot through. Soldiers dropped their cover and leapt to their whistlers, the war mounts calm under the incoming fire.

The soldiers urged their beasts into motion. Some rode up onto the south side, but the bluecoat infantry had already deployed into firing ranks and the first volley sent the riders back toward the creek. But the creekbed slowed them with its mud and thick growth.

"To the north bank," Storm Arriving shouted, and the men, long habituated to command, complied.

A shout went up from the cavalry riders as they saw their quarry reach level ground on their side of the stream, but Storm Arriving and his soldiers had faith in their whistler mounts and kicked them into their fastest pace. The beasts leaned forward, necks extended, tails straight out behind them. Their tough, flat-clawed fore-feet drooped to the seedheads, and with powerful rear legs, they pumped across the flat terrain, impelled by the shots from their pursuers' rifles.

Distance grew between the mounted groups, but not quickly enough. The carbines the cavalry bore were re-peaters, and they sent shot after ill-aimed shot after the soldiers. With so many, some were bound to find a mark, and as they did, whistlers howled and men cried out.

"Heel left," Storm Arriving shouted, and they did, holding onto the ropes of their riding harnesses and leaning into a sharp left turn around a grassy rise. Rifle shots tore through their exposed flank, but quickly the rise was between them for protection. "Prepare!" he or-dered. Rifles came out of sheaths. "Halt!"

They reined in and wheeled to face the oncoming cav-alry. Whistlers ducked down into the grass, their chame-leon skin fading to green blotches. Soldiers leapt down behind them, using their size and coloration for camouflage.

It was no longer a matter of victory for Storm Arriv-ing. It was a matter of escape and survival. "Aim for their mounts," he said, and heard the agreement of others.

When the bluecoats appeared around the rise, both sides opened fire. Shooting from atop a galloping horse in a turn, any bluecoats who found a mark did so by luck. For Storm Arriving and his soldiers, luck was not needed. Horses screamed as bullets hit sweaty flanks and froth-spattered breasts, and those not hit shied and reared. Bluecoats fell or were thrown. Some kept their saddle seats, but as Storm Arriving sent his third round into them, the cavalry was tossed into chaos.

"Away!" he shouted. Holding the first rope of his rid-ing gear, he let his whistler pull him up as it rose. He tucked his feet into the harness loops and sped away. Looking back, he saw four whistlers had been left be-hind, wounded beyond recovery. The soldiers, though, had been picked up by fellows, as had the wounded, and they fled the confusion they had created, heading for the safety of the prairie's gentle folds. A final look back told him that the bluecoats had broken off their pursuit, unable or unwilling to continue with their reduced force. He was just as glad.

They headed north for several miles until they reached their camp in the woods along Broken Leg Creek, a favored spot with plenty of cover, water, and deadwood for cookfires. Here they found the supplies and riding whistlers they had left in reserve, and men set to the tasks of tending their wounds and caring for their beasts. Storm Arriving was inspecting his whistler's feet for injury when a group of soldiers came up to him. Mosquito was with them. Storm Arriving glanced over at Whistling Elk, but the man-becoming-woman merely shrugged, not knowing what the men wanted. Storm Arriving stood to meet them.

"It is time for us to go home," Mosquito said.

Storm Arriving looked at the group. Ten men, all seasoned veterans, a tenth of his remaining strength. "How am I to wage this war without men to fight it?" he asked.

"That cannot be our concern," Mosquito replied. "We cannot fight forever. We have to return to the People."

"No," Storm Arriving said. "You will stay here and fight. As you agreed."

"We did not agree to fight all year," Mosquito said, anger making his face darken with blood. "No one expected to fight all year!"

"Sharp Knife will return soon with the Crow People. Already the Crow soldiers will outnumber our own. Do you want to let the Crow defend our lands?"

Mosquito's features twisted in distaste. "Fighting *with* the Crow? We should be fighting *against* them! If such trash is truly coming to the fight, it is only another reason to return home. And if you still believe that they will honor their agreement, you are a bigger fool than I thought."

"Fool?" Storm Arriving said, stepping forward in anger. "Better fool than coward."

"Is it a coward who wants to feed his family?"

"A coward runs home to his wife when the fighting gets tough."

"At least I know where my wife is, and with whom."

Whistling Elk stepped in between the men before they clashed. One hand against each man's chest, he pressured them apart. Storm Arriving glared at Mosquito. He wanted to pummel the man's blunt features, wanted to throttle him until his eyes boggled in his head.

"Stand back, both of you," Whistling Elk said, and to Storm Arriving alone, "Fighting the men you lead will not help."

The words sank in and Storm Arriving swallowed his anger. He stepped back away from Whistling Elk's barring hand. Mosquito did likewise.

"You cannot tell me what to do," Mosquito said, uttering the ultimate phrase of the People's independent spirit.

"No," Storm Arriving said. "I can only tell you what you agreed to do. What you *all* agreed to do."

Glancing from Storm Arriving to Whistling Elk, Mosquito decided not to respond. He turned and stalked off toward his mount and supplies. The men with him, some sheepish in rebuke, others still fuming with their own anger, followed him.

"Some will stay," Storm Arriving said to Whistling Elk.

"Yes," the man-becoming-woman said. "But how many? And for how long?"

He watched as seven soldiers packed up their gear and rode off toward the north.

"Sharp Knife will return soon with reinforcements," Storm Arriving said.

I hope, he added to himself.

Toward evening, riders came in from the other battle groups in the region, bringing reports of heavy bluecoat activity, word of the Council's continued refusal to send any soldiers, and news of departure of more men heading home to family, lodge, and the summer hunt. Storm Arriving sat near the small fire he shared with Whistling Elk and Knee Prints by the Bank. The lean carcasses of two rabbits hissed over the searing coals. Looking past the fire into the darkness of the wood beyond, he considered the information the riders had brought.

"The bluecoats are out in greater numbers," he said.

"Like today," Whistling Elk said. "That was not a simple supply train."

"No," Knee Prints by the Bank said. "Nor was it a group of new recruits. Those were seasoned men."

This information pointed Storm Arriving toward an uncomfortable conclusion that he had been avoiding since sundown, but now he had to face it.

"They have changed strategies," he said. "The bluecoats no longer merely protect their own settlements and harry us with small raiding parties. Now they send large forces marching across our lands. Now they hunt us."

Whistling Elk held the sleeve of his dress out of the fire as he reached out to turn the rabbits on the spit. "Look at it this way. With fewer numbers, we will be harder to find."

Storm Arriving sighed, his concerns deeper than his friend's humor could affect. "Not us," he said. "The People. They hunt the People." He looked and saw the stunned faces of the two men he had come to trust above all others in this war. He shrugged and stared back into the darkness. "It is the only thing that makes sense."

Knee Prints by the Bank scowled. "It is as it was for my people," he said. "What the *vé'hó'e* cannot subdue, they work to destroy."

"How will we stop them?" Whistling Elk asked.

Storm Arriving lifted his head and looked once more into the forest darkness that hid his battle group. Small fires like his own were tended by tired soldiers, filling the wood with globes of wavering light encased in glimmering green, but there were too few—desperately too few to make a difference against a full regiment of bluecoats. He needed more men, and he closed his eyes to do what he had not done for a long time.

Sitting up straight, he felt the pull of skin on the scars he bore on his chest, the scars he had earned through the skin sacrifice, a daylong ordeal spent hanging from skewers that pierced his flesh. He felt the tightness of the scars and remembered, after it was over and the stretched skin had been sliced away, the feeling that had suffused him. He had felt the nearness of the spirit world in that moment, and had been sure of its existence.

Though his belief in it had waned, he reached back into that time and that moment, and sent a prayer onward into that other world: Help us.

His whistler rumbled from his spot nearby the fire, a low, chest-filling pulsation like fingers on a drumhead. Whistling Elk's mount picked up the reverberating call, as did others. The hackles on Storm Arriving's neck stood tall as he understood that the whistlers' thrum was not a warning, but a message of homecoming.

He stood. Others did, also. Men and whistlers looked to the northwest, toward the wind and home. Past the radiant spheres of campfires, the forest was black. But the whistlers sensed that out there, someone was coming, some of their own were coming in.

The call of welcome growled through the trees and then, pale as spirit riders, men on whistlers appeared between the boles. Storm Arriving felt his heart leap in his chest as he saw their clothing, their headgear, their weapons, and their faces.

Crow.

From amid the ghostly company, Sharp Knife rode forward. Storm Arriving raised his hand and the Little Bowstring soldier came ahead to meet him. The Crow warriors stayed at the limit of vision. Sharp Knife dismounted and clasped hands with his friends.

"I am glad to see you," Storm Arriving said. "We are in great need of what you bring."

"It is a relief to be back among my own," the veteran warrior said in a wistful tone, "but I am afraid I have not brought you what you wanted."

"What?" Storm Arriving said with a laugh and a sweep of his hand toward the Crow. "Are these riders only spirit men?"

"No, they are real."

"Then what is it I wanted that you have not brought?" Storm Arriving asked with a jovial slap to Sharp Knife's shoulder.

"Enough of them," Sharp Knife said.

Storm Arriving's laughter died in a throat gone dry. Sharp Knife's scowl of concern had not faded. Storm Arriving looked at the firelight's limit and the ragged line of riders that stood along it. They were fierce-eyed men, some young, some mature, but none of them green, none of them inexperienced in war. They were just the type of men Storm Arriving had hoped for, but Sharp Knife's worry dug a pit in his belly.

"Tell me what you mean," he said.

Sharp Knife hesitated, looking back at the riders himself before he spoke. "That is all there is. They are all that came."

Storm Arriving felt every muscle tighten. He swallowed with difficulty. "Then tell me there are those I cannot see behind them."

The Little Bowstring soldier hung his head. "I cannot."

Knee Prints by the Bank spoke in a hiss. "This is treachery. There are barely forty of them."

"Grey Feather promised two men for every rifle we sent him," Storm Arriving said, unable to keep his voice low. "What happened to Grey Feather's promise?"

"Quiet," Whistling Elk said, a hand on Storm Arriving's arm. "Quiet, or you will lose even the few he has sent us."

Storm Arriving looked and saw the defiance in the Crow. Their bitter expressions spoke of old pain and little caring.

"This was all Grey Feather could send right now. It's the hunting season, and his soldiers had to put aside meat for their families. These men, they have no families."

As they spoke, the news spread through the camp. Standing there, hearing Sharp Knife's words, Storm Arriving also heard the words of indignation that began to rise from others.

"This is all they sent?"

"The Crow People have gone back on their word."

"I have a family, too."

Storm Arriving closed his eyes as the discontent rolled through the forest, swift as wind, destructive as wildfire.

"Welcome in our new friends," he said to Sharp Knife. "Ask them to make camp among us. I will not have them feel that they were any different from our own."

Sharp Knife signed his agreement and went to do as he was asked.

"How can you be so calm?" Knee Prints by the Bank asked in a whisper.

Storm Arriving took a deep breath and smelled the scents of woodsmoke, cooked meat, and wild onions. "What choice do I have?" he said.

He did not eat that night, waving away any offer of the spitted rabbit. Instead, he sat next to his whistler, on the dark side, away from the fire, leaning against his mount's spice-scented skin. From this shadowy spot, he could look out over the forest camp, and could see and hear everything.

Sharp Knife had done as he had asked and set the Crow warriors in camps among their own. Keeping the tribes separate could have delayed the inevitable, but he wanted to force the situation and see the result as soon as possible. And so, as he sat against his drake's warmth, he listened to the arguments, the insults, and the challenges that were tossed between the campfires. As the night deepened, he heard the imprecations, the complaints, and the justifications as those tired of their futile war built the strength they needed. Toward morning, he heard the grumbling of whistlers as they were prodded awake, and as their soldiers, convinced of their own righteousness but not brave enough to face their commander, stole out of camp before dawn would show their faces.

When the sun rose, weaving its golden light around the tree trunks, Storm Arriving stood on stiff legs and walked through the encampment.

Men were waking up, eyes bleary with too little sleep, their worried dreams giving way to worried thoughts. As he passed by, Storm Arriving signed a silent greeting. "Thank you for staying," he said to the men of his own tribe, and, "Thank you for coming," he said to the Crow soldiers. Of the men who had stayed, he saw widowers, orphans, and those who, like Knee Prints by the Bank, bore a hatred of the bluecoats that outweighed everything else. There was a resolve in their features that hardened them. Eyes dark and expressionless, mouths set in grim lines, skin tight across jaws—they were faces carved by pain and loss, and in the Crow men he saw the same.

They were a hundred men, forty Crow and sixty of the People's soldiers. It was a small group, but a group dedicated to the purpose ahead. As he returned to the ashes of his own campfire, he knew there would be no further dissensions. Those who were with them would stay with them until the end, whatever end that might be.

And what of me? he asked himself. Neither orphan nor widower, what keeps *me* here?

The answer, however, was clear. He was just like these men: hard, bitter, and alone, a man without family or connections. His mother and father were dead, his wife and child and sister were off seeking a white man, and his father-in-law stood in public opposition to his every move.

But I am a soldier, aren't I? Isn't it my duty to be out here, protecting my tribe?

He did not know but, as he looked out over the fighting men who would follow him beyond this place, he didn't know that it really mattered, as long as the goal was the same.

CHAPTER 17

Moon When the Whistlers Get Fat, Waxing
Fifty-seven Years after the Star Fell
Off the Coast of Cadiz
Land of the Iron Shirts

Speaks while Leaving stood on the ship's deck with—and apart from—the other passengers. The twenty or so *vé'hó'e* who had traveled with her on the *Hija Del Viento* had become accustomed to her presence, but they still did not know what to do about her. At first, their rudeness had exceeded anything she could have imagined. They gaped at her with openmouthed stares, their pallid features twisted in disgust. Within a few days, they began to hide their whispers behind their hands, their stares turned to long glances, and their retreats diminished to less evasive maneuvers.

The trip might have gone more smoothly had either One Who Flies or Alejandro been able to act as a liaison between her and the other passengers. A word, a gesture, even their mere presence might have lessened the horror of these people. But wishing and wondering did not change the fact that Alejandro had spent the entire voyage belowdeck, ill from the ship's constant rocking; One Who Flies had been likewise incapacitated, though for a different reason entirely.

With Vincent's help, One Who Flies had managed to gain access to the liquor that had debilitated him so thoroughly. But Vincent had remained behind in Cuba, and since then Mouse Road had taken in hand the care of One Who Flies. The ocean crossing had not been easy on him.

Not that Speaks while Leaving regretted the situation.

Though her journey had been spent mostly in solitude, it had given her time to spend with her daughter without caring about the things that normally filled her life: preparing the next meal, fetching the day's water, setting up the family's lodges, butchering kills, tanning hides, drying meat, gathering wood and chips for the fire, making clothes, weaving ropes, and tending to the newborn, the aged, and those afflicted by the illnesses and accidents that were part of everyday existence on the Plains.

The past moon had been a time of unbelievable luxury. Water was brought to her, food was presented, and even the eliminations of her own body were whisked away by others whose only purpose was to serve her and those with her. She hadn't had to concern herself with anything but the care and feeding of her daughter, and even that had been eased tremendously by the continual supply of clean cloth, ample water, and foods prepared by unseen hands. And, had she desired it, even the most basic tasks of feeding and bathing her daughter could have been delegated to others.

But she had not so desired. The time had been an unexpected gift that she had no wish to waste. She watched Blue Shell Woman grow plump with the generous feedings. She was enchanted anew by her daughter's silly babblings. Not needing to keep her hands free for daily work, she put aside the cradleboard and instead carried her daughter about, holding her on her hip as she showed Blue Shell Woman the world around them. She had learned of her daughter's inquisitiveness, of how birds and the waving branches of trees always made her laugh. Aboard the ship, the two of them had fallen into a new rhythm: waking early to enjoy the dawn and the empty decks before the other passengers awoke, then eating something sweet and warm and creamy, then a nap in the sunshine. When gulls flew with the ship, she took Blue Shell Woman to the rear deck and they laughed as the big birds wheeled and spun, their snow-white plumage bright in the sunlight. In the afternoons, Speaks while Leaving told her daughter stories and tales, taught her of the spirits and the world. During the nights when the ship's movement made it hard for them to sleep for longer than a hand's breadth of time, she spoke at length of the girl's father. Even though it was a tender subject, her daughter had a right to be proud of her father, and in the darkened cabin room, she could tell her of his achievements and her tears would not show.

And through these languorous days, this yearling babe whom she thought she knew was revealed to her as a completely new person with her own moods, thoughts, likes, dislikes, and even—she thought—dreams.

She stood at the rail, Blue Shell Woman happy at her hip, both of them squinting into the morning brilliance that hid their destination. Nearby but still at a discreet distance were the *vé'ho'e* passengers: men in dark suits and women in frocks of striped cloth. Now and again, one of the women would glance in her direction, as if wondering what Speaks while Leaving might do next. Suddenly the woman gasped and stared at her. Others near the woman looked and they, too, stared at her and Blue Shell Woman. Then Speaks while Leaving heard someone behind her make a rude noise. She turned to find Mouse Road, up from belowdecks, her fingers pulling at her cheeks and at the corners of her eyes, her tongue wagging like a bull in rut and her rear end swaying from side to side.

Laughter burst from her lips even as she moved to hide her sister-in-law from view.

"Stop that," she said, barely able to speak for laughing.

"Why?" Mouse Road asked, wiping her mouth with her sleeve and peering around to look at the *vé'ho'e* women. "I'm just giving them what they want, something to stare at."

Speaks while Leaving laughed again. "Yes, you certainly did that," she said, wanting to change the subject. "How is One Who Flies?"

"See for yourself," the younger woman said, turning.

One Who Flies emerged from the stairway, stepping up onto the deck and taking a look around. He saw the women at the rail and raised a hand in greeting.

He looked better than when they had departed, with some color in his cheeks and eyes that were once more sharp and alive with thought. He had shaved off his whiskers and moustache, and looked like a human being again, despite his *vé'ho'e* clothing, but his mouth was dour and there was a harrowed pinch to the intelligence in his eyes. He may have been purged of the imbibed poisons, but he was not happy.

"What is wrong with him?" Speaks while Leaving asked her sister.

"Ask *him*."

One Who Flies came up to them, bowed, and joined them at the rail.

"It is good to see you," Speaks while Leaving began.

"Thank you," he said.

"But you look distressed. What troubles you?"

"Nothing," he said as he squinted into the rising sun. "I am fine."

"You see?" Mouse Road said. "It is practically all he ever says."

"And what would you have me say?" There was something new in his voice as well: a bitterness Speaks while Leaving had never heard there before.

"I would have you tell me what it is that troubles you." She turned to Speaks while Leaving. "He barely sleeps, though the tremors have nearly left him. He paces at night; I hear his footsteps. He will not speak unless spoken to, nor offer an opinion on anything, not on what he wishes to eat or if he cares to take a walk up in the sunshine. He says neither what he wants nor what he needs. It is like talking to a stone. A whistler would be better company."

"Then you should have picked your companions more carefully," he said. "It was not I who insisted on this journey."

"*Eya!*" Mouse Road said, signing surrender with her hands. "My fault. As if I had forced you to come along."

"And you didn't?" he asked. " 'I can't let her go alone,' you said. 'I need you,' you said."

"And I do."

"For what?" he said, turning to face her. "To fail again? To ruin everything again?"

"No," Speaks while Leaving said, jolting them both out of their disputation. She looked at them both, saw Mouse Road's frustration and the pain that One Who Flies wore like a trophy. To speak of her vision and the role she was sure One Who Flies was to play would only anger him further. "I need you to try," she said. "That is all. Only to try."

He stood a bit taller and glanced at her. "And if I do fail?"

"Then you fail," she said. "But you will fail having tried, and not lying in the mud, reeking of *vé'ho'e* poisons."

That shamed him—she saw it in the way his stance rounded and his gaze turned vacant—and she regretted her words. Shaming him had not been her intent. She needed him strong of spirit as well as of body. She tried to undo the damage.

"Will you try?" she asked him.

Quietly, he said, "Yes," and turned to look once more toward the land of their goal.

"How long will it take to reach their queen?" she asked.

"I do not know," One Who Flies said. "But here is someone who can answer you. *Buenos días, señor.*"

"Buenos días." It was Alejandro, pale and unsteady on his feet, but on his feet at last.

"How do you feel?" Speaks while Leaving asked him.

"Better just to be within the sight of land," he said as he peered at the sun-bright waters and white buildings ahead. "Brilliant Cadiz. Salty and clean, the Gate to the New World."

"Can you tell us, Don Alejandro, how long it will be before we can meet your queen?"

Alejandro shrugged. "It is hard to say. Tonight, we shall stay in a small place my wife's family owns nearby, along the Guadalquivir. From there we will take a carriage to Utrera where we will board a train for the trip. By train, it will be four, perhaps five days; were we to travel by horse or carriage, it would be closer to two weeks before we reached the regency court."

"Two weeks?" Speaks while Leaving wondered aloud. "Your land must be as large as ours."

Alejandro held up a hand. "Hardly, my dear. A horse-drawn carriage is not a whistler, not by quite a margin, and even a whistler with a travois would quickly outpace a heavy carriage on a bad road. But the train shall save us that particular torture." He turned back to the view. "For myself, though, I would walk barefoot all the way to Madrid if it meant an end to my ocean voyaging."

And I would do the same, Speaks while Leaving thought, glancing at One Who Flies, if only I could know that what I am doing is right.

The city of Cadiz looked much like Havana, from what they were able to see of it. With low houses crammed up along the shore of a deep harbor thick with tiny boats and tan-skinned, dark-haired people working busily at tasks she could barely fathom, Speaks while Leaving would not have been able to tell the two towns apart had not the sun driven a different course through the sky in relation to the surrounding hills. Such comparisons were brief, however, as they quickly left the bright city on its sparkling bay and headed into those hills.

The carriage Alejandro hired proved a rough ride, bouncing and jostling as it traveled along the pitted road, and the air within grew close with the scents of four people ripe from two weeks at sea. The thing that Speaks while Leaving had missed most from her normal life was her daily bath in the rivers near camp. On the ship, where the large *vé'ho'e* basins weren't available for bathing, she had missed them most intensely.

The road was dusty and, once they had crossed over the scrub-covered ridges and left behind the refreshment of the ocean breeze, the air grew warm and thick. They wound through the hills for hours, stopping at a small building every hand or two of time to water the four sweaty horses that pulled the carriage. Eventually, the hills dropped away and they began to meander their way down their sloping sides. Speaks while Leaving could see the lowlands ahead, a dark green fen laced with curving streams, stretching into a hazy distance.

"Las Marismas," Alejandro labeled it. "The delta of the Guadalquivir and breeding ground of the best fighting bulls in the world."

"Fighting bulls?" she asked.

"Yes." Alejandro's voice was filled with admiration. "The corrida, or bullfight as you might call it, is a national sport in Spain. One man, one bull, in a contest to the death—usually the bull's. Perhaps you shall see a corrida during your stay."

One man against one bull did not sound like anything worth watching to Speaks while Leaving. During the buffalo hunt, a lucky man might bring down two bulls in a single day, and that while riding amid the entire herd. One man against one bull did not sound like a contest at all, but she kept her opinion to herself as it was obvious that Alejandro took great pride in it.

They reached the marshy lowlands and drove a twisting route along their limit. The road kept close to the hills like a child not wanting to stray from its mother, and from the look of the wet, swampy land beyond, Speaks while Leaving could see the reason for it. Every step through this land would bring solid ground and spongy muck in equal proportion. Greenery could just as easily cover a sink as a stone here, but what captured her attention were the birds that inhabited the fen. Everywhere—on water and on the soggy land—birds congregated.

Ducks and geese were the only birds of a shape familiar to her, but were of types she had never seen. There were troops of long-legged birds—like herons but smaller and blazing white. Flocks of smaller birds filled the air, flying between the gnarled, dark trees that marked the patches of more solid ground. And above, dark-winged against the blue sky, large birds soared on the rising air, circling like the little-teeth along the shores of the Big Salty, the feathers of their wingtips spread like fingers to catch the wind.

While Blue Shell Woman slept in her arms, Speaks while Leaving stared out the dusty window, marveling with Mouse Road at the variety of birds large and small, pale and dark, unadorned and painted in the brightest of colors, all of them new and unfamiliar.

It was late afternoon when they arrived at the villa where they were to spend their first night, and despite the dust of the road, they unlatched their windows and slid them downward so that they could lean out and get a better look at the place. It was a long, low building of pale stone, nestled beneath the branches of tall, dark trees, which shaded it from the westering sun. But for the breeze of their passage, the air was calm, hot, and thick with the smell of the swamps: moist, green, fecund.

The carriage drove up along a path of packed earth and pulled up near the villa's main entrance. Black timbers supported the deep eaves and the wrought-iron grillwork gated the entryway.

The heavy front doors opened. Two men in simple cloth shirts, striped pants, and sandals came out and opened the iron gate. Then from the shadows within the house came a dark figure. It was an old woman, short and squat, clothed in a black skirt and a black shawl over a white blouse. She had a cane in each of her gnarled hands, and as she slowly emerged into the afternoon sun, Speaks while Leaving could tell that she was a relative of Olivia and Victoria, the two sisters who had married Roberto and Alejandro. Though advancing years had withered her beauty and bent her frame, her eyes still carried the dark spirit that Speaks while Leaving had seen in her younger relations.

Alejandro greeted the woman warmly, speaking to her rapidly in his own language. The woman spoke little, accepting his kisses on each of her cheeks, but her eyes never left the three guests who stood waiting to be introduced. When Alejandro did turn to present them to her, the old woman's appraisal was frank and unflattering.

"Please allow me to present Dona Señora Albina Augustina Álvarez de Baca, aunt to my wife, and our hostess for the night."

One Who Flies bowed, and Speaks while Leaving and Mouse Road curtsied as Alejandro had instructed them.

Squinting at One Who Flies, the old woman leaned toward her nephew and asked a question. Alejandro laughed, a little forcefully. "Dona Albina asks if you are a Catholic," he said, embarrassed by the question.

"No," One Who Flies answered him. "My mother is a Presbyterian, and that is the faith in which I was raised."

The woman was quite displeased by the answer. Speaks while Leaving could not understand more than a few of her rapidly lisped words as Dona Albina railed, pointing to One Who Flies, pointing at Speaks while Leaving and Mouse Road. She used the word *católico*

repeatedly in relation to One Who Flies, but for the
women she used a different word—*pagana*—and she
used it with disgust. Alejandro tried to quiet her diplo-
matically at first, then with glowers delivered between
glances of apology for his guests.

"*Paganas, en mi casa,*" she went on, and then berated
Alejandro himself on some subject that involved his
wife, Victoria.

"*¡Ya basta!*"

Birds flew up from the trees as if blown into the air
by Alejandro's shout. The old woman looked at him,
jaw slack, eyes wide. He said something else, quietly,
and though Speaks while Leaving could see that he
would win the argument, she also knew that he would
smart for it when word traveled back to his wife.

Alejandro ushered them into the coolness of the house
with a drove of apologies. "She is a very devout
woman," he said, and, "She is very old. She doesn't have
many guests," he added, and finally ended with, "It is
only for one night."

Speaks while Leaving did not understand how simply
sitting all day in a box that bounced along the roads
could make her so tired, but it had. Her companions
were similarly affected, and when she and Mouse Road
were shown to the room they would share, they did not
care about the chair, the table, or the door that led to
the small garden patio. They saw nothing but the bed
piled high with quilts and coverings, and immediately
they collapsed upon it, Blue Shell Woman between
them. Together, they slept, the day's dissipating warmth
their only blanket. They awoke to find it full dark outside, and the room filled with the aromas of meat. By
the light of a single candle, Speaks while Leaving could
see that on the room's simple table, food had been laid
out, left for them by silent servants.

"I don't think the old woman wants to see us for the
evening meal," Mouse Road said.

Speaks while Leaving laughed. "That is fine with me."

The three of them kept to their small room at the end
of the long house, eating a dinner of thick stew and
brown bread that only brought on another wave of

sleepiness. Even Blue Shell Woman seemed to be happy to return to sleep.

In the night, Speaks while Leaving wrestled with dreams of recent events.

She awoke to the grey light of dawn. Mouse Road and Blue Shell Woman still slept, a thin blanket pulled over them against the night's chill. She slipped gently off the bed, made water in the small bucket the *vé'hó'e* supplied for the purpose, and then, grabbing her moccasins and a blue-and-white striped blanket that lay on a chair, she let herself out the narrow door that led to the small garden.

The air was cool, almost cold, and made the skin on her arms turn to gooseflesh as she stopped to put on her moccasins. Bricks paved the patio in a circular whorl, in the center of which was a small table and two chairs. Plants surrounded the small area, and enclosing the whole garden were walls made of the same brick as the pavers. Vines climbed the walls of both garden and house, tendrils grasping mortared joins. In one corner, a pillar of thorny canes sprouted up like a flowered geyser, the pink blooms unnaturally bright in the pre-dawn gloom. She walked over to smell one of the flowers and her nose and mouth were filled, honeyed, and her stomach growled, made hungry by the scent.

To one side she saw a small gap in the enclosing wall. Squeezing through the ivy-thick opening, she emerged at the side of the house. The sky was still indeterminate, a starless grey that could mean either a clouded or brilliant day ahead. The dark trees that protected the house stood silent in the still air. Beyond them, birdsong beckoned.

She chafed her arms to brush off the chill and wrapped the blanket like a shawl around her shoulders before she headed down through the trees. As she left the trees behind, the vista widened, revealing the same broad landscape that had filled the carriage's windows the previous day. Flat and unobstructed but for the infrequent top of a large and contorted tree, the twisting paths and waterways stretched out before her through a veil of morning mist. Birds swooped through the mist, and she heard the morning squabbles of waterfowl.

A well-worn path led toward the waters, and she headed down it. At the far side of the drive, she climbed the stile over a split-rail fence and walked into a world filled with movement and life.

The pale path wound its way into the fen, twisting around pools and slow-moving waters thick with weed. Though it was chilly, the waters looked inviting. Grass stood tall near the waters, heads heavy with seed and stalks already paling with the approach of summer. In the distance, a stalk of white egrets waded through the dark water. Nearer, ducks paddled the streams on either side, but she did not know them with their curious colors and stripes and speckles.

"Who are you all?" she asked them as she walked along. "Do you know any from my world?"

No, they said to her, winking their golden eyes. Where is your world?

She laughed at the ducks' question. "I do not know," she told them, "other than to say 'west, across the water.'"

The thought filled her with a sudden sadness, for never before had she not known where her home was. Never before had she not known how to go home. She pulled the blanket a little tighter around her shoulders.

She came to a place where the path turned to skirt a larger pond. The waters were covered with tiny green leaves that shone in the growing light of dawn. The golden-eyed ducks paddled out into the pond, nibbling at the floating plants, leaving dark wakes in the still waters. There grew in the air a flow of warbles, whistles, and cackles that came from the shrouding mist until a swallow flew close, skimming over the pond and the low-lying land. Another joined it, and then another. They were three, four, eight, fifteen. Speaks while Leaving was surrounded by a swirl of the tiny, sharp-tailed birds, all sweeping, gyring, calling out in wild conversation.

They flew past her as she walked, flitting near her feet, past her hips. She heard the flap of their wings near her head, and felt the wind of their passage on her face. They spun around her, white-breasted blurs, black-backed darts. When she stopped, they swept the pond's surface, discomfiting the ducks, but when she took another step, they returned, eager for the gnats and bugs disturbed from the grasses at her feet. She walked along with this corona of flight surrounding her, following her. She held out a hand as she walked, and one of the birds lit there, its throat rapid with breath, its wide mouth agape, panting. A second landed on her shoulder. They stared at her with beaded eyes.

"Do *you* know my world?" she asked them.

No, they said between breaths. You are a stranger to us here.

"*¿Señora?*" said a voice, and the swallows dispersed as quickly as autumn leaves in the wind.

A man was poling along the waterway in a flat-bottomed boat. He was staring at her as if at a spirit suddenly made flesh. "*Señora,*" he said again. "*¿Estás espíritu o estás real?*"

She did not know what he might have meant, and so she simply smiled and raised two fingers in the sign that meant *friend*. The man in the boat asked his question again, a little more urgently this time. Afraid she might have inadvertently broken some rule of this strange land, she turned and headed back into the mist, walking back the way she had come. It was just as well, she knew. Mouse Road would be awake by now, and Blue Shell Woman would need her attention as well. She only hoped that the man in the boat did not cause any difficulty.

Back at the villa, she found Mouse Road and Blue Shell Woman at their ablutions. The little girl stood in a basin of warm, steamy water, holding herself upright by keeping a pudgy grip on Mouse Road's arm while Mouse Road bathed her. Blue Shell Woman smiled and gurgled as she saw her mother come in.

"Good morning, Little Pot Belly," she said, coming to help bathe her child. "Aren't you in a good mood this morning?"

"I am glad she is," Mouse Road said. "Everyone else in the house seems to be rather sour."

"We shall be on our way soon enough."

"And I'm glad of that, too."

They bathed the little girl and played games with her nose until she was clean. As Mouse Road took her niece off in a cotton towel to get dry, Speaks while Leaving tossed the basin water out into the garden greenery and then took the ewer to ask for more warm water. She opened the door, seeking one of the servants, and spied two of them down at the branching of the corridor, whispering in earnest gossip. She went toward them, hoping the pitcher would make her desire clear enough—for none of the household spoke the Trader's Tongue—but so deliberate were they that they did not notice her approach. She cleared her throat.

Startled out of their conference, the two women clung to each other for support. Seeing her, they immediately touched their heads, chests, and shoulders in the warding sign of their faith. Speaks while Leaving presented the empty pitcher to them, but they only stared at her.

"Pardon," she said to them, holding out the pitcher. *"Je vous en prie, donnez-moi plus d'eau?"*

The women warded themselves again and bobbed in quick curtsies. One, understanding either her words or gestures, reached out for the ewer, taking it with tentative hands as from a dangerous creature. The maid started off to fill it, leaving her companion standing there in the hallway, staring. Coming back, she grabbed the other woman's sleeve and pulled her along. The second maid followed, though her gaze clung to Speaks while Leaving as long as possible.

"Merci," Speaks while Leaving said absently, not knowing what to make of the women's odd behavior. She went back to the room. "They *are* acting strangely today," she said to Mouse Road. "But not sour-faced so much as, well, as a little crazy."

Mouse Road shrugged. "Who can say of *vé'hó'e*? They never seem to know how to act."

It was an old adage, but generally accurate. In this odd house, in this odd land, it seemed particularly so.

The water was brought by another wide-eyed serving woman who smiled and stared at Speaks while Leaving as she curtsied her way to the dry sink to fill the water basin. Hands free, she made that same, four-pointed warding but with a smile still on her face and her eyes still fixed on Speaks while Leaving, as she made her way out the door.

"I think they are all simple in the head," Mouse Road said.

"I think you may be right."

It was a short time later that there was a knock on the door and One Who Flies and Alejandro entered. Speaks while Leaving saw her friend's look linger on Mouse Road, and she was glad to see that some of his old affections seemed to be returning. Perhaps with those affections would come some of his old strength as well.

"The house is in an uproar," One Who Flies said. "What have you been doing?"

The two women glanced at each other, then shrugged.

"Nothing," Mouse Road said.

"Have you been in here all morning?" Alejandro asked.

"Not all morning," Speaks while Leaving said. "I went for a walk earlier."

"Out in the marsh?"

"Yes."

He pointed to the blue-striped blanket on the chair. "With that?"

"Yes. Was I not supposed to?"

"What *happened* out there?"

Speaks while Leaving did not understand their concern. "I went for a walk. It was cold, and I took the blanket. I walked along the water's edge; I . . . looked at the plants and . . . listened to the trees and . . . spoke to some of the birds there."

"You what?" Alejandro asked sharply.

It was a thing she had not expected Alejandro to understand, and looked to One Who Flies for support. "There were birds all around, in the water, flying around me as I walked—a few even landed on my arm. I-I spoke with them."

"You spoke to the birds?" Alejandro asked.

Her embarrassment gave way to annoyance. "Yes. Haven't you ever listened to the world around you? And if you listen, why can't you speak to it? I was lonely, and I was thinking of home. There were many birds around me, and I asked them if they had ever been to the land of the People."

One Who Flies walked to the window, taking in her words. "And had they?" he asked in the language of the People.

"No," she said. "But I didn't talk to very many. I wanted to ask the egrets but this man came along in a boat and—"

He began to laugh.

"One Who Flies," Alejandro said, "this is not a laughing matter."

He waved a hand as he laughed, moving to a chair to sit. "Oh, but it is. It is." He laughed some more and when he looked up at Speaks while Leaving, he began to laugh again.

Speaks while Leaving put her hands on her hips. "I am beginning to get angry."

One Who Flies got his humor under control. He looked at Alejandro. "She does not understand—"

"I would like to," Speaks while Leaving told him.

He wiped his eyes as his laughter subsided. "You, see, my dear, sweet lady, you have created quite a stir."

"How?" she asked. "I only went for a walk."

"The man in the boat?" he said. "He came back with the most incredible story. He says that when he was out there, a woman appeared out of the mist. She looked like one of the houseguests, but she was dressed all in blue and white, and was surrounded by a swirling cloud of swallows, like a halo of sorts. Some of the birds had landed on her hand, and the woman spoke to them. And when the man asked, 'Are you spirit or are you flesh?' she only answered with her hand held up in benediction." He held up his hand, two fingers extended upward in the sign that among the allied tribes meant *friend*. "And then she disappeared into the mist."

Speaks while Leaving still did not understand. Other than the man misunderstanding the sign she had made, it was precisely what had happened. Her perplexity must have shown on her face.

"He thinks you were the Virgin Mary," One Who Flies explained. "The Mother of God, of *their* god. The mother of the *vé'ho'e* god who died and lived again."

"*Me?*" Speaks while Leaving asked.

One Who Flies signed with his hand. *You.*

Now she laughed. She looked at Mouse Road, who still held Blue Shell Woman wrapped in a soft towel. "They think I am a spirit mother," she said, and they both laughed.

The three of them laughed together. Only Alejandro remained snappish. "You have to understand," he said quite seriously. "These are a very religious people, especially the country folk, and they take such things very seriously. Word of this is spreading."

"Yes?" she said. "And how is that any matter to us?"

"It matters to us, because word of this will travel with us. It may outpace us, as a matter of fact. We must be careful to neither encourage nor discourage it."

"Why?"

"It is delicate," he said. "If we encourage it, we are being disrespectful of the Catholic faith, using this misunderstanding to gain an advantage. We will lose credibility with these people and thus with those who govern them." He shrugged. "On the other hand, we cannot deny what actually occurred, and if we discourage it too strenuously, the perception is that we are treating the possibility of such a vision as impossible, and again, we seem disrespectful of many other such visions that fill Catholic history."

Speaks while Leaving sighed. "Then what do you suggest we do?"

Alejandro thought about it. "I don't know, exactly. Though for a start, I'd suggest you curtail your conversations with the local wildlife."

The carriage provided by the Señora de Baca was larger than the one Alejandro had hired the day before, and so their traveling promised to be more comfortable by a similar margin. As they prepared to embark, Speaks while Leaving turned to their hostess. The old woman's demeanor was less acerbic today, more somber as she regarded her departing guests.

"I thank you for your hospitality," she said, and Alejandro translated her words from the swallowed tones of the Trader's Tongue into the lisped staccato of the Iron Shirts. "It was a pleasant rest."

The old woman, her withered skin nearly as pale as

her white hair, regarded Speaks while Leaving with a directness that would have been an insult among the People. With the members of her staff looking on with eyes widened in near adoration, Dona Albina considered her words carefully. "Blessings upon you," she said, "and good fortune in the tasks that lie ahead of you."

"May the great spirit watch over you as well," Speaks while Leaving said, and then turned toward the carriage. Many of the servants, she saw, made the sign of their faith as she passed by them.

Alejandro kissed his aunt on both cheeks, and climbed inside the carriage. The driver's whip cracked, the team of horses stepped against their collars, and the iron-rimmed wheels creaked into motion. As the carriage turned around to head back down the drive, the staff waved: a V of men and women, in aprons and working clothes, ranked to either side of their mistress, hands raised in farewell. Speaks while Leaving liked the look of them all—a small community of folk living on the edge of this grand, alien marshland—and she waved back, bidding them and the villa goodbye.

The carriage rocked its way up the slopes to meet the rising sun, and within a few hands of time, they were rolling into a town filled with smoke, shouts, and the bustle of people, carts, horses, and donkeys. They debarked at a long, low building where the air, thick with the smell of machines, was filled with so much sound that it made Speaks while Leaving wince. She tried to protect Blue Shell Woman from its harsh edge, but the barrage of metallic shrieks, thunders, and percussive clanks could not be turned away and the baby added her wail to the din.

"This way," Alejandro said, leading them into the press of people. With his tall stature and imperious eye, he cut a swath through the throng and One Who Flies ushered them after him, the servants following behind with the luggage. They walked through a shadowed, echoing hall and then back out into the sharp noonday light where Speaks while Leaving halted at the sight before her.

She had heard of the iron roads the *vé'hó'e* built across the land, and of the huge, black beasts of metal that rode along them, but she had never seen one before now. She had always imagined them to be dark things, massive like boulders, but this creation stunned her. It *breathed*.

At the end of a line of cars, it crouched, steaming and breathing and hissing as it waited to be released. It was a living thing—but a dead thing, too—and it petrified her. She stopped, unwilling to move forward, unwilling to approach further until One Who Flies returned to her and, with a gentle hand on her arm and a whispered word of encouragement, drew her toward it. When they settled into their compartment and the door was closed, blocking out the press of sound and vibration, she finally allowed herself to take an easy breath.

She had just gotten Blue Shell Woman quiet again when, with a jolt and a crunch, the train started off. She looked out the window, staring at the world as it began to slide past, and told herself it was all perfectly safe.

It's just like riding a whistler, she told herself.

But it wasn't. When one rode a whistler, you felt the beast beneath you, felt its muscles flex and its bones move. You felt the wind in your face, smelled the grass through which you sped, and saw the land you traveled.

This was different. It was like being inside and outside at the same time, like being still and in motion at once. The seat on which she perched vibrated and shuddered with the clacking of the wheels. She waited for everything to break apart, but it didn't, though it swayed and bucked as they picked up speed. It was a bilious experience, and the only good thing she could see in it was when the rhythm of the rails lulled Blue Shell Woman into a happy slumber, but that one good thing was enough, and slowly, Speaks while Leaving allowed her body to unclench.

By morning's end, they had passed up out of the hills and entered a land that made the strangeness of Las Marismas seem as familiar as the banks of the Red Paint River. They were in a tableland where the heat was already oppressive. Despite the dust, they slid the windows down to allow the air some room to move, and Speaks while Leaving draped a cloth over her shoulder and arm as a shade for Blue Shell Woman. Outside, the land to either side was a sere, dun-colored waste of plains and low, undulating hills. Tough-leafed shrubs grew in dark patches, breaking the monotony of the view between the roadbed and the mountainous horizon, and here and there a tree stood up against the sun's tyranny, but for hours Speaks while Leaving saw little more than cracked earth, dry grass, rocks, and the shimmer of the heat above the baking ground.

"This is a harsh land," she said, more to herself than anyone else. "The deserts of our southlands have more life than I see here."

"This," Alejandro said, "is La Extremadura. It is a tough land that breeds tough people. Most of the men who conquered the New World came from here."

Speaks while Leaving could understand why. Growing up in a land like this would make a man angry enough to subjugate anyone who got in his way.

La Extremadura, as Alejandro had named it, went on for hours, marking the end of their first day and filling most of their second. They passed through stretches of land where dark-headed trees spread their branches to create pools of hot shade. Some of the trees had black trunks, while others were grey, red, and even bright orange.

"Cork trees," Alejandro explained. "The farmers strip off the thick bark. The brightest trunks are those most recently harvested. It takes many years for it to grow back, so the harvest rotates from tree to tree over the course of nearly a decade."

Speaks while Leaving knew of such harvesting, and had done some herself, taking strips of black willow bark as medicine, or making needle pouches out of steamed birchbark. Ten years was a long time to scar a tree in such a way, but by the size of some of the cork trees she saw, the practice had not hurt them.

As Alejandro explained the world beyond the window, One Who Flies translated for Mouse Road. In turn, the young woman asked questions about everything that Alejandro had left out of his explanations. What is that plant? That bird with yellow wings? Look at that bright red rock! What is that man out there doing? Is that tiny building his home?

But while Mouse Road peppered the men with her inquiries, Speaks while Leaving merely stared at the trees and the land around them. She had never been to a place where she could not identify a single plant or animal. Not only could she not find her way home from this place, but she would not know how to survive here. Left alone in this land, she would not know what plants could be eaten, or which should be avoided. She would not know where to find water, or the best places to set a snare. While the foreignness of the land excited Mouse Road, it frightened Speaks while Leaving. She felt a gripping within her breast, a small but insistent chill on her heart.

She closed her eyes and listened to the land, wanting to hear its spirit as she often listened at home. She listened for the spirit wind that blew across the prairie, and the spirit heart that beat strong like the heavy steps of a buffalo bull, deep within the world. She listened for the tread of the Thunder Beings, for the hum of *nevé-stanevóo'o*, the four powers that protected the corners of the world. She listened for the voices of Coyote, of Bear, of Eagle, Hawk, and Blackbird. She listened for the hum of Dragonfly, the peep of Frog, the song of Cricket.

But all that came to her ear was a panting breath, as if the land itself was tired out. Knowing this only made her feel farther removed from her homeland. Even in Las Marismas, she had been able to hear the land whisper, but in this place the land had no voice, and the farther into it they traveled, the quieter the land became. Was there nothing of the spirit powers in this land? Or did it simply speak in a language that she could not understand, could not even hear? Was it like this in all *vé'ho'e* lands? Was this why they were so different? Was this why *vé'hó'e* did not understand about the earth they trod? Was it not that they ignored the voice of the land they inhabited, but that, in the lands of their creation, there had never been a voice to hear?

Her thoughts made her want to weep, and her dread grew. Blue Shell Woman fretted, sensing her mother's distress, and Speaks while Leaving worked to control her emotions.

I must think of the People, she told herself. I am here for them, to bring One Who Flies before the queen of the Iron Shirts, so that we may build a greater alliance. To protect the People. Surely a few lonely moons in a lonely land are worth that?

They stopped their second night in a small village and stepped down onto the graveled bed with muscles made sore from hard seats and hours of confinement.

Villages in this harsh land were all memories of the same thought, each with a small circular plaza that was the nexus of business and attention for the inhabitants. Speaks while Leaving, Mouse Road, and Blue Shell Woman drew long stares from the local folk as they followed Alejandro to the inn where they ate a meal and were met with a combination of servility and disparagement as the ownership dealt separately with Alejandro and his guests. They were shown to their rooms, where Speaks while Leaving slept heavily, ensnared by dreams of fiery lands and orange trees where dark-eyed people stared at her every move.

By morning, however, the change had set in. From the footman that accompanied them to the porter who handled their baggage and thence to the stationmaster, from the stationmaster to the smith to the shopkeeper, and finally around to the innkeeper the word had spread. Walking back to the station, suddenly it was Speaks while Leaving who was given the greatest deference. She and her daughter were greeted with smiles and nods. Women would kiss their fingers and touch her sleeve. Men would remove their hats and, covering their hearts, bow to her as she passed. Children stared at her in awe, their eyes as dark and shiny as their glossy black hair.

Alejandro spoke to the footman on several occasions, requesting that he refrain from spreading tales, but the man shrugged off his suggestions.

"I have seen what I have seen, and I have heard what I have heard," the gray-whiskered servant said. "I do not need you to tell me what is true and what is false."

When Alejandro glanced at Speaks while Leaving as at an errant child, she, too, shrugged off his concerns.

"What would you have me do?" she asked him. "How

can I prove that I am not this spirit woman they want me to be?"

Now it was Alejandro who shrugged. "How indeed?"

After a third day in La Extremadura, they left it, climbing up into higher, more fertile land. Speaks while Leaving was glad to see it go, her eyes and ears hungry for the gifts of a more forgiving landscape, but even as they passed the tilled lands of farm crops, herds of cattle and sheep, even as the carriage rumbled beneath the thick boughs of dark forests filled with birdsong, still the land lay mute around her.

It was all so different that, in time, it all became the same in its difference. The roads, the towns, they wove of themselves a tapestry of unearthliness. The places, the people, the creatures were all anonymous, but all part of the same foreign cloth. Mouse Road's enthusiasm grew with each new town, each ridge crossed, and each new valley below. For Speaks while Leaving, the land only made her wish for home, hearth, and husband.

On the fourth day, Alejandro said something that lifted her mood.

"Today we will arrive at Court," he said as the car that had become their home jounced and reeled around a particularly bad turn. "I would have enjoyed introducing you to the beauties of Madrid, but our queen keeps court up in the mountains during the summer heat. Still, if there is a place that inspires awe, it is El Escorial."

One Who Flies translated not only the words, but also Alejandro's inflection, first of regret and then of zeal.

"What is that? What is El Escorial?" Mouse Road asked. During the long journey, Mouse Road's interest in everything had infected One Who Flies, bringing him up from the depths of his troubled mind. Speaks while Leaving was glad to see it, not only as it gave her hope for the task that lay before them, but also as evidence of a healing in their troubled love for one another. Speaks while Leaving knew well the misery of a difficult courtship, and she hoped that her sister-in-law and her friend found an easier path than the one she and Storm Arriving were following.

She shook off that last thought. Thinking of him only

made her worry after his safety, only made her heart
ache for him. Her nights had been lonely enough without
his warmth, without his strength beside her; and her days
were already filled with enough anxiety without adding
such worries.

Mouse Road's question was answered as Alejandro
turned to look out the window. Squeezing the latches,
he slid the window down, stuck his head outside, and
then sat back in his seat with a broad grin on his face.

"That," he said, hooking one thumb toward the view,
"is the town of El Escorial."

The train slung to the left around a curve in the track,
and before them, across a shallow, tree-thick valley, a
small town spilled down the hillside, its red roofs, whitewashed walls, and brown, twisted streets a jumble of
patchwork color. But the town, with its bright houses
shining beneath the summer sun, was not the thing that
drew the eye. No, the thing that commanded every attention was the edifice that stood atop the hill.

"And that," Alejandro said, "is the Palace of San
Lorenzo."

It looked as out of place as anything Speaks while
Leaving had ever seen. Like jackrabbit ears on a whistler, like fish in the sky. Every town they had visited had
its cathedral—sometimes more than one—and whether
they had been graceful things of delicate lines and
upreaching curves or unpretentious blocks that stood out
simply because they were taller than the buildings
around them, to her they had still seemed part of the
town in which they stood, like the Council Lodge and
the Sacred Lodges: taller than the lodges around them,
but still part of the tribal whole.

The Palace of San Lorenzo was not part of the town
of El Escorial. It was not part of the land around it. It
was an alien thing in an alien land.

It did not merely stand atop the hill. It towered. It
commanded.

It loomed.

The palace walls were flat, straight, and tall. As the
carriage headed down into the valley, Speaks while
Leaving could see two of the walls that formed its mas-

sive square. At least forty feet tall, the walls were a bowshot long, with towers at each corner. Massive, huge, lacking the decoration and ornament of every other edifice she had seen in this land, she felt her heart pound at the sight of it.

With part of her mind, she heard Alejandro explain to One Who Flies and Mouse Road the history of the palace, built nearly three hundred years before. He told of how unusual it was in Spanish architecture, constructed in the shape of the square grille upon which its namesake, Saint Laurence, was martyred. But most of her mind was consumed by the sheer immensity of the creation before her.

They passed into the forest at the foot of the hill, the crowding branches and thick leaves hiding the palace from her.

And she despaired.

How can the People hope to overcome creatures that build such things?

The trees ended, and the town began, but even as they switched from the train to a carriage, even from within the twisted streets, the palace dominated. They drove over the cobbles, and it grew larger and larger. At no time could it not be seen; down the street, between the buildings, even over the rooftops. It grew as they approached, taller with each turn in the road. She wanted to look away—wanted *it* to go away—but like a moth to the firelight, she was drawn.

How can we hope to defeat these creatures? We must seem as small, as inconsequential—as bothersome—as a fly at a whistler's nostril, she thought.

A sob broke through her breathing, and she realized that she was weeping openly. Mouse Road touched her.

"What is it?"

"How can we defeat these *vé'hó'e*?" she asked, her gaze filled with the foreboding structure. "How can we even combat them?" She turned to the others, saw Mouse Road's concern, Alejandro's incomprehension of her words or her emotions. But it was in the face of One Who Flies that she saw an unexpected calm.

"That is why we are here," he said as he glanced

toward her and then back out at the bulk of stone. "To see that this is not the palace of our enemy, but of our ally."

Mouse Road put an arm around Speaks while Leaving and laid her head upon her shoulder.

"Do not fear, sister," Mouse Road said to her.

She smelled the scent of Mouse Road's hair, and heard the whisper of her breathing. One Who Flies held out his hand. Mouse Road put her hand on his, and with a nudge, she encouraged Speaks while Leaving to do the same. Fingers entwined, flesh warm against flesh, she felt the pulse of her own heart and of theirs. The pulses deepened, strengthened, until she heard it in her ears, and though her eyes were filled with the sight of the palace's frightful walls, in her mind she heard the drumbeat of the Grass Dance, the pumping of a whistler's legs, and the pounding of the herds across the prairie.

CHAPTER 18

Monday, June 23, A.D. 1890
Palacio de San Lorenzo
El Escorial, Spain

George sat on a marble bench in the shade of a glossy-leafed camellia, the heat of the Spanish summer already building despite the forenoon hour. The meticulous palace gardens were extensive, stretching from the northern side of the huge square foundation around the east and southern faces. On the north, where the palace's shadow ameliorated the sun's intensity, was a broad palazzo and low hedges that kept open the vista to the gentle hills in the distance. On the east and south sides, however, where the sterile palace walls nearly doubled the day's light, masonry walls and archways separated the gardens into small courtyards, providing interest and shade, creating verdant rooms, each with its own personality and charm.

It was in such a courtyard that George now sat. Colorful finches sang amidst the camellia's thick leaves and scentless flowers. They flew from branches to the stone lip of a lily-clad pool, therein to dip their beaks before returning to the shady boughs. Around him, flowered stalks of blue and pink, as tall as a man, looked down on the shorter, more delicate blooms of lavender and rosemary. Fat bees floated lazily from flower to flower, and a jeweled hummingbird buzzed in through a columned archway to work his precise craft on a spear of larkspur.

George thought back on the journey that had brought him to this odd, magnificent place. For over a year, he had been away from any place he might call home. He had traveled to Albuquerque and San Francisco in New Spain, to Washington and New Republic in America, to Cuba's Havana, and now to this remarkable place in the heart of the Old World. But those were mere cities, spots on a faded map. His greater journey had taken him from the pinnacles of elation and pride and hope, to fear, deepest grief, and a drunken despair that even now dogged at his heels.

A good night's sleep had helped that, but, oddly enough, not nearly as much as had spending the better part of a week sitting in a hot, cramped railcar. Despite its discomforts, their journey from Cadiz to El Escorial had done a great deal to lift his spirits. Translating question after question for Mouse Road, he had seen the inner workings of her mind as never before. There was a sharpness to her inquiry that went beyond mere curiosity. Any dullard might be curious about what things were, but repeatedly she had asked *why* things were, often with an incisiveness that had made Alejandro think before providing her an answer. Why were the bulls of Las Marismas the best? Why do people who are so poor stay in such a hard land as La Extremadura? Why did Philip II want to build his palace in the shape of an instrument of such terrible pain? Watching her bright mind explore this new world, he had been reminded of another "why"—why he had come to love her—and sitting across from her, seeing her cherubic smiles, seeing her dark eyes soak up the view, made for as pleasant a week as he could remember, regardless of its physical discomforts.

But that journey had ended at El Escorial, and now, after a night's rest in sumptuous surroundings, George faced the purpose of their coming. How many other, similar meetings had he had on behalf of the People and their hopes for a peaceful future? He recalled his first such "meeting," riding giant lizards into the Capitol Building in Washington. He remembered, too, and too well, critical meetings with Canadian arms dealers, the viceroy of New Spain, and his own father, the President of the United States. Prior to every one of those meetings, he had felt a confidence in his purpose and in his ability to handle it. And every one ended with a failure.

How now, then, as he prepared to meet with a queen? And when he felt so unequal to the task? Would he fare better, for feeling worse?

He looked up and saw Mouse Road standing in the archway. The bleached buckskin of her dress shone like the pale stone beside her, but her skin and hair were gathered shadow, dusky despite the noon.

"How long have you been there?" he asked.

She shrugged. "Not long." She came over and sat beside him in the shade. She sat close to him, closer than the bench required, and her nearness fired a forge within him. He reached out and took her hand in his.

"I want to tell you how much I appreciate what you did for me . . . aboard the ship." She had been a kind and patient nurse during his recovery from the debilitation he had brought upon himself.

"I am just glad to be with you again," she said. "I . . . I am sorry for the way I spoke to you . . . that day."

He knew the day of which she spoke. He remembered her words clearly, spoken through rain and anger, just as he had told her that he was preparing to leave on yet another diplomatic mission. Though nearly a year had passed, her slicing rebuke still hurt.

How long, One Who Flies? How long will it be before you can be a whole man?

"What you said to me . . . your brother said the same thing." He touched his shirt where, beneath, he bore the medicine bag from the tribe's late chief. "As did Three Trees Together."

"Then perhaps they knew what I have only just realized," she said, surprising him. "That you are not a normal man, that it is something you cannot be. I have accepted this, now."

He heard her words, and something within him tightened near to breaking. Whereas before she had been angry, now she was resigned. Her judgment of him, so long withheld in hopes of him changing, had now been rendered, and he had been found lacking. He had thought things were going well between them.

Glancing over at her, their gazes met and lingered. In her eyes, he believed he could see an affection for him, even love. He wanted to reach around her, pull her close, and rest his soul upon her heart. He wanted to make her happy, but her words, her acquiescence of what he also had to admit was his basic nature, drove a wedge between them.

"I do not think I can ever be that kind of man," he said, and quickly—too quickly—she signed her understanding and agreement.

He looked up at the blazing walls of the palace, blinking in the brightness to hide sudden emotion, trying to mask the despair that had crept back into his heart. Mouse Road, however, seemed unperturbed, even serene as she sat there, letting him hold her hand in his. Her lack of sadness could mean only one thing: There was no future for them together, and any hope of such was in vain. Intellectually, he could not deny that it was the wisest course. They were so different, their worlds so different. For years, now, he had tried to believe that he, having rejected his own world, might fit into hers, but time and again, he had met with resistance and difficulty.

As his mind was reeling with these thoughts, Mouse Road gently lifted his hand and brought it to her face. His palm caressed her jaw, his fingertips her cheek. She closed her eyes at his touch, confusing him utterly.

"Mouse Road," he began. "I . . . I don't know what you want of me."

She smiled and released his hand.

"Ah, here they are," Alejandro said as he strode into the courtyard, Speaks while Leaving at his side.

George blinked and looked at them as if awakening from a slumber. He saw Speaks while Leaving share a knowing glance with her sister-in-law.

"I wanted to talk to you before the audience. We meet with Her Majesty in less than an hour, you know?"

The last thing George wanted to do in an hour was to go before the Queen Regent of Spain, but could see no way to avoid it. "Yes," he said. "I know."

"Good," Alejandro said as he bade Speaks while Leaving sit on the bench opposite George and Mouse

Road. He, too, sat down, his gaze taking in the garden's colors. He took a deep chestful of the herb- and bloom-scented air before returning to business.

"While our dear María Cristina is our ruler," he said, "she is not the one we need to impress."

George tried to bring his mind back to the day's purpose, tried to flush from his memory the commotion Mouse Road had wrought. "She is not?" he asked, catching up with Alejandro's words.

"No. The ones we need to impress are her ministers, Sagasta and Cánovas. They are the ones who speak for the *real* government of Spain." He crossed one leg over the other and leaned forward against his knee as he explained. "After our own . . . troubles, back in '68, the monarchy was restored, but only in connection with a civil government. That government is ruled by two parties, one liberal, one conservative, each presiding for a handful of years, at which point control is given over to the other party." He shrugged. "It makes long-term planning difficult, as policies change radically from administration to administration, but it can be done."

"And these two men?" George asked.

"Ah, sí," Alejandro said. "Sagasta speaks for the liberal party and is our current Prime Minister, and Cánovas leads the conservatives. To win the queen, however, we must win them both, for their opinions are the opinions of the government; and to win them both, we must play to their disparate interests. For Sagasta, we need to stress the arguments of freedom and liberty for the Indian peoples. It will appeal to his egalitarianism. For Cánovas, however, we need to concentrate on how this alliance will strengthen the Spanish Empire."

George sighed and stood up. This talk of politics and strategies made him nervous, and he had trouble believing he could pull it off. He began to pace, slowly marking off the length of the shade made by the camellia's glossy leaves.

I can't do this, he said to himself. Even if I had it within me, I couldn't do this.

"One Who Flies?" Speaks while Leaving asked. "What is wrong?"

George turned and paced off the shadow again. Not wanting to speak of his personal deficiencies, he spoke instead of the defects in their political arguments.

"Why would Spain do this?" he asked. "What *would* an alliance with the Cheyenne bring? I'll tell you: the anger of the United States, that's what. Grief. War. That's what it will bring. This is folly. What can we offer the Spanish crown that would make it worth such a risk?"

"There is much we can offer," Speaks while Leaving said, switching to her own language.

"What?" George asked her. "Our undying gratitude? Our friendship? And don't say gold. The moment we offer them gold we'll simply be overrun by *vé'hó'e* of a different sort." He realized that he was using the word *we,* including himself once again with the People, but he could not bring himself to say *you,* and thus exclude himself. Whether he liked it or not, whether the bond was complete or not, he *was* part of the People, and would remain so until his end.

"There are other things we can offer," she said. "The Council has given us their full support."

He turned in his pacing and saw signs being passed between Speaks while Leaving and Mouse Road, though he did not catch their meaning.

"The Council gave *you* their support?"

"Yes," Speaks while Leaving said.

"I thought you said that the Council was divided. Torn between war and peace, and unsure about an alliance with any of the *vé'hó'e.*"

Speaks while Leaving shrugged, and George saw another glance pass between the two women. "That is true," she said. "But it is much like Alejandro's mission here. His *viceroy*"—she used the foreign word, as the People's language had no construct for such hierarchical titles—"supports his mission, although he does not endorse it personally. Just so, while the Council could not decide for itself whether to follow the road of war or the road of peace, it was willing to let us try once more to form an alliance with the Iron Shirts. Some look to *Ma'heo'o* and the spirit powers for guidance, while others look to the world of men. If we succeed, the chiefs will take it as a sign of which path we should walk."

"And if we fail?" George asked.

"You are wrong about what this alliance will bring," she said to him. "War will not come if we form this alliance, One Who Flies. War will come if we fail."

He thought about what she said for several long moments. Alejandro, though not understanding the exchange, was content to let Speaks while Leaving plead her case.

"Perhaps it is as you say," George admitted as he recommenced his measured pacing. "But support or no, I still do not see what we can offer the Iron Shirts."

"Anything," she said.

That stopped him. The surprise he saw on Mouse Road's face mimicked his own. Perhaps she had not been privy to the Council's final decisions. "What do you mean, 'anything'?" he asked.

"Anything," Speaks while Leaving said again. "Any peaceful concession required to forge the alliance. They can build their iron roads, we will set aside lands for settlement, and yes, we will even let them dig for the yellow chief-metal."

"But Speaks while Leaving—" Mouse Road said.

"Quiet," Speaks while Leaving told her in a tone that was uncharacteristically brusque. "Any peaceful concession that you can devise, we must offer."

George was skeptical; it was too vague, too openended. He remembered the offer that he and Three Trees Together had prepared in proposal to the United States. Specific lands had been delineated, and particular amounts had been calculated. But, he had to remind himself, that was Three Trees Together. He did not know the personality of this new Council; he had not been home to meet with the new leadership. If the Council was as fractured as he had been told, this might be the best they could agree upon.

"They leave it up to us, then?"

"Yes," she said, with another silencing glance at Mouse Road. "As long as it is a peaceful concession. We must avoid war and violence. That is the vision . . . of the Council."

"Railroads, settlements, resources," George said, mulling it over, pacing once more. "There is much there to trade, though we must keep ourselves safe as well. We must be sure we do not trade the yoke of the Horse Nations for a new one owned by the Iron Shirts."

"Yes," Speaks while Leaving said, excitement growing in her voice as he took hold of the idea.

George looked up at the towering mass of the palace, at the square, cross-topped tower at the corner. "And there are other things, other resources that might interest the Iron Shirts." He turned to Alejandro and switched to French.

"Tell me, sir. What else should I know before we are received by Her Most Royal and Catholic Majesty?"

When the hour of their audience came, George and Alejandro were escorted through the palace, down long, lofty-ceilinged hallways, past priceless works of art, to a room that made George gape. While no grand throne room, broad and echoing, it was still one of the most amazing rooms he had ever seen.

While only fifty or so feet across, it was easily three times that in length: a long, narrow room paved with marble tiles placed in a cross-and-square pattern of white and charcoal grey. The walls, between the many open doorways that let in light from the south, were lined with pilaster-flanked bookcases, each twice the height of a man and each filled with hundreds of books. George stared at the bindings—old, thick, worn, yet bright with gilded decorations framing titles in Spanish, Latin, Portuguese, French, German, and even English. Hundreds of books crowded each glance, thousands as he turned his head, tens—perhaps a hundred thousand—as he slowly rotated to take in the entire room.

And above him, a ceiling to rival the Florentine masters. Atop the bookcases, panels supported a semi-cylindrical vault that ran the length of the long library. The vault itself was divided by arches carved and gilded with the interlocking geometry of Greek keys, and between the divisions, on the panels and on the curved ceiling, were frescoes.

George stared at the massive, baroque work above him. The panels—ten in all—showed scenes of piety, trial, and martyrdom, any one of which would be considered a masterpiece. Over the panels, scenes of biblical figures arched across the apex, bordered and buttressed by prophets and patriarchs. The more George looked, the more he saw. Between the golden supports were carved and gilded placards, icons of the saints. Oval bosses of stamped gold shone like gentle suns from the beam joinings, and in corners and peaks throughout the room hovered a host of plump, winged cherubim.

"¡Madre de Dios!" Alejandro whispered, his voice filled with a reverential awe, as if they had been ushered into not a library, but a cathedral. "I have heard of the wonders of this place—as a child I sat at my father's knee and heard the tales of Philippe Segundo—but never did I imagine even a tenth of such glory."

They walked slowly, almost lethargically, down the long book-lined hall, staring. Chairs and small tables were arranged in small groups to either side, tall candelabra standing guard with fat candles upraised. Precious miniatures from the reaches of the Spanish Empire stood on shelves and reading tables: intricately carved jade statuettes, porcelain figurines of exquisite detail, carved boxes of bloodred cinnabar. Pieces of free-standing artwork commanded the middle of the hallway—a bronze eagle on a marble pedestal, a carved Apollo, and at the end, an ancient armillary sphere nearly as tall as George. Every glance brought richness to the eye; from the wealth of knowledge and literary thought to the magnificence of gold and art, the room was a staggering trove of captured talent.

As George stood, wordless amid the splendor, he wondered if there was a more extraordinary room in the palace. Had they been brought here to be impressed? Humbled? Or simply because it was convenient?

The sound of heavy, booted footsteps and the clank of metal echoed through the passageways. George and Alejandro straightened and stood side by side, old military habits responding to the unmistakable tread of approaching soldiers. Four men in ceremonial uniform entered, their crested morions and cuirasses buffed to a high polish. They wore puffed pantaloons, tight leggings that tucked into their hard, high boots, and carried pikes wrapped in the colors of Spain. At each man's hip,

George noticed, was not rapier, dirk, or a pistolier to match the period of their costume. There, the ever-practical Spanish military had placed a modern revolver in holster, a fact that told him that these men were not just here for decoration.

The first two soldiers took position on either side of the door, while the other two crossed the room and stood behind George and Alejandro. George felt the hair on the back of his neck stand up, but forced himself to keep his gaze on the doorway. If the soldiers wanted to make him nervous, fine; but he'd be damned before he'd let it show.

A thin man wearing a black suit and an orange sash entered. He carried a long walking stick and, as he stopped at the door, he struck the tiles with it three times. The wood rang like a bell, and the man, in Spanish even George could follow, announced, "Her Glorious Catholic Majesty, María Cristina Deseada Enriqueta Felicidad, Queen Regent of Spain." He struck the tiles again and with a bow, backed away to the side.

The woman who entered was neither tall nor regal, but she walked at the head of her entourage with the stately grace that befitted a queen. Her dress was, neck to floor, a widow's deep black, made of taffetas and silk. The cuffs and bodice seams were frilled with black lace, and black pearls and beads of faceted onyx had been sewn into a cross-hatch pattern across the leg-o'-mutton sleeves. The only color she wore was the chain of double-linked gold around her neck, and the delicate, black-and-gold Damasquinado cross that hung from it. She was short, small-waisted, her still-dark hair done up in braids coiled into a bun. Her face was rather plain, with overlarge eyes that accentuated the impression of mourning, though in those eyes George saw no hint of sadness. Evaluation, he saw there, and skepticism, perhaps, but with Alfonso XII, dead these five years past, he would have been surprised if her weeds were more than a sartorial nod of respect for her late husband. This was, George reminded himself, the woman who had the presence of mind and personal charisma to convince her country to name her regent for a child she still carried in her womb. Had Alfonso XIII been born female, he wondered what might have happened to the Spanish monarchy. As Queen María Cristina and her entourage approached, George and Alejandro bowed deeply and held it until she stopped before them. Straightening, George saw that four men had entered with her, all fair-skinned, unlike the peasantry he had met during their journey, all with moustaches or beards, all in dark suits. Two of them stood to one side of their queen while the other two—most likely aides—hung back.

"Welcome, Don Alejandro," the queen said, as casually as if greeting an old friend. "We are pleased to see you in El Escorial. Our viceregal cousin, Lord Serrano, has told us much of your aspirations concerning the natives of the New World." She spoke French—ostensibly for George's benefit—though her clipped diction betrayed her Austrian upbringing and told George that María Cristina was likely more comfortable speaking in *lingua franca* than in the tongue of the country she professed to rule.

"Your Majesty is most kind to take notice of my interests, though I assure Your Majesty that my aspirations are for nothing but the greater glory of Spain."

The tiniest of smiles touched the corner of her mouth. "Indeed," she said, neither question nor statement, but equal portions of both.

"Your Majesty," Alejandro said, "may I introduce the man I have come to know as 'One Who Flies,' the acknowledged ambassador from the Cheyenne Alliance, George Armstrong Custer, Jr., son of the President of the United States."

The mention of his father took George by surprise, though he knew he should have expected it. He bowed, a little late, but not egregiously so.

"Welcome, One Who Flies," the queen said. "We were shocked to hear of the attack on your father's life, but gladdened to learn he has survived it. His recovery, we are assured, is well underway."

There was a look that passed between the queen and Alejandro that George could not interpret, so he simply nodded, acknowledging her notice. "I thank Your Majesty for the news. It was a bad business that cost both sides dearly."

"Yes," she said thoughtfully. George, working against years of courtesy among the Cheyenne, made himself look the queen in the eye as was the etiquette among *vé'hó'e*. She regarded him frankly, chin up, head cocked slightly, studying him. "We heard that one of the native chiefs had also died in the attack. He was a friend of yours, we take it?"

George was acutely aware of the fringe of the medicine bag he wore beneath his shirt. "He was a great friend, Your Majesty. A great friend and a wise leader."

"A terrible loss, then," she said. "Our condolences."

George nodded, accepting her commiseration.

"¿Su Majestad?" said one of the men who had entered with her. The tall, bespectacled gentleman then asked the queen a question in a tone so peremptory that it surprised George. The man stood by one of the reading chairs, offering it to her.

"Yes, of course," the queen said as she moved toward the chair. "By all means, to business. You gentlemen know Don Antonio Cánovas del Castillo, of course, our advisor from the conservative faction? And this," she said, gesturing to the other prominent man beside her, "is our Premier, Práxedes Mateo Sagasta. You may speak freely before them, as their opinions weigh heavily in any of our decisions." She lowered herself slowly onto the chair and sat on the edge, poised, as if ready to leap up on the moment. "Don Alejandro, if you will translate for us?"

"Un placer," Alejandro replied with a bow.

"Speak to us of your proposals," she said, and as Alejandro translated, he stepped back, leaving George to lead the negotiations.

George spoke to her of the Alliance's desire for peace with the United States, especially after a lifetime of war. The queen regent listened attentively as he outlined the situation, the forces arrayed, and the current prospects for the allied tribes. But while the queen's attention was given solely over to him, and while she nodded in response to his recitation, it was not she who asked the pointed questions.

"Do you expect Spanish troops to solve your problems?" Cánovas asked.

"Not at all, sir," George replied. "I hardly need point out that the military prowess of the Cheyenne and their allied tribes have kept both American and Spanish colonists at bay for three hundred years, and without help from either side."

"Then what *do* you expect?" the tall man asked.

George noticed that María Cristina did not look from questioner to responder, as would most anyone following a conversation. Instead, she watched only him.

She knows the questions already, he said to himself. She is not ruled by these men, though she lets others believe so.

"We expect nothing," George said, now aware of who was actually in control of these proceedings. "We only hope. And what we hope for is support, friendship, advice, and a fighting chance to protect our lands from those who would take them away. Your Majesty, gentlemen, for a thousand years the Cheyenne and their allies have lived lives that are independent of any technology or industry beyond that which a man or woman can perform with their own hands. The time for that culture is fading, and though they have been able to forestall the inevitable, the tribes must change in order to survive. They must learn a different way of life, keeping what they can of the old as they adapt to the new." He looked directly at the queen regent. "But in order to survive long enough to effect this change, we need the help of Spain. Without it, a culture, a way of life, and an entire people will surely be wiped out."

The queen did not react to his plea. Her features remained calm and composed, with a look of general but unexcited interest, and George suddenly doubted his earlier assessment. Perhaps she *was* just a puppet, and these men beside her the puppeteers.

Or perhaps, he thought, she has already made up her mind.

"But why should Spain assay this risk?" Sagasta now asked, his lilting Castilian words and his high, effeminate voice at odds with his appearance. Where Cánovas was tall and aristocratic, with silk lapels, thinning gray hair, and moustache and beard trimmed in a classic imperial, Sagasta was short and unassuming, his blunt chin and wide mouth covered by a rough gray beard, and the dark waves of his hair ruffled and unkempt. "What you ask for seems easy enough to give—friendship, support, advice—but even such innocuous bestowments will earn us the ire of your eastern neighbor. To make friends with you will surely make us an enemy of the United States. What inducements are there to such a situation?"

"The ruling Council of the Cheyenne Alliance has empowered us to offer many things to the Spanish crown in return for their promise of support. This will not be Spanish charity, but a true alliance, with benefit seen by both sides."

"What sort of benefits?" Cánovas asked, pressing for more detail.

"Railroad easements," George said. "Permanent settlements. The lands we were prepared to cede to the United States, we might cede to Spain instead. And there is another resource that Spain might find of interest."

Alejandro cleared his throat and, glancing over, George caught his querying look. Inwardly, George smiled; were he to tell the queen and her men about the mineral riches in Cheyenne lands, he could expect an alliance to be made on the spot. He could also expect it to be broken with the first Spanish foot set in Alliance territory.

"What resource is this of which you speak?" asked María Cristina.

"Souls, Your Majesty."

For the first time since the audience had commenced, she looked to her ministers. It was an answer that none of them had expected.

"Do you mean . . . ?" Sagasta began.

"Sir, while many of the Cheyenne people are quite devout in their own faith and their own beliefs in a higher power, there are, just as with any people, those whose faith is not as strong. There are those who are unsure, shaken, and disillusioned with their faith, especially so in times of crisis such as this. Such people might find comfort in the Catholic faith."

"The Cheyenne leaders would allow this?"

"The Cheyenne have had a long history of tolerance toward other religions. How could they not? Their neighboring tribes often have very different views on God and other matters spiritual. Itinerant priests have traveled in their territories for centuries. In order to co-exist, they have learned to be tolerant, and they accept that a man's conscience is his own domain. And while it was not discussed in specific, I'm sure the Council will agree to grant safe passage to all Catholic missionaries for the purposes of spreading the Word of God, provided that they receive in return assurances that the . . . excesses of zeal . . . that have marred past centuries will not be repeated."

It was his last card, and he had played it as well as he could. The queen regent looked over at her two ministers. Cánovas and Sagasta whispered briefly together and then nodded to their monarch. María Cristina seemed to take something from that nod, and that something did not please her. She stood, her expression thunderous, her mouth twisted as if the words she held within were bitter.

"We thank you for your pains in bringing these proposals before us, but we have heard nothing here that persuades us. Spain's place in the New World is firm, and the balance of power there is set. What you ask will surely upset the scales, and that is not something we desire."

George felt the blood drain from his face as she spoke.

"We are sorry you have traveled so far to hear this, but your proposal is rejected." She turned and walked from the room, her footsteps as clipped as her accent. Her ministers followed her, as did their aides, and finally, with a clatter of metal, the armed and armored soldiers.

The two of them stood there, alone in the immense hall of words and knowledge, staring at the empty passageway. George could hear his own breathing, felt his pulse pounding in his throat. When he finally moved, the scuff of his shoe against the tiles was overloud, rasping and harsh in the silence that beat down upon him.

George thought back on his previous failures: on the

battlefield, in Washington, in San Francisco. With Mouse Road. This was just another in a long string of deficiencies, another disappointment in his catastrophic history.

"Aaugh!" he bellowed through gritted teeth, startling Alejandro.

"My boy," Alejandro said, "I am as frustrated by this as you are."

"Somehow, Alejandro, I doubt that very much." He walked away down the long hall.

"We must tell the women," Alejandro said after him. "We must break the news to Speaks while Leaving."

"You go," George said. "You tell her. I have something else to do."

The palace was big, a labyrinth of hallways, a perfect place in which to lose oneself. George wandered the corridors, blind to the grandeur at every turn, interested only in the turns themselves. He walked, deeper and deeper into the belly of beast, until he found a small sitting room. When a maid happened by, he flagged her down like a cab.

"¿Sí, señor?" she asked.

"Whiskey," he said, sure that the word would be understood in any language.

It took a while, but eventually it arrived: a crystal carafe on a silver tray brought by an underbutler. George took the bottle, filled the glass, slammed back the drink, and poured another while the first still burned down his throat.

"Encore," he said, indicating the carafe. The butler bowed and retreated.

In that tiny, windowless room, George hid and drank. The liquor at first warmed him, soothed him, and stifled the shivering anger that had gripped him from the moment the queen regent had left him standing there, jaw agape, his mind a foam of anguish. Then, and quickly, too, the whiskey began to work its other magic, numbing him, driving out the thoughts that plagued him, but before it did, before it could shove every trouble into that dark closet of drunkenness, it first had to open that closet. He saw every inadequacy he'd ever faced, every failure he'd ever known. He saw the destruction of the airship that had taken him into Cheyenne territory, saw the death of Mouse Road's older sister, saw the disappointment in Storm Arriving's face when he failed to return with the weapons he had promised. He saw his own gullibility at Vincent's subterfuge, saw his father's chest red with blood, saw the ashen face of Three Trees Together as his voice was silenced for all time. He saw his mother's condemnation. He saw Mouse Road's resignation.

He wept as these anguishes washed over him, especially the last one, for while the others spoke of a failed past, Mouse Road's disappointment spoke of an empty future. He saw no future, none at all; only the void lay before him, without purpose, without a goal, without a family, without a nation, without a home. He drank again, felt the burn, and waited for the troubles to be corralled and packed away into that closet of secrets, of pain, of failure.

"What are you doing?"

He turned his head and the room slewed around him. The glass was taken from his hand, the carafe removed from his reach. His gaze traipsed behind the person until she slowed down long enough for it to catch up.

"Mouse Road," he said, the Cheyenne syllables slipping around in his mouth before he could utter them. Then he laughed, for the troubles had been banished, tucked into their alcoholic beds. "I'm celebrating."

"Celebrating? Alejandro told us that the woman-chief of the Iron Shirts refused us."

"Yes," George said, though the Cheyenne word—*héehe'e*—came out as more giggle than agreement.

"Then what is there to celebrate?"

Now he did giggle, and raised his glass, though realizing he no longer held one only made him giggle the more. "I'm celebrating an unbroken record. There is not one thing I have tried to do for the People that has worked."

She stood before him, hands on her hips, her almond-shaped eyes narrowed by the intensity of her disapproval.

"And to think," she said, "that I wanted to be your wife."

"That was a long time ago, sweetheart."

"That was this *morning,* you fool."

The grin slipped from his face. "What?"

"Where have you been, these past weeks?" she asked him. "On the boat, and on the iron road? Where were you?" She made an indelicate sound. "Swaddled in your pity is where you were. Deafened by your own whines and wails, and blinded by the hands you held over your own eyes, that is where you were. Too consumed by your hatred of yourself to see my love for you."

He knew by her tone and words that he should be contrite. This was the point to apologize and turn over a new leaf, start a new chapter and move forward. This, he knew, was his last chance with her.

But he couldn't bring himself to care. "What does it matter?" he asked.

"Not to you, that's clear enough, but it matters to me."

His head wobbled as he tried to keep her in focus. "Why?"

She came forward and knelt at his feet. He could see the tears in her eyes, now, and the anguish that from a step away had seemed to be disgust. "Because I still love you," she said. "Because I still want to be your wife."

"But you told me yourself," he said. "I cannot be a normal man. You said you had accepted that."

"And I have," she said, leaning against him. "And it is part of what makes you special to me, that you are *not* a normal man. You are driven, brave, and passionate, unsatisfied with inaction, and yet somehow empty of any personal ambition. You love the People better than many who are born to the blood. You will not be a normal man, not ever. You are One Who Flies, son of Long Hair. You will lead an extraordinary life, and I wanted to be part of it."

"Wanted?" he asked.

"Yes," she said. "Wanted. When I thought that it was me whom you loved." She pushed back away from him and stood. "But not now."

"Why not?"

She went to the sideboard and retrieved the carafe and glass. "Because, when things were the worst for you, you ran to this, and not to me." The liquor sloshed within its crystal as she clunked it down on the sidetable. "I have been replaced, and I won't be wife to a man who loves me second best. Second wife is for widowed sisters, old women, and men-becoming-women. Not for me. I will not be second wife."

She put the empty glass back in George's hand and he concentrated on holding it, not wanting to drop it on the hard floor. In his encroaching stupor, it took him a few moments to realize that she had gone.

He was alone in the small room.

The lamplight glinted from the facets that ran around the base of the glass. He felt its smoothed ridges and polished edges beneath his fingers, and reached for the carafe.

I will not be second wife.

He considered the half-emptied carafe and the amber whiskey it still contained. His head swam with liquor already consumed, and he could still taste its sharpness, the grit of charcoal, the musk of peat. More would bring oblivion and, quite possibly, forgetfulness. More would ensure that this moment would not become yet another moment he would have to battle, but is that what he wanted? Did he want to forget everything she had said, or just the last thing she said?

He reached for the bottle.

CHAPTER 19

Moon When the Whistlers Get Fat, Waxing
Fifty-seven Years after the Star Fell
Palace of San Lorenzo
El Escorial, Spain

Speaks while Leaving had listened to Alejandro's description of his audience with the queen regent, but all she had really heard was that their proposal had been rejected. That one fact drove from her mind any other thought she might have had.

Rejected. Denied. Refused.

She held back tears as Mouse Road had asked after One Who Flies, held them back as Alejandro had asked if there was anything he could do, and held them back as he bowed himself out of the room and Mouse Road left in search of the man she loved. Then, alone with her daughter, Speaks while Leaving had finally let the tears fill her eyes and slip down her cheeks. Blue Shell Woman fretted with her mother's emotion. Speaks while Leaving stood and took her to the window where they both could look out through the rippled glass.

The window was one of many that opened out onto a courtyard that sat entirely within the palace walls. Four pools of clear water flanked a shrine, and the sun high overhead spilled down into them, flashing off the backs of fat orange fish that glided beneath the lily leaves. The sun and its heat beckoned to her, and, with Blue Shell Woman on her hip, she went down in search of it.

Servants bowed to her as she made her way through the halls and stairways. Several made the sign of their faith as she passed, but she cared nothing for that now. She wanted to think of nothing, right now, nothing but the feel of the sun on her face, on her hair, on her shoulders. Making her way past statues and paintings and murals, she found the courtyard and stepped out into it.

She could smell the heat rising from the stones, and she walked from the shadows into the blinding sunlight as a thirsty man toward water. Closing her eyes, face upturned, she felt the sun's heat and saw the red as it tried to penetrate her eyelids.

The courtyard was square and walled by two tiers of tall, arched windows. On the north side, three square towers commanded the rooftops, and to the south, she could see one of the palace's corner towers. Along the outer edge of the court, bushes grew in a thick border, though they were kept unnaturally low and square by the trimming of vé'ho'e gardeners. Within that border, two low steps led to a raised stone platform at the corners of which were the four pools. Standing tall in the center of everything was a stone shrine.

Blue Shell Woman cooed in the warmth, and Speaks while Leaving took her to one of the pools. They sat down on the stone edge and the baby immediately reached for the fish. Speaks while Leaving let her splash her hands, but kept an arm beneath her belly so she wouldn't go headfirst into the water.

The shrine cast a sharp-edged shadow across the pool, and the fish wove their way from light to dark, keeping their distance from the baby's splashing hands. Her ripples shattered the sunlight, sending shards dancing on the shrine. Speaks while Leaving watched the play of light along the shrine's columns. Four tall openings made the shrine into a sort of stone gazebo, its domed top supported by four columned niches. In each of the niches was a life-sized man made of stone. The nearest statue held a book to his chest and wore robes like many of the vé'hó'e in the paintings she had seen. His face was bearded, too, as many of the vé'hó'e were and as the men of the People could not be, even had they desired it. His expression, however, was a puzzle to her. He looked either sad or sleepy or perhaps fearful. His head was cocked a little to one side, but his eyes were looking upward to the sky, as if he were afraid something was about to fall upon him. He held his free hand upturned, prepared to catch that which was coming down.

What was he thinking about? she wondered. What was he afraid of?

The stone man embodied all her feelings about the *vé'hó'e*. They were cold, pale, stiff, and entirely incomprehensible. She felt tears building again within her and there, in that quiet courtyard, with her daughter playing happily at the water's edge, she let her grief flow, and her tears fell onto the hot stones, each one evaporating, its damp circle shrinking to nothing even before the next tear fell.

The vision—or at least her interpretation of it—was dead. There would be no peaceful solution. War would come, was already on its way, and it would take those she loved and the life she loved with it, burning it away like a wildfire. And Storm Arriving, already in the vanguard of that war, already aching for that contest, would likely be one of the first consumed by war's gluttony. Blood would spring from the land, as if the earth itself were injured. The *vé'hó'e* would come onward, with nothing to slow them down but the People's bravery and indignation.

How many would die? How many would survive? Any? Would anything of the life she knew survive the onslaught that was sure to come? Would she? Would her daughter?

For the first time in her life, she actually wished for a vision to come upon her. Never before had she ever wanted to feel the chill of the spirit powers, but now she did. She wanted to know, wanted to understand what was coming, but as she opened her mind to the other world, it was veiled, dark, silent. She could not feel it, not here, not in the center of a stone courtyard surrounded by stone walls surrounded by even more walls, all set atop a rocky hillside inside a harsh country. Here, she was utterly cut off from the People, from the land, and from the powers that coursed through it.

Blue Shell Woman's joyous giggle brought her back to the sun-drenched court, and as she reached to take a lily leaf from her daughter's mouth, she was startled to find a woman standing in the shadowed opening of the shrine.

"I beg your pardon," the woman said in the Trader's Tongue. "I heard the child's laughter. I hope I am not disturbing you."

Speaks while Leaving wiped tears from her cheeks as she regarded the small woman. Her fine, black clothing accentuated her pallid skin; the only color she bore was the gold of a large cross that hung at her breast. She stood, hands clasped before her, but while her words had been polite, there had been no apology in her tone.

"Your Majesty," Speaks while Leaving said, guessing her identity. She picked up Blue Shell Woman. "We were just leaving."

"No," the queen said, stepping forward but remaining within the shrine's shadow. "Please, don't leave on my account."

Speaks while Leaving looked the queen in the eye, hoping this *vé'ho'e* woman took it as the challenge she intended it to be. "I *do* leave on your account. My people will perish, on your account."

"Please," María Cristina said as she sat down on the pool's stone rim, unconsciously arranging the ample hems of her skirts.

Speaks while Leaving glared at the queen a while longer, allowing herself to feel the antagonism that she might otherwise have held back, and hoping that her feelings showed upon her face.

"Is this your daughter?" the queen asked.

It was the only question that had a chance of breaking through her scorn. She fought the impulse to relent and pulled Blue Shell Woman close in a double-armed embrace, but that only made the little girl laugh.

"Yes," Speaks while Leaving said. "My daughter."

"How old is she?"

"A little more than a year."

"That is a good age."

That the queen wanted to talk was obvious, and Speaks while Leaving was suddenly curious as to what would bring her out into the heat. "Your Majesty has children?" she asked, keeping the conversation alive.

The queen smiled. *"Vraiment,"* she said and chuckled. "Two daughters, the Princesas Mercedes and Teresa, and my son, who will be king. A son who most likely

saved my life." She held her hands out toward the baby.
"May I?"

She let the queen take Blue Shell Woman into her
arms and watched as she cradled her, made bubbly
sounds, and waggled two fingers along the infant's lips.
Speaks while Leaving was taken off guard by this woman's easy manner. "How is it your son saved you?"

"My husband died while I was still pregnant," she
said. "It was a troubled time here, but I was able to
have my son crowned king before he was even born.
Had he been another daughter, the succession would
have been open to question, and the Federalists would
likely have had me exiled. Or killed, along with my children." Sitting there, smiling into Blue Shell Woman's
laughter, the queen told her the rest of the story, of
Spain's troubles as the pendulum swung between a monarchy and a republic, and of the uneasy compromise that
had been struck between the two.

"So you have had to negotiate for your survival?"

"Yes," the queen said, regret touching her voice. "I
have."

"That is what I am doing. Only I negotiate not just
for myself, but for my nation. How can you turn your
back on our request?"

The queen smiled as she glanced up at Speaks while
Leaving. "Because I had to. At least right then, I had
to."

Speaks while Leaving frowned. "I do not understand."

Blue Shell Woman reached for the hand-sized cross
of gold that hung at the queen's throat. She unpinned it
and gave it to her. The baby immediately put the cross
into her mouth.

"I had to refuse the offer. It had been decided. But
the men who made that decision are concerned only with
their own power and the power of their factions." She
laughed again, a low, throaty sound that seemed out of
place coming from such a small woman. "It is ironic.
These men are prideful of their peasant bloodlines, but
the higher they rise, the less they hear what their own
peasantry is saying."

The queen leaned close. "I listen," she said. "I hear

the tales they tell. I know what the people want their leaders to do. I hear what the people say."

"And what do you hear?" Speaks while Leaving asked, daring to hope.

"I hear them speak of a brave people who have stood up to the might of Spain and now struggle against the American upstarts for their very existence. I hear of armies killing women and children. I even hear the tales they tell of a most remarkable *corrida* that took place in San Francisco. But right now, all I hear is the tale of a young mother to whom the birds flock, and with whom she converses; a woman who preaches peace, for her people and others; a woman who has visions, and who carries about her an aura of holiness the like of which has not been seen since the days of the saints."

Speaks while Leaving lowered her gaze, embarrassed by the comparison. "I did not intend any disrespect," she said, acutely aware that her daughter was teething on the symbol of the *vé'ho'e* religion. "I was just out for a walk when—"

"My dear." The queen reached out into the sunlight to touch her hand, her skin shockingly pale against Speaks while Leaving's darker flesh. "Do not think that I blame you for any of this. The people of Spain are a simple people. They are strong, independent, and incredibly devoted to their Church. As a result, they see things that might not truly exist." She retreated into the shade once more. "Ironic, is it not? That I, a Grand Duchess of Austria and now Queen Regent of Spain, born of a long line of royal blood, should depend on the love and support of the lowest classes? You see, governors and politicians can be removed from office and cast down in disgrace. Royalty, on the other hand, must be killed."

But she had not said it. She had not said what Speaks while Leaving had heard hiding within her words, the logical culmination of her thoughts and meaning.

"Your Majesty, I beg your pardon, but was there something you wanted to tell me?"

The queen regarded her, a small smile on her lips. "I don't impress you, do I?"

"No, Your Majesty, except as a woman who has been

able to manage her destiny, alone in a world of men, and as a woman who works hard to protect her family."

"A woman alone in a world of men. You know something of this, don't you?"

"My people have a saying. 'Decisions are not made in the Council, but in the lodge.' "

She laughed again her low, almost manly laugh. "Meaning that while men do not make the decisions, we must let it appear as if they do."

"Yes, Your Majesty, which makes it difficult for a woman who does not have a man to act on her behalf."

"Yes, it does," María Cristina said. "Unless that woman is a queen. You see, we have a saying, too, that I think is appropriate."

"What saying is that?"

" 'Changing her mind is a woman's prerogative.' "

CHAPTER 20

Monday, June 23, A.D. 1890
Palacio de San Lorenzo
El Escorial, Spain

Alejandro had just put pen to paper when he heard running footsteps and the jouncing wail of an unhappy baby. He rose and stepped to the door, opening it just as Speaks while Leaving was about to knock.

"She has agreed!" she said, breathless and beaming with excited joy. Blue Shell Woman seemed less than pleased by the news, though she quieted now that her mother had stopped running.

"Who?" Alejandro asked. "Agreed to what?"

"María Cristina! To everything!"

"No! To everything?"

"Yes," she said with a laugh. "I hardly believe it myself."

"But—but how?" He stepped back and gestured her within but she waved off the invitation.

"I was outside, and she came, and we began to talk." The words spilled from her mouth. "We talked of home and children and I told her she did not impress me much and then suddenly we were talking of how we could help each other, of how she could help save the People and how the People could help Spain."

"*¡Dios mío!* And she agreed? On what terms?"

"She said we would work out the details tomorrow. For now, she has agreed to assist the People in any way she can in return for settlements, railroads, and safe conduct for her missionaries."

"Mining rights," Alejandro said. "Did she mention anything about mining rights?"

"No," Speaks while Leaving said. "And I wouldn't say anything about that when you meet tomorrow." Her glee was infectious, and Alejandro found he was grinning broadly. "I need to find One Who Flies," she said. "And Mouse Road. They will be so happy!" She turned and ran down the corridor toward her own rooms, her daughter once again taking up the job of siren, wailing to clear the way. Servants stood back to let her pass.

He watched her go, stunned by her news. Finally, he crossed himself not once, but twice.

"*¡Gracias a Dios!*" he whispered, and then, still grinning, a thought occurred to him.

What if she was mistaken? What if she had misinterpreted the queen's intention? Perhaps the queen only *wanted* to help, but had not actually agreed to anything. Speaks while Leaving was desperate for this alliance, but did she want it badly enough to have merely heard what she wanted to hear? Alejandro hoped he was mistaken, but better to get some confirmation on this miracle rather than to move forward on faith.

He put on his coat, checked himself in the looking glass, and headed in the opposite direction down the corridor. Speaks while Leaving had run off toward the private apartments, but Alejandro wanted the business end of the palace. That was where he would find either Cánovas or Sagasta.

Like tributaries to a greater river, the narrow hallways of the apartments led him to the broader corridors that ran the palace's grid. He walked with a stride lengthened by equal parts triumph and alarm, hoping Speaks while Leaving had actually done the impossible, fearing that she had not.

As he reached the main cross hall that would take him to the governmental offices within San Lorenzo, a liveried servant stopped and bowed to him as he passed.

"Congratulations, Señor Silveira," the man said.

The simple phrase stopped him in his tracks. He turned, and the servant smiled and bowed again.

"Thank you," Alejandro said quietly before starting once more on his way.

As he walked, other servants bowed as well, giving him their congratulations, good wishes, and a great deal more respect than they had upon his arrival. Speaks while Leaving seemed to have been correct, and in typical Spanish form, word was traveling quickly through the palace.

"It is wonderful news," a guardsman said when he asked the whereabouts of either Sagasta or Cánovas.

"Yes," Alejandro said. "Wonderful news."

"God is certainly with that woman. It is clear that He has taken a hand. Please permit me to offer my congratulations, señor."

"My thanks," he said, becoming more than slightly embarrassed at receiving such praise for something he had not done.

"You will find Prime Minister Sagasta in his offices. Down the hallway, turn right, the fourth door on your left."

Alejandro nodded and walked down the hall, his footsteps muffled by the red and gold carpet. He stopped outside the heavy door, a door that was probably centuries old. Sagasta was likely to be unhappy at having been overruled by his queen's change of heart. Did he want to go in? He hardly needed confirmation of the queen's decision, but on the other hand, he would have to speak to Sagasta or Cánovas sooner or later.

He knocked on the door.

"Sí."

Alejandro entered.

Sagasta sat at his desk, reading through papers written in his small but efficient hand. The offices were cramped—as were many of the ancillary rooms in this ancient building—but were richly appointed nonetheless with red carpets, an arras of brocade on one wall, and a shield with crossed halberds and drapes of red and gold fabric on the other. The desk at which he sat was of burled walnut with inlaid ivory and silver wire along the edges. A narrow doorway was open through which Alejandro spied another small room, the footboard of a small bed, and the end of a dressing table.

"Your savage friend has bewitched our regent," Sagasta said, his tenor voice and his acculturated lisp heightening the bitterness of his tone. "I have no other explanation for her contravention of the advice of both myself *and* Señor Cánovas. You are either incredibly shrewd or incredibly foolish, Don Alejandro."

"But she is in earnest?" Alejandro asked, stung, but ignoring the veiled insult. He still wanted to hear from an official source that this was indeed true.

"In earnest? Oh, yes. Very much so. She is convinced in the potential of such an alliance. She thinks it is an important symbol of the benevolence of the Spanish Crown." He laughed: a single, sharp exhalation that held more contempt than humor. "I fear the Americans will think it more than merely symbolic."

"I should think they would see it as an act of aggression."

Sagasta's bushy eyebrows lifted upward. "Ah, so you're not a fool."

"No, Prime Minister. I am not," he said.

He leaned forward, an elbow on his desk. "Then you must think that there is something worth our trouble in this savage land."

Alejandro realized he may have let himself say too much. Though born of common stock, the prime minister was a sharp-eyed man, and little got past him unnoticed.

"Surely the settlement lands alone—" Alejandro began.

"No," Sagasta said. "Taking on such a risk for the possibility of a few settlements and trade opportunities is ludicrous. What else?"

"It is a fertile land, Prime Minister. Agricultural trade—"

"No, we could feed the world out of the valleys of Alta California." Sagasta peered at him, and Alejandro got the uncomfortable impression that the prime minister could hear the klaxon bells of warning inside his head, could read the words imprinted on his mind, words he did not want to utter or even acknowledge.

"Minerals."

Alejandro felt the blood drain from his face. "Prime Minister, I don't know what you might mean."

Sagasta stood and, hands clasped at the small of his

back, he began to walk a slow circuit around Alejandro. "You can't go back to playing the fool, now, my friend. You have already proven yourself otherwise. No, it all makes perfect sense. I wondered how you had brought the Americans so close to an agreement with the paltry ten million in gold we allowed that fop of a viceroy to promise you."

He came back to his desk and sat on the edge of it. "How was that meeting, Don Alejandro? How was it, being so close to the man who cost you your career, your position in society?" Alejandro's shock must have shown on his face for the prime minister reacted with a smile. "Oh, yes, we were well aware of your history with Custer and your loss to him at the Battle of El Bracito. Tell me, what was it like to stand next to him? To watch as he was gunned down before your very eyes?" Sagasta's smile became an unpleasant thing as he leaned a little forward, as a conspirator. "Was it all you had hoped for?"

Alejandro's temper boiled over. "Señor Sagasta, I will not stand for such insinuations. You have touched my honor, sir, and I will have satisfaction!"

Sagasta held up a hand. "I apologize, my friend." He shrugged. "Call it a bad joke. I have often been told that my sense of humor is somewhat unpleasant. Please, Don Alejandro, accept my apology. I meant no disrespect."

Though the prime minister's words were conciliatory, his insincerity showed in his knowing smile and the squint to his eye. Still, Alejandro had no recourse. He bowed.

"Apology accepted."

"Good, we are friends again." He stood and clapped a hand on Alejandro's shoulder. "And to prove it, I have the perfect gift. This new alliance; how would you like to be the one to inform the Americans? Would that appeal to you?"

The idea was more than appealing, and Alejandro allowed himself to be distracted. He agreed at once, and within the hour, he was back in a carriage, heading back down the mountains toward Madrid and the Embassy of the United States. In his pocket were the papers desig-

nating him "special envoy" for the Crown. Though the
ink was barely dry and the wax seal still warm, it would
gain him entry without appointment to see the American ambassador.

As they drove over the final ridge, Alejandro leaned
out the window. Past the vineyards and olive groves,
across the dark ribbon of the Rio Manzanares lay the
expanse of Madrid. Painted yellow by the westering sun,
it was as faceted as a raw crystal, bristling with the ta-
pered spires of cathedrals and churches. The carriage
clattered down the roadway, rattled across the Ro-
manesque stone bridge, and plunged into the dense forest of buildings. The driver knew the way, but Alejandro
did not, never before having been to the heart of New
Castile. Shops, schools, banks, and apartments flew past
in a cloud of blurred impressions. Despite the late hour,
the streets were thick with pedestrians, all out on the
evening's post-siesta business. The sun's slanting rays
turned the sky purple, the clouds orange, and the rooftops red, but left the deep streets to glow yellow with
lamplight. The carriage turned sharply onto a narrow
street lined with well-trimmed houses standing shoulder
to shoulder. Then the street debouched into a small circle with a central fountain. The carriage veered around
it, making nearly a full circuit before the driver reined
in before a tall square house of red brick. As with most
Spanish homes, it had a fence and gate of finely wrought
iron, black and coiled and twisted in graceful patterns,
but behind the gate was something no other home had:
a flagpole with the stars and stripes of the American
flag. Two serving men, their black suits made darker and
their white shirts whiter by the gloaming, worked the
ropes at the pole, retiring the flag for the night. The
driver descended from the cab and hailed them. One
came over and exchanged words and gestures as the
driver explained who his passenger was. The serving
man opened the gate while the driver returned to his
carriage to help his passenger debark.

Alejandro felt his stomach tighten as he walked
through the gate and up the path with a confident stride.
He had seen so many of his plans go awry in his
lifetime—military career ruined, social position lost, even

his revenge against Custer soiled by an assassin's whim—
that he could hardly believe that something was about
to go right.

He was ushered into a den or smoking room; he could
never tell with the ornate way in which Americans of
the Gilded Age outfitted their homes.

"The ambassador will be with you shortly," the butler
said, and withdrew, leaving him to inspect the room.

Every flat surface and most of the vertical space either
held or was covered by something that was intended to
be decorative but generally only attracted the eye long
enough to repulse it. Gaudily framed pictures, flowered
vases, figurines, bunting-draped mementos, doilies, fussy
glass lamps, cut-glass ashtrays, plants in brass pots, and
other such pieces of gimcrackery filled the room, making
it so that a man could hardly tell the room's purpose,
much less discern its main furnishings, hidden as they
were beneath the clutter. It was as furious a collection
of junk as Alejandro had ever seen, surpassing even the
more egregious examples he had seen while working as
New Spain's representative in the States. Amid the litter,
he spied one item that seemed of genuine interest. It
was a medal in a velvet box. He had to move a small
ceramic turtle and a piece of shirred lacework before he
could see it clearly. A Maltese cross struck in bronze,
with a circlet of laurel leaves surrounding a Confederate
flag. Somewhat green with the patina of age, it had obviously been kept clean by a loving hand.

"The Southern Cross of Honor," said a man at the
doorway, his words made slow and elastic by his Georgian accent. "Awarded to my father, Colonel George
Anderson Boudoin."

Alejandro turned to find the ambassador entering the
room. The man had obviously just come from dinner, as
betokened by the serviette he was removing from its
place tucked into his collar.

"I am Henry Boudoin. My man said you wished to
see me?"

"Excellency," Alejandro said with a bow. He retrieved
his papers of office from within his coat and offered
them to Boudoin. "Permit me to introduce myself . . ."

Boudoin did not take the papers. "I know who you

are, Silveira, and I know what you are. I have accepted you into my home out of respect for your government, but do not expect any courtesy. I'm told you have an important message. Please deliver it, and be on your way."

Alejandro clenched his teeth. Had the man been a Spaniard, had he been anyone *other* than the United States ambassador, he would have crossed the two steps that separated them and struck him across the face, such was the affront to his honor. The fact that Boudoin, as ambassador in Spain, was aware of how the Spanish cherished their honor, and had made the insult intentionally only infuriated Alejandro the more.

But he controlled his anger and his indignation. Instead of rising to the bait, he bowed again, though more shallowly, as to an equal. He put his letter of introduction back into his coat pocket and retrieved the second piece of paper he had brought, the one with the official message from the Crown, penned also by Sagasta. The paper, folded thrice, held the image of the royal crest embedded in its wax seal. He held it out to Boudoin.

"Mr. Ambassador, my message comes directly from Her Most Royal and Catholic Majesty, María Cristina, Queen Regent of Spain. Her Majesty wishes to inform your government of the Crown's distress and dismay at your treatment of a group of people whose rights and lives you should be working to protect, namely the native tribes known as the Cheyenne Alliance. Her Majesty wishes to inform your government further that, upon great deliberation and in an effort to alleviate the suffering of these people, the Crown has decided to ally itself with the Cheyenne and their affiliated tribes."

The ambassador's mouth opened and closed without a word passing his lips. He snatched the letter from Alejandro's hand, broke the seal and opened it. His jaw gaped once more as he read, and his ire rose until his cheeks were as florid as young wine, and the look in his eye was as raw and acidic.

"This is lunacy," Boudoin said, reading it again from the beginning. " 'Aid, succor, and support'? Has your Austrian queen finally gone mad?"

"Sir," Alejandro said, letting his anger show at last.

"You may impugn my honor all you wish and for your position and station I will allow it, but do not dare to presume that I will let insults to my sovereign go unanswered."

Boudoin collected himself, standing tall. "Very well, Señor Silveira, then hear this: Any alliance Spain attempts to forge with the Cheyenne can only be an empty gesture, for there is no Cheyenne nation with which to ally." He gripped the royal message in his fist as tightly as he might a saber. "And if Spain so much as sets one *foot* on American soil, there will be Hell to pay at the end of it."

Mustering all his diplomatic skill, Alejandro smiled. "Of course, Mr. Ambassador, of course. The Spanish Crown would never dream of abrogating the sovereignty of territories controlled by the United States," he said, putting especial stress on the word *controlled*. Boudoin heard the inflection, and understood it. He pointed at the door.

"Get your treacherous ass out of my house."

Still smiling, and feeling not at all unsatisfied by the encounter, Alejandro did just that.

It was late when he arrived back at San Lorenzo. The broken dish of a moon flew high up between the wind-blown clouds, painting them with silver light as they passed within reach. The palace was a dark monolith pierced by four tiers of windows like ordered caves in a mountainside. A few of the caves held the banked fires of lamplight as some clerk toiled over a report, some aide read a novel, or some minister enjoyed just one last sherry before retiring for the night. But as Alejandro entered the building, servants were ready and waiting for him, asking if he needed anything, offering him some refreshment, and informing him that Her Majesty was waiting for him in her apartments.

"What?" he said in surprise.

"Right this way, if you please, señor."

He followed, calm as a lamb, through what seemed like a mile of corridor, up flights of stairs, and past the watchful gaze of alert and armored guards, until he was at last brought to a small, unmarked door. The door was built of layers of wood, carved and shaped by hands long

dead. His guide nodded to the guard who stood outside
and the guard rapped heavily on the thick wood. A voice
spoke from within the room beyond, a syllable that the
guard took as permission granted. He opened the door.
The servant retreated. Alejandro swallowed and slowly
entered the room.

As a royal apartment, it did not live up to Alejandro's
expectation. He expected gold throughout in metal and
leaf, jeweled fabrics, attendants and ladies in waiting. He
expected plush furnishings, intricate carpets, and nothing
less than the glory of Spain.

What he found instead was an anteroom with floors
of simple parquetry, hardwood chairs of clean lines, and
on the walls of the room, blue and white tile had been
set from the floor up to the height of a man's waist to
create a porcelain wainscoting that kept the otherwise
dark room bright and cheerful. A modest chandelier of
wrought iron hung from the white coved ceiling, bathing
the room with a gentle glow. Above the tiling, pictures
had been hung on the walls—some of which were no
doubt priceless treasures, but most of which were small,
unassuming portraits of family members, past rulers, and
landscapes of local scenery.

"In here, Don Alejandro."

"Your Majesty?"

"Yes," she replied. "In here."

He walked forward, toward her voice, and found her
at a desk in a small adjoining room. She sat straight-
backed on the edge of her chair, writing in the light from
an oil lamp. A bookcase stood atop the desk, giving the
queen little room to write her letters, but she did not
seem to mind. On the wall around her were again more
small pictures, most barely larger than his hand. The
queen, dressed in her customary black, put her signature
on the bottom of her letter and put the pen back in
its inkpot.

"There," she said, setting the letter aside, and,
"Please, Don Alejandro. Come in. Be seated."

There were three chairs along the wall behind her. He
moved toward them, hesitated, not knowing if he should
take the one closest to her or the one nearer the door.
She made up his mind for him, offering the chair nearest

to her. He bowed, and took his seat while she turned her chair around to face him.

"So tell me," she said, "how did that Georgian boor take your news?"

The queen had left off using the royal "we" in her conversation, and it unsettled him. He reassessed his surroundings. Sitting in the private apartment of the queen, having a personal conversation with her five paces from her bed, sitting close enough to touch her, he was suddenly quite glad that he had left the door to the hallway open. The guard standing outside in the corridor would be able to vouch for the propriety of the meeting, should a rumor start. He had not heard such rumors about María Cristina, but he'd also spent his life in New Spain, not the Old, and some types of news got squashed before they could travel too far.

He cleared his throat, smiled a nervous smile, and related to her the main points of his meeting with Boudoin.

"And he didn't insult me once?" she asked.

The heat of blood flushed his neck and face.

The queen laughed in hearty humor. "I can see that he did, and that you defended me." She reached out and put her hand on his. "And honor and modesty kept you from telling me of either. How sweet, Don Alejandro."

"Your Majesty," was all he could manage to say. While she was not an unattractive woman—in a Germanic way—the sheer magnitude of her position frightened him beyond any masculine response. Of course, the touch of the royal hand might have been nothing more than a gesture of thanks, as between close friends, meant to put him at his ease; but he wasn't her friend and he didn't feel at ease, much as he tried to appear so.

"What do you think the Americans will do?" she asked, leaning back a little in her chair.

Alejandro was glad for the change in subject to one that required some thought. "It will depend entirely upon what you actually decide to do, Majesty. At the very least, they will denounce this alliance, just as Boudoin did this evening, and that is if you do nothing. If you do anything openly such as send in arms or supplies, I expect they will react more strongly, perhaps with a limited blockade of the Tejano ports. If you send troops in . . . I think you know what reaction that will bring."

She nodded, a pleased expression still gracing her youthful features. "Turning the tables, they say, is fair play, no? The Americans have been backing, supplying, and promoting the rebels in Cuba for twenty years, trying to overthrow the Crown and build an independent state . . . an independent state that would naturally want to join the Union to which it owed so much. And so I say, what they do in the hills above Havana, we can do in the plains of their West."

Alejandro tried to calm his excitement at the prospects opening before him. "It is dangerous, Your Majesty. As I've said."

She laughed again, reached forward and caressed his cheek and jaw with the palm of her hand. Then she took his hand and stood, drawing him to his feet. "You cannot fool me, Don Alejandro. You are too wily and too intelligent not to want this alliance, regardless of the cost." She walked him out to the anteroom and there, before the open door, where the guards without were sure to hear, she said, "Go, Don Alejandro Silveira-Rioja. I make you Special Ambassador to the Cheyenne, free to negotiate with them on behalf of the Spanish Crown."

He dropped to one knee before her without thinking, bowing his head in gratitude. "My humblest thanks, Your Majesty."

She stepped forward and lifted his chin so that he would look at her. Tiny thing that she was, as he knelt he still came up nearly to her shoulder. She leaned forward and kissed him on both cheeks.

"Sow us a friendship, Don Alejandro, and we shall reap a nation."

Then she drew him once more to his feet, and escorted him to the door.

The guard closed the door behind him. Alejandro, more than a little stunned, stood in the hallway, collecting his scattered thoughts.

Special Ambassador. Had it truly happened? And what of her attentiveness? Had any of *that* actually happened?

Thrown into deep confusion, he headed down the hallway, toward the main corridors. He walked without thinking of where he was going, following the path of least resistance, drawn downward from the upper stories to the main floor. Slowly, a desire, a thought formed in his mind, accompanied by a purpose and a goal. Looking up, he saw where he was and, recognizing it, turned right and walked onward.

He entered the darkened basilica. The architects of the Palacio de San Lorenzo, acceding to the wishes of Philippe Segundo, incorporated the secular as well as the religious within its walls, building into the palace's heart a grand basilica of soaring height. The columns and arches of gray stone, carved and fitted with immense precision, echoed Alejandro's crisp footsteps as he walked down the ash- and ivory-colored tiles of the nave. With chapels and shrines on either side, he passed the grille and stepped out from beneath the choir loft. The columns ascended into darkness, so high he could barely see the circle of the rotunda in the weak light of candles and oil lamps.

As he approached the altar, his eyes and the dim light worked in joint effort to bring out the wonders around him. Angels emerged from the darkness. Arched ceilings shimmered with divine blue and gold and, as his steps slowed, slowly, too, did the multitude of figures begin to appear in the frescoes that hung a hundred feet above him. He could almost hear their wondrous song, the harmonies of heaven. He halted at the steps that led up to the altar. To either side stood a tall, domed pulpit from which the priests gave their sermons, and ahead, the wall behind the altar glowed with the softness of candlelit gold. He stared upward at the portraits of the saints and the martyrs, feeling insignificant and unworthy before such grandeur.

For the second time that day, he knelt and, overcome by events, lay himself prostrate before the altar, his arms stretched out to either side. The tile floor was cold along the length of his body, and its chill seeped into his limbs, his torso, the flesh of his cheek.

"Dear Lord," he began, but halted, the words of personal prayer so long unused that he did not know how to utter the thoughts that roamed in his head.

Is it wrong for me to pray for war? Is it a sin to work so hard for something that will cause the death of men? What if, out of it, comes an ultimate good? Is it a sin to bring glory to the Church, or souls to the paradise of Heaven?

But he knew that his motivations were far from such a noble—and justifiable—cause. No, his motives were for personal gain: position, power, money. But if he created enough good, would God forgive him his more temporal goals?

He brought his arms beneath him and clasped his hands, still prone before the altar. "Dear Lord in Heaven," he began anew, "if I succeed, it will not be for myself alone. It will be for You as well. The Church will benefit from my desires. If You only will help me and guide me, I will give back to You as I have never done before. I will dedicate chapels, build whole churches among these Cheyenne. I will use my position and wealth to benefit the poor and destitute. I will expand Your Church on Earth. If You only give me the tools I need to forge this new nation, as my queen has commanded me."

He lay there a while longer, the cold seeping into his joints, thoughts of what was ahead filling his brain. María Cristina, Custer, One Who Flies, Speaks while Leaving, himself—they were all inextricably bound, woven together by acts and desires. But acts and desires were not enough to build a nation.

To build a nation took blood.

CHAPTER 21

Moon When the Whistlers Get Fat, Full Fifty-seven Years after the Star Fell South of the White River Alliance Territory

Storm Arriving soared above the sacred mountains. The warm wind, lush with the scents of tree and grass, sunshine and river, buoyed him, lifting him higher. He could feel the wind pass through the fingerlike feathers of his outstretched wings, and riffle across the sleek, flat plumage of his body. He clenched talons that were eager to grip and opened his shiny beak to shout his desire to the world: Wife of mine, where are you?

A screech from below echoed his own, answering him in a different voice. His eagle's sight found her at once—a thousand feet below, the sun bright along her glossy back. She craned her feathered neck to fix him with her gaze, then snapped her black-tipped beak before loosing another rough-tongued cry of ardor.

He stooped, folding wings tightly against his ribs, tucking curled feet up under his tailfeathers. With movements as small as thought, he aimed his body at her, shifting his course through the fluid air. Shallowing, he approached, extending rasplike legs, talons open. She rolled, her back to the world, and met him claw for claw. Wingtips touching, they fell in taloned embrace, mating in brilliant, sunlit freedom, bodies entwined, heedless of up or down. He filled her with his light and they screamed as one being, one thought, until the wind caught up to them and separated them with its powerful hand.

They flew together, and he rolled under the sun's plea-

sure, happy, his wife beside him, sleek and beautiful. She
screeched again, a thought that was not for him, and she
wheeled toward the south. He flew to catch her, to keep
pace with her flight, but could not. He called after her:
Stay! Don't leave me.

Her winged form dwindled, an undulating curve that
disappeared in the atmospheric haze, taking with it his
desires for lodge and family, leaving behind his aching
breast and a growing desolation.

He cried out one final time, and let rest his pinion
arms, giving himself up to the earth's inexorable pull.
Bereft of his lifemate, he would return his body to the
earth and send his spirit to the stars. But as he fell, his
body changed, and though he let his arms droop, still he
flew, lower and lower, until he was skimming above the
prairie's pelt. His despair turned to fear as his arms and
legs became pendant sticks armed with hooks. His
breathing chest became rigid with blue armor. His view
of the world was not downward but all-encompassing,
and he could see at one time both the brown water flow-
ing through a tawny land, and the double-pair of glassy
wings that sprouted from his back.

He had become one of the little-whirlwinds, a blue
dragonfly born of blue waters, quick and hard to kill. He
stopped above a meandering river, hovering, breathing
without breath, feeling his body buzz beneath shivering
wings. To the north were the sacred mountains, the
teaching places of his people, but he did not want to go
there. There was nothing for him there. To the south,
there was the memory of what was and what might have
been, and as his fear faded, he knew that neither did he
want to go searching for ruined pasts or lost futures.

He pivoted eastward and shot forward. The flat land
became hilly as he left the Plains and approached the
borderlands. His fear melted away, replaced with a vi-
brating rage. He heard the sound of other wings, and
without turning saw others like himself joining him.
Blue, green, red, black, and striped yellow, they flew
toward the *vé'ho'e* lands, close to the ground, pulling
behind them the vortex winds that gave them their
name. The whirlwinds grew, combined, and when they

reached the banks of the Big Greasy, they drew destruction in their wake.

The vision flew apart, broken into pieces of light as a hand shook him awake. He blinked. He lay in a deep bed of sweet flag, the air heady with the scent of its crushed leaves. The sun was rising and the blade-tips and flowered spikes were aflame with a light as orange as glowing coals.

It was Whistling Elk who shook him awake. He stayed in a low crouch, his gaze fixed on the distance.

"Bluecoat patrol," he said.

Storm Arriving rubbed his eyes, still caught between dream and reality. "We must—"

"Quiet," Whistling Elk said. "We knew what to do."

Gunfire erupted in a volley and men shouted, screamed. Storm Arriving remembered the eagle of his dream and frowned. A few more shots and the screaming stopped. Whistling Elk looked, was satisfied, and stood. He offered his hand. Storm Arriving took it and rose.

The remnants of his battle group had bedded down along a shallow creek whose waters had been swallowed up by reeds and sweet flag, providing ample cover. Beyond the creek, the tall prairie grasses stretched toward the horizon, a golden hide studded with green outcrops of buckbrush and yellow dabs of mustard flower. Horses ran, riderless, toward the southeast, and eight soldiers walked back toward the creek, their hands full of rifles and supplies taken from the bluecoats who undoubtedly lay dead in the deep grass.

"We should leave," Whistling Elk said. "The main body won't be far behind them."

Storm Arriving tasted bile. "We are reduced to scavenging and raiding," he said. Along the creekbed, his hundred men prepared to depart, but for where? For what?

"It is all we can do with so few against so many," the man-becoming-woman said. "It is better for the People if we live and fight than die in glory. You taught us that."

"Yes," Storm Arriving said, half to himself. "But we do nothing. We achieve nothing this way."

"Then what?"

Knee Prints by the Bank came over to them. "The messengers are ready to take word to the other battle groups. What are your orders for the day?"

He felt the wind rise, coming in from the west, pushing at his back as he watched the land glow beneath the rising sun. From the south would soon come the column of bluecoats they had been harassing for a moon and more, a lance of men thrust deep into Alliance territory. On horse and on foot they would come, hundreds strong, armed with rifle, pistol, and heavy gun. The two other battle groups followed similar columns, keeping pace, wreaking what havoc they could, but always retreating to spare their own forces. They buzzed around them like yellow jackets at a cookfire, but onward would the blue-coats come, and soon—very soon—they would find the People. That meeting would mean the end. Of everything.

"Storm Arriving?" Knee Prints by the Bank said. "Your orders for the day?"

The wind pushed again, a spirit hand urging him eastward.

"If we cannot turn the lance, we must turn the hand that wields it," he said, and his voice seemed far away to his own ears.

Knee Prints by the Bank cleared his throat. "Yes. That is good advice, but hardly the kind of orders that the other groups will understand."

Storm Arriving brought his focus back to the men who stood by him: Whistling Elk, whose dual nature provided insight into men's hearts; Knee Prints by the Bank, whose resolve and respectability commanded men's minds; and the men themselves, each blooded of body and soul, each willing to follow and fight.

"Send out the orders," he said. "Ride east, and let them see us ride east."

They mounted up. He led them south, heeling left just in sight of the bluecoat advance. They rode over a gentle sigh of land and halted in disarray, as if surprised to meet their enemy. The bluecoats reacted swiftly, running to form defensive ranks, but Storm Arriving kicked his mount into motion, avoiding a battle most surely lost, but drawing his foe's interest away from northern targets. The column did not follow, but he hoped to change that in time.

The whistlers' lungs sucked in the prairie air and their powerful legs pressed them forward, eastward now. They rode for a day, sent out messengers at sunset, and rode on through the night. With each mile, with each moonlit rise they topped and each star-filled stream they crossed, he felt his blood cool and thin. He flew in the darkness, soaring through the night. The wind flew with him, and his body tightened, hardened. Dream armor encased him, and his heart slowed. They all flew, skimming the ground from whistlerback, as silent as the little-whirlwinds; soldiers no longer, they were weapons themselves, living darts with which to prick a massive bear. He looked back, half expecting to see a twister, but only night pursued, thunder-dark and ghostly.

That, he said to himself, will be good enough.

By noon, the land had rumpled itself into unkempt folds. Woods filled gaps between larger streams and grasses competed with sharp-fingered juniper and fields of prickly milkweed, their downy heads dancing in the westerly breeze. They rode through this, too, not pausing but to give mounts and men brief rests for water. Messengers came and went, linking the three forces as they ranged eastward, and toward evening, as his forces drew near his goal, Storm Arriving sent out his final orders.

He reined in on a knoll, deep in lands he had not visited in years, lands that had changed a great deal in that short time.

All around them were the square, dark homesteads of *vé'hó'e,* their windows glowing with lamplight, the land around each home torn and cleared of native growth. The forests that packed the water-rich land only a half-day west had here been felled by an appetite for wood: to build, to fence, to burn. Now the lands that rolled toward the Big Greasy were naked and broken, torn into corrugated squares and planted with lines of corn, wheatgrass, and many plants that Storm Arriving could not even identify.

Farther, more settlements gathered along the banks of a river, changing it, too. Where he had known broad, sandy banks and quiet, tree-canopied eddies, lodges and structures now crowded side by side. Along muddy shores where hardbacks had splashed and grumbled, grazing on waterborn weeds, boats of every size now rested or sat bobbing at anchor, tugged by the great river's sluggish summer current. It was a town divided by a river, linked by ferryboats, and it was the focal point of every *vé'ho'e* settler for miles and miles.

Whistling Elk nudged his mount next to Storm Arriving's. "I am afraid I know what you are thinking."

Knee Prints by the Bank laughed from the other side. "It does not take any special wisdom to see it."

"Do not do this," Whistling Elk said. "There is no honor in it. It is shameful. The Council has forbidden it."

"The Council has forbidden us to do anything," Knee Prints by the Bank said.

"But even Three Trees Together agreed—you told me that before he died, he had promised the *vé'hó'e* not to do this sort of thing."

Storm Arriving sneered as he stared at the only thing his enemy seemed to value. "Before he died," he said. "Before he was *murdered*."

"Died, murdered, yes, but he promised not to do this thing."

"And Long Hair promised not to do *that* thing," Storm Arriving shouted, pointing back to the west, to the bluecoats, and their advance on the People. "*Vé'ho'e* promises," he said, "are like water in your hand. You can drink of them now, but you cannot save them for tomorrow. They slip away, until nothing is left but your thirst."

"But it is wrong," Whistling Elk said, begging him.

He was silent a moment. "Do you know what the *vé'hó'e* call us? They call us savages. They call us animals. This is nothing more than what they expect of us."

"But these are *families*." Whistling Elk grabbed his arm, tears on his face. "Families, not soldiers. Not bluecoats. These are wives and children. What if they were yours?"

He glared at the man-becoming-woman. "I have no wife," he said. "I have no child. The *vé'hó'e* have taken them." Then he jerked his arm out of the other's grasp and addressed his soldiers.

"Start with the farms," he commanded. "And take fire to the town. Kill the men. Use the women if you wish. Leave the children to starve. Let's go!"

Riders scattered, spreading out in threes and fours toward the lamplit homes. Whistling Elk did not ride forward. Storm Arriving glanced over as the first sounds of murder could be heard.

"It is only what they expect," Storm Arriving told him. Then he nudged his whistler into motion, leaving Whistling Elk to hold the knoll alone.

CHAPTER 22

Tuesday, July 8, A.D. 1890
White House
Washington, District of Columbia

The cursive letters evaded Custer's will, twisting as he attempted to set them on the page. He wrestled with them, with the pen itself, the mere feel of it alien in his left hand. It was nothing but an ink-dipped stick, but it spun and bucked within his grasp, seeking escape, a goal it had already achieved twice this morning as evidenced by the stains and smears on his desktop blotter. Inanimate yet willful, it felt both stiff and rubbery in his clumsy fingers, but he strove against its dominance, gaining ground with each letter, gaining confidence with every word.

He sat back and stretched the cramping muscles of a neck and shoulder unaccustomed to attacking a piece of paper from the left. Morning sunshine streamed into the library, bouncing up from the floor to fill the coved ceiling with wood-grained light. A wet breeze moved sluggishly in and out through the open French doors. Custer looked back down and regarded the two lines it had taken him a quarter hour to write:

> *My dearest Sunshine Girl,*
> *   It is the first day of Spring, and you sit by the*
> *window, bathed in Sun's sweet glory.*

It was a belated letter, one of the many he had composed for Libbie and stored in the shelves of his memory, but the words and the moment—now months behind him—had remained crisp and vivid. Committing these long-held thoughts to paper was not only good practice for the President's recalcitrant body, it was the least he could do for the woman who had stood by him through the past difficult months. Though he had been able to communicate to her through the slurred speech of his handicap, he had never been able to utter the words of love and devotion that had been so much a part of their relationship. For twenty-five years, from courtship and through wars and politics, he had forever spoken frankly of his adoration for Libbie Bacon, the prettiest girl in Monroe, but from the day an assassin's bullet stole his loquacity and turned his words into sounds best fit for a farmyard beast, he had been unwilling to bear hearing the words of his devotion so perverted.

And so he had saved those words. Until now. Until the time when the faculty of the written word was once more within reach of his inept fingers.

He regarded the product of his efforts. The penmanship was atrocious, but he had to learn how to forgive that, so he decided instead to pride himself in the fact that the slowness of his hand had enabled him to achieve perfect spelling. A simple attainment, perhaps, and one better suited to a schoolhouse pupil than a nation's leader, but it was a start. With diligent work, he would be ready to return to the tasks of his position. A few things needed to be brought into play first, though, his strength and stamina not the least of them. With attention to every move, he reached over and redipped his nib in the ink, tapped it twice against the pot's rim, and brought the pen smoothly back to the page.

Three knocks sounded at the library door.

"Yeh," he said, still unable to manage a good and sibilant "s" with his stroke-palsied tongue. He had learned to forgive himself for many things during this past difficult year. "Come in."

He glanced up as Jacob entered. "Good morning, Jacob," he said as he returned his attention to his letters.

"Good morning, Autie," he said as he took a seat in the chair before Custer's worktable. He looked troubled, with splotches of color in his pudgy cheeks and eyes peering out from beneath a wrinkled brow. Even his mouth—usually so ready with a smile—was bunched up under his moustache, giving him the aspect of a terrier denied the chase.

"I know that look," Custer said. "That look means trouble."

Jacob put a small stack of papers on the table. Custer recognized the half-sheets of telegraph transcriptions and the densely typed, oddly indented foolscap of military reports. Jacob, as Secretary of War, often had such papers in hand, but his demeanor gave Custer a bad feeling about what today's report contained.

"Things are bad out there, Autie."

"How bad?"

"Very bad." He stabbed the papers with a daggered finger. "Homesteaders killed. Whole families slaughtered. Towns burned to the ground. Your Cheyenne have gone mad, Autie."

Custer frowned and paused in his writing. This was not good news, not at all, but gone mad? "No," he said, working hard to make his diction crisp. "Not mad." In his entire experience, the Indian had never been the crazed killer depicted in novels. They had often been incomprehensible to white men, but their motives, once known, had always been logical.

But this time . . . he couldn't see what they were doing. Attacking the homesteads and tiny hamlets of the newly settled southern region would gain them nothing except the immediate retribution of the garrisons and forces already in the region. He could not decipher their goal, unless . . .

"Wait. Where?" he asked. "Where are they?"

"Along the eastern borderlands," Jacob said with the exasperation of a man who cannot get his point across. "They've even crossed the Missouri. They're attacking towns and homes in Santee Territory and Yankton. We weren't prepared—"

Custer laughed.

"Autie, I don't see that this is a laughing matter!"

He waved his ink-stained hand to calm Jacob's indignation. "Brilliant," he said.

"Killing women and children can hardly be called brilliant."

Custer laughed some more. "Why not?" he asked. "We did it."

"Our soldiers did not scalp and rape and burn!"

Custer shook his head. "Jacob. Are you sure of that?"

Jacob swallowed his next retort. "No, I'm not." His anger melted into petulance. "I still don't see the 'brilliance' of this."

"Come, Jacob. Think back to West Point." He jabbed a finger down on the tabletop. "You are here, hidden and protected by miles of prairie." Now he drew a line from the side toward that spot. "And here I come toward your position. You can't get away. What do you do?"

"I draw you off with a flanking maneuver."

"And if I don't take the bait?" He drew a new line back behind the oncoming force.

"I move behind and attack you from the rear."

"And if that fails?" He extended the line farther back to the rear of the advancing column.

"I attack your supply lines."

"Yeh. Now what if you can't? What if you know at the beginning that your numbers are not enough to achieve a victory in direct combat?"

Jacob puzzled at it but shook his head. "I don't know."

Custer drew the line even farther back. "If I can't keep you out, I make you want to leave." He brought a clenched fist down on the table. "I hit what you must defend. I draw you back."

Jacob's frown deepened. "That's despicable," he said.

Custer gave a one-shouldered shrug. "It's war. Did you tell Morton yet?"

"Hm? Morton? No, not yet."

"Good," Custer said and put his hand on the reports. "Let me."

Jacob reached out for the papers. "Autie, I have to tell him. It's my duty."

"No, your duty is to get the information to him. Leave it here. I'll make sure he's told."

"Autie . . ."

Custer didn't push further. "What other news?"

"Psh," Jacob said with a dismissive wave. He sat back in his chair. "Everything is bad. Morton has the navy prowling the southern coasts to ensure 'free navigation' from Spanish privateers—not that we've seen any—and we have reports of trading caravans making their way up from Tejano into the Territory. Heavily guarded caravans. And we're pretty sure that the guards are more than just guards."

"Military?"

"Undoubtedly. I tell you, I think that man is doing everything he can to get us into a war. If he's not thumping his chest about 'Spanish arrogance,' he's thumbing his nose at the Spaniards with guns and supplies to Cuba. Did you hear that he's dispatched warships to Havana to 'protect United States interests in the region'?"

Custer nodded. "And in return?"

"In return, Spain has dispatched a fleet of her own. Havana harbor is going to be stacking them in like sardines. Our ships will be cheek-to-jowl with the dapper dons."

Custer grimaced. "That won't be good," he said.

"No," Jacob agreed. "It'll be a powderkeg." He shrugged. "It serves us right for running you with a businessman and not a politician, I suppose."

Custer lifted his right hand, already twisted and starting to wither like an apple left too long on the tree. "How could we have known?"

The news was disturbing. Events were culminating more swiftly than Custer liked, and sooner than he feared he could handle them. He brought his pen back to Libbie's letter.

"War is coming, Jacob, but it is not inevitable," he said, taking extra care with the multisyllabic word.

"But Autie, with Spanish ships in the Gulf, Spanish soldiers in the Territory, and the Spanish weapons in Cheyenne hands . . ."

"We could lose the Interior," Custer finished. "I agree. And that is why we will work to avoid this war

Morton is heading for." He frowned in concentration as he drew the intricate curls of a capital *D*.

"The Cheyenne are one thing," he went on. "Spain, entirely another. We are not prepared to go to war with Spain. I need you to prepare a meeting, Jacob. In a week. Maybe a little longer."

"Of course, Autie. With whom?"

He glanced up from his work and gave Jacob his best rendition of the old Custer wink. "With the Cabinet."

Jacob swelled with excitement at the prospect. "It will be my pleasure."

Custer nodded. "Keep it quiet, though. I don't want Morton to know until I'm ready." He nodded. "Thank you, Jacob."

Jacob stood. "Thank you, Mr. President." He reached for the stack of papers but Custer touched them first.

"Leave those with me," he said.

Jacob hesitated, ready to insist. "You'll see that Morton gets them?"

"I will personally make sure that Morton is informed of the situation."

Jacob knew his old friend and commander, and probably knew what Custer was thinking. After a long moment of consideration, though, he relented. When he left the library, however, he did so wearing an expression quite nearly as troubled as the one he'd worn on the way in.

Yes, Custer thought, you know me. And you know that I didn't say I'd tell Morton. You're walking down the hall, now, trying to think it through, trying to remember precisely what it is I *did* say I'd do.

He put down the pen and picked up the reports that detailed the Cheyenne attacks and their results. He thumbed through them.

Civilian casualties, they read. Depravities visited upon women. Mutilations. Livestock slaughtered. Homes burned. Shops burned. Towns burned. Langtree. Homeview. Westgate.

He let the pages fall back into place and closed his eyes. He hadn't seen reports like this for nearly a score of years, but the images of torn bodies, bloodied fields, and the smoking ruins of homes were all too real, all too easy to recall.

What are you doing? he asked the unseen warriors of the prairie. What changed you? Why this sudden cruelty?

He shook his head, resigned to the fact that, most likely, he would never know the answer to those questions. Then he took the reports and put them under a pile of other papers, off to the side of his worktable.

Morton would be informed, all right. He promised Jacob, and he intended to keep that promise. And in a few days, when the story hit the papers, he would make sure that Morton saw the reports. Waiting a few days would not change the outcome in the West. People would die, homes would be burned, livestock would be killed, but no more tomorrow than if he told Morton today. What *would* be different was the public reaction to the news. Hearing such news with a sympathetic leader on hand to tell them that steps had been taken to crush the violence would soothe the situation, but hearing it and then seeing that leader caught flatfooted by the reports, that would lead to outcry, and public outcry was just the pry-rod Custer required to get Morton out of his chair.

"*My* chair," Custer muttered, and then, looking at his writing, "Aw, Hell." He had misspelled *Darling,* and while penmanship might be somewhat out of his control, he would accept damnation before he'd accept less than excellence in the things he *could* control. He crumpled the letter, brought out a fresh sheet of paper, redipped his pen, and started anew.

My dearest Sunshine Girl . . .

CHAPTER 23

Moon When the Whistlers Get Fat, Waning
Fifty-seven Years after the Star Fell
The Docks
Cadiz, Spain

The carriage's iron-rimmed wheels clattered and banged along the rough cobbles that led to the wharfs. The streets were lined with townsfolk, all come to bid farewell to their country's newest friends. They waved hats and kerchiefs in the bright sunshine, standing on tiptoe to catch a glimpse of the travelers.

Speaks while Leaving and Mouse Road rode in an open carriage with a nursemaid who held Blue Shell Woman. A second carriage rattled on behind them, bringing Alejandro and One Who Flies. Speaks while Leaving waved to the well-wishers who called to her and blessed her and made their signs of the cross as she passed. Mouse Road waved, too, though without enthusiasm, and Blue Shell Woman, propped up and made to wave by the nursemaid, cried in small, percussive coughs of unhappiness.

"*Pobrecita. Ella gruñón,*" the nursemaid said in a sympathetic tone.

Speaks while Leaving understood the intention if not the words, and hoped that they would arrive soon, ending the jarring, noisy trip that had taken them from the manor where they had spent the night, high up in the hills over the shining town, down to the sea where their ship awaited.

Their ship. The phrase filled her with hope and excitement, for "their ship" would take her back to her homeland where, bright with good news, she could begin the

difficult work of convincing men to follow a woman's
advice. The weariness of the weeks they had spent in
this land hung upon her like a weight. The long arguments with One Who Flies, the long meetings with the
queen's ministers, the long days riding in hot carriages
and railcars, and the long, drawn-out ritual of dining
with every magistrate in every town through which they
passed—it had all sapped at her strength, draining it
lower and lower each day until, now, she felt barely able
to keep awake. Their ship—and the two-week ocean
voyage—promised a spate of time wherein she might
recuperate. She looked forward to the lazy, shipboard
days ahead; days filled with rest, siestas, easy food, warm
sunshine, and the ever-nearing shores of home. She intended to indulge in the luxury of their journey and in
the time it would provide her with Blue Shell Woman
for she knew that, reaching home, all such leisure would
end. There was no time for afternoon naps in life among
the People, no time for quiet strolls with her daughter.
The shores of home meant a return to family, friends,
and loved ones, but it also meant a return to the work
of living, and the work of surviving, both as a person,
and as a People. There would be no rest, once she rode
back into Alliance territory.

But that work was still half a moon away, and the
pleasure of the sea voyage lay ahead. The two carriages
swung around the final curve, passing houses that had
been whitewashed for so many years that the repeated
coats of lime had rounded every corner and edge. They
passed through the final gap in the close-set streets and
emerged into the dazzling light of the sun-sparkled quay.
The carriages circled around, and the crowds pressed in
as they drew to a halt. The driver helped his passengers
descend, and Speaks while Leaving stepped down into a
throng of men and women, their skin tanned by sun and
toil, their features rough but their eyes wide, their faces
smiling. They reached out toward her, and as she
touched each hand, it recoiled, retreating to its owner
like the hand of a hungry man given food. Her skin was
dark, like theirs, and her braided hair was dark, like
theirs and her eyes were dark, like theirs; but these were
a different people. As she thanked them and made her

way to the pier, she saw in their dark eyes the image that they superimposed upon her. Her touch gave them joy for no other reason than it gave them hope and belief, contact with the spiritual, and their misplaced faith saddened her.

"Madonna," one old man said as he held his hat over his heart, gazing at her with eyes brimming with emotion.

She wanted to tell him that he was wrong, that it was all a mistake, but instead she merely touched his hand and smiled as his tears spilled.

Alejandro and One Who Flies came up from their carriage and escorted them through the crowd. They made their way to the dock and across the gangway to the ship. The passengers who had preceded them aboard stared at the spectacle. The women whispered to one another from behind parasols and gloved hands, but the men, Speaks while Leaving noticed, regarded them with a kindly eye. News of their mission and their success had traveled along with the legend of the "Madonna of the Swallows." They stood apart from the new arrivals, as if there was a barrier between them. Then, one gentleman stepped forward, tipped his hat to Alejandro, and introduced himself. The rest surged in after him, as though a dam had been breached, swamping them with eager interest.

Speaks while Leaving took her wailing daughter from the nursemaid and let her return to the dock. Then she turned to One Who Flies and Alejandro.

"I will take her to our quarters," she said. "She is probably just tired. She did not sleep well last night."

The ship's horn blasted a huge note above their heads, making everyone jump and sending Blue Shell Woman into renewed displeasure.

"She has been unhappy today, hasn't she?" Alejandro noted. "She's usually such a cheerful traveler, but today I could hear her cries all the way from the mayor's villa." He motioned to one of the ship's waitstaff and spoke to him in Spanish. The steward bowed to Speaks while Leaving.

"He will escort you to your stateroom," Alejandro told her.

"Many thanks," she said with a small nod.

Alejandro tipped his hat as she left. One Who Flies bowed, but said nothing. He had said little since El Escorial. Toward her, he had been civil but unfriendly, but toward Mouse Road, he had seemed mostly just embarrassed.

She turned to Mouse Road. "I am going below. You can stay here if you wish."

"No," the young woman said. "I will go with you."

The steward led them away. The ship—the *Santa Luisa*—was a steamer with one smokestack amidships and two masts for sails, one fore and one aft. While her hull was painted black above the waterline, her wooden decks gleamed with care and polish, her brasswork shone, and the white paint of the structures abovedeck was brilliant in the summer sun. Speaks while Leaving squinted against the glare as the steward led them forward.

The brightness from abovedeck made the shadowed interior all the darker. Stepping carefully down the steep stairs, they came to a narrow companionway that twisted around pipes and squeezed through bulkheads. Blue Shell Woman's cries were magnified by the small space, focused by the close, hard walls. As they passed open doors, Speaks while Leaving saw some of the other rooms: small, efficient spaces where some of the other passengers were already settling in. They looked up as her baby's wails approached, and she saw their eyes widen as they passed, surprised to see not a pale servant or lady of means with a pampered infant, but a dusky-skinned woman in an elkhide dress with her feather-haired daughter.

Their walk took three turns in quick succession, passing several other rooms—some open, some closed, all seemingly identical. Speaks while Leaving hoped she would be able to remember which one was theirs. Each room had a label on its door, and when the steward opened one such door for them, she made note of the curved squiggles that distinguished theirs from the others.

Inside, it was gloomy, partly because her eyes still had not relaxed after the day's brightness. She saw that their traveling cases—a gift from the queen—had already been brought inside. The queen's gift had been impossible to refuse, even though everything Speaks while Leaving and Mouse Road carried could fit inside just one of the brass- and leather-bound cases. Nor had she seen any use for them when she returned to the People. Heavy, ungainly, and overlarge, they would be useless on whistlerback, and would outweigh any amount of goods she could possibly fit inside them. And yet, they were here, neatly stacked and strapped into the corner.

There were also two narrow beds, one of which was folded up against the wall, as well as a dry sink with pitcher and basin, and, in the corner opposite their luggage, a small table before an elbow-shaped bench. Between the furnishings there was barely enough room to pace out six steps, and would be even less when the second bed was unfolded.

Speaks while Leaving sat on the bed and laid her daughter down upon the rough blanket. Mouse Road sat on the bench at the table and rested her forehead on her pillowed arms.

"What is it?" Speaks while Leaving asked as she went over to their luggage. "Are you still upset about One Who Flies?"

"No," Mouse Road said. "I am tired."

Speaks while Leaving pulled out the case that held their meager belongings and opened it. She took out the rolled pelt of elkhide and untied it. Soft as a breath, the fur was both warm and cool to the touch. She laid it out on the bed and set Blue Shell Woman upon it. The familiar touch quieted the baby's squalling and she rolled over and clutched a handful of fur in her chubby fingers. Speaks while Leaving stroked her daughter's back, quieting her further.

"Everyone seems tired today," she said, wondering if Mouse Road was hiding something from her. "Even One Who Flies. He has been sullen since we left El Escorial." She glanced over, but Mouse Road did not raise her head.

"He feels useless," Mouse Road said.

"Useless?" she said dismissively. "After all his help working out the details of the alliance?"

"Details you told him." She lifted her head and peered over her folded arms. "Details that the Council will be surprised they have approved, I might add. But maybe *useless* is the wrong word." Her head sank back onto her arms. "*Unnecessary* is better. We've both been unnecessary. Only I don't mind. He does."

Speaks while Leaving unlatched the other bed and set it onto its drop-down legs. She smoothed out the blankets. "Here," she said. "Lie down. Rest. Blue Shell Woman is sleeping. You sleep, too."

Reluctantly, as if even moving to a more comfortable place was too much effort, Mouse Road allowed herself to be put to bed. Though a bit stuffy, the room was still pleasant and cozy. Speaks while Leaving left the two of them there to sleep and went up on deck, taking care to retrace the path the steward had shown them.

Most of the passengers were also abovedecks, milling near the portside rail as the crew prepared to cast off. There were only thirty passengers on this voyage, the bulk of the ship's space and interest having been given over to the more lucrative use of hauling cargo bound for Cuba and New Spain. What space that the *Santa Luisa* had saved for passengers was sold at a premium; this was no voyage crammed with steerage-class immigrants. The people Speaks while Leaving saw on deck were the well-to-do of Spain's better classes. Businessmen, financiers, professionals, perhaps even an aristocrat or two made up the passenger list. As she walked, blinking in the lively light that bounced from fixture, deck, and shiny wavelet, she passed round women in pale traveling dresses standing at the rail, waving to the friends they were leaving behind. The women wore hats with broad, curving brims and thin veils decorated with sparkling crystals, and the lacework frills on their parasols fluttered in the westerly breeze. The men stood stoically beside their mates or chatted in dark-suited knots, Spain already forgotten, business the subject ahead.

She saw Alejandro in the center of one such cluster, standing tall and proud, surrounded by men who leaned forward to glean all they could from his words. He saw her and raised a hand in greeting, but did not stop the thread of his discourse. She looked further, but did not

see One Who Flies, and so she went to the rail alone
and watched as the crew cast off.

The sun was happy in a deep blue sky studded with
thistledown clouds. The breeze was clean and salty. The
crew, in their blue shirts and blue-and-white striped
pants, coiled ropes and lowered the gangway. Smoke
boiled up out of the tall stack amidships. She jumped as
the steam whistle howled, sounding three deep notes
that echoed around the cove. The rail trembled beneath
her grip, the women waved handkerchiefs with renewed
energy, and the *Santa Luisa* edged away from the dock.
Many of the people on the dock and upper pier seemed
to be waving in her direction. She raised her hand in
farewell and a shout rose from the crowd.

Two more shots from the whistle, and Speaks while
Leaving felt the surge of power as the ship pushed forward, turning her bow to the west and the open sea. The
breeze strengthened as they moved against it, and seagulls hung on curved wings, slipping back and forth
across their path as effortlessly as children playing on an
icebound pond.

She was heading home.

Mouse Road and Blue Shell Woman slept through all
of the first day and most of the second; unusual behavior
for both of them. The second night, Blue Shell Woman
was fretful, but Speaks while Leaving put it down to her
having slept through the daylight hours. The next morning, the baby awoke in tears and Speaks while Leaving
took her out of the room so as not to disturb Mouse
Road. Up on deck, she carried her daughter on her hip,
cooing to her as they made their circuit alongside the
rails.

The sea was calm, and the ship plowed through the
gentle swells with a languorous pitch and roll that reminded Speaks while Leaving of coursing over the prairie on whistlerback.

"The prairie is like an ocean, too," she told her daughter. "An ocean that the People have sailed for generations. The People left the Sweet Waters of the north and
walked out onto the Plains to follow Buffalo, to whom
our destiny is tied. There we met all sorts of new friends,

like Whistler who in turn tied his destiny to ours. And
we met Drummer Grouse who brings in the spring with
his dances, and Red-Topknot Crane who tells us when
winter is coming." She told her story in a calm, soothing
voice, but Blue Shell Woman would not be appeased.
She wavered between whimper and wail, breaking her
mother's heart.

Speaks while Leaving kissed her daughter's forehead
and recoiled at its heat. She put her hand on the baby's
cheek, then on the nape of her neck. She put her palm
on the skin of her own cheek and felt its relative
coolness.

"Poor thing," she said with more calm than she felt.
"No wonder you are so unhappy."

She went forward to the lounge and found a steward
who understood her French and brought her a cup of
water. Blue Shell Woman fussed at it, but eventually
agreed to drink.

The threat of fever hung over every mother's child
and Speaks while Leaving felt fear begin to gnaw at her.
She stayed for a while in the empty lounge, keeping her
daughter out of the ocean breeze, and praying for her
symptoms to ease. When other passengers began to
rouse and drift into the common areas, though, Blue
Shell Woman was still crying, and Speaks while Leaving
rose and returned to their quarters.

Mouse Road lay on her bed and moaned as Speaks
while Leaving brought the fussing baby into the small
room.

"It's time you got up, anyway," Speaks while Leaving
told her.

"I don't feel well," the young woman said.

Speaks while Leaving sat down on the edge of the
bed. She put her hand on Mouse Road's forehead.

"My throat is sore."

"You have a fever as well. So does Blue Shell Woman.
I should have thought of that."

"Thought of what?" Mouse Road asked, opening
her eyes.

Speaks while Leaving frowned and went to the other
bed. She put Blue Shell Woman down and got some of

the cloth the *vé'ho'e* nursemaid had given her to use as diapers.

"You haven't spent much time around the *vé'ho'e*," she said as she changed her daughter's swaddlings. "I have. I have already had most of their diseases. You haven't." She swallowed against a throat gone stiff and thick. "Neither has Blue Shell Woman. I should have thought of that before I agreed to let you come."

Mouse Road laughed weakly. "*You* agreed to let *me* come? Wasn't it the other way around?" She sat up, moaned, and reclined again. "You had no choice."

Speaks while Leaving took a cloth to the dry sink and wetted it in the basin. She brought it back and began to swab at her daughter's skin. "Perhaps," she said. "Still, I might have insisted, and as for this one—" She stopped, staring at the red splotches on her daughter's legs and groin.

"What is it?" Mouse Road asked, rising up on one elbow.

She continued cleaning Blue Shell Woman. "Nothing. A rash. She has a rash. Probably from the soiled cloth against her skin." She finished cleaning the baby and wrapped her in a clean cloth.

The changing soothed Blue Shell Woman, and she lay quietly on the bed, looking up at her mother with large, dark, tired eyes. Speaks while Leaving felt her forehead again. Still hot.

"She will be quiet for a while, now. Let me go and get some food and drink for you both."

She bundled up the soiled cloth and left. A steward was in the hall and she gave him the bundle.

"*¿Lavar, por favor? ¿Para niña?*" It was almost all the Spanish she knew, but words she had found frequent use for during her time among the Iron Shirts.

Then she went up on deck.

She didn't know where One Who Flies had been settled, but she knew where she would find Alejandro. He would be ill through most of the trip, sickened by the ship's constant motion. The leeward rail was his place of refuge during the days aboard ship, if the weather allowed it, and today the weather was fine, with a sharp blue sky, streamer clouds high above, and a brisk salt breeze coming in off the port bow. She walked around to starboard where the ship's structure broke the wind's strength and the air fluttered in gentle, incoherent puffs.

Alejandro lay on one of the long chairs set away from the rail. He stood as she approached, slowly, but with dignity. She noticed a spot on his lapel.

"Good morning, senora," he said with a bow. "Or should I say, 'Madonna'?"

"You know better than that," she said. She took the handkerchief out of his pocket and wiped the spot of vomit from his lapel, then folded the cloth and returned it to him. "Having trouble already?"

He smiled weakly. "I fear so. It seems the better I live prior to a journey, the worse I fare en route." He gestured to the chairs. "If you don't mind?"

"Of course." She sat, and Alejandro reclined gratefully in his chair. "Perhaps we should shorten our journey."

Alejandro laughed, then coughed, covering his mouth with the handkerchief. "Shorten it? If only we could."

"I want to turn around and go back to Spain."

He stared at her, then caught his rudeness and looked out to sea. "We cannot simply 'turn around,'" he said. "And besides, why would you want to do such a thing?"

"The girls are ill," she said. "They have both come down with a fever and a sore throat."

With closed eyes, he took a deep breath and let it out slowly through pursed lips, controlling his nausea. "A fever and a sore throat," he said. "A common child's complaint. It is certainly no reason to turn around."

"I fear it may be more than that."

He motioned toward the vastness around them. "And what will turning around do for us? Even if we could convince the captain to do so, it would still be nearly three days before we returned to Cadiz. They will probably be recovered by then." He burped and his face contorted at the taste of it. He laid his head back against the chair's cushion and closed his eyes once more. "Don't be foolish. They have caught a summer chill. It happens to every child."

Neither his words nor his attitude pleased her, but she couldn't argue with him. Likely, it was just a common fever.

"Where is One Who Flies?"

"Now don't you go and trouble him about this."

"No," she said innocently. "It is just that I haven't seen him since we departed."

Alejandro pulled his watch from his pocket and opened the case. He peered at the numbers. "He should be sitting down to brunch about now. He tends to rise late, these days."

She stood. "He is not drinking, is he?"

Alejandro squinted up at her. "Not that I know. And you've seen him. I don't think he has had a drop, not since that one night at El Escorial."

"Yes," she said, then pointed toward the bow. "In the dining room, you said?"

"Yes, dear. If not, he is in cabin number eight. *Ocho.*"

"*Ocho,*" she repeated. "Thank you." She rose and headed forward.

The dining room was broad, with a low ceiling of dark wood. At night, the lamps on every table were lit to give the room a warm glow, but now, during the day, long windows let the sunshine stream in. The tables sparkled as clean daylight glinted from crystal glasses, silver utensils, and gold-rimmed china painted with buxom roses, but most of the chairs stood empty. Waiters in bright linen doublets stood to the side, and one stepped forward.

"Would you care for a seat, madame?" he asked her in his accented French.

She spied One Who Flies, sitting across the room with his back to the light. His face in shadow, it was made grimmer yet by the scowl he wore. He stared at his steaming cup of coffee, shoulders tight, hands flat on the tabletop.

"I think my friend is expecting me," she said.

"Of course, madame," he said, and ushered her across the room.

"Good morning," she said in Cheyenne.

One Who Flies looked up as if slapped.

"May I join you?" she asked.

He gestured to the seat opposite. The waiter pulled the chair out for her.

"Coffee?" the waiter asked. "Tea?"

"Water, if you please."

The waiter bowed and left.

They sat in silence as the waiter returned with a goblet and pitcher, set the former down and filled it with still water from the latter. When he retreated, they remained silent. It was a longtime custom among the People for guest and host to enjoy long moments of stillness, visiting without words, but this was not such a moment. The tension in One Who Flies shouted through his quietude. She could hear his spirit cry out, howling, raging against the bastions of his control. That this man, the man in whom so much of her past and even more of her future was entwined, that he should be clouded over with such anger for her made her heart ache, but before she could think of words to say, One Who Flies spoke.

"What do you want?" he asked, and in that small phrase, she heard his bitterness and anger.

"What makes you think I want something?" she asked in reply.

"You always want something from me," he said.

The denial was on her lips, nearly spoken, when she thought about it and relented. "I suppose that is true," she said, but her accession did nothing to mollify One Who Flies.

"So, what do you want?" he asked again.

He was obviously not in any mood to grant requests or help her in any way, but to not ask was not an option. "I want you to convince the captain to turn the ship and head back to Cadiz."

"No."

His refusal, though expected, surprised her with its speed and simplicity. "Don't you even want to know why I want you to do this?"

"No," he said.

"You refuse then because it is I who ask it."

"No." He leaned forward and looked at her directly. "I have done everything you have ever asked of me, and more. You *and* your People. I have done it regardless of whether I thought it could be done, or whether it could be done at all." He leaned back again, but held her with his gaze. "I have learned, finally, to pick my battles with greater wisdom. This thing you ask, perhaps someone could do it, but not I. The captain will not listen to me. And *that* is why I refuse."

Still not meeting his challenging gaze, she asked him, "And you do not care the reason?"

"The reason is irrelevant," he said. "It has no bearing on my ability to succeed, only my pain at failing."

She looked up into his blue eyes, so pale, so unlike her own. "To not try is to fail."

He smiled, but it was not a pleasant thing to behold. It was a weak thing, twisted and full of loathing. "Then I have failed you again, Madonna."

She looked away, unable to face his wrath. "Do you hate me that much, then?"

"Oh, no," he said. "Not you. Only me."

His self-pity emboldened her, and she looked up at him again. "What is wrong with you?" she asked. "You used to be so fearless, so strong. I could *feel* the power in you. And now you do nothing but whine and mope. 'Poor me. Poor One Who Flies.' *Eya.* You sound like an old woman, and not the man who fell from the—"

He raised a warning finger. "Don't say it. Do not speak of visions or Thunder Beings or of my falling from any cloud."

"What?" she asked, taken aback. "Why not?"

"Because it is not true."

"It is."

"No." He put his hand back down on the table, anger subsiding. "It is not. It is a story created to fit a dream, no truer than the story of the Madonna of the Swallows."

"I see," she said. She pushed back her chair and stood. The waiter came forward to assist her. "There was something else I wanted," she said to One Who Flies. "I wanted to tell you that Blue Shell Woman and Mouse Road have taken ill."

For the first time she saw an emotion other than anger or bitterness cross his face. He looked up, eyes filled with genuine worry and care. "Mouse Road? She is ill?"

He looked back down at his hands. "I hope it is nothing serious."

"Yes," Speaks while Leaving said. "Hope that, will you? Surely you cannot fail in doing that." She walked away then, her heels pounding the deck through the softness of her moccasin soles.

She stole back within the room. The two of them were sleeping again—the best remedy they could take at this point—and she sat at the bench and table so as not to disturb them. She lay forward, resting her head upon her arms, and listened to the ship.

Out in the hallway, she heard the lighthearted words and passing conversations of fellow travelers as they strolled to and from their rooms. Between them were the efficient steps of the crew, walking with purpose, delivering laundry or tea or other services with a sharp, double-rap on the door.

When they had gone, there were only the sounds of the three of them, breathing, the sound of her own heart in her ears, and the constant yet variable sounds of the moving ship.

She heard the rumble of the engine, pushing them forward into the wind. She heard the brassy creak of the gimbaled lamp and the subtle groan of wood and metal as the ship rose and fell through green water. Prow-waves curled back from the bow, their *shish* blending with the hum of lines that held up the empty masts. Beyond that, she imagined the mew of distant terns, the gossip of porpoises, and the silent dreams of fish scything their way through the cold deep. The porpoises swam closer; they were right alongside the ship, laughing and playing just beyond the hull, chattering, chattering.

She awoke. The chatter was a baby's plaintive cry. Blue Shell Woman was on her stomach, up on her elbows, looking toward her and crying weakly in short, gasping bursts of anger and misery.

Speaks while Leaving rose and went to her. Mouse Road moaned and stirred in the other bed. Speaks while Leaving felt her daughter's forehead. Still feverish. She chided herself again for not bringing her medicines and herbs. A little willow bark would help lessen her daughter's suffering. Mouse Road, at least, could be told that it would be fine; the baby knew only her pain and discomfort, and took nothing from Speaks while Leaving's words of encouragement. She went to dampen a fresh cloth.

When she removed her daughter's diaper, she saw at once that the rash had spread. Her heart quickened. The blotches had grown, merged, reddened, and now covered her thighs, groin, and belly. She pulled the baby's clothing farther up. The rash glowed angrily across her round belly, up her chest. She pulled her daughter's shift over her head, and Blue Shell Woman's cries became bellows. The rash flushed the skin of her armpits and spilled down her arms. Mouth dry, Speaks while Leaving moved to the other bed and began untying the laces at the shoulders of Mouse Road's dress.

"What?" the young woman complained in a croaking voice.

Speaks while Leaving pulled at the leather ties, baring her sister-in-law's collarbone and breasts.

"Stop," Mouse Road demanded, but Speaks while Leaving pushed her fever-weak arms away and pulled the dress down to her waist. Mouse Road's skin raged with the rash's fury, bright as paint on her arms and torso. She stared, not wanting to believe what she saw, then leapt up and lifted the oil lamp from its gimbaled sconce. Mouse Road was staring at the rash that covered her, tears streaming down her cheeks.

"We have—"

"No," Speaks while Leaving said. "No." But when she brought the lamp close and raised the wick, she knew that her denial was a lie. In the lamp's white glow, she could clearly see the rash's scarlet color and the skin's rough, sandy texture.

"Red fever," she breathed.

Red fever. As a member of the Closed Windpipe band, a band that dealt frequently with *vé'hó'e* at the trading posts along the Big Greasy, Speaks while Leaving had been exposed to the red fever early in her youth. Mouse Road, however, was of the Tree People, a band more reclusive than hers, and she probably had had little exposure to sufferers of the disease.

But I gave her that chance, she berated herself. Mouse

Road and my daughter both. I brought them here. This is my doing.

Mouse Road looked up at her and the fear was wide in her eyes. "Will we die?"

"No," Speaks while Leaving said, praying that this denial was not a lie. "No. Many live through the red fever. I had it as a tiny girl, myself." She forced a smile onto her face. "You needn't worry."

"But Blue Shell Woman," Mouse Road said.

The smile faltered. "Yes," she said, "she is in danger."

Willow bark would not help this fever. What she needed was bloodroot and the bark of the black-cherry tree, but all she would be able to hope for was what was available from the ship's stores. She went to the door.

She called to a passing steward and asked him to bring water and fruit as quickly as possible. He bowed and left to comply, and Speaks while Leaving turned back to the room and her two charges.

Red fever, with its sore throat and scarlet rash, was a killer, weakening the heart and torturing the kidneys. It filled the body with poisons and, absent any bloodroot or the diuretic properties of black-cherry bark, her only hope was to flush her patients' bodies with fluids. She picked up her naked daughter and held her as Blue Shell Woman whimpered against her shoulder. Her red skin was dry and rough where the rash burned. She took a dampened cloth and daubed it at the baby's cheek and forehead. There was nothing else she could do.

A double-rap sounded at the door.

"Sí," she said, and it opened.

The steward came in with a small tray, on which were a bowl of cut fruit, two glasses, and a small carafe of water.

"No," she said, trying to remember the Spanish words she needed. *"Más."*

The steward, a small man with a thick moustache, stared at her in concentration.

"Más agua. Mucho más agua, por favor."

He nodded in comprehension, and then took a step back as he noticed the baby. Recognition and fear spread across his features. "Sí, señora," he said. "Sí." He left hurriedly.

Speaks while Leaving only hoped he would bring more water.

She took the small carafe, filled the glass half-full, and then handed the carafe to Mouse Road.

"Drink," she told her sister-in-law. With the glass, she entreated her daughter to do the same. Mouse Road cried out in pain as she swallowed against the sore throat brought on by the fever.

"I can't," she said and handed back the carafe.

"Drink," Speaks while Leaving ordered her. "You must. I know it hurts, but it will help to flush the fever from your body." She turned back to the task of trying to convince her daughter to drink, but Blue Shell Woman knew nothing of flushing a fever. She knew only that her throat hurt, and that drinking made it hurt more, and so refused the water.

"Come, Little Pot Belly," she said. "You must."

There was another knock on the door.

"Sí," she said, but the door did not open. She went and opened it herself.

A tray with two pitchers of water and a pitcher of fruit juice sat outside the door. The steward was nowhere to be seen. Unable to blame him for his fear, she put Blue Shell Woman on the bed and retrieved the liquids, silently thanking him for doing what he had.

Blue Shell Woman adamantly refused to take any water, but the juice the steward brought was sweet, and, with patience and some spillage, Speaks while Leaving was able to get some fluid into her. Mouse Road was a better patient, drinking when requested to, and taking care of her own needs as best as possible.

The rash soon covered the whole of their torsos, upper arms, and thighs. They lay in fitful misery, red as blood up to their necks, hot and cold in stages as they fought the fever through the night.

It was early the next morning, when Mouse Road was shivering beneath a blanket and Blue Shell Woman was turning her head away from the prospect of swallowing more juice, that there was another knock at the door.

"Sí," she said, hoping it was the steward with some more water, but this time the door opened and she looked up to find One Who Flies standing in the doorway, Alejandro at his back. One Who Flies wore a frown of concern while Alejandro, pale from another stint at the leeward rail, looked befuddled.

"Water," One Who Flies said to Alejandro. "Water, towels, a large basin. Ice, too. Chipped. And get the physician. What was his name?"

"Garcia-Fuentes?"

"Yes. Get him."

"It's awfully early," Alejandro said.

"I don't care. Wake him," One Who Flies said with force, and Alejandro disappeared.

One Who Flies went first to Mouse Road. He felt her forehead and cheek, and put fingers to the pulse in her neck. "Why didn't you tell me they had scarlet fever?" he said as he turned to Blue Shell Woman and felt her skin as well.

"I did not know then," she said quietly. "Would it have made a difference?"

He stood, removed his jacket, and tossed it on top of the luggage. "Of course," he said as he rolled up his cuffs. "My sisters had scarlet fever when they were young, when my father was away on campaign. I helped my mother get them through it. I can help you get these two through it, as well."

She looked up at him. He was wide-eyed, alert, and full of purpose. He was transformed from the stiff and stony man she had seen the previous day. He tossed a cloth into the basin and upended a pitcher of water over it. This was once again the man she knew, the man she had seen in her visions.

Then she looked down at the daughter she held in her arms. In contrast, Blue Shell Woman was listless, groggy, and weak. Mouse Road was no better, incoherent with the fever.

"I mean, are you sure you want to try this?" she asked him. "Are you sure this is a battle you can win?"

He paused in his ready movements, halted by her words: by his own words.

"I was wrong," he said without turning to face her. "There are some battles that must be fought, whether they can be won or not." He glanced over his shoulder,

toward the sleeping Mouse Road. "Some things are
worth the battle alone."

A knock sounded at the door and One Who Flies rose
to open it. Alejandro stood outside, and with him was a
rounded man dressed in shirtsleeves, trousers, and a
dressing gown. Alejandro ushered him within.

One Who Flies shook the man's hand. "This is Señor
Federico Garcia-Fuentes," he said, introducing the man
to her. "He is a physician, and he has agreed to see if
there is anything he can do."

Speaks while Leaving stood. *"Muchas gracias,"* she
said.

Garcia-Fuentes bowed. "I only hope I can be of help,"
he said in perfect French. He carried a black satchel,
which he deposited on the bench behind the table.
Speaks while Leaving saw him look about the tiny room,
his sharp eyes taking in the ewer, the basin, the pitchers
of water and juice, the glasses near the bedside, One
Who Flies standing with the wet towel in his hand, and
even Speaks while Leaving herself; considering all else
before moving forward to the two patients.

"You have done well," he said. "I couldn't have done
more in your place."

"Thank you, señor."

She watched as he examined Mouse Road, pushing
aside the sheet and blanket here and there to inspect
her skin, yet mindful of her modesty. He pointed to his
bag and One Who Flies brought it to him. He pulled
out a long flared tube, one end of which he put to Mouse
Road's chest. Leaning over her, he put his ear to the
other end. She moaned as he gently listened to her
breathing and pulse. Then he turned and came to Blue
Shell Woman.

The baby mewed weakly as he took her. Speaks while
Leaving recognized the sound, having heard it in a
dream: the call of terns, light as air, slicing through the
wind bound for distant shores. She blinked, and tears
fell from her eyes. Garcia-Fuentes glanced over at One
Who Flies, and then looked up at her.

"They are in the worst of it," he said, "and there's
little we can do." He put the flared tube back into his

bag and pulled out a wooden box. He undid the brass
latch and opened it, revealing many small compartments
lined with red velvet. In the compartments, fit snugly
into the depressions, were square bottles of dark brown
glass, each sealed with cork and wax. He lifted first one,
then another, checking the handwritten labels wrapped
around each bottle until he found the one he sought.
Taking it out, he closed and latched the box. With his
fingernail, he scored the wax seal and pulled out the
cork, then sniffed the contents.

"This is sanguinaria. Give them one drop of this on a
lump of sugar . . . just one drop," he said, handing her
the bottle. "Once in the morning, once at noon, and
once in the evening. Just one drop. Otherwise, continue
treating them as you have been. Some warm broth might
be good, too."

Speaks while Leaving took the bottle, looking at the
long looped words that described its contents. "One
drop," she echoed, and pulled the cork to smell the contents as he had. Her nose wrinkled at the scent: it was
nauseous, vile, the odor of warm rot.

She smiled. Bloodroot!

"One drop only," Garcia-Fuentes said again. "Any
more will cause vomiting."

"Yes. One drop." Bloodroot. He had given her a bottle of bloodroot. She pointed to his box. "Do you have
any black-cherry bark?"

Garcia-Fuentes stood and put the box back in his bag.
"Señora, I am a physician, not some scoundrel selling
tonics."

She blinked, not understanding his bristled attitude. It
did not matter. Bloodroot was what she wanted, and
bloodroot was what he had given her. It would help the
soreness and constriction in their throats, and allow
them to take in more liquid. "Thank you, señor."

He bowed to her, bid adieu to One Who Flies, and
left. One Who Flies whispered something to Alejandro
as he took the towels and pitchers of water and ice.
Then he closed the door and went to Mouse Road. He
laid the dampened cloth on her forehead. She moaned
but did not move. He prepared another for Blue Shell
Woman.

"Alejandro brought some lump sugar, too," he said, offering her the damp cloth.

Instead of taking the cloth, she handed him the baby. He took her in his arms gingerly, as if she were brittle and likely to snap. Speaks while Leaving went to the table and set two lumps of sugar on the table. Then, with care, she loosened the cork in the bottle and tipped it, watching as the dark liquid seeped out, building up a bead on the lip of the mouth. She could smell its foulness, a stench that she knew well from preparing it as a red dye and as a paint, as well as a medicine. The bead became a droplet, and the droplet eased out until, with a small tap, she made it fall onto the sugar cube, soiling its sparkled whiteness, turning it the color of dried blood. She prepared the second cube as the first but shook off a smaller droplet, coloring only the top half of the cube.

The first dose she gave to Mouse Road, propping her up and bringing her to semi-awareness. She winced at the awful taste, despite the sugar's sweetness, but the cube quickly melted away. But a whole cube would be too large for Blue Shell Woman to take, so she crushed the second dose between two spoons and gave the result to the baby while One Who Flies held her. Blue Shell Woman complained but could not rid herself of the medicine.

Then she sat on the bed next to One Who Flies.

"There is little else to do, now, but make them comfortable, and get them to drink as much as possible."

"You could probably use some sleep," he said.

"No," she lied. She hadn't slept but a few, dream-filled moments since their departure from Cadiz. "I am fine."

"You are not. Here." He patted the bed. "Lie down. I'll hold the baby. As you said, there's little else we can do."

She sighed, but he was right. She lay down on the bed, lying close to the wall so he would have a place to put Blue Shell Woman down when she got too heavy.

Sleep closed her unwilling eyes, and she dreamt of fire in the sky. Smoke burned her eyes and she heard the sounds of war screaming across the land.

She awoke and blinked away sleep. Her eyes had crusted over, and she rubbed at them. One Who Flies was pacing slowly back and forth in the small room— three steps one way, three steps back—holding Blue Shell Woman in his arms. His hair ve mussed and there was stubble on his chin. In the windowless cabin, she knew not if it was night or day.

"How long?" she said.

"All day," he said. "It is nearly nightfall."

"How are they?"

His expression told her. They were not good. She rose quickly and reached out for her daughter.

"I gave them both their medicine for the evening. Mouse Road has taken some juice, but I can't rouse the baby enough to get her to drink."

Her daughter's skin was gritty, hot, and dry. Her breathing was labored, her eyes rolled up in her head. Putting a hand on the baby's breast, she could feel her heart; a rapid flutter, as fragile as a bee in straw. And as dangerous.

She had seen this. From times spent tending the sick of her own band, and even some *vé'ho'e* children, she had seen this. A single glance at One Who Flies told her that he had not. He had helped his sisters through the red fever, but they had survived. This, he had never seen.

Mouse Road was sleeping, and from the regular rise and fall of her breast, Speaks while Leaving could tell that the fever had passed over her. She sighed, trying to control her emotions a little longer, glad at least that the price of her foolhardiness would not be doubled.

"Thank you, One Who Flies. I can watch over them for a while. You look like you could use a walk around the deck or a splash of water on your face."

He rubbed at the stubble on his chin and then raked back his hair. "Yes. I probably could. Would you like something to eat? I can bring something from the galley."

She smiled, but knew that her sadness showed through. "Something to eat," she said. "Yes. Fine."

"Fine," One Who Flies said, glancing at her, gauging her mood. "Are you sure? I could stay."

"No," she said and shooed at him with her free hand. "You go. I'll be fine alone with them for a little while."

"If you're sure," he said, and then gathered up the soiled and sodden towels, the empty pitcher, the bowl of water that had been clean chips of ice, and took them all away.

She bolted the door behind him.

She sat down on the empty bed, up in the corner against the wall, her daughter in her arms, her legs folded together and to the left in the manner proper for a woman of the Closed Windpipe band. As the ocean rocked the ship, the ship's motion rocked the cabin, the cabin rocked her, and she in turn rocked her baby. She sat straight-backed in her corner refuge, denying her desire to collapse, curl up, and weep. The time for that was close enough. For now, she could maintain a dignified vigil. It would not be long.

She retraced the steps that had brought her to this place, following the path of small decisions she had traveled, revisiting the bright hope that had banished the qualms lurking in the crevices of her mind. At what point should she have turned away? At what juncture should she have turned left instead of right, gone back instead of forward? At Cadiz? In Cuba? In the *vé'ho'e* town?

At home?

Should she have never left? Should she have listened to the counsel of her fear and let Mouse Road go ahead on her own? Should she have gone back to sleep in her empty bed?

Her empty bed. The image set her mind a-reel, for with it came its opposite, accompanied by memories of the man who made the difference: her husband, the man of whom she had not thought for days, even weeks. She had spent too much of her life unmarried, too many years alone, and had fallen back into those patterns that had set her apart from normal people and led her across the prairie searching for the truth of her visions. She had always followed her visions, trusting the gift of the *ma'heono* over the advice of men, over the wisdom of chiefs, and now, over the cries of her own heart. Following those visions had cost her—in love, in time, in the closeness of family and friends—but now, as her daughter lay dying in her arms, now and for the first time, she regretted it.

Blue Shell Woman's head hung back, her mouth slack and open, her lifepulse rippling along the gentle crease of her throat. Her small body jerked with each inward breath, her lungs sucking air through a throat nearly swollen shut and letting it seep out again in a gurgling rattle. Speaks while Leaving watched her, counting the moments between each spasmodic breath, counting first to five, then six.

I did not know, she told the spirits. I did not know that this was part of the price.

Seven.

Had I known, I never would have agreed to pay it.

Eight. Nine.

"I am sorry, my daughter. I did not know."

Ten.

And no more.

Above, she could hear the night wind cry out as it was sliced by the ship's mastlines. She heard ancient thunder in the engines below. The night closed around her, swallowing her, swallowing light, wreathing her in its depthless void. The cry of the wind became her own voice, keening as grief cut through her, and the thunder from below became the pounding on her door, a pounding that grew louder with her mourning wail, rising to a peak as she began to sing the words of her daughter's death song.

At dawn, she stood on deck against the ship's rail. One Who Flies held her tightly, keeping her steady as well as keeping her upright. Her throat was raw from crying, and her sobs now were only croaks as she held out the shrouded body of her daughter to Dr. Garcia-Fuentes. The doctor took the body from her, but still she reached out after it, grasping the air.

Alejandro stood close by, the events of the previous day making him paler than his own discomfort obliged, and with him was the ship's captain, who quietly read words she did not understand from a small, leather-bound book. The doctor took the body to the rail and, at a nod from the captain, dropped Blue Shell Woman into the sea.

Words were beyond her capacity to form, but her mind seethed with them—words of shame, of guilt, of grief—as well as wordless things: sharp claws of pain, freezing fires of regret, and the black shards of broken dreams. Her daughter's shrouded form bobbed on the waves—so small a thing held in the expanse of the ocean's palm—and Speaks while Leaving prayed that her spirit would find its way from this wide place to the star road that even now had not faded completely from the sky. The burial cloths grew heavy with water and began to drag at Blue Shell Woman's body. As the swells rolled over the body and the pale shroud grew dim beneath the dark waves, Speaks while Leaving knew that it was more than just a daughter she had lost here. It was a past, and a future as well. More had died here than her child, but she would have to wait until she returned home before she knew what else she was burying beneath the waves.

CHAPTER 24

Thursday, July 24, A.D. 1890
The White House
Washington, District of Columbia

The chair's right front wheel squeaked like a mouse on the rack as Douglas brought Custer down the back hall of the White House. Custer had thought often about that squeaky wheel, hating it just in and of itself, and hating what it represented. Many times, he'd thought of getting it fixed, but each time he had relented, always deciding to leave it as it was. The squeak, annoying as it was, served his purposes, for with each shuttle from the residence to the library, just as with each noisy and ignominious trip in the small elevator, he was reminded of his incapacitation and goaded into further action. The squeak had become a prod, and today—especially today—he was grateful for it.

He straightened in the chair as they came around the corner, heading toward the kitchen: several staff members, in aprons and in servant's black-and-white, stopped and stood against the wall to give him room to pass.

"Good morning, Mr. President," each said in turn, and Custer returned their warm smiles with a wink and a nod as Douglas and the squeak ushered him down the hall.

Just outside the kitchen door, he raised his hand and Douglas stopped. The swinging door stood just ahead, still rocking slightly to and fro from the last person through. Custer took a breath to calm himself, then gripped the thick wood handle of his cane in his left hand. Douglas set the stops on the chair's wheels and came around to help, but Custer waved him off. With his feet on the thin and well-traveled carpet, he leaned forward, got his weight over his knees, and pushed upward with legs and on the cane.

Standing there on his own, having got there on his own, he saw Douglas's small smile.

"Feeling feisty today, Mr. President?"

"You bet," Custer said.

Douglas stepped back toward the door and pushed it open.

Walking, Custer had learned from his many training ambulations taken around the library's oval floor, was mostly a matter of falling forward, but doing it slowly so that one's head didn't outpace one's rear end. He did it now, tipping forward slightly, feeling the brief but definite lilt of his gut as he passed from stability to precariousness, and then set his legs and cane in motion to keep pace. He walked to the door, pushed against the cane to turn right, and entered the kitchen.

The White House kitchen was a large, bright room with tables, stoves, ovens, and cabinets. Pots and pans and cooking dishes hung from hooks on the right, while ladles and utensils of metal both bright and dark hung on the left. In the middle was an open working space filled with the scents of blooming yeast, chopped herbs, and cleanliness. Normally, it would also have been filled with Cook's staff of twenty, all busy putting food to the fire or meat to the knife, and the din of orders, instructions, and banter would have bounced from the walls. This morning, however, it was quiet, empty, and ominous.

At the table farthest from the door sat seven men: Samuel, Jacob, and five other secretaries from Custer's Cabinet, all sitting silently, staring at their cooling cups of coffee. Wearing their dark suits and beetled frowns, they seemed more out of place in this room than ballerinas on a busy street corner, but as Custer walked into the kitchen, their frowns eased and with a scrape of chairs and the rattle of china, they stood.

Inwardly, Custer smiled. At least to these men, he was still the President.

Samuel pulled out a chair for him as he made his halting way to the table. Custer saw the appraisal in their eyes. His limp and his halting step were marks against him, and his still-imperfect speech would not help the matter. He had to show them his inner strength and his ability to command.

"Good morning," he said, intelligibly but with impediment.

"Good morning, Mr. President," they answered. Glances flickered around the table as the Cabinet members saw both how far he had come, and how far he had yet to go in his recovery.

"Please, gentlemen, be seated." They sat along with him. "I note that a few are not in attendance," he said.

"Er, yes," Jacob said, offering Custer a cup of coffee. When the cup was refused, he went on. "The Secretary of State is currently in New York, engaged in trade talks with the French."

"And Hawkins?"

"The . . . the Secretary of the Treasury sends his regrets, but is unable to attend."

"Ha," Custer said with a wink. "Well, we knew which side of the fence he was on, now, didn't we?"

The others chuckled and the mood relaxed. Jacob nodded. "We did, indeed, Mr. President."

"No matter," Custer said. "The men I want are here. The men I trust are here. Let's get the ball rolling. Jacob?"

"Yes, sir. Of course." He took a piece of paper out of his coat pocket, unfolded it, and laid it out on the table before him. Custer saw that his friend's hands trembled a bit; if the others saw it, they didn't show it. On the paper were a few simple lines of notes. Jacob cleared his throat.

"Gentlemen, we have brought you here because we are at a pivotal point. The crises that have been building for the past months are about to crest and break. The Cheyenne response to Morton's war is costing us more in civilian casualties than in military, and populations and investment in the regions have begun to drop. The legislature is demanding action. As one senator succinctly put it, 'Business needs people.' "

He nodded to Samuel and Custer's aide produced copies of a report, which he handed to the others.

"As you will see in this dispatch," Jacob continued,

"the rebels in Cuba, emboldened by the new influx of cash and arms provided at the Vice President's direction, have succeeded in burning or severely damaging three sugar refineries in the Havana area, including the complete destruction of one American refinery, in which three Americans perished."

Jacob warmed to his task and Custer was glad to see it. His Secretary of War had been an able soldier and had proven to be a good administrator, but public speaking was not where his strength lay, except when he got his hackles up. Jacob calm was a trustworthy man, but Jacob riled, with the tension that growled in his words and the dark, deadpan gaze that showed most clearly the pitiless resolve of which he was entirely capable, *that* Jacob was a man of whom to be wary.

"We now have Spanish troops in the borderlands," he told them. "We have Spanish warships prowling the Gulf, and we have a Spanish railway pushing north out of Albuquerque. Spain has allied itself with the Cheyenne, in spirit if not in fact, and in response, Morton has sent our warships to Havana—over my objections and the objections of Secretary Fairchild—to protect our interests in Cuba. What good a thousand sailors will do against those rebels is any man's guess." He reined in on his acrimony with visible effort, taking his notes from the table and returning them to his breast pocket.

"In short," he concluded, "we are on the brink of war."

Custer took advantage of the pause that followed that pronouncement. "Your thoughts, gentlemen?"

Temperance Fullerton, the Secretary of the Interior, a thin, overweening New Englander, was the first to offer an opinion. "I cannot disagree with a single point."

"Things are bad," the Postmaster General said, "but are they as bad as that? I mean, is it war?"

Fairchild grumped. "War or no," the Secretary of the Navy said, "it's sure that it's Morton's doing. The man is spoiling for a fight, and I can't fathom the reason for it. He seems determined to antagonize the entire world, one nation at a time."

"And that is precisely why Secretary Dickerson is up in New York," Jacob said. "The French are furious over this new import tariff that Morton has imposed on them for allowing Spanish importers to use French ports to avoid the tariff he imposed on *them*."

"The French, angry with us?" Fairchild said. "Hardly a new situation. They've barely forgiven us for not backing their own revolution."

"But the last thing we need is a trade war with France on top of a shooting war with Spain," Jacob said.

"True," Fullerton said, and the others agreed.

Custer cleared his throat. "Can I take it, then, that I have your support to return to my duties as President and avoid this war?" His words were thick, but intelligible.

Fairchild was the first to speak. "Taking the tack that Hawkins would take, if he'd had the guts to show, I'd say that war isn't always undesirable, Mr. President. It's good for business: factories are busy, people pull together, and patriotism feeds domestic investment."

"Perhaps," Fullerton said, "but what if, despite this financial boon, we lost territory to the Spanish? We must defend the western territories from Spanish aggression and imperialism."

"Hear, hear," Jacob said. "After all, Fairchild, whose side are you on?"

"Who said there are sides, here?" Fairchild asked.

"Gentlemen," Custer said, breaking in before the heat got too high. "It's never a crime to disagree, and Secretary Fairchild raises defensible points. However, I believe he will agree that the overriding precept here is this: Never get backed into a war."

Nods went around the table.

"Absolutely," Jacob said. "We must defuse this situation and defuse it now. If we're to fight the Spanish, we should do it in a time and place of our choosing. As it is, we're about to get caught with our trousers down around our ankles."

Custer looked at them all. "And so I ask it again. Do you support my resuming my duties as President?"

Simpson Bayard, the Attorney General, had not spoken through the meeting. Now he coughed genteelly. A Southern diplomat from an old and established line that had spawned three senators and a president, he commanded and received the respect of his fellow Cabinet members.

"Mr. President," he said in his slow, Virginian drawl, "it is hardly up to us. This is strictly a matter of law, of Constitutional law. If you are pronounced fit to resume your duties, you may do so, sir, and without a by-your-leave from the Cabinet."

"Correct," Custer said, "as always. But I want—no, I *need*—more than the law." He plopped his useless right hand on the table, and to illustrate his point, he banged it a few times. "This," he said, raising the crippled limb, "and this"—he thumped his hand against his right leg— "and this"—he motioned toward the slack side of his mouth. "They are what people see. For some, they are *all* that they will see. And they will wonder if my mind is likewise afflicted." He raised his twisted hand and let it fall into his lap. "And so, the law is not enough for me. I am not asking for your permission, Mr. Bayard. I am asking for your support. Your *public* support. Do I have it?"

Jacob did not hesitate. "Of course, Mr. President."

Fullerton chimed in next, followed by Fairchild and the others. Only Bayard remained.

"Simpson?" Custer asked, his tongue lisping over the sibilants in his name.

The Attorney General gave his President a long, level stare. Custer did not flinch from it, but withstood his regard. The moment stretched out to the point of discomfort. Finally, Bayard nodded.

"Yes, Mr. President. I believe I can say with confidence that not only are you fit to resume your presidential duties, but that despite your infirmities, between you and the Vice President, you are the fitter of the two."

It was what Custer wanted to hear, and it set his resolve in steel. He stood. The Cabinet officers stood with him.

"Then if you will kindly follow me?"

Setting his cane, he walked to the kitchen door. Douglas set the door open and then went to the wheelchair, ready to help Custer.

"No," Custer said, and smiled at the old chair with its squeaky right front wheel. "That is one horse I'll not ride again." And with the Cabinet at his back, he headed down the hallway.

They passed the kitchen staff, all lined up along the wall where they had waited for the meeting to end. He winked to Cook as he passed, and Cook winked back. He walked down the back hall to the elevator. It was a tight squeeze, but they all got inside and, with the gate closed, the electric motor clunked into motion, lifting them slowly—too slowly for Custer's whirling mind—to the second floor.

The gilded accordion gate banged open and Custer led the way—still too slowly—down and around to the wide cross hall, and thence to the left, toward the offices. Behind him, the men of his Cabinet were silent, their tread measured like pallbearers at a funeral. Custer rejected the image, filling his mind instead with the picture of a returning Caesar, and suddenly their slow progress took on the attitude of a procession of might.

Outside the door, he stopped to straighten his waistcoat and jacket. Samuel came forward to open the door, and Custer strode in like a conqueror. The aide who ran Morton's outer office stood from behind his desk and watched without a word as Custer and the Cabinet walked in and opened the door to the inner office.

"Damn it, Blake," Morton said as they entered. "I said I wasn't to be—" He swallowed the rest of his sentence, seeing that not only was it Custer who disturbed him, but most of the Cabinet as well.

Morton stood behind his desk, looking all the shorter for its oversized width. Standing from their seats before the desk were Morton's two advisors, Chaucer and Yancy. Yancy, Custer had been told, was the man responsible for pushing Morton toward this confrontation in Cuba. He brushed the thought aside.

Old news, he told himself, and concentrated on the man behind the desk.

Morton was fuming like a kettle on the fire. His knuckles whitened as he leaned forward onto the desk. Custer noted the flag on its stand behind him, and the trappings of high office: portraits of predecessors, maps with notations, and the glint of gold from pen, tray, and blotter. Small silver-framed photographs of his wife and family were lined up along the credenza like audience members at a recital. Custer inspected these items slowly, without hurry, giving the Vice President time to come to a full boil.

"Mr. President," Morton finally said, his calm tone unable to mask the acid he most surely tasted. "What is the meaning of this intrusion?"

Custer turned around and looked at the men behind him. Samuel stood at parade rest, bouncing slightly on the balls of his feet. Fullerton, Fairchild, and the others were grave but at the same time buoyant, shoulders back and heads high. Jacob, stalwart old friend and supporter, looked Custer in the eye and winked.

He turned back to Morton. "I beg your pardon, Levi," he said, "but I believe that you are sitting in my chair."

Morton blanched, a feat that Custer would have thought impossible for the already pale New Yorker. His features wavered between indignation and sheer disbelief, but when Jacob sniggered, he decided on the former.

"This is outrageous!" he shouted, but his overexcitement made it sound more an adolescent whine than a condemnation.

"What is outrageous," Attorney General Bayard said, "is the disgraceful situation in which you have embroiled this country."

"But there are protocols," Morton said, now in full complaint. "His doctors must pronounce him fit—"

"And they shall," Custer said. "In due course, they shall. For now, however, I suggest"—he paused as the word gave him no small trouble—"that you go home and pack. That will give me some time to think of a place to send you, an emissary to some place where you can do us no further harm."

Morton stood there, his eyes glancing from face to face for support but finding none, not even in the sycophants that he had gathered around him.

"Well?" Jacob said. "You heard the President, didn't you?"

But Custer raised his withered hand. "Have a care, Jacob. He outranks you." He turned and addressed the men who had accompanied him.

"Samuel, contact the ambassadors of Spain *and* France. I want to see them both tomorrow at the latest."

"Yes, Mr. President."

"And Temperance, would you get a wire to Dickerson in New York, please? His meeting with the French is not needed."

"Yes, Mr. President," the Interior Secretary said. "At once."

"Jacob and Fairchild, I want all the latest on our deployments. And to the rest of you, I'll be entertaining recommendations for a new Secretary of the Treasury."

"Yes, Mr. President," they said, and "Thank you, Mr. President."

Custer followed them out of the room, leaving Morton and his cronies behind, engulfed in an uncomfortable silence that he was sure would last mere moments after his exit. He went through the outer office and had stepped into the hallway when the inner office door slammed with enough force to make the paintings dance on the walls. He smiled, but not without a twinge of melancholy. Morton had done a poor job, of that there was no question, and he roundly deserved censure. But more than that lay ahead for the former New York banker turned politician. Time and again, Custer had seen it played out: it had happened to his dear General McClellan in both the military and political arenas. The public was fickle in its favor, and the press was merciless, eager to jump on any fault, perceived or real. It was the drama of everyday life that lay ahead for Morton, and Custer did not envy him his future. Not in the least.

"You all right, Mr. President?" Douglas asked, coming up from the station he'd taken outside Morton's office.

He took a deep breath as the officers of his Cabinet headed off on their assignments.

"Yes, Douglas. I am fine."

CHAPTER 25
Saturday, July 26, A.D. 1890
La Ciudad de la Habana, Cuba

Palm fronds twitched in a slow breeze thick with the smell of rot as the *Santa Luisa* approached the harbor in Havana. Alejandro stood on deck with the rest of the passengers, waiting in the heavy heat, watching the somnolent streets slip past the rails. It was siesta, and Havana slept, torpid in the oppressive humidity and heat. No man worked, no child played in the streets. Not even a dog barked as the ship cruised up the channel. The city was as still as a graveyard populated with ghosts.

He stood to one side, away from the others in his party, unable—or unwilling—to stand too close to such raw emotion. Everyone, passenger and crew alike, had been disturbed in some measure by the overheaping volume of grief that had afflicted Speaks while Leaving. Even now she wept, as she had done without surcease since her child's death. She cried in silence, her voice having long given out from wailing. Her hair, brutally shorn of its long braids in an expression of grief, hung forward, thick and lank as a mop, hiding her tearful features.

Standing next to the grieving mother was Mouse Road, alive but weak still from her bout with scarlet fever. The skin on her hands and arms was peeling from the fever, and she looked like some scabrous waif as she nestled, hollow-eyed, within the protective embrace of One Who Flies. One Who Flies had also been changed by the fever. He had become once more the man Alejandro had first met on the shores of the Gulf of Narváez: decisive, clearheaded, and in command. After kicking in the door of the cabin, he had been tireless in his protection of the women, overseeing their every need, even providing the knife with which Speaks while Leaving sawed through her thick braids and cut the skin of her forearms. But through the death of Blue Shell Woman, One Who Flies had been reborn. He stood now, his arm around Mouse Road's shoulder, his blue-eyed gaze a sharp thing that he wielded like a rapier: quick, agile, and dangerous.

The other passengers milled about on the deck, politely ignoring the grief-stricken trio. The sun poured its light down upon the ship, the excess splashing back up from the green waters in sharp glints that blinded the eye. The women protected themselves with parasols of net and lace while the men could only fan themselves weakly with their hats. Some passengers would be continuing on toward Veracruz and La Ciudad México, while others would be changing ships and heading to La Puerta del Norte. Still others, like himself, would be staying in Havana, but all would be glad to depart, at least for a time, this ship of tragedy and savage, blatant mourning.

As the *Santa Luisa* chugged its way past the bulk of the Castillo La Cabaña that brooded like a troubled brow high up on its hill, the harbor came into view. Mutters and exclamations rose from the other passengers, and Alejandro looked to see what it was that evoked their interest. He saw it at once.

Deep inside the harbor, lined up like piglets at a sow's belly, were four, six, no, seven warships. They bristled with spars and guns, and while some flew the red and yellow of Spain, others had hung the red, white, and blue ensign of the United States from their rear gaff. What had happened while he had been away? American warships frequently made ports-of-call to Havana, as did Spanish ships, but three American ships at once, and four Spanish ships? Never had he heard of such a gathering, not since . . .

He frowned. Not since the Tejano conflict. Not since

the *end* of that war. He imagined the messages that had passed beneath him, tapping their way along the transatlantic cable down in the ocean muck while he, deaf and dumb to the world, had sailed across on the waves above. He took a deep lungful of the sultry air and let it out slowly as the *Santa Luisa* maneuvered her way toward the wharf.

The ship's horn blasted twice, bringing sluggish shoremen down the pier's dark planks and crewmen to their posts on deck, hawsers ready. It also brought out a scurry of men in pale, rumpled suits and white, straw hats. Alejandro recognized their breed at once—newspapermen—and he looked over at Speaks while Leaving. He might be willing to visit war upon her people for Spain's benefit, but the least he could do was spare her this battle with the press. He walked over to One Who Flies.

"The newspapers are here," he said. He saw fire flare in the young man's eyes and held up his hands to forestall any action. "Don't worry," he said. "I will take care of them. You stay behind with the women and come down last. I will go down first and draw them off. Capitan!"

The captain came over, and Alejandro drew him toward the rail. He withdrew several bills from his pocket and tucked them in the captain's hand.

"I need a few of your men to protect my guests from those vultures," he said, pointing to the reporters. "Will you take care of it?"

"It is done, Don Alejandro."

"Thank you, Capitan. I knew I could count on you." He said his final farewells to his fellow travelers as the ship was tied off and the gangway set in place, and then he returned to the rail and marshaled himself for the fray.

He disembarked first, gathering the reporters' attention. "Yes, yes, this way, over here," he said as he led them toward the end of the pier, away from the other departing passengers. A few crates were stacked nearby, and he stood on one of them, looking down on the reporters' eagerness.

"You will excuse me, gentlemen," he said, "but while

I will gladly answer all your questions, I must remind you that I have been aboard a ship for the past two weeks, and have little in the way of any new information."

"Did you know that President Custer had resumed his duties?" asked an American reporter in English.

Alejandro kept the smile on his face. "Why, no," he answered in Spanish. "I was not aware of that, though I am pleased to hear that President Custer has recovered sufficiently from that dastardly assassination attempt." The passengers had disembarked and One Who Flies and the women were now descending, preceded by four crewmen and followed by four more.

"Will you be traveling immediately to meet with the Cheyenne?" a Cuban reporter asked.

"Not immediately, no," he replied, keeping an eye on his guests as they made their way up the pier. "I will be staying in Havana for a few weeks, setting my affairs in order. A meeting with the Cheyenne leadership takes some logistical planning, as I'm sure you can appreciate."

A few questions later, and One Who Flies was nearly at the wharf.

"One last question," Alejandro said.

"How will your mission be affected, now that President Custer has reopened negotiations with the Cheyenne?"

Alejandro blinked and his smile grew stale on his face. "I'm sorry," he said. "Reopened negotiations?"

"Yes," the reporter said. "He has called for new negotiations. How will this affect your mission to the Cheyenne?"

"Her Majesty the Queen Regent," he said, trying to recover quickly from his shock, "in the name of her august son Don Alfonso the Thirteenth, has given to me the office of Special Ambassador to the Cheyenne people, for the purposes of aiding them in their conflict with the United States government. If President Custer has broken off hostilities in the region, and is willing to parley once more with the Cheyenne leadership, this can only make my mission easier. I am more than willing to once again act as liaison between the two nations."

One Who Flies had reached the wharf and was being bundled into a carriage.

"And now, if you will excuse me, gentlemen?" He ignored their further questions and walked at a brisk step toward the ramp that led up from the pier to the wharf. The reporters dogged him, keeping pace, some in front of him walking backward, all peppering him with their questions. He ignored them with a pleasant smile, pushing past the ones who got in his way on the ramp. He motioned to the driver of the carriage, and the man climbed up into his seat. The reporters noticed the others in the carriage too late, and their questions to One Who Flies came just as Alejandro stepped up into the box. The stair was folded up, and the driver snapped his horses into motion. The reporters followed the carriage for a few feet but quickly gave up, fanning themselves with their notebooks as Alejandro rode away.

They rode in silence to the governor's mansion and arrived there to find the entire household turned out to greet them. Alejandro's heart sped up as he saw his wife and daughter waiting with broad smiles. Isabella waved with exuberant energy, and Alejandro glanced at One Who Flies, Mouse Road still close at his side, their hands entwined. Isabella was about to have her romantic hopes dashed.

The carriage turned in through the gate and drove around the curve of the graveled drive. The somberness of the arrivals affected their reception immediately, as those gathered before the mansion's colonnade sensed the incoming mood. Roberto looked particularly concerned, stepping forward but bidding the others remain where they were. He met the carriage, his dark eyes locked on Alejandro.

"What is it?" he asked. "What has happened?"

"Much," Alejandro said.

"Ha. Here, also," Roberto said with his usual brevity.

One Who Flies helped Speaks while Leaving from the carriage and Roberto, seeing her condition and noting the absence of her child, gave his brother-in-law an inquiring glance.

"We need to talk."

Roberto beckoned to his wife and Olivia came to his

side. "Get everyone settled in." He glanced at the two Cheyenne women and their watchful companion. "Quietly. No questions."

"Of course not," Olivia said. Having also deduced the crux of what had transpired, her tone spoke of her distaste at such an uncouth idea as prying into the affairs of their guests, but it was also filled with sympathy for their plight. "Poor dears," she said as she went to the women. "Let's get you inside. Victoria, will you assist me?" She tried to draw the women away, but One Who Flies would not be separated from Mouse Road. Olivia glanced over and Alejandro gave her a nod. "And One Who Flies," she said. "Would you be so kind as to accompany us?"

Alejandro watched them go, watched the household staff file slowly back inside, and watched his daughter view with increasing displeasure the obvious bond between One Who Flies and Mouse Road. She looked to her father, her expression pleading, but he was powerless and glad to be so. His helpless shrug sent her into tears, and she ran into the house. Though he thought that all had left, Alejandro noticed that one person still remained. In the shadows of the mansion's archway, leaning up against one of the whitewashed columns, stood D'Avignon. The wiry old man sauntered toward them, hands in his pockets like a backcountry farmer.

"Do you want him with us?" Alejandro asked.

"Oh, indeed," Roberto said, and put his hand on his brother-in-law's shoulder. "He is very helpful."

Together, the three of them walked around the side of the house. Roberto led them through a shaded garden heady with the elegance of jasmine and the blousy scent of roses. Their footsteps mingled with the birdsong and the plash of water in the fountain, but rather than seat them at the padded chairs nearby, he opened a door and ushered them into a small room.

It was a small workroom, Alejandro saw as his eyes adjusted to the less brilliant light of the interior, and one in which he'd never been before. Barely fourteen feet square, it held a large table in its center, and the walls were lined with cabinets and countertops. From the beams and rafters hung bundles of herbs and drying flowers, and on the shelves were a broad variety of vases and urns.

"Very well," Alejandro said. "What has happened?"

"Custer is back," Roberto began. "Tensions have . . . eased."

D'Avignon laughed through his teeth. "That's a tepid way to put it."

Alejandro ignored him, not a little bit peeved at having to put up with this rascal. "What do you mean, Roberto, eased? I heard that he has reopened negotiations with the Cheyenne."

"Correct," Roberto said.

"But what of his soldiers in the Territory?"

"Recalled."

"And the hostilities?"

"Ceased."

"But . . . but . . ." There were too many questions, but the biggest one lay at anchor in the harbor. "What about those warships in the harbor?"

"Shore leave," Roberto said.

"'Shore leave?'" he echoed. "Do you mean that there are American sailors at liberty in Havana?"

"At liberty?" D'Avignon said. "Hell, man, the sailors are drinking and whoring up a storm in the low quarter. And the captains are copying the Spanish dons and giving tours of their ships to townsfolk."

Alejandro leaned forward, resting his forearms on the worktable and putting his head in his hands. "This is not good," he said. "This is not good."

"No," Roberto said.

"Not good?" D'Avignon repeated. "You gentlemen, I must say, have a considerable talent for understatement."

"How would you put it?" Alejandro asked.

"Heh. I'd say you got a root up your bum is what I'd say. I'd say you had been outflanked and outmaneuvered by that wily old man. I'd say this pretty well ruins our plans!" He punctuated the last with a thump of his fist on the tiled countertop.

Alejandro moaned, seeing the truth of it.

"But there are gains, too," Roberto said. "You are favored of the queen. The viceroy must acknowledge you. Your position has risen. You are Special Ambassador to the Cheyenne."

"Do you think I wanted that?" Alejandro said with a snarl. "Favor? Position? Do you think I want to go back out into that God-forsaken wilderness and *talk* to those people?" He stood and raked his fingers through his hair. "What will position do for me when I'm out on the prairie, Roberto? What will the queen's favor buy me when I'm out among those illiterate savages?" He jabbed a finger toward the outside. "Did you see that woman we brought in here? Did you see what her grief has turned her into? She hacked off her hair and cut her arms with a knife, Roberto. She refused food and water. She smeared herself with ashes."

"She lost her child," Roberto said.

"She lost her mind!" Alejandro thundered. "She lost all sense of dignity." He shook his head as he paced the small room. "I traveled with her for a month and more. She spoke French like a white woman, and was nearly as smart as a man. She charmed our queen and the entire countryside as well with her simple, unassuming manner. But it's all a façade, Roberto. It's all for show. Scratch the skin, and underneath they're all savages. Do you think I want to spend time with them? All the position and power in the world would not make it worth my while."

"But your family," Roberto said. "Don't forget about them. Position and power—"

"Won't buy them food, won't buy them clothing," Alejandro said. "Position and power won't keep a roof over their heads. No, you don't remember what it's like, my dear governor. You have been too successful for too long. You don't remember how fickle position can be, how it can be taken from you at the whim of another, or how it can be destroyed by the wrong word in the right ear." He shook his head. "I don't forget my family, Roberto, but position and the queen's favor will not help them. Money will help my family. Gold will help them, and *that* is what I want."

"Then you are lost," Roberto said. "Without war, Spain has no reason to enter the territory, and without a reason to enter . . ." He shrugged. "You are lost."

"*He* is lost?" D'Avignon said. "You mean that *we* are lost. I had a stake in this, too, remember? And I won't give up on it that easily."

"What?" Alejandro said with a laugh. "Do you mean to start a war on your own?" He laughed some more. "Be serious."

"I am serious . . . Ambassador," he said, putting extra emphasis on the final word.

Alejandro remembered the trouble this man was willing to cause and stopped laughing. As long as D'Avignon proved of service, Alejandro would have to suffer the man's presence. He was just as uneasy thinking about the kind of service the man would most likely provide.

"Very well," he said. "Tell us what you are talking about."

D'Avignon nodded and stood up straighter, accepting their renewed truce. "Well, sirs, I was just thinking that all Spain needs is a push."

"A push?" Roberto said. "Into war?"

"Indeed," D'Avignon said.

"How?" Alejandro asked.

D'Avignon glanced left and right theatrically. "I've been able to mingle with the American newspapermen here in Havana. They tell me that they're here to report on the losses at the sugar mills and on the situation with the rebels up in the hills. The Americans have made those rebels into a ready-made scapegoat."

"I don't see how," Roberto said.

D'Avignon looked at him with a frown. "Do you *read* the newspapers, Governor?"

"No," Roberto said. "And certainly not the American ones. I speak English but I won't read it."

"Pff," D'Avignon said. "Well, if you had, you'd know that those rebels are funded and supplied by America—"

"We know that without reading any newspapers," Alejandro said.

"—and you'd also know that Morton's efforts these past months have helped that image along, especially in the States."

Alejandro put his hands down flat on the worktable. "And how does this help us?"

D'Avignon winked. "There are reporters out there who are aching for a story, even if we have to make one. You say the word, gentlemen, and within a few days I'll create a situation that neither Spain nor the United States can ignore. I'll have them at each other's throats by the end of the week."

Alejandro was stunned, and he frankly did not know whether or not to believe this man. He looked at Roberto. "He has spoken of this to you?"

Roberto shrugged. "In brief."

"And is it possible?"

"Oh, yes," Roberto said. "But men would die."

Alejandro could not suppress a chuckle. "If we're talking about starting a war, my friend, we can hardly avoid that. But, still . . ."

"If you are still undecided," D'Avignon said, "let me attempt to tip the scales a bit. You know that there is gold in the Cheyenne Territory, yes?"

They nodded.

"And you know that I worked to help One Who Flies work the one deposit that he found, yes?"

Again, nods.

"And did I ever mention that just from that one deposit, and in just one year, we took out a quarter million U.S. dollars' worth?"

They stared.

"And that the one site we worked was just one of at least a dozen promising spots I prospected with One Who Flies?"

"No," Alejandro said with a breath. "You failed to mention that."

"Well I'm mentioning it now," D'Avignon said. "And I'll mention, too, that we will never ever get that far into Cheyenne Territory without either their permission or an army at our back. Now, either we're all in this, or none of us can be, because when you two say 'go,' I'm going, and we can't turn back."

Alejandro considered it all, and from his beaded brow of sweat, he could tell that Roberto was considering it as well. This might be beyond his brother-in-law's reach, for though Roberto talked a tough game, he was really quite a gentle man.

"Position," Alejandro said, as if musing, "is transitory. I've seen it myself. You know this, Roberto. I was once an honored military leader, a respected member of the elite of New Spain. When the winds changed, I was spat upon and cast down and it took me twenty years to climb back. Position is transitory. You cannot hold onto it, you cannot protect it."

Roberto's eyes were interested but his frown told of his reluctance.

"What would happen, Roberto, if the viceroy smelled out our plans? Would you still live in this fine house?"

"No," Roberto said. "I would have to leave, and return to my ranch in Solano."

"Exactly," Alejandro said, feeling more convinced himself as he spoke. "Because the viceroy can take away your position. But gold . . . gold and money, *that* can be protected, and if the viceroy tried to take that from you, you could go after him with impunity, could you not?"

Roberto's frown eased. "Of course," he said. "With impunity."

"Position is transitory," Alejandro said, sure of himself. "Wealth is power."

Roberto nodded in agreement.

Alejandro turned to D'Avignon.

"What is the plan?"

CHAPTER 26
Tuesday, July 29, A.D. 1890
Havana
Cuba

Seagulls wheeled and spun overhead, and clouds rolled on the wind like tumbleweeds. Crewmen raised nets filled with luggage and cargo from the pier onto the coastal steamer *Gracia de la Mar*. Passengers hugged their relations and said their goodbyes before boarding for the three-day journey to La Puerta del Norte.

George stood on the pier and, for the first time in what seemed years, did not fear his future. Mouse Road stood beside him and held onto his arm for support both physical and emotional. Having her so close fired him, and her love drove him. He cursed himself for having been an idiot for so long, and thanked the spirits that, between himself and Mouse Road, at least one of them had been stubborn enough not to give up. He caressed her hand with its flaky skin, and she squeezed his arm with affection returned.

The ship blasted a steamy note. George turned to Alejandro and Roberto.

"I suppose we should get aboard now."

"It's time," Roberto said.

George stuck out his hand to the governor. "Thank you for your gracious hospitality," he said.

Roberto shook his hand. *"Un placer,"* he said.

"And you," George said, turning to Alejandro. "What can I say? Without your help, none of this would have happened."

Alejandro was looking down the wharf. He blinked as

he realized he was being spoken to. "Hm? Oh, it was nothing, I assure you."

"No, sir. Don't you realize what you've done?" George tried to put into words what he felt at that moment. "You have changed the future of an entire people. You have remapped the destiny of tens of thousands." He extended his hand. "It has been an honor to be a small part of that."

Alejandro actually blushed at the praise. He clasped George's hand and shook it. "I wish you all the best," he said incongruously.

"Is something wrong?" George asked, sensing Alejandro's distraction.

"Forgive me," Alejandro said. "My mind is full of things this morning. There is so much to prepare for."

"Of course," George said, understanding. "But don't worry about things on my end. I will set up the regular couriers immediately. One every four days, between the Council and your outpost at the border. Are you sure the telegraph will have reached that far in time?"

"I am assured that it will be operating within the week."

"Fine," George said. "That will be plenty of time." He looked around for Vincent but did not see him. He searched for him up at the wharf where Roberto's men barricaded the press, but did not find him there, either. "Where is Vincent?"

"Vincent?" Alejandro said. "Oh, D'Avignon. He is . . . er . . ."

"On an errand," Roberto said with a prim smile.

"Oh," George said. "Too bad. I was hoping to see him before we left. Would you tell him we said good-bye? And tell him I said thanks for the kick in the ribs."

"Yes," Alejandro said. "Of course."

The ship blasted another note, and the clumps of people on the pier began to separate into passengers and well-wishers.

"Thank you, again," George said.

"*Muchas gracias,* señores," Mouse Road said, and received a nod of acknowledgment from the two men.

They turned and headed toward the ship. Speaks while Leaving stood at the end of the pier, looking out at the harbor and the water that led from beneath her feet out to the sea and out to the ocean where her child's body lay entombed. They walked to her and gently George touched her.

Her hair hung in twisted hanks, uncombed and unwashed in an expression of mourning, but through them he could see that her cheeks were dry. George wondered if she had finally cried herself out, at least for now.

"It's time to go," he said to her.

She allowed him to lead her away from the pier's edge and steer her toward the ship. They climbed in silence, walking up the ridged ramp, first Speaks while Leaving, then Mouse Road, and George last. Mouse Road held George's hand as she climbed, and he smiled as he felt the strength of her long-fingered grip. The experience of her illness had forged a bond between them. Having seen her so close to death had shown him that, despite all he had lost in recent years, there was still more he could lose—much more. More importantly, it allowed him to see what it was that he had gained during those same years: a new life, the respect of leaders, and the love of a sweet and devoted woman. Feeling the brush of the medicine bag he still wore beneath his shirt, he thought he might finally have learned the lesson that Three Trees Together had been trying to teach him.

On deck, Mouse Road's hand curled around his arm. The suppleness of her body filled him with yearnings beyond the mere emotional, and he strove to maintain his composure. Speaks while Leaving walked to the rail, drawn by the green waters, and George took advantage of the relative solitude.

"Mouse Road," he said, "before anything goes any further between us, I wanted to talk to you."

"Yes," she said, as if she had been expecting it.

He turned to face her, but could not look at her, and so he held her hands in his and stared at them. He saw the peeling skin on the backs and palms of her hands, remnants of the fever that had nearly taken her from him.

"I would like you to be my wife," he said, blurting the words out all at once, and then laughed, embarrassed and relieved at having spoken so boldly.

The hands he held squeezed his. "And I would like you to be my husband," she said.

He could not keep the smile from his face and he felt the sting of tears in his eyes. "Good," he said. "That is good. But . . ." There were things he wanted to say, things that needed to be said. "But you need to know, you need to realize . . . life with me won't be the kind of life your mother led."

"I know this."

"It will be busy. I will have to travel. And if things go the way I hope, it may be like that for years."

"I know this, too," she said.

"And that means I won't be home very much at all."

"Then neither will I," she said.

He looked up at her and saw the smile, the cheeks round as plums, the long eyes, dark-lashed and bright with happiness. "You will travel with me?"

"I am never letting you go anywhere without me again," she said.

He embraced her, propriety be damned, and she held him tightly. He felt the silk of her hair against his cheek, smelled the sunshine warmth of her skin. He took her by the shoulders and pushed her to arm's length.

"Are you sure?" he asked, challenging her with a level stare.

Her smile broadened. "Yes," she said. "You will show me the *vé'ho'e* world, and we will bring peace to the People."

He reached to hug her again but she put a hand to his chest, smile waning. "My brother will not approve," she said. "Storm Arriving will never approve."

"No," he said, and his gut tightened into a knot of the old fear. He remembered the rituals that had brought Storm Arriving together with Speaks while Leaving, rituals in which he had played a part. He had acted as a liaison, and visited Speaks while Leaving's father to offer the chief the bride-price and ask for his permission on behalf of Storm Arriving. He remembered sitting with Storm Arriving through the night as they awaited either the return of the bride-price—and the implicit refusal of his suit—or the appearance of the wedding party bearing gifts of their own, including the bride herself. Now, with Mouse Road's father long passed on to *Séáno,* Storm Arriving was the only one who could grant a man permission to marry his sister. But George had already pressed his suit and been refused that permission, and he had no reason to expect that Storm Arriving had changed his opinion on the matter.

"What can we do, then?" he said.

"It is simple," she said brightly. "We must elope."

"Elope?" George had spent a lot of time among the People, but they had always been very close-lipped in matters concerning the sexes. "How do we elope?"

She shrugged. "We run away together."

"But . . ." He chuckled. "But we have already done that."

She giggled—an incredibly girlish sound—and leaned into his embrace. "Yes. I know."

"Then we are . . . I mean, there's no ceremony . . . no . . ."

"No," she said, and now her voice was deep and womanly against his chest. "So, if you want to be married, we can be."

"As simple as that?"

"As simple as that." She looked up at him. "Of course, when we get home, you should offer my brother a bride-price."

He swallowed against the tumult of emotions. His love for this tiny woman, and his gratitude for that love, threatened to overwhelm him. He had always admired the relationship his parents were so willing to show the world—partners in life as well as in love—and now it seemed as if he was to be similarly blessed.

"I don't have enough to pay for such a treasure as you," he said. "No man does."

She laughed once more, and he felt the closeness of her body draw him like a magnet. "A single blanket is a fortune if it is all a man owns."

"I think I can arrange for a little more than that."

They walked to the aft rail where the passengers had begun to gather. They sidled in among the men and women who stood chatting excitedly, prepared for one last farewell wave to friends and family.

"Have you ever lain with a woman?" Mouse Road asked.

George felt the blood rush to his cheeks and he was glad that Mouse Road spoke the language of the People and no tongue that might have been overheard and understood. He glanced down at her and saw her looking up at him with an expression of innocent curiosity. The choice of lying to her occurred to him, but he decided against it, as one lie always led to others.

"Yes," he said, "but it was a long time ago."

"But you learned what you need to know? About men and women?"

He cleared his throat, now regretting his decision of honesty. "Yes," he said.

"Good," she said, and leaned against his arm. "Then I won't have to teach you."

His breath caught in his throat and he coughed. She could hardly have surprised him more.

"She was a *vé'ho'e*?" she asked.

George, still trying to regain control of himself, looked out over the docks and the milling people and signed with his hand. *Yes.*

"Was she prettier than me?"

He looked at her, surprised again by her quicksilver mind. "Was she . . . prettier?" he said. The answer required no thought, but still he gave it thought as he realized for the first time that, as he looked at Mouse Road, he was looking at his wife.

Her long black braids, supple and warm as satin, shone in the sunlight. Her skin, from brow to jaw to the exquisite length of her neck and the shelf of her collarbone, glowed with youth and beauty. Was she prettier? Remembering the tired, waxy features of the small-town whore he had slept with, the question did not deserve consideration, not on that level or on any other. Even taking into account the young women of society whose company he had enjoyed—daughters of judges, congressmen, and generals, women of fine breeding and wealth— he could not in any earnest manner compare them to the woman at his side.

Mouse Road's beauty surpassed that of anyone he'd

known or wished to know, but so did the other features that drew him to her: her exuberance, her resolve, her intelligence, the devotion and loyalty that had driven her to search for him, the passion that she had shown in berating him for his weaknesses, and the alluring femininity that pervaded her every move, every word, every thought.

"No one is as pretty as you," he said, and her smile was bashful, happy, and loving, all at once.

The ship blasted three long notes as the last passengers boarded and the gangway was removed. George felt the deck tremble as the giant engines below fired to life. The others at the rail called out and waved goodbye to those who were staying behind. George spied Alejandro and Roberto on the pier. He waved and Roberto waved back. So did Alejandro, after a jab and a pointing finger brought his attention back to his departing guests. Smoke gushed upward from the stacks, in white and black, and the *Gracia de la Mar* got under way.

"When will I get to meet your parents?" Mouse Road asked, bringing laughter out of him as an answer. "Is that funny?" she asked.

"No," he said, grinning, but then thought of how that meeting might go. "And yes, it is." He waved again and breathed deeply of the warm tropical air.

There was a scuffle behind them, and they turned to find Speaks while Leaving stumbling toward the rail. George reached out to steady her. Her eyes were wide, staring out toward the harbor, but not seeing. He called her name. The passengers retreated. Her knees buckled and George caught her as she fell.

"No," she said. "Leave me alone." Her eyes stared up into the sky.

"It is the *Ma'heono*," Mouse Road said.

"Leave me alone. I do not want to see it. I do not want to see it!"

George felt the fear that swirled around them like a whirlwind. He saw the frightened faces of the *vé'ho'e* passengers. "It is fine," he said, hoping someone among the Spaniards understood his French. "She has fainted. A swoon. That is all." He heard a man's voice translate his words and looked back at Speaks while Leaving.

"I am in a dark place," she said.

"It is all right," Mouse Road said. "We are with you. Just tell us what you see."

Once before, George had been present when the *ma'heono* had come upon Speaks while Leaving with a vision. Just as she had then, she told them now what it was she saw in the spirit world.

"I smell rusted metal and sour water. I smell *vé'ho'e* machines. It is dark. Wait. There is a light," she said. "A tiny fire. I see Vincent."

"Vincent?" George said. The ship had begun to slowly pull away from the pier, and George saw both Alejandro and Roberto, standing, stretching their necks to see what was happening.

"The fire begins to sparkle. I run. I am in a cave, or a tunnel. There is another with us. We climb a ladder. *Vé'ho'e*. In blue and white."

"Vincent," George said again. "On an errand."

"There is light, now. And others, men and women. And water. We walk down the ramp."

Vincent. An errand. Sparkling fire.

George remembered Vincent's expert instruction to him and the others as they mined for gold up in the Sheep Mountains. He remembered Vincent's lessons on fuses and explosives, lessons that had helped them in mining and in war.

He stood. Alejandro and Roberto still stood on the dock, Roberto shading his eyes with his hand. Beyond them, behind them, was the wharf, and beyond that, the other piers for the larger ships.

Vincent. Sparkling fire.

The warships of Spain and the United States stood side by side, American ships to the south, Spanish on the north. George saw men and women on board, taking tours given by captains glad to have their crews on liberty instead of at battle readiness.

"Oh, no," George said. "What have you done?"

Lying on the deck in Mouse Road's arms, Speaks while Leaving shouted. "I see fire!"

A booming sound wrung the air and George felt it in his chest. The aft deck of the northernmost warship blew upward, tossing planks, sailors, and the Spanish flag high into the air. Fire gouted upward in a smoky billow.

Screams came from everywhere—the ship, the wharf, the pier, and from the passengers around George as they piled to the rail. People ran, those near the warship running away, and those distant running closer. A second detonation crumped deep within the ship and the superstructure was thrust up and forward like the metal of a sardine can. Screams of munitions joined those of people as the ship's battery caught, and now no one ran toward the warships. All fled. Shells exploded in popcorn reports, and George saw fire break out on the warship next to the first, as well as the cargo ship on the other side.

Sailors dove off into the harbor's green water. The warships at the end of the line, the American ships, sent heavy smoke up from their stacks as they brought their engines on line. Fire spread, on the piers and from ship to ship. Explosions multiplied, propagating like fiery weeds.

Vincent. Sparkling fire. An errand.

George stared at the two men on the pier, growing smaller as the *Gracia de la Mar* poured on the steam to get herself clear of any possible danger.

"What have you done?" George shouted at them. "Alejandro! What have you done?" But as the first Spanish ship started to go down at the aft, its graceful bow rising up out of the water, he knew what they had done. He slid down along the rail until he sat on the deck next to Mouse Road. Speaks while Leaving blinked her eyes, returning from the spirit world.

"I had a vision," she said.

George listened to the screams of dying men and frightened townsfolk, the shouts of orders and of rending metal.

"No," he said, unwilling to watch any more, having seen too much already. "No vision. You saw the truth."

"Do you know what her vision means?" Mouse Road asked.

The captain of the *Gracia de la Mar* sent his ship cruising out of the harbor, not willing to risk crew or cargo to the disaster behind him. George, sitting on the deck, surrounded by weeping passengers and cursing Spaniards, knew exactly what the vision meant.

"It means war," he said. "And no one will be able to avoid this one. Not even my father."

CHAPTER 27

Wednesday, July 30, A.D. 1890
The White House
Washington, District of Columbia

With the fork a clumsy lever in his right hand, Custer pinned the slab of breakfast ham in place while with his left he did his best to cut it with the knife. His grip slipped and the tines screeched like fingernails against a blackboard slate, raising the hair on the nape of his neck and making Lydia and Maria shudder at the sound. No one moved for a moment as the memory of the sound faded, and then Libbie cleared her throat.

"Autie, Senator Tibbets is having a dinner party on the fifteenth next."

"At last," Maria said. "Finally, something to look forward to."

"Maria, we have yet to accept the invitation," her mother reminded her.

"But Mother, this year was so dreadfully dull. I only went to three balls all season."

"There are reasons, dear, not the least of which has been your father's health."

"But can't we at least go to the Tibbetses?"

"That's what I'm asking your father." She turned to Custer. "Autie? May we? You know how the girls love dining at the Tibbetses."

"Indeed," Custer said as he maneuvered a piece of meat from the plate to his mouth.

"Can we go, Father?" Maria's eyes were wide at the prospect of a dinner party—and the new frock that it would require—but Custer's eye was on his eldest daughter.

"What do you think, Lydia? Do you want to go to a dinner party at the Tibbets place?"

Lydia blushed as she studied the food on her plate. "I wouldn't mind," she said.

"Wouldn't mind?" Maria laughed. "Why, she's been dreaming of nothing but for a fortnight, ever since she heard that Richard Tibbets is back from his tour of Europe."

Lydia's blush burned up from her cheeks to her hairline and she threw a daggered glare at her baby sister.

"Richard Tibbets would be quite the prize," Libbie said.

"Mother," Lydia whispered. *"Please."*

"No, no," Custer said. "She's quite right."

"I don't believe this," Lydia said.

"Young Tibbets would be quite the conquest," he continued, enjoying his daughter's discomfort, "but in comparison, I think that our Lydia would be the prize."

"May we please change the subject?"

"No!" they all said together before breaking into laughter. Lydia lifted her gaze to heaven and gave an infuriated "Augh!" that only added to the merriment of the others.

Custer was still chuckling when the dining room door opened. Samuel stepped inside and tugged at his ear, the sign that the President was wanted. Libbie caught the sign and sighed.

"It seems as though Samuel has come to your rescue, Lydia."

Custer put down his utensils. "If you will excuse me, ladies?" He stood and took his cane when Douglas handed it to him. As he walked past Libbie, she reached out and took his hand. Her smile was bittersweet as she gazed up at him.

"I became quite accustomed to our leading a normal life," she said.

"I know you did, Sunshine." He leaned over and kissed the smooth sweep of her dark hair. "So did I." Then he turned to follow Samuel.

"My apologies, Mr. President. You know that I wouldn't interrupt unless it was important."

"I know," he said, and he did. Samuel was not one

for histrionics, and if he chose to interrupt the family dinner, he had reason.

As Samuel led him from the residence dining room, he wondered whether he preferred this life to the one he'd known in the months following the shooting. Never before had he had the leisure that the months of recuperation provided: the freedom to read, the release from responsibility and command, the time to enjoy family and friends without the looming presence of politics and "business."

Business. It had become a bad word during Morton's stewardship, a word that connoted all the worst of rampant industrialization at the expense of the worker. That, too, was something that the past months had shown him. Business, as the conglomerates defined it, was steel and machines and cash flow and seven-figure finances. It was the engine of the economy, but it ran the common man under its wheels as it moved ahead, and Custer wondered at the wisdom of his party's strong affiliation with the captains of American "business."

But such ruminations were a luxury he had little time for now, and as Samuel ushered him into the parlor, they vanished, for Jacob was waiting there, and Jacob never came at breakfast unless it was a crisis.

"What has happened?" Custer asked.

Jacob handed Custer a handful of telegraph messages, all written in the block letters of the operator's hasty hand.

HAVANA HARBOR, it read. THREE SPANISH WARSHIPS, TWO SPANISH FREIGHTERS, DESTROYED BY EXPLOSION AND FIRE.

"Aw, Hell," Custer said as he read the other messages. "Spanish warships? What about the ships Morton sent there?"

"The USS *Boston* and the *Chicago* escaped harm, as did one of the other Spanish warships. Better for us, though, if we'd lost them."

"Why? What do you mean?"

Jacob grimaced. "It wasn't an accident. The Cuban rebels have been fitted squarely with the blame for the initial explosion."

"The rebels? How have they figured that?"

"They caught one of them," he said. "And he told them that they were provided with explosives and instruction by an American posing as a reporter or something."

"Is it true?"

"The rebels would say anything to—"

"I asked, is it true? Do we have men down there?"

"I don't know, Autie! Reports are confused and spotty. Information is still coming in."

"Aw, Hell," Custer said as he sat down heavily onto a velvet-covered chair. He looked through the telegraph messages. The block letters shouted at him, but though they said no more than Jacob had already told him, they could not exaggerate the importance of the words. Three ships of the line sunk in Havana harbor. Two Spanish freighters, loaded with sugar. One captured rebel with a tale of an American spy posing as a newspaperman. And all the meetings, all the backroom maneuvering he'd done, none of it would come to anything.

"That's it, then."

"Sir?" Jacob said.

"That's it. There's nothing else we can do."

"Mr. President?" Samuel leaned forward, concern in his eyes. "Are you all right?"

"God *damn it*!" he shouted as he pushed himself to his feet. "Of *course* I'm not all right!" He tossed the messages and they bloomed into a fluttering dahlia of paper, which floated to the floor. He staggered and caught himself on the back of the chair, then shoved at it, tossing it forward into the side table. "God *damn it*!"

"Autie! Settle down!"

"Settle down?" he rasped at Jacob, limping toward him. "Why in all Hell should I settle down?" But his weak foot caught on the carpet edge and he toppled, crashing forward into the divan. Jacob and Samuel reached for him but he snarled and waved them back. He lowered himself onto the floor, leaning back against the divan's upholstered satin, the taste of metal in his mouth.

He stared at the floor as his mind filled with the memory of the last time he had sat on the floor. Last Christmas, it had been, downstairs in one of the sitting rooms.

He had sat cross-legged on the floor in front of the fire. Across from him had been his old friend, his old adversary, Three Trees Together. On that day, the old chief had given him a buffalo robe he had painted with the scene of the massacre at Kansa Bay, and on that day, Custer had decided that he needed to work toward peace with the Cheyenne. Remembering the reunion with his son that had followed, he was reminded of all the many and complicated reasons that had led him to that decision.

And now those decisions, those reasons, and all his work since that day were for naught. All his hopes now lay at the bottom of Havana's harbor, sunk with those warships and papered over with the telegraph messages that littered the floor.

He wanted to weep, but he had not the time.

"Autie?" Jacob said.

He looked up at his old friend and saw reflected in his eyes the pain that he felt. Samuel, too, was affected, quietly gathering together the strewn messages, his face dour.

"We're going to war, Jacob."

"I know, Autie."

"Mobilize our forces."

"Yes, sir. What do you think they will do?"

He took a deep breath to clear his head. The maps unrolled in his mind, and he saw the theater laid before him. "It's obvious," he said. "Rightly or wrongly, they've got evidence that we have been working to usurp their control over Cuba. They'll return the favor." He looked up at his two closest advisors.

"We've been backed into a war, my friends. Against Spain *and* the Cheyenne. In the Territory."

CHAPTER 28

**Moon When the Cherries Are Ripe, Waxing
Fifty-seven Years after the Star Fell
Near the Red Paint River
Alliance Territory**

They rode northeast, following the swath of churned earth that marked the buffalo's path through the land. The wind blew in from the west, the direction of beginnings and birth, and Speaks while Leaving leaned into it. It turned her shortened hair into tiny whips that lashed her face with relentless zeal, and it made the grass lie down, even where it had not been trampled or grazed down by the passage of the buffalo herd. She could smell the weather on the wind's shoulders, clouds piled up beyond the world's rim, pregnant with rain. She could smell, too, the dusty dung chips left in the wake of the buffalo herd. The coming rain would soften them and they would seep down through the hoofprints, returning to the land to renew the soil. Life sprung from the buffalo, and the land sang the song of the herd.

Ahead to the north, rising from the horizon's edge were the Sacred Mountains, dark with trees and distance. The Teaching Mountain was there, and the Listening Mountain, and the Mountain of Whispers, too, though she could not make out their individual profiles across the hazy miles. But they were there, she knew—purpled guardians of the People—and their presence gave her a rock of stability in a life that had gone entirely too far out of her control.

Mouse Road and One Who Flies rode side by side, their whistlers as close as a mated pair. Watching them over the past weeks, during the journeys on sea and on land, she had seen them grow stronger together. For nearly a moon, they had rarely been separated, spending their days with each other, a pair now, instead of two persons. Together, they were impervious to the pain around them, their mutual love softening the blows of grief and disappointment that she knew they felt. Their devotion warmed her heart as any true love might, but it also tasted of bitterness, bringing home all the failings of her own love for Storm Arriving. Where they had formed a partnership, she and her husband were still only two people, a man and a woman who had more yearning than satisfaction, more history than future.

The future. She could not see it, and she dreaded it. It was a future now of war and conflict, a future she had been trying to avoid, but there was also another future, a closer future, into which she did not want to travel. Every wave on the sea and every roll of the land beneath her whistler's feet brought her closer to an immediate future that she *could* see, and too clearly. As the land began to slope down toward the meandering Red Paint River, as they neared the moment when they would spy the first outlying lodges of the tribe's circular encampment, she wished for the courage to flee, to turn her back on everyone and ride away.

But such courage would only delay what must come, not avoid it. That, too, she could see, and so she summoned a different courage.

"You will hear it soon enough," she said.

Mouse Road and One Who Flies jerked on their reins, startled at the sound of her voice. She had not spoken for several days—had barely spoken at all since Blue Shell Woman had been laid into the broad salt waters— and so she understood her companions' surprise. They prodded their mounts and came closer.

"You will hear it soon enough," she said again, gesturing toward the river's path. "When we ride in, you will hear it, but it will be better if you hear it now from me."

"Hear what?" One Who Flies asked, without concern, and the lack of suspicion in his voice sharpened the edge on the guilt that cut her heart.

Her whistler rumbled deep in her breast and paled the skin on her flanks, sensing her rider's fear. Speaks while Leaving reached forward to scratch between her shoulders and soothe her anxiety, a motion that also gave herself time to muster the will to proceed.

"I have lied to you," she said.

"About what?" One Who Flies asked.

She dragged at the words, pulling them from her mind to her lips. "The Council never authorized us—no, they never authorized *me* to negotiate with the Iron Shirts."

Mouse Road had known this and grew ashamed of her own silence. One Who Flies looked at his new wife and then back at Speaks while Leaving, not understanding the ramifications of her words.

"They knew none of it?" he asked, incredulous. "They didn't approve of the terms? The concessions we offered? The concessions the Iron Shirts accepted?"

She signed with her hands. *No. None of it.*

One Who Flies spoke distractedly, dreamlike. "But you said . . . the Council was divided . . . an alliance would convince them . . ."

"Yes," Speaks while Leaving said. "Divided between peace and war."

He laughed at the irony. "They don't have to worry about *that* decision anymore. It has been made for them."

"Not by me!" Speaks while Leaving shouted, and then reached forward again to calm both her mount and herself. "Not by me," she repeated quietly.

"No. Not by you," he said, "though by whom does not matter. War is a faithful hound, and comes no matter who calls it home."

"I am sorry," she said. "I was not thinking of what it might cost you two."

Mouse Road toed her whistler forward and touched Speaks while Leaving on the shoulder. "It did not matter," she said. "I would have gone looking for him with you or without you."

"And I," One Who Flies said, coming up on her other side, "if you had not come, I would still be lying in the mud." A cloud crossed his features. "Or worse."

"You gave us a gift," Mouse Road said, and Speaks while Leaving saw her exchange a glance at her beloved for a smile. "Any pain I have known is outweighed."

"And for me as well," One Who Flies said.

She burst out with tears she did not know she had left. She thought that she had cried all she would ever cry, but now, with their easy acceptance of her transgression, she found that she had more tears she could shed. Sobs broke in her chest, making it impossible to speak until she controlled them.

"What of the Council?" she asked.

"What about them?" One Who Flies asked in return.

"The alliance with the Iron Shirts. The promises I made to María Cristina. What can I do about that? War is coming. It follows us like a stench. How can I tell them what I've done? What should I tell them?"

One Who Flies patted her arm. "My dear sister-in-law," he said. "Isn't it clear enough? You must turn your lie into the truth."

"But war . . . my vision . . ." She could not explain it to him, how the vision had led her, how her visions *always* led her. This vision had spoken to her in images of peace, trade, and cooperation. She had not felt the bite of war; she had not smelled the smoke of death in it. But war was coming. Was the vision wrong? And if the *vision* could be wrong, was it a vision? Were any of them visions? "I cannot see," she said, panicking, feeling the blindness approach as confidence in her prescience dimmed. "The vision . . . I cannot see . . ."

A hand gripped her arm and she was jolted back to awareness, back to the prairie, to the wind, and to the blue eyes of One Who Flies, his gaze stern, his hold on her arm bruising.

"You *can* see," he said. "But sometimes it takes more than dancing to bring a vision into being. This is one of those times."

She blinked at him. "More than dancing?" she said.

"Yes," he said. "A great vision takes great work."

Could it be? Could the vision be true and war still come? She looked at One Who Flies, and saw the hope and belief in his eyes.

"Yes," she said, wanting to believe as well and feeling her dread lessen. "Peace is the goal, but perhaps not the path."

He smiled at her, and hope filled her heart.

They started off again, following the subtle folds of land that marked the limits of the Red Paint River. In wet winters, the rivers that flowed through the gentle land would rise from their shallow banks and flood the land for miles. In summertime, though, these unassuming heights merely gave a rider a longer sight, and when the sun had only a hand of sky left in the west, they saw the first lodges of the Great Circle of the People. Smoke rose from the conical homes, and at the western edge they saw the shadow of whistler flocks.

They saw outriders heading toward them and waited for them near an upthrust of pale rock. Waiting, they saw, too, that the camp's circle was broken by gaps where some of the bands should have been. Whether they had left early, or never arrived at all, Speaks while Leaving did not know, but it was a sign that all was far from well.

Eight riders stopped at a hundred yards, rifles ready. "Who are you?" one of them shouted.

With the sun at their backs and One Who Flies in his *vé'ho'e* clothing, Speaks while Leaving understood their caution.

"I am One Who Flies," he shouted to them. "Of the Tree People band, with Speaks while Leaving and Mouse Road."

The riders peered at them, conferred, and then two riders sped back to camp, yipping with the news. The other six came forward to meet them.

Speaks while Leaving knew a few of the men, especially Silver Cloud, a cousin on her father's side from the Hair Rope band. He rode closer, studying their faces and her cut hair.

"You bring bad news," he said, for there was no question.

"Yes," One Who Flies said. "And good news."

Silver Cloud glanced at Speaks while Leaving. "But mostly bad news."

"Yes," One Who Flies agreed.

"Is my husband home?" she asked Silver Cloud.

He signed: *Yes, he is in his lodge.*

She turned to One Who Flies and Mouse Road. "I

will wait for him here. He will have much to tell me, and I would not have him do it in the heart of camp."

One Who Flies signed his understanding, and Silver Cloud and the others escorted him and Mouse Road toward camp.

Her whistler grew fractious, watching the others depart, being so close to home and flock and yet kept behind, alone. She dismounted and with a slap on her flank, sent the hen running. The whistler sang as she headed toward the flock and her family, a yodeling call that was echoed in the distance by others welcoming her home.

Speaks while Leaving sat down to wait at the base of a speckled boulder, facing the setting sun. The wind was in her face, rushing past her ears with the sound of waves on a shore. A few clouds had rolled up into the sky, and the sun painted them blue and yellow and orange, the day's final chore as it drifted down toward slumber.

The earth sang. She heard it in the ground beneath her and in the stone at her back. The silent, truculent land of the Iron Shirts had bothered her deeply, but here, despite a heart still raw with grief, she was gladdened by the conversations that surrounded her on every side. From the sky to the earth and in the water that linked them both the songs of life rang and buzzed and trumpeted through her mind, and when she closed her eyes, her other sight opened. Though she felt the soft rays of the setting sun on her face, life around her gleamed with its own shining brilliance. She moved through the light, listening, watching, tasting the dreams that filled the world's heart.

The crying wind kneaded clouds that hummed in rainbow hues. The grass yawned, sleepy after a long season in the sun, ready for the approach of autumn it felt in its rooted feet. A field mouse winked black bead eyes and cleaned his whiskers, preparing his bravery for his twilight rounds, while a gopher organized his burrow with modest pride. Atop the speckled boulder against which she sat, a wren landed and speared the air with three sharp notes, impatient for tomorrow's sun though today's had yet to depart.

She put her hands on the ground and felt its heartbeat, heard the rush of its lifeblood in the waters of the Red Paint River. She saw everything in lucid detail, from the depths of every cloud to a single hair on the mouse's face, but when she turned to look at herself, she saw only vapor and fog. She was a nebula in a world of clarity, a figure wrapped in doubt. Despite the light of life around her, she waited in shadow, and the shadow grew, darkened, chilling her. She heard the rhythm of a rider's approach, and when a whistler sang a question, she opened her eyes.

Before her was one of the largest drakes she had ever seen, his withers a head taller than a man. Aggressive bars of red and white flared along his muzzle, and his flanks wheeled with shapes of clashing color that flaunted his confidence. Astride this grand beast sat Storm Arriving, imperious and fearsome.

The right side of his head was freshly shaven. He had drawn a line of black paint along his hairline, and four streaks of black dragged downward beneath his right eye: black, the color of victory. Bloody sunlight sizzled on the seven rings of white silver that pierced the rim of his ear, and twin eagle feathers were tied to the top of his braid with a black leather cord. His leggings dripped with a luxuriant fringe that seemed to move with the colors of his drake's display, and tied to his leather shirt were the scalps of his victories—at least twenty in number, she could not count them as their tufts of blond, red, and brown hair crawled across his shoulders and chest like living things in the wind.

He was magnificent, and she stood, wanting to tell him so, but the purpose in his eyes was as dark as their color, and his mouth was a tight line: a rope pulled near to snapping. She could not speak to him. He was part spirit and part man. He was War, and he was Death, and she could not speak to such a creature. She could only stand before him, gazing at him through her tears, and wonder at the transformation of the man she had once loved so dearly.

He unhooked his feet from the loops in the riding harness and slid down the whistler's side, landing on both feet. Then he strode toward her and without a word swung a wide, backhanded blow that struck her across the face. She stumbled backward against the boulder, and caught herself there, one hand on the warm stone, one on her hot cheek. She blinked away new tears and looked up at him. He stood, wide-stanced, his chest expanding and contracting with angry breaths. He stabbed a finger at her.

"You have failed me as a friend," he said, his voice trembling with emotion. "And you have betrayed me as a wife. But now, with your stubborn arrogance, you have killed our child." He looked up and shook his fist in the wind's face. "Blue Shell Woman! My daughter! Forgive me!"

When he brought his gaze down upon her once more, she felt it like a weight. She saw in his eyes the wound that threatened to tear him open, and she knew she had put that wound there. Beyond any other change that she saw, *this* change was of her own making. She curled around the pain in her heart, cowed by the wrath she had created.

He turned and pulled himself up onto his war drake's spine. He set his feet in the harness loops and toed the mount around to face back toward the camp.

"The Kit Fox will be dancing tomorrow. I will dance with them, and I will strike the drum and throw you away. Tonight, I return to the Tree People. Tomorrow, I am no longer your husband." He kicked his whistler into a run. She heard its heavy footsteps recede, gathered up by the wind and blown away.

She lay there, curled against the cooling stone, as the day was extinguished and night poured across the sky. The wind pushed the clouds, and the clouds brought a pattering of rain. The raindrops were warm on her arm and on her shoulder, but cool on her stinging cheek. Swallows flew through the last of twilight, their garrulous chatter crisp in the deepening dark.

Speaks while Leaving wept. There was nothing else she could do.

CHAPTER 29

Moon When the Cherries Are Ripe, Full Fifty-seven Years after the Star Fell Along the Red Paint River Alliance Territory

Mouse Road stepped out of her lodge and into the early morning air. Her lodge. *Her* lodge. A married woman now, she no longer had to share a lodge with her relations, and had returned once more to the lodge that had been her mother's. She took a deep breath, smelling the dew that beaded the grass and the seams of the lodgeskins, and wrapped her arms about her shoulders.

The doorflap opened behind her, and One Who Flies joined her in the blue light of dawn. He wrapped his own arms around her, and nuzzled her neck with his cheek. She laughed and recoiled from the scratchiness of his overnight beard. He was such a strange thing, this man who used to be a *vé'ho'e*. He was not built like one of the People. His legs were thicker, his arms thinner. He had pale hair on his limbs and dark hair on his chest, and hair grew on his face as quick as grass in springtime. And his skin! In the places where the sun did not touch it, his skin was as pale as a plucked grouse, but where it was exposed, it had darkened to the golden color of skillet bread. His head had the softest hair she had ever known, coming in dark at his scalp and paling to nearly white at the ends, ends cut short in his grief over Three Trees Together, and still not long enough to pull back into a braid.

"You are up early," she said.

"I meet with the Council today. Remember?"

"Yes. Though I thought it might have been a cold bed that woke you." She reached behind and grabbed his hips, pulling him close up against her. He held her tightly and she laughed again, slapping away a hand that grew too bold.

"You must be patient," she said. "We do not want a baby so soon, do we?"

"I don't care," he whispered into her hair.

"You will," she chided him. "When you want to go off with Alejandro we won't want to have to bring the child . . ." Her voice trailed away as she realized what she was saying.

"Alejandro?" One Who Flies said. "I don't think I'll ever be able to trust that man again. This war is all his doing, and who knows what other tragedies he has had a hand in." But her attention had been diverted, and she looked over at the neighboring lodge that she used to share with Speaks while Leaving and Storm Arriving.

Storm Arriving had been absent since their arrival, choosing to avoid her defiant elopement by staying in the Kit Fox soldiers' meeting lodge. One Who Flies wanted to make things right between them, but she had counseled patience out of respect for her brother's grief over the death of his daughter.

And as for Speaks while Leaving, neither had she returned to the lodge, and it was another morning when no smoke rose from the smokehole.

One Who Flies saw where she was looking. "She is still out there," he said. "It has been four days."

"And that is long enough," Mouse Road said. She walked to the whistler that they kept tied near the lodge and unknotted the halter rope. One Who Flies said nothing, knowing her mind, and worked instead on tightening up the keel-rope and pad of the riding harness. He helped her up onto the whistler's back. She slipped her moccasins into the riding loops and tucked her knees under the first-rope.

"Stand up," she told it, and the whistler rose with a muttered complaint.

"Bring her home," One Who Flies said. Then he took her hand and kissed it, another strange habit from his *vé'ho'e* life.

"I love you," she said, squeezing his hand.

"And I love you," he said, releasing her.

She rode out of camp, heading through the empty places at a run. Her yearling whistler called to the flocks as they rode past, and the matriarchs replied with a two-note encouragement.

The air was thick and somnolent, with a mist that hung above the ground and graced even the plainest of plants with a web of moist jewels. She rode through its coolness, gathering gems in her hair, looking for the rock where Speaks while Leaving had made her hermitage. No one had bothered her during the four days since her return. Grief and mourning were respected, and the cause of hers was a story that had been well-told throughout the camp. But after four days with no word, Mouse Road worried that she might have moved from grief to despair, and done herself harm. She promised herself that she would only see that Speaks while Leaving was well, and then would return.

The mist thickened as she rode toward the higher ground, raising a wall of gray cloth that kept pace with her as she traveled. The outcrop was near, she knew it was, but finding it proved a challenge. The uphill slope of the land shifted downward and she knew she had ridden too far. She retreated, found the height, and directed her mount to walk along the barely perceptible ridge.

They proceeded, wrapped in the shroud of fog, seeing only the tired grass and an occasional patch of milkwood plants. She guided her mount slowly, listening to the muffled morning, alert for any sound of distress until the fog shredded like a dream and there, a stone's throw ahead through the coiling streamers of mist, was the gray-green pile of bouldered granite. She toed her whistler forward but reined in again as one of the boulders twisted and looked her way. Three other boulders grew heads and turned to see who it was had come, and Mouse Road felt her breath grow short with a gut-taut fear.

Pitted eyes stared out from beneath crevice brows. Their features were blunt and rough, their hair the mottled green of lichen. The mist swirled, and she blinked her eyes, seeing only four lumps of stone, boulders cold and immobile. Then she heard a voice from the other side of the outcropping. She kicked her whistler into motion and rounded the rocks to find Speaks while Leaving lying supine on a small patch of ground protected by an arc of stones.

"Yes," Mouse Road heard her say. "I will. I will."

Mouse Road slid off her whistler's back and ran to her. Speaks while Leaving was rigid, her breath sharp and shallow. Her lips were drawn back and her eyes had rolled white, and Mouse Road recognized at once that she was in the grip of another vision. She took her hand and yelped when Speaks while Leaving grabbed both her hands and gripped them with a terrible strength.

"They are here," Speaks while Leaving said, uttering the words with rapid breaths. "They are all around."

"Don't worry," Mouse Road said. She looked at the stones that stood around them. They leaned in toward the two women, eager, and Mouse Road wanted to run, to take Speaks while Leaving and run away from this place. A low sound began, coming from all around.

"I see," Speaks while Leaving said. "Yes, I see. I see."

There was a rumble in the ground. The whistler cried out and bolted, halter rope trailing into the mist. Mouse Road called after it and tried to stand but was unable to free her hands from Speaks while Leaving's relentless grip. Boulders creaked and moved, the earth trembled, and then Mouse Road felt a popping in her ears and a lifting in her innards. She shouted at the rocks around her, and everything went quiet. She heard her own breath, raw and dry. A stone clattered. A blackbird asked a trilled question. Another answered.

She looked down. Speaks while Leaving lay quietly, her eyes looking up into the clearing mist, her hands relaxed. She looked up and smiled a tired smile.

"Are you all right?" Mouse Road asked.

"I am fine," Speaks while Leaving said, and slowly sat up. She reached out and caressed Mouse Road's cheek. "You have been given a hard path, haven't you?"

Mouse Road looked down at her hands. "Not as hard as some," she said, thinking of what Speaks while Leaving had gone through in her life.

"Perhaps," Speaks while Leaving said, and then reached out and embraced her. "Remember," she whispered. "No matter how hard it is, remember that it will all turn out fine."

She pulled away from Speaks while Leaving and looked her straight in the eye. "Are you all right?" she asked her again.

Speaks while Leaving took a deep breath and looked up into the clearing sky. The sun grew bright. "Don't worry," she said. "I am fine. Help me get up, will you?"

She stood and helped her former sister-in-law to her feet. Speaks while Leaving was weak-kneed from her days of abstinence.

"Let me go for a whistler."

"No," Speaks while Leaving said. "I don't want to be out here alone anymore. I'm tired of being alone."

Mouse Road took her arm over her shoulder and together they began walking back toward the camp. "Do you think my brother will take you back?"

"Eh?" Speaks while Leaving said, not quite following her question. "Ah, that. No, Storm Arriving will not take me back any sooner than I will return to him. It will be some time before we are able to forgive one another. No, what I meant is that I've been alone too much. Out following my visions instead of building a future of my own." She sighed. "I've been a selfish woman. Hardheaded and stubborn, just as your brother always said I was."

"No more than he is," Mouse Road said, and Speaks while Leaving laughed. "But what about the People? How will you help the People if you don't follow your visions?"

Speaks while Leaving leaned against her and pointed ahead. The mist had burned away and the camp was laid out before them, lodges forming the incomplete circle, broken where families and bands had failed to gather. "The People have been torn apart by my visions, and I have not helped by leaving them alone. I was wrong to think that I could bring these visions into being by myself. I cannot do it alone. I need the help of others, just as the People need the help of other tribes."

Mouse Road thought of what Speaks while Leaving

had been saying when she found her up at the rocks. "Is that what you saw up there, at the rocks?"

Speaks while Leaving was gazing ahead, toward the camp and home. "Yes," she said. "The *nevé-stanevóo'o* came from the corners of the earth today. That is one of the things they told me."

"What else did they tell you?" she asked, remembering, too, her words about the hard path that lay ahead.

"They told me that war is coming," Speaks while Leaving said. "They told me that we must prepare." And then she waved at someone.

Mouse Road looked and saw a rider headed their way, bringing two extra mounts with him. His short, pale hair bounced with his whistler's strides, and his smile could be seen in spite of the distance.

"I believe your husband has come to bring us home," Speaks while Leaving said.

"Yes," Mouse Road said, feeling the conflict of happiness and apprehension. If war was coming, if a hard path still lay ahead of her, she was glad at least that she would not be alone and, as her husband rode up to them, the morning sun flashing from his unearthly blue eyes, she smiled.

Cheyenne Pronunciation Guide

There are only fourteen letters in the Cheyenne alphabet. They are used to create small words that can be combined to create some very long words. The language is very descriptive, and often combines several smaller words to construct a longer, more complex concept. The following are simplified examples of this subtle and intricate language, but it will give you some idea of how to pronounce the words in the text.

LETTER	PRONUNCIATION OF THE CHEYENNE LETTER
a	"a" as in "water"
e	"i" as in "omit" (short *i*, not a long *e*)
h	"h" as in "home"
k	"k" as in "skit"
m	"m" as in "mouse"
n	"n" as in "not"
o	"o" as in "hope"
p	"p" as in "poor"
s	"s" as in "said"
š	"sh" as in "shy"
t	"t" as in "stop"
v	"v" as in "value"

x   "ch" as in "Bach" (a soft, aspirated *h*)
'   glottal stop as in "Uh-oh!"

The three vowels (a, e, o) can be marked for high pitch
(á, é, ó) or be voiceless (whispered), as in â, ô, ê.

Glossary

Ame'haooestse
: Tsétsêhéstâhese for the name One Who Flies

Bands
: Cheyenne clans or family groups. Bands always travel together, while the tribe as a whole only gathers in the summer months. Bands are familial and matrilineal; men who marry go to live with the woman and her band. The ten Cheyenne bands are:

- The Closed Windpipe Band (also Closed Gullet or Closed Aorta)
- The Scabby Band
- The Hair Rope Men
- The Ridge People
- The Tree People (also Log Men or Southern Eaters)
- The Poor People
- The Broken Jaw People (also Lower Jaw Protruding People or Drifted Away Band)
- The Suhtai

- The Flexed Leg Band (also Lying on the Side with Knees Drawn Up People, later absorbed into Dog Soldier Society)
- The Northern Eaters

The Cloud People	Tsétsêhéstâhese phrase for the Southern Arapaho
The Cradle People	Tsétsêhéstâhese phrase for the Assiniboine
The Crow People	Tsétsêhéstâhese phrase for the Crow
The Cut-Hair People	Tsétsêhéstâhese phrase for the Osage
Eestseohtse'e	Tsétsêhéstâhese for the name Speaks while Leaving
Grandmother Land	Tsétsêhéstâhese phrase for Canada
The Greasy Wood People	Tsétsêhéstâhese phrase for the Kiowa
Haaahe	A Tsétsêhéstâhese phrase of greeting, from one man to another
Hámêstoo'êstse (sing), *Hámêstoo'e* (pl)	Sit!
Héehe'e	Yes.
He'kotoo'êstse (sing), *He'kotoo'e* (pl)	Be quiet!
Hó'ésta	Shout!
Hohkeekemeona'e	*Tsétsêhéstâhese* for the name Mouse Road
Hová'âháne	*No.*
The Inviters	Tsétsêhéstâhese phrase for the Lakota
Iron Shirts	Tsétsêhéstâhese phrase for the Spanish conquistadors
Ke'éehe	Child's word for grandmother
The Little Star People	Tsétsêhéstâhese phrase for the Oglala Lakota

Maahótse	The four Sacred Arrows of the People
Ma'heo'o (sing), Ma'heono (pl)	A word that can be loosely translated as "that which is sacred," referring to the basis of Cheyenne spirituality and mystery
Mo'e'haeva'e	*Tsétsêhéstâhese* for the name Magpie Woman
Moons	In the world of the Fallen Cloud, the names for the yearly cycle of moons are slightly different. The winter-to-winter cycle in these books is as follows:

- Hoop and Stick Game Moon
- Big Hoop and Stick Game Moon
- Light Snow Moon
- Ball Game Moon (or Spring Moon)
- Hatchling Moon
- Moon When the Whistlers Get Fat
- Moon When the Buffalo Are Rutting
- Moon When the Cherries Are Ripe
- Plum Moon (or Cool Moon)
- Moon When the Ice Starts to Form
- Hard Face Moon
- Big Hard Face Moon

Néá'eše	Thank you.
Néséne	My friend (said by one man to another)

Nevé-stanevóo'o	The Four Sacred Persons, created by Ma'heo'o, who guard the four corners of the world
Nóheto	Let's go!
Nóxa'e	Wait!
The Sage People	Tsétsêhéstâhese phrase for the Northern Arapaho
Séáno	The happy place for the deceased
The Snake People	Tsétsêhéstâhese phrase for the Comanche
Soldier Societies	The military organizations within the tribe. Membership in a society was voluntary and had no relation to the band in which one lived. The six Cheyenne soldier societies are:

- Kit Foxes (also Fox Soldiers)
- Elkhorn Scrapers (also Crooked Lances)
- Dog Men (or Dog Soldiers)
- Red Shields (or Buffalo Bull Soldiers)
- Crazy Dogs
- Little Bowstrings

Tsêhe'êsta'ehe	Long Hair (General G. A. Custer)
Tosa'e	Where?
Tsétsêhéstâhese	The Cheyenne people's word for themselves
Vá'ôhtáma	The place of honor at the back of the lodge
Vé'ho'e (sing), *Vé'hó'e* (pl)	Lit. spider, from the word for "cocooned," and now the word for whites
Vétšêškévâhonoo'o	Fry bread

| The Wolf People | Tsétsêhéstâhese phrase for the Pawnee |
| The Year the Star Fell | In the year 1833, the Leonid meteor shower was especially fierce. The incredible display made such an impression on the Cheyenne of the time that it became a memorable event from which many other events were dated. |

About the Author

Kurt R. A. Giambastiani has had short stories published in *Dragon Magazine, Talebones,* and *Marion Zimmer Bradley's Fantasy Magazine*, among others. He is currently a lead analyst in the Seattle area, where he lives with his wife and two cats.

S.M. STIRLING

**From national bestselling author
S.M. Stirling comes gripping novels of
alternative history**

Island in the Sea of Time
0-451-45675-0

Against the Tide of Years
0-451-45743-9

On the Oceans of Eternity
0-451-45780-3

The Peshawar Lancers
0-451-45873-7

"FIRST-RATE ADVENTURE ALL THE WAY."
—HARRY TURTLEDOVE

To order call: 1-800-788-6262

R922

Roc Science Fiction & Fantasy
COMING IN FEBRUARY 2004

SON OF AVONAR
by Carol Berg
0-451-45962-8

Seri, a Leiran noblewoman living in exile, is no stranger
to defying the unjust laws of her land. But she may have
gone to far in sheltering a wanted fugitive who possesses
unusual abilities—a fugitive with the fate of an entire
people in his hands...

OMNIFIX
by Scott Mackay
0-451-45960-1

An alien invasion left part of Earth's population deterio-
rating from alien viruses. The drug called Omnifix
replaces the victims' DNA with microtechnology, saving
their lives at a cost of their humanity. But now, the
aliens have returned...

MECHWARRIOR: DARK AGE
FORTRESS OF LIES
by J. Steven York
0-451-45963-6

Duke Aaron Sandoval is trying to convince the governors
of the Republic to forge a coalition against the House
Liao in an attempt to seize power for himself. And he's
willing to sacrifice anything or anyone—including his
nephew Eric—who stands in his way.

Classic Science Fiction & Fantasy
from
ROC

2001: A SPACE ODYSSEY by Arthur C. Clarke
Based on the screenplay written with Stanley Kubrick, this
novel represents a milestone in the genre.
"The greatest science fiction novel of all time." —*Time*

0-451-45799-4

ROBOT VISIONS by Isaac Asimov
Here are 36 magnificent stories and essays about Asimov's
most beloved creations—Robots. This collection includes
some of his best known and best loved robot stories.

0-451-45064-7

THE FOREST HOUSE by Marion Zimmer Bradley
The stunning prequel to *The Mists of Avalon*, this is
the story of Druidic priestesses who guard their ancient
rites from the encroaching might of Imperial Rome.

0-451-45424-3

BORED OF THE RINGS by The Harvard Lampoon
This hilarious spoof lambastes all the favorite
characters from Tolkien's fantasy trilogy. An instant
cult classic, this is a must read for anyone who has ever
wished to wander the green hills of the shire. And after
almost sixty years in print, has become a classic itself.

0-451-45261-5

Available wherever books are sold, or
to order call: 1-800-788-6262

Penguin Group (USA) Inc.
Online

Your Internet gateway to a virtual environment with
hundreds of entertaining and enlightening books
from Penguin Group (USA) Inc.

*While you're there, get the latest buzz on
the best authors and books around—*

Tom Clancy, Patricia Cornwell, W.E.B. Griffin,
Nora Roberts, William Gibson, Robin Cook,
Brian Jacques, Catherine Coulter, Stephen King,
Ken Follett, Terry McMillan, and many more!

**Penguin Group (USA) Inc. Online is located at
http://www.penguin.com**

PENGUIN PUTNAM NEWS

Every month you'll get an inside look at our upcom-
ing books and new features on our site. This is an
ongoing effort to provide you with the most
up-to-date information about
our books and authors.

Subscribe to Penguin Group (USA) Inc. News at
http://www.penguin.com/newsletters